ICON READERS' GUIDES

Salman Rushdie

Midnight's Children
The Satanic Verses

EDITED BY DAVID SMALE

Consultant editor: Nicolas Tredell

D1202940

ICON BOOKS

Published in 2001 by Icon Books Ltd.,
Grange Road, Duxford, Cambridge CB2 4QF
e-mail: info@iconbooks.co.uk
www.iconbooks.co.uk

Sold in the UK, Europe, South Africa and Asia by Faber & Faber Ltd.,
3 Queen Square, London WC1N 3AU or their agents

Distributed in the UK, Europe, South Africa and Asia by Macmillan
Distribution Ltd., Houndmills, Basingstoke RG21 6XS

Published in Australia in 2001 by Allen & Unwin Pty. Ltd.,
PO Box 8500, 83 Alexander Street, Crows Nest, NSW 2065

Distributed in Canada by Penguin Books Canada, 10 Alcorn Avenue,
Suite 300, Toronto, Ontario M4V 3B2

Consultant editor: Nicolas Tredell
Managing editor: Duncan Heath
Series devised by: Christopher Cox
Cover design: Simon Flynn
Typesetting: Wayzgoose

ISBN 1 84046 253 1

Printed and bound in Great Britain by
Biddles Ltd., Guildford and King's Lynn

Contents

'It Was and It Was Not So . . . It Happened and It Never Did': History, Historicism and Nation

Assesses Rushdie's engagement with historical debates and Indian nationhood. The first extract is by the prolific Uma Parameswaran who sets out to examine the veracity of Rushdie's depiction of Indian history in *Midnight's Children*. This is followed by a short essay by Rushdie himself in which he challenges the institutionalised distinction between historical and fictional narratives and emphasises the importance of memory in *Midnight's Children*. Aruna Srivastava argues that Rushdie does not reject historical objectivity outright, but places it alongside a number of different philosophical approaches to history. Rukmini Bhaya Nair discusses the linguistic qualities of *The Satanic Verses* and suggests that its use of 'gossip' as a narrative form to express history allows it to encompass a realm excluded from official and authoritative discourse.

'Mutability of the Essence of the Self': Writing the Migrant Experience

Explores Rushdie's treatment of migrancy and cultural hybridity in his writing. Timothy Brennan describes Rushdie as a 'Third-World cosmopolitan' and points to complex relations of affiliation and compromise expressed in his fictions through the figure of the 'chamcha'. Homi K. Bhabha provides two intellectually challenging, yet rewarding, extracts in which he suggests that something 'new' may emerge out of the 'difference' of the migrant experience. The chapter concludes with an extract from Vijay Mishra who, while drawing upon many of Bhabha's ideas, suggests that *The Satanic Verses* clearly reveals that multiple and frequently divergent discourses have emerged out of the postcolonial diaspora.

'How Are We to Understand My Too-Many Women?': The Issue of Gender in Rushdie's Fiction

Explores an important, but for the most part rarely discussed, aspect of Rushdie's writing. Most critics prefer to discuss Rushdie's status as a postcolonial writer, but by doing so act as though gender issues do not play a part in those debates. Extracts from Nancy E. Batty and Charu Verma, and an article in full from Catherine Cundy, go some way towards compensating for that lack.

'And if Rivers of Blood Flow From the Cuts His Verses
Inflict': The Politics of Fiction

Examines the politics and political consequences of Rushdie's fiction.
Katherine Frank's discussion of the libel suit taken out against Rushdie
by Indira Gandhi following the publication of *Midnight's Children*, illustrates the controversial nature of even Rushdie's earliest writing. This
chapter then goes on to plot the development of the 'Rushdie Affair' and
chart the range of political, religious, literary and academic responses to
it. This Guide concludes with K.M. Newton's scholarly reading of the
'Rushdie Affair' through the lens of literary criticism.

INTRODUCTION

THE SHEER volume of criticism surrounding Rushdie's work is aston-ishing if one considers that it is just over 25 years since the 1975 publication of his first novel *Grimus*. Now largely overshadowed by his more recent works, *Grimus* is interesting for the manner in which it prefigures many of the stylistic and formalistic qualities characteristic of Rushdie's later novels. Liz Calder, an editor at Victor Gollancz, said of the novel: 'I liked it. I responded to its extraordinary use of language. I mean, it was just wild. I hadn't read anything like it. And although it was barmy in some ways, all over the place, I thought it was amazing.'[1] Rushdie had entered *Grimus* in a science-fiction competition sponsored by Gollancz, but the novel failed to impress the judges. Despite its lack of success, Gollancz offered to publish *Grimus*, and Rushdie used the proceeds to spend the next five months travelling across India and Pakistan. He returned to England for the publication of the novel. Yet, for all its exuberance and formal experimentation, *Grimus* was very poorly received. According to Ian Hamilton, it was 'a forbiddingly anonymous affair: one could deduce from it almost nothing about the author's background.'[2] Rushdie himself was aware of its flaws, and in his interview with John Haffenden admit-ted: 'What I didn't like about *Grimus* was that it was too easy to use a fantasy that didn't grow out of the real world, a kind of whimsy.'[3] Rushdie was forced to 're-examine everything I had thought about writing and put it back together another way.'[4] He resolved that his future works would 'come out of something real', something that reflected his own know-ledge of the world, and his recent journey across India provided him with, or reminded him of, just the 'reality' he was seeking.[5]

Rushdie immediately began work on a novel entitled *Madame Rama*. Set in India, and containing a central character loosely based upon Indira Gandhi, *Madame Rama* engaged with the politics of the Indian Emergency period.[6] To Rushdie's surprise, Gollancz turned down the novel. Yet this work was to provide Rushdie with much of the material for his next project, *Midnight's Children*. Despite some initial doubts about the novel, *Midnight's Children* was accepted by Jonathan Cape, then London's most prestigious publisher of literary fiction. Less than 2,000 copies of the book were printed, but, following enthusiastic reviews, it soon became apparent that *Midnight's Children* was to be Rushdie's first success as a novelist.

Not only had Rushdie tapped into a rich vein by turning to India for his inspiration, he had, according to some reviewers, also turned to a subject very much to the taste of an English readership – for it seems that big books about India are popular with the English.[7] It is certainly true that books about India tend to do well when it comes to literary competitions. In 1981, Rushdie was awarded the Booker Prize for *Midnight's Children*. The competition had been running for just thirteen years, yet Rushdie was the fourth author to win the prize for a novel set in India. In 1993, *Midnight's Children* was considered to be the best prize-winning novel of the competition's first 25 years and was awarded the Booker of Bookers.

But though the English literary establishment has rewarded Rushdie, his position within that establishment remains unclear. The Booker Prize is an annual award, open to all writers within the Commonwealth. As such, it implicitly promotes the existence of what are loosely termed 'Commonwealth writers'. Rushdie, however, throughout his writing career has resisted attempts to categorise his work, and he has serious problems with such a label. In his essay '"Commonwealth Literature" Does Not Exist', for example, Rushdie points to the dangers of such a term, arguing that it represents a false category that serves to obscure the proliferation of a new sort of English literature, one that has very little to do with the English themselves. Rushdie writes that the English language 'ceased to be the sole possession of the English some time ago. Perhaps "Commonwealth literature" was invented to delay the day when we rough beasts actually slouch into Bethlehem. In which case, it's time to admit that the centre cannot hold.'[8] Rushdie sees himself as very much a part of this new sort of English literature, operating outside the constraints and assumptions of a central establishment unaware of its own demise.

Following the award of the Booker Prize, Rushdie became a public figure. Not only did he find himself fêted by the literary establishment (he was awarded a £7,500 Arts Council bursary to enable him to become a full-time writer), but the press and media sought his views on subjects ranging from racism in Britain to the state of Indian politics. Rushdie had by this time developed a clear sense of the political function of literature. This is perhaps best expressed in his essay on Günter Grass when he writes that an author should: 'Go for Broke. Always try and do too much. Dispense with safety nets. Take a deep breath before you begin talking. Aim for the stars. Keep grinning. Be bloody-minded. Argue with the world.'[9] Rushdie certainly applied this philosophy to his third novel, *Shame*. If *Midnight's Children* engages with Indira Gandhi's policies in India, then *Shame* represents a direct and more damning attack upon the government of Pakistan. In this novel, Rushdie laments the separation of post-independence India into the separate states of India and Pakistan. Rushdie describes such a division, organised along religious lines, as an opportunity not realised, as 'a failure of the dreaming mind.'[10] Rushdie also

condemns the political oppression and abuse of both the civilian governments and military dictatorship experienced by Pakistan by lampooning
such figures as General Zia ('Old Razor Guts'), Zulfikar Ali Bhutto and
his daughter Benazir Bhutto ('the Virgin Ironpants'). Though *Shame*, like
his previous novel, has its comedy elements, Rushdie admits it is 'even
nastier than *Midnight's Children*, or at least the nastiness goes on in a more
sustained way.'[11] The Pakistan government banned *Shame*.

Rushdie's fourth novel, *The Satanic Verses*, represents yet another shift
in emphasis, for it is as much about England as it is about India. In this
novel, Rushdie's attention broadens to include the hybrid experience of
migrancy. Yet, as Ian Hamilton has observed, there is also a sense that the
novel has other concerns – that its many Eastern references suggest that
a large portion of the intended readership of *The Satanic Verses* lay
'elsewhere'. Consequently, 'few Western critics picked up on the book's
"offensive" elements.'[12] *The Satanic Verses* was published on 26 September
1988. The controversy that was to be so overwhelmingly associated with
this work had, however, already achieved some momentum in India after
early reviews of the novel had revealed its potentially offensive nature. It
was to reach unprecedented heights when, on 14 February 1989, Ayatollah
Khomeini issued the fatwa against Rushdie.

The controversy associated with Salman Rushdie has far too often overshadowed the literary qualities of his fiction. The 'Rushdie Affair' as it is
now called, which was always more about politics than criticism, has
established something of a barrier between readers of Rushdie's novels
and the works themselves. Indeed, such has been the nature of this controversy that many potential readers have been turned away from an
appreciation of one of the most gifted writers of the twentieth century.
Conversely, many readers have been attracted to a novel such as *The Satanic
Verses* not because of its literary merits, but merely because of its status as
a scandalous text. This Guide acknowledges the contentious nature of
Rushdie's writing, yet does so by first placing it, or re-placing it, within
the literary realm. Focusing for the most part on his two most famous
novels, *Midnight's Children* and *The Satanic Verses*, this Guide provides a
clear and structured introduction to Rushdie's writing through the
tremendously stimulating body of criticism it has generated. The formal
brilliance of Rushdie's writing has drawn an equally exciting response
from critics, and readers of this Guide cannot fail to appreciate the range
and quality of this work, nor can they fail to benefit from it. Not only
does such criticism reveal the variety of debates existing within the literary realm, but it also provides the necessary illumination required for a
full and intelligent understanding of the politics surrounding Rushdie's
fiction.

The first chapter of this Guide explores the initial responses to *Midnight's
Children* and *The Satanic Verses*. In many ways, these reviews anticipate

much of the academic debate later to be associated with the novels. Some reviewers of *Midnight's Children* sought to locate it within Western literary concerns such as the supposed crisis in the novel by suggesting that Rushdie's formal innovations offered a positive response to that crisis. Other reviewers pointed to the popularity of Indian writers, either to suggest a rather cynical commodification of India for a Western readership, or to argue that *Midnight's Children* represented an important example of the postcolonial 'voice'. Reviewers of *The Satanic Verses* were also divided. The novel's stylistic qualities were almost without exception admired. Yet by this stage of Rushdie's career, reviewers were also fully attuned to the political nature of Rushdie's writing. For many reviewers, *The Satanic Verses* was a novel about the migrant's experience of institutionalised racism in Britain. For others, it depicted a more hopeful hybrid experience. In the months following the publication of *The Satanic Verses*, however, Rushdie's alleged insult to Islam inevitably influenced responses to the novel.

Chapter Two of this Guide explores the critical effort that has gone into attempts to locate Rushdie's works within literary and cultural traditions. This approach to Rushdie's novels is particularly interesting inasmuch as the impulse to provide a formal context for *Midnight's Children* and *The Satanic Verses* clearly has political connotations that impact upon a critical reading of the novels' thematic concerns. Some critics, such as Philip Engblom and Patricia Merivale, place Rushdie firmly within a Western literary tradition, pointing to the influence of writers such as Laurence Sterne, Jonathan Swift and Günter Grass. Other critics, including C. Kanaganayakam and Feroza Jussawalla, perhaps rejecting what they regard as Western assimilation of Rushdie's works, respond by identifying both novels' use of myth and their numerous references to Eastern classics such as the *Mahabharata* and *Ramayana*.

The third chapter of this Guide assesses Rushdie's engagement with history, historicism and nationhood. These issues are central to postcolonial debate, and are frequently raised by critics as a means to examine Rushdie's status as a postcolonial writer. While Uma Parameswaran's article restricts its discussion of *Midnight's Children* to an examination of the novel's historical veracity, many critics prefer a more sophisticated approach to Rushdie's work. Rushdie is seen to mobilise historical discourse so that he may then interrogate its authoritative role in the construction of both nationhood and selfhood. He places different understandings of history alongside each other, deconstructing the institutional distinction between historical and fictional narratives. Rushdie is seen to offer a more fluid conception of history, one rooted in memory and the oral storyteller's art.

Chapter Four of this Guide explores the relationship between Rushdie's fiction and his complex treatment of migrancy and hybridity. Rushdie himself repeatedly draws attention to this aspect of his life and work. The first two extracts included in this chapter are taken from

Timothy Brennan's excellent *Salman Rushdie and the Third World*, where he presents a sophisticated reading of both *Midnight's Children* and *The Satanic Verses* to support his description of Rushdie as a 'Third-World cosmopolitan'. For Brennan, Rushdie occupies a problematic space both inside and beyond the culture he depicts; appearing both compromised by Western affiliations, and yet empowered to criticise the very power that privileges him. This chapter also includes two challenging, yet stimulating, extracts from Homi K. Bhabha. In these extracts, Bhabha examines Rushdie's treatment of cultural hybridity in *The Satanic Verses*, suggesting that out of the postcolonial diaspora something 'new' has emerged.

Chapter Five of this Guide examines Rushdie's engagement with gender issues – particularly his depictions of women. This approach to Rushdie's work tends to be somewhat eclipsed by postcolonial debates, but certainly deserves recognition. The character of Padma, from *Midnight's Children*, receives special attention. Her role as foil to Saleem's narrative is discussed from a number of conflicting perspectives. Numerous critics acknowledge Padma's structural importance. Yet, while some critics argue that Padma acts to undercut Saleem's pomposity and thereby both expose his subscription to Western values and reveal their vulnerability, others propose a less favourable reading. Charu Verma, for example, suggests that Rushdie's depiction of Padma does little more than perpetuate masculine/feminine binaries that support the oppression of women. The chapter concludes with a less damning, though still critical, article by Catherine Cundy. This article, included in full, presents a thoughtful examination of Rushdie's gender politics in both *Midnight's Children* and *The Satanic Verses*.

The final chapter of this Guide acknowledges that it is impossible to ignore the political, and potentially offensive, nature of Rushdie's writing. It opens with Katherine Frank's discussion of Indira Gandhi's libel suit against Rushdie. Her article raises the question of authorial accountability – a question that would be asked in more ominous tones following the publication of *The Satanic Verses*. This chapter then provides a carefully plotted account of the reasons behind, and the development of, what would later be termed the 'Rushdie Affair'. Though much of the final chapter is dedicated to the political fall-out that resulted from the publication of *The Satanic Verses*, its conclusion, provided by K. M. Newton, relocates Rushdie's writing within literary debate.

CHAPTER ONE

'Rising from My Pages Comes the Unmistakable Whiff of Chutney': Reviews of *Midnight's Children* and *The Satanic Verses*

ALMOST ALL reviewers of *Midnight's Children* point to an English, and more broadly Western, fascination with India as an exotic land of mysteries, myths, and marvels. Salman Rushdie, however, argues that he is not merely seeking to cater for a Western taste for the exotic. In *Midnight's Children*, India is more than a colourful background; India is the active subject of the novel.[1] Yet if India is the subject of Rushdie's work, then so too is literature itself. For Rushdie is a 'literary' writer in the sense that he is very much concerned with the form and evolution of the novel. Rushdie himself is seen to be an important contributor to that evolution. Valentine Cunningham, for example, in his review of *Midnight's Children* for the *Times Literary Supplement*, suggests that such is the scale of India in terms of its geography and population, and so diverse are its cultures, that: 'a novel pretending to India as a subject can't avoid the question of how novels in general may claim truthfully to cope with the daunting vastnesses, the multiplicities of things and persons.'[2]

The first review included in this chapter is Anita Desai's 'An Oriental Fantasy', published in *The Book Review* for July/August 1981.[3] Desai is an Indian novelist herself. This adds an extra dimension to her review, for she is both a practitioner and critic.[4] Like Cunningham, Desai points to Rushdie's engagement with the form of the novel, but in a more detailed manner examines Rushdie's problematic status as an Indian writer employing an essentially European literary form. For Desai, *Midnight's Children* represents an example of much needed innovation during a period of crisis for European literature.

■ With Salman Rushdie's novel *Midnight's Children*, the Indian novel has at last come of age. It is a giant that soars above all those flat little social documents, those childlike rural tales, those quasi-philosophical rambles that have made up the Indian fictional scene. Of course the novel never was an Indian literary form: it was an import from the West and the earliest Indian novels were faithful copies of their Victorian counterparts, acts of homage rather than of plagiarism. The Indian novelist of today continues to search despairingly for tradition – a tradition that does not exist here, that he feels has to be captured abroad and somehow brought back alive. Not having lived through the experiences of the twentieth century in the West, he is unaware that the tradition he seeks was demolished by the war, blown to smithereens by the atomic bomb.

Rushdie has arrived on the literary scene when the tradition has already long been in shreds. Picking up the shreds he has forged a new style, a kaleidoscopic manner in the new tradition created by [Günter] Grass in Europe, Philip Roth in America, stopping just short of their macabre surrealism and infusing his work with an Indian philosophy, an Indian light. 'I was being sucked into a grotesque mimicry of European literature,' he confesses, and 'perhaps it would be fair to say that Europe repeats itself in India, as farce.' The tone of this farce, if that is what he chooses to call it, is European, but the fantasy is Oriental, the mixture of the two explosive. In this explosion, India is seen in the form of a dust-storm, yet it is not without shape. 'Everything has shape if you look for it. There is no escape from form.' His memory is the shaping influence: 'I have become, it seems to me, the apex of the isosceles triangle, supported equally by twin deities, the wild god of memory and the lotus-goddess of the present.'[5] □

Desai, however, expresses little hope for the novel's reception in India itself.

■ It is not surprising that Rushdie himself now lives in London. It is tragic to think that this book, which may be considered a *tour de force* in the West but is obviously of major interest to Indian readers, has not been published or distributed in India and may never be read in the land that prefers to avert its eyes from the intolerable reality and gaze upon maya, the shimmer of illusion. Rushdie asks 'Is this an Indian disease, this urge to encapsulate the whole of history? Worse: am I infected too?' Actually it is not, and he is wrong: the Indian habit is to ignore what is close and gaze into the distance where nothing is visible and nothing can distract from soothing reverie. He himself is an exception – his gaze always intense, sharply in focus, his mind in complete command. Witness the precision of his observation: 'a muslin dupatta wound miser-tight around her head', 'the sharp aroma of despotism. It smelled of burning oily rags,' and in an occasional lyrical moment, 'The world was new again. After a winter's gestation in its egg-shell of ice, the valley had beaked its way out into the open, moist and yellow.' His spirits remain high, his humour ribald and very, very localised (the liveliest chapters [are] those about Bombay, written practically in the uncouth and hilarious tongue of that city).

Reading this novel, one is dazzled by the many gifts of this writer of courage, sheer stylistic brilliance and the power of both imagination and control. Underlying the hilarity and the hysteria, there is always the wholly serious purpose and the searching conscience. 'Be Fair!' he reminds his readers. 'No body, no country has a monopoly of untruth' and quotes from the Urdu poet Iqbal: *Where can one find the land that is foreign to God?* The book is not only a national allegory but is as universal as the fables of Cervantes, Swift, Kafka and Grass. Like all the greatest books, it can be read as a comedy, a fable, a farce, and yet it is a tragedy as well: the tragedy of individual lives harried and wrecked by history, and of history harried and wrecked by individuals.[6] □

Clark Blaise's 'A Novel of India's Coming of Age', published in *The New York Times Book Review*, similarly recognises Rushdie's influence on 'the Indian novel'. Blaise, however, includes Desai herself in the very tradition challenged by Rushdie's work.

■ The literary map of India is about to be redrawn. The familiar outline – E.M. Forster's outline essentially – will always be there, because India will always offer the dualities essential for the Forsterian vision: the open sewer and the whispering glade, Mother Theresa and the Taj Mahal. Serious English-language novelists from India (often called Indo-Anglians), or those from abroad who use Indian material, have steered a steady course between these two vast, mutually obliterating realities; hence the vivid patches of local color provided by the timeless South India of R.K. Narayan's novels and the cool pastels added by the later fiction of Anita Desai. The Indian novels of Paul Scott and Ruth Jhabvala also fall comfortably between these two poles. For a long time it has seemed that novels from India write their own blurbs: poised, witty, delicate, sparkling.[7] □

Rushdie is, for Blaise, a very different sort of writer; coarser, more aggressive, and more ambitious in his handling of India as literary subject matter. Rushdie himself admits that in *Midnight's Children* he attempted to move on from the sort of 'delicate' books about India that Blaise describes. Rushdie regards such books as dated, out of touch with his conception of India as an 'elephantine place'.[8] *Midnight's Children*, according to Blaise, depicts a thoroughly modern, urban, India. As much as it marks a maturing of books about India, so too does it seek to depict India itself 'coming of age' from 'its special, gifted infancy to its very ordinary, drained adulthood.'[9] Such a comment is designed to draw attention to the text's political engagement with the 'betrayal and corruption, the loss of ideals, culminating with "the Widow's" Emergency rule.'[10] It also allows Blaise to link *Midnight's Children* to a tradition of politically allegorical novels about 'growing-up', such as Laurence Sterne's *Tristram Shandy* (1759–67), and Günter Grass's *The Tin Drum* (1959). In this respect, Blaise follows Desai's example, and that of so many reviewers and critics of Rushdie's works. Though Rushdie himself frequently admits to the influence of writers of this sort, such connections should be cautiously made. To his credit, Blaise willingly admits this, suggesting that overemphasis on such influence obscures the true range of *Midnight's Children* and Rushdie's own originality. Blaise writes of Rushdie's novel:

■ Its characters speak in many voices: 'Once upon a time there were Radha and Krishna, and Rama and Sita, and Laila and Majnu; also (because we were not unaffected by the West) Romeo and Juliet, and Spencer Tracy and Katherine Hepburn.' Much of the dialogue (the best parts) reads like the hip vulgarity – *yaar!* – of the Hindi film magazine. The desiccated syllables of T.S. Eliot, so strong an influence upon other Anglo-Indian writers, are gone. 'Midnight's Children' sounds like a continent finding its voice.

How Indian is it? It is slangy, and a taste for India (or a knowledge of Bombay) obviously heightens the response. Here is a description of a cafe where Saleem's mother goes secretly to meet her dishonored first husband: 'The Pioneer Café was not much when compared to the Gaylords and Kwalitys of the city's more glamorous parts; a real rutputty joint, with painted boards proclaiming LOVELY LASSI and FUNTABULOUS FALOODA and BHEL-PURI BOMBAY FASHION, with filmi playback music blaring out from a cheap radio by the cash-till, a long narrow greeny room lit by flickering neon, a forbidding world in which broken-toothed men sat at reccine-covered tables with crumpled cards and expressionless eyes.' Very Indian.[11] □

Such is the sheer scale of Rushdie's subject matter, however, that while reviewers applaud Rushdie's stylistic brilliance, many find difficulty with what they regard as the structural looseness of his writing. Blaise, however, affirms that *Midnight's Children*, despite some faults, is a fundamentally integrated work:

■ Of course there are a few false notes. There is a shorter, purer novel locked inside this shaggy monster. A different author might have teased it out, a different editor might have insisted upon it. I'm glad they didn't. There are moments when the effects are strained, particularly in the early chapters, when an ancient Kashmiri boatman begins sounding like 'The Two-Thousand-Year-Old Man.' On a more serious level, Mr. Rushdie at first has a difficult time endowing the villains of Indian politics with mythic stature (Grass's Germany made it so easy); petty household intrigues seem more momentous than the misaffairs of state ([Gabriel García Márquez's] Latin America made it easy too). But with Ayub Khan, the Bangladesh war, 'The Widow' and her son, the later pages darken quite handsomely. The flow of the book is toward the integration of a dozen strongly developed narratives, and in ways that are marvelous to behold, integration is achieved. The myriad personalities of Saleem, imposed by the time, place and circumstance of his birth ('So much, yaar, inside one person,' remarks a Pakistani soldier, of the Saleem then known as buddha, the tracker, 'so many bad things, no wonder he kept his mouth shut!'), are reduced to a single, eloquent, ordinary soul. The flow of the book rushes to its conclusion in counterpointed harmony: myths intact, history accounted for, and a remarkable character fully alive.[12] □

Rushdie's engagement with the politics of India's period of emergency rule is examined in more detail in Robert Taubman's review 'Experiments with Truth', published in the *London Review of Books*.[13] Though Taubman's review is for the most part positive, it does signal the sort of approach to *Midnight's Children* adopted by many of the novel's detractors.

■ Despite ambiguities, and despite its special concern with the pathos of lost causes, there's no mistaking the book's serious commitments: to harmony and conciliation, against war, tyranny and obscurantism. It is in the old tradition of heart-felt indignation at *l'infâme*. And, in keeping with that tradition, the satirical animus is directed against particular targets – most notably, Indira Gandhi. Of course, this is a limitation, if one looks in a political novel for something more searching about the condition of a country. It is partisan rather than diagnostic, and in comparison with radical satire of the kind Günter Grass brings to bear on modern Germany, *Midnight's Children* may look inadequate to its subject. One recalls 18th-century satire, however, and the animus directed by Pope and Swift against some small, personal targets. There is satire that rises above immediate provocations and survives them without losing its point, and this is the kind of art to which *Midnight's Children* aspires.

But something else modifies its satire – a view of life that is one Westerners have long recognised as peculiarly Indian, and tend to find admirable in its idealism, though baffling in its disregard of the consequences. The version of it probably best-known in Western literature is the Krishna and Arjuna passage in [T.S. Eliot's] 'The Dry Salvages', with its prohibition: 'And do not think of the fruit of action.' In *Midnight's Children* all good causes are hedged around with warnings not to expect the success of these causes: indeed, what throws into relief the book's commitment to certain ideals, such as love, justice and hope, is its very insistence on human failure in all these directions. It seems to me that this is probably an impossible basis from which to launch political satire to any telling effect. But it affords the book something else: its considerable range of moral interests. Imagination is one of these moral interests. So we have the paradox, in this work of true imagination, that imagination is regarded as a value only so long as it remains potential.[14] □

Having argued that *Midnight's Children* lacks the satirical temper of European works such as *The Tin Drum*, Taubman attempts to mitigate such a lack by comparing Rushdie's work favourably to that of Grass, but it is debatable whether such a comparison does in fact favour *Midnight's Children*. Taubman writes: '*Midnight's Children* can even be seen (what one wouldn't easily say of Grass, or most modern literature) as paying a compliment to human nature.'[15] Taubman's overall enthusiasm for *Midnight's Children*, however, tends to cloud the less positive implications of his review; rather than support Rushdie's status as a politically engaged writer he prefers to discuss him as a fantasist. Yet, for Rushdie, the power of literature to describe the world is a deeply political act and he suggests that it is a peculiarity of Western criticism to read his novels simply as apolitical works of fantasy.[16] Rushdie seems very aware of the danger of this approach to literature; with more than a little irony he writes: 'I am only telling a sort of modern fairy-tale, so that's all right; nobody need get upset, or take anything I say too seriously. No drastic action need be taken either. What a relief!'[17] People do, however, take what Rushdie says seriously. Events surrounding the publication of *The Satanic Verses* bear dramatic testimony to this.

Like Saleem, Rushdie himself is one of India's 'midnight's children', or at least very close to being one. He was born just eight weeks before the 'birth' of Indian independence (this occurred immediately after the stroke of midnight, on the morning of 15 August 1947) and the coincidence of these two births gave rise to a family joke that in time matured into the idea for *Midnight's Children* itself.[18] Rushdie, however, left India at the age of fourteen to pursue his studies in England. He went to Rugby, a prestigious English public school, and achieved his degree at Cambridge University. He continues to live and work in England (Rushdie has recently returned from a much publicised, yet clearly temporary, move to New York). Consequently, his status as an 'Indian writer' is a problematic one.

S. Krishnan's review, 'Midnight's Children: An un-Indian book about all things Indian', observes of Midnight's Children:

■ Its popularity perhaps lies in the fact that it is a very un-Indian book about things Indian. In other words, it is not the kind of book Indians write about India. It is a rich and lush book, full of invention, fantasy and a wonderful mix of the beautiful and the grotesque that, of all countries in the world, only India seems to offer to the Western world, to the latter's complete, if morbid, satisfaction. It is a book that explores the mysterious sexuality of, and also its non-existence among, Indians – a subject other Indian writers tend to skirt. It is a chiaroscuro of the lovely and the ugly, the gentle and the horrible, the fragrant and the foul, that make up Indian life. It is also an endless panorama of extraordinary characters, exotics always associated with India, such as conjurers, peepshow-men, monkey trainers, snake-charmers et al, who are however presented in an unstereotyped fashion, which in itself is quite an accomplishment. Above all Rushdie has an almost manic and ferocious virtuosity with words, and keeps them flowing relentlessly, creating one exaggeration after another, which grip the reader and hold him in their thrall. He seems incapable of writing a single sentence without an unexpected, and usually delightful, modifier in it. Rushdie has a love-hate relationship with the country of his origin. If this leads him to excesses in judgement, it also lets him dwell lovingly and lyrically on those things Indian he cares for. He is a gifted writer, if not a glittering one, and though Midnight's Children has been overpraised, there is no doubt that it is certainly the most diverting and unusual fiction of India since G.V. Desani's All About H. Hatterr [1948]. It is certainly a very hard act to follow, and we will all be interested in seeing what Rushdie does for an encore.[19] □

The last review of Midnight's Children in this chapter, Aparna Mahanta's 'Allegories of the Indian Experience', is one of the most damning of all the attacks aimed at the novel by reviewers.[20]

■ In the lack-lustre world of post-war British fiction, Salman Rushdie's exotic fantasies have made a deep impact, his novel 'Midnight's Children' winning the Booker Prize for 1981, and his second, 'Shame', being short-listed for the same in 1983 (the prize eventually going to a South African novelist). Not that exotic fantasia is alien to the tradition of British fiction. Indeed it has a very respectable lineage going back to Swift and Sterne and coming down to Waugh and Greene, a patrimony which our Rushdie has been able to emulate very successfully. As Britain's imperial domains expanded so did the imagination of her novelists, who used all the available resources of language and fancy to fill up the empty spaces, empty for them, even though packed with the incomprehensible dark faces. Naturally with the passing of the empire, this strain has waned except for occasional flashes from the new breed of jet-set adventurers. Rushdie now steps into the gap, coming in the wake of the reigning nostalgia for the Raj, and decked with all the trappings of wit, humour and satire, that were the hall-marks of British Fiction in the grand old days. Which, again, only goes to prove that the Raj isn't dead after all. The pseudo-sons, the Saleem Sinais are there to take over.[21] □

Mahanta's opening paragraph seems to position Rushdie in terms similar to Gayatri Spivak's notion of the 'privileged native informant'. For Spivak, such a figure can be seen to draw upon knowledge of their culture merely to present incomplete, prejudiced, or simply stereotypical representations of that culture.[22] As such, these representations are not only alien to that culture's view of itself, but alienating in the broader context of processes of orientalisation. Mahanta's approach to Rushdie's novel is reminiscent of Edward Said's attack upon the writer V. S. Naipaul when he accused him of allowing 'himself quite consciously to be turned into a witness for the Western prosecution and by doing so denied himself the capacity to operate within Third World literary discourses.'[23] Mahanta's review sets out to establish Rushdie as such a 'witness', describing him as an alienated Indian writer, who, when not catering for a Western taste for the exotic, is writing for equally alienated Indian readers.

■ Leaving aside what the British find in Salman Rushdie, the question is what do we Indians find in him. By 'Indian' here I, of course, mean the English-educated Indian, though even the ordinary English-knowing Indian would find it hard to follow Rushdie's sophisticated and literary style, full of allusions, quotations, echoes, resonances, as well as the sudden and unexplained shifts between fantasy and reality, particularly in 'Midnight's Children'. 'Shame' is easier if only because it is out and out fantasy. Even leaving aside the fact of his not knowing English, Rushdie's novels are not for the ordinary Indian. In the first place ordinary Indians don't figure in these novels, except as that familiar sea of dark faces, the sea of humanity beating against the ubiquitous citadels of the white man's presence, the European clubs (*vide* 'A Passage to India' [E. M. Forster, 1924], Orwell's 'Burmese Days' [1934], etc). In Rushdie's case, these citadels are those taken over, lock, stock and barrel from the departing Angrez, the mansions of Bombay seaside, Flashman's hotel, the Residencies for the new brown Civilians, but their functions remain the same, to isolate, cut off, preserve, pickle, entomb. The difference in Rushdie's case, and it is an important difference, is that, looking out, [like] his predecessors, from his reserved fastnesses at the dark, swelling, sometimes angry and jeering mass, he cannot, like them, just react with loathing and fear or even with the twinge of guilt of a liberal [Forster], nor can he dismiss it as an alien monster, because, as 'Shame' makes clear, he is part of that monster, indeed that monster is himself, it exists within us all.[24] □

Mahanta's review adopts an almost apologetic tone as it argues that Rushdie's works are directed at a very particular, privileged readership. Mahanta appears to include herself in a readership comprising 'a tiny stratum of India's and Pakistan's elite, inheritors of the British mantle, the deracinated, speaking English, thinking English, dreaming English, Indians terrified, horrified, revolted by Indians and India, yet unable to escape the umbilical bonds.'[25] Emigration provides no escape from such bonds.

■ Even when, like Rushdie, they settle abroad, they cannot keep away, like the snake swaying to the snake-charmer's gourd or more appositely, like the vultures hovering over the rotting carcass. Rushdie happens to be more sensitive than his fellow expatriates, and despite the ever present temptation to sensationalise to satisfy British palates, which he is not always able to resist, his concern for his subject is genuine. In the midst of his loathing and revulsion he does try to understand and to make some sense of the swarming mess, even if he has often to throw up his hands in despair at the doings of this mad continent. Rushdie articulates the Western educated, liberal Indian's inability to comprehend the Indian reality, an inability revealed in Rushdie by his recourse to allegory and fantasy. Where the ordinary Indian, whose home after all is India, suffers, passively or with burning indignation, for him there being no choice except acceptance or revolution, the intellectual, particularly the Westernised intellectual, tries to bring a system into the disorder, to construct the algebraical formulas for the teeming misery, whether with the dutiful conscientiousness of a Victorian Bluebook compiler or with the zany humour of a Rushdie.[26] □

Having implicated herself as a privileged reader of *Midnight's Children*, Mahanta feels free to mount an attack on Rushdie's work for its emphasis on despair and Rushdie's inability to overcome his alienation – an attack that rather disingenuously elides a similar alienation in herself.

■ 'Midnight's Children' hovers between allegory and realism. On the personal level reality is a cluster of comic mischances – Dr Aziz bumping his nose against a frozen tussock, Amina Sinai caught robeless in a bathroom, Saleem trapped in a clothes basket. The point where realism ends and fantasy begins is not always clear, confusingly so for those unfamiliar with this type of writing, where realism is used as a jumping-board for fantasy. Fantasy at its best is intended to be a mask for reality, the gateway to a more intense reality, but sometimes it can become an excuse for unreality or lack of understanding. In parts of 'Midnight's Children' it seems as if Rushdie gets out of his depth in attempting to encompass the whole of the Indian sub-continent's historical and geographical diversity, even if only in an allegorical framework. The agonies of partition, the trauma of nations unable to stand on their feet being forced to run, the incompatible marriage of the two Pakistans, the festering ghost-haunted marshes of Bangladesh, the former East Pakistan that was, to the arid brick-stone wilderness of the North-Western Frontier, the Pakistan that is – can all this be comprehended by a bird's-eye view, even a hawk's or an airman's? The result is aetheralised abstractions which are no good in a novel which as a genre thrives on solidity, even if of a fantastic kind. Rushdie is defeated where Sanjay Gandhi was – in the eyesore slums of Luyten's New Delhi – by the many-headed Indian Ravana – the hungry but insistent generations. After this point 'Midnight's Children' falls off as allegory merges into a surrealist nightmare. Nausea is what Rushdie intends, nausea at the stinking, horrible mess of the emergency, of raw entrails cooked in the jails of free India. But nausea is only endurable as transmuted art as in Kafka, not raw as in Rushdie where fantasy uneasily rubs shoulders with the unendurable. [. . .]

As a political allegorist Rushdie is schematic and abstract, dealing with surface impressions rather than probing, giving a brilliantly impressionistic picture rather than any sound analysis. As a political analyst he can think no further than in terms of disintegration and explosions to unstick the pressures that suppression has built up. But his importance nonetheless is that he is symptomatic of a new breed of Indians – an elite nurtured and brought up in English, reluctant, shamefaced inheritors of the colonial traditions, cut off from the living, throbbing reality of deprivation and struggle. Like grandfather Aziz of 'Midnight's Children' these new Indians have a hole where the [heart] should have been, they are frozen and atrophied, creatively impotent like Sinai, mannequins like Isky Harappa and General Hyder, playthings of history. With no traditions except those sneeringly thrown at them by the departing Sahibs of Methwold's by the ballroom-dancing denizens of Flashman's Hotel they are cut off from their roots, aerobic plants, exotics with aerial roots. They, like their creator, are not of their own making, or so they believe. For them there is no release except explosion. Rushdie's novels are about these Indians and Pakistanis, and are for them so they can see their faces in it [*sic*].[27] □

Despite the criticism directed at *Midnight's Children* by some reviewers, Rushdie claims the book was well received in both India and Pakistan. Rushdie was somewhat nervous that his contested status as an expatriate writer working in Britain, with links to both India and Pakistan, might have led to a less than positive response to his novel.[28] In an interview with Michael T. Kaufman, Rushdie explained that: 'In Pakistan there is suspicion because I'm Indian and in India because I'm Pakistani. Both sides wish to claim me. Both sides find it hard that I don't reject the other side. So I was expecting hostility or fear.'[29] Yet Rushdie's lecture tour was very well attended, and his audiences generous in their praise of both author and novel: 'The book was written as a way of reclaiming India, and this was like India and Pakistan doing the same thing back.'[30]

Reviews of *Midnight's Children* point to Rushdie's status as a controversial literary figure. Following the publication of *The Satanic Verses* on 26 September 1988 the discussion surrounding Rushdie and his works took on an altogether different order of magnitude. While the reviews contained in the second half of this chapter represent the initial reception of Rushdie's novel, they also prefigure the 'trouble' that was to follow.

By the time *The Satanic Verses* was published, Rushdie was established as an important figure on the British literary scene. His third novel *Shame*, published in 1983, had been shortlisted for the Booker Prize. Though Rushdie had been considered favourite to win, the award went instead to the South African author J.M. Coetzee for his novel *Life and Times of Michael K*. However, *Shame* did win France's Prix du Meilleur Livre Étranger. Rushdie had also by this time acquired a reputation as a politically vocal writer. In numerous articles and interviews (many of which are referred to in this Guide), Rushdie engaged with political and social issues ranging from the politics of Indian partition to Thatcherism and racial oppression in Britain.

It is perhaps inevitable that such a prominent figure should attract critics. It is certainly the case that Rushdie was unpopular in some quarters of the British, specifically London, 'cultural scene'. Rushdie's media status and literary success were not universally celebrated. The cynicism surrounding Rushdie is clearly evident in some of the reviews of *The Satanic Verses*. Iain Sinclair, for example, describes the publication of *The Satanic Verses* as though it were a calculated financial event. He sees Rushdie as a one-man public limited company, dedicated to the cultivation of literary prestige merely as the means to secure ever-greater sales figures. Sinclair writes, 'What we've got here isn't a mere novel . . . It's an investment. The arrival, the second coming, after all the teasings by supplement, the foreplay of retrospective interviews, the mugshots of Salman coyly hiding behind cheques, is inevitably something of a downer.'[31] Though Sinclair might just as easily be describing the avarice of the publishing industry itself, the reader is left with a less than favourable impression of the writer fêted by such an industry.

For some commentators, this very personal criticism of Rushdie indicates the continued presence of racial prejudice in British culture, even within supposedly intellectual circles. Angela Carter, for example, identified a sense of resentment against Rushdie that contained 'a strong element of racism . . . very similar to the attitude to the Jews.'[32] Roger Woddis argues a similar point when he suggests that such prejudice shifts over time and Rushdie happens to fall into the racial group currently under attack. Woddis writes with cutting irony: 'And now it's the Asians. I mean they come over here and appropriate the English novel, win our literary prizes, take our women and our publisher's money. Why can't they stick to their own language?'[33]

Like *Midnight's Children*, *The Satanic Verses* was attacked for its structural looseness. Robert Irwin in his review of *The Satanic Verses* for the *Times Literary Supplement*, for example, voices his dissatisfaction with what he describes as the 'confusingly arbitrary' development of the novel's plot.[34] Patrick Parrinder, however, argues that the novel's fluid structure represents an attempt to bypass the forces of censorship that might otherwise be directed against a novel so deeply concerned with 'the global resurgence of Islamic fundamentalism.'[35]

■ Gibreel's dreams, in particular, 'name the unnamable' by portraying a bloodthirsty Imam's seizure of power, the tale of a pilgrimage of Indian villagers who end up drowning in the Arabian Sea, and some ungodly goings-on in Jahilia, the fictive equivalent of Mecca. As Mahound and his followers return from their flight to Yathrib to take over the city, we see two writers – the satirist Baal and his own Persian scribe Salman – becoming the prophet's mortal enemies. (Meanwhile, the inmates of the local brothel cheekily impersonate the prophet's 12 wives.) Salman finally admits to having changed the wording of some of Mahound's revelations, but saves his own skin by betraying Baal. Is there any way of escaping this fundamentalist universe – the universe as dreamed by Gibreel – or is a little verbal tinkering the best that can be done? Saladin Chamcha finally leaves behind his demonic powers, going off with a woman whose last words are 'Let's get the hell out of here.' Another woman, Gibreel's ex-lover Alleluia Cone, has turned herself into an intrepid mountaineer and Everest-explorer in order, as she hopes, to rise above good and evil: but she fails, so far as we can tell, since Gibreel in the end sends her prematurely to paradise. In a reversal of the story of *Paradise Lost* [John Milton, 1667] it is Gibreel who gradually degenerates into a bringer of death, while Saladin finds some sort of redemption: but this, after all, is the Devil's version. It is all damnably entertaining, and fiendishly ingenious.

   Rushdie wrote in *Shame* that 'every story one chooses to tell is a kind of censorship, it prevents the telling of other tales.' His own profuse and multiple-branching fictions do not give the impression that anything has been prevented from being told.[36] □

Rushdie himself admits that the novel might seem to lack structural coherence, but the reasons he suggests for this are different from Parrinder's. When interviewed by Sean French for *The Observer*, he points out that *Midnight's Children* is lent structure through its engagement with Indian history. *The Satanic Verses*, however, is for Rushdie a novel about identity and transformation and 'since it's so much about transformation I wanted to write it in such a way that the book itself was metamorphosing all the time. Obviously the danger is that the book falls apart.'[37]

   Many reviewers and critics of his work discuss Rushdie's examination of migration and metamorphosis. Malise Ruthven's 'A Question of Identity', for example, responds directly to the growing controversy surrounding *The Satanic Verses* by adopting such an approach to the novel.

■ *The Satanic Verses* . . . is as much about changing identities as loss of religious faith: many of its devices, such as the use of the same names by more than one character (or perhaps the same character in different guise – one cannot be sure), add emphasis to this central preoccupation. The migrant's dilemma – to change, risking loss of faith and identity, or to try to hold on to a consistent idea of selfhood – lies at the novel's heart, and provides its unexpected denouement. It is Saladin Chamcha, the 'creature of selected discontinuities, a willing re-invention of himself', who, by watching his father die (in what is a remarkably moving yet clear-eyed description), recovers his former, unassimilated selfhood as Salahuddin Chamchawala, the Bombay bourgeois; it is Gibreel, the 'untranslated man' whom the world considers 'good' for wishing to remain 'continuous', who is finally destroyed, unable to contain the eruptions of a religious megalomania which leaks into and overwhelms his waking self, 'making him that angelic Gibreel he has no desire to be'.

   The rage with which this magnificent, challenging novel has been greeted by a number of Muslim organisations proves that Rushdie has touched upon some extremely raw nerves in a community experiencing the very dilemmas and transformations he portrays.[38] □

The Satanic Verses certainly touched upon 'some extremely raw nerves'. Rushdie was perceived to be directly attacking the foundations of a world religion. The publication of *The Satanic Verses* coincided with massive shifts occurring in world politics. As a result of the break-up of the former Soviet Union, tensions between the Cold-War powers were easing and

Western fears were shifting from Russia to the Middle East. Rushdie's perceived attack upon the Muslim faith was seen to be all the more acute, since for many Muslims it not only originated from one of their own, but also came at a time when their faith was rapidly emerging as the latest bogeyman of the Western nations. Edward Said voices the question posed by many Muslims:

■ Why must a Moslem, who could be defending and sympathetically interpreting us, now represent us so roughly, so expertly and so disrespectfully to an audience already primed to excoriate our traditions, reality, history, religion, language, and origin? Why, in other words, must a member of our culture join the legions of Orientalists in Orientalizing Islam so radically and unfairly?[39] □

Before the publication of *The Satanic Verses*, Rushdie had been at the forefront of anti-racist debates in Britain. He frequently made use of his high media profile to support the cause of ethnic minorities by attacking the policies of the then-Conservative government. Indeed, according to Michael Dummett, Rushdie was something of a hero among members of the ethnic minorities. Dummett argues that following the release of the novel, however, 'Much as you might want to, you can never again play that role: You can never again assume the stance of the denouncer of white prejudice. For now you are one of us. You have become an honorary white.'[40]

The figure of the religious fundamentalist gripped the Western imagination. Fundamentalism was, moreover, not only something to be feared but also became something uniquely Islamic. In an interview published in *India Today* for September 1988, Rushdie admitted that one of the major themes of *The Satanic Verses* was religion and fanaticism. Rushdie added, however, that if he appeared to focus on the Islamic religion it was simply because 'that is what I know the most about. But the ideas about religious faith and the nature of religious experience and also the political implications of religious extremism are applicable with a few variations to just about any religion.'[41] Though Rushdie claimed that the novel was opposed to all forms of orthodoxy, his reply when he was asked if he feared reaction from the Mullahs seemed to suggest that he expected some sort of backlash: 'Even *Shame* was attacked by fundamentalist Muslims. I cannot censor. I write whatever there is to write.'[42] Within the novel, this refusal to censor the self is expressed by the young satirist Baal who declares: '"A poet's work [is to] name the unnamable, to point at frauds, to take sides, start arguments, shape the world and stop it from going to sleep." And if rivers of blood flow from the cuts his verses inflict, then they will nourish him.'[43] Rushdie knew that *The Satanic Verses* would draw a response from Muslims. He could not, however, have anticipated the enormity of that response.

The following review, by Professor Syed Ali Ashraf, expresses the outrage felt by many Muslims after the publication of *The Satanic Verses*. It also represents an early response from the Islamic establishment to Rushdie's novel. Professor Ali Ashraf was at this time Director-General of the Islamic Academy in Cambridge.

■ Rushdie has written a negative satire on life. It is nihilistic. There is no positive norm. Love is presented as either sentimentality or lust. Selfishness dominates. Angels and Satan and the devils are man-made fabrications. Religious consciousness is shown only as superstition.

Rushdie then goes to the highest domain and tries to pull it down to prove that the Prophet of Islam (Peace be upon him) was not at all the perfect man history tells us of. He sides with the orientalists because that is convenient for him so that he can distort history as much as it suits him to do so. That is why he concocts a new kind of myth and turns a sexual pervert into an angel but an angel who himself does not know what message he pours into the heart of the Prophet. [. . .]

What is most satanic in this venture of Rushdie is that he has written this novel to satirise the Prophet and his Companions, to ridicule [the] religious consciousness of people, to remove from the hearts of people any sense of reverence for angels, prophets, holy books, and hence any faith in God and the Hereafter. He has intentionally and deliberately distorted the history of the Blessed Prophet and his Companions though he has retained the names of the Companions and chosen the name that vicious missionaries in the Middle Ages used to give to the Prophet (peace be upon him) only in order to tell people that he was not writing history. [. . .]

The method that he has adopted to achieve his goal is also confusing and unsuccessful from the literary point of view. How could the two characters Gibreel (Gabriel) and Saladin fall from the sky and still be alive? How could they get transformed and how could they become normal again? How could they have the normal human body and how could they at the same time move about and influence people across space and time?

Rushdie tried to learn some Sufistic terminology and some Hindu and Buddhistic terms and started playing with them in a childish way. He wanted to be realistic and fantastic at the same time. Where he failed miserably is in portraying people's feelings when they see the transformation of Saladin or Gibreel as if these are normal things. In a normal situation, these abnormal things do not happen. In a fairy tale they do. His attempt to mix normalcy and fairy tale myths created by him [does] not carry conviction. Had we been transported into the imaginary world completely, as C.S. Lewis does in children's tales or as is done in fairy tales, it would have been convincing. [. . .]

Rushdie is thus a practitioner of black magic who turns things upside down. Does he see anything great or good in human nature? Rushdie succeeds in portraying a large number of characters of which the two are the most prominent, Gibreel and Saladin. The characterisation of the Prophet, his companions and The Imam is highly twisted and incompetent. In his attempt to theorise and present a distorted version of history it was not possible for him to have any norm of behaviour which would show, as sometimes he wanted to, a conflict between good and evil. It is his incapacity to understand or respond to human greatness that makes him highly confused. Men and women may be led by superstition but Religion is not superstition. Ayesha and her followers are destroyed by their false beliefs which they sincerely held. This type of religiosity is present in human society but this should have been presented as an aberration and not genuine religious sentiment or beliefs. As against this type of pseudo-religion presented as religion, he does not present any truly religious character or even a predominantly 'good' (to use the Aristotelian concept) character in the whole novel. When the Prophet and his Companions are confused or corrupt or hypocritical like politicians where can he find a really 'good' character?

There is thus no relief in this novel. It is mentally disturbing, almost paranoic, in its love of a corrupt society. To use his own words it is [the] '*locus classicus* of incompatible realities. Lives that have no business mingling with one another sit side by side upon the omnibus' of his novel. 'One universe, on a zebra crossing, is caught for an instant, blinking like a rabbit, in the headlamps of a motor vehicle in which an entirely alien and contradictory continuum is to be found.' If that is his only intention in writing this novel, he may be said to have succeeded in presenting such contradictions in human nature. His strength as a novelist lies in his ability to portray such minds. But when we go a bit deeper into his characterisation we notice that nearly all these characters are repeating the same side of human nature I shall term satanic, i.e. the world of passions and lust and selfishness not for a moment relieved by a desire to struggle with such devilish enchantments.[44] □

Though protesters against the novel received no satisfaction from British law, *The Satanic Verses* was banned in India, Pakistan, Saudi Arabia, and South Africa. The immediate response of the British media to this was somewhat muted. When the novel was banned in India in October 1988, for example, *The Times* dedicated just five lines, and the *Guardian* a mere four lines, to reporting the event. Despite the growing unrest surrounding *The Satanic Verses,* the literary community exhibited little sense of the enormous political storm building on the horizon. Some reviewers even attempted to dismiss the developing controversy. Jonathan Yardley, for example, argued that the response to the novel suggested 'nothing so much as the human capacity to overreact.'[45] Yardley is referring both to the banning of the book by the Indian government of Rajiv Gandhi, and the decision in Britain to award the novel the 1988 Whitbread Prize. For Yardley, these decisions were ill considered; by banning the book, the Indian government simply increased its appeal, and by awarding such a prestigious prize, the Whitbread judges merely demonstrated sympathy for Rushdie.

Yet the controversy surrounding *The Satanic Verses* continued to grow. In interview, Rushdie questioned how the novel could outrage Muslims, and how the Indian government could ban it:

■ [M]ost people, including those in the government have not read it. [Prime Minister] **Rajiv Gandhi** said quite openly that he had not read it and that he did not intend to read it. The Muslim groups who have pushed for the ban in India said openly that they did not need to read it; 95% of what has been written about the book in India has been by those who have not read it.[46] □

Interviews also afforded Rushdie the opportunity to defend his status as a writer and the novel itself. The following interview, 'Bonfire of the Certainties', was recorded on 27 January 1989, but broadcast on 14 February 1989, the very day the Iranian religious leader Ayatollah Khomeini declared the fatwa against Rushdie.

■ *Did you expect such a powerful reaction to this book?*

I expected that the mullahs wouldn't like it. But I didn't write it for the mullahs. I've seen what the mullahs have done in Pakistan over the past 11 years – the level of oppression instituted there by islamisation. I've seen, too, how almost all the poets in Pakistan were in exile in England during that period. Only now are they beginning to think about going back.

Obviously I have a view of the world which is not theirs. I insist on my right to express it as I think fit.

It's very simple in this country. If you don't want to read a book, you don't have to read it. It's very hard to be offended by *The Satanic Verses*, it requires a long period of intense reading. It's a quarter of a million words.

The controversy, in a sense, has been about your acting on the historic text of the Koran and playing with that. How much of that was based on historical fact?

Almost entirely. Almost everything in those sections – the dream sequences – starts from an historical or quasi-historical basis, though one can't really speak with absolute certainty about that period of Mohammed's life. The records are very partial and ambiguous. But he is, after all, the only prophet who exists even partially in history. As with all the other prophets, we only have legends and stories written hundreds of years later. The interesting thing about Mohammed is that there is objective information about him other than sacred text. It seemed to me, when I studied it as an historian, that that makes this whole phenomenon an historical as well as a spiritual one, and the relationship between the people involved is absolutely fascinating.

Islam is, after all, one of the greatest ideas that ever came into the world – I suppose the next idea of that size would have been Marxism – and the chance to study the birth of a great historical idea is interesting. The one thing you learn as an historian is just how fragmented and ambiguous and peculiar the historical record is. So I thought, well, let's not try and pretend to be writing a history. Let's take the themes I'm interested in and fantasise them and fabulate them and all that, so that we don't have to get into the issue: did this really happen like this or did it not?

The themes are huge. Basically, there's two questions that the book seeks to answer. When an idea comes into the world, it's faced with two big tests: when you're weak, do you compromise; when you're strong, are you tolerant? Those are the questions that those sections of the novel seek to dramatise. It shows that (and, as far as we can tell about Mohammed's life, this is also true) the answer to the first question is that, when weak, there seems [in the case of Mohammed] to have been a brief flirtation with a possible compromise – about monotheism – which was very rapidly rejected.

Now I don't think this diminishes Mohammed. All prophets face temptation. When Gibreel [the archangel] comes to Mohammed and tells him that these verses are satanic verses and should be removed – and here are the real verses – he forgave him. He said, 'Never mind, it's understandable, things like this have happened before.' I mean, it seems that Gibreel is more tolerant than some of these people attacking the book.

When Mohammed returned to Mecca in power, he was very, very tolerant. And I think, if I remember correctly, only five or six people were executed after the re-taking of Mecca. And of those five or six people, two were writers, and two were actresses who had performed satirical texts. Now there you have an image that I thought was worth exploring: at the very beginning of Islam you find a conflict between the sacred text and the profane text, between revealed literature and imagined literature. For a writer, that conflict is fascinating and interesting to explore. So that's what I was doing, exploring.

Do you think the opposition to the book is based on people feeling weak or feeling strong?

It seems to me that nothing I can do can destroy Islam. They keep announcing that 900 million people in the world are Muslims. What can I do? How can I unmake Islam? It's not possible. So even if it were my desire, which it isn't, the idea that, somehow, a book should exist which takes a different point of view from that of the imams and be such a dangerous thing, is not convincing to me.

It seems to me completely legitimate that there should be dissent from orthodoxy, not just about Islam, but about anything – from Conservative politics, that's a kind of orthodoxy under which we all live at the moment, it's important that there should be dissent from that. If radical politics were the orthodoxy in this country I think it would be important that there should be dissent from that too.

One of the things that a writer can do is to say: Here is the way in which you're told you're supposed to look at the world, but actually there are also some other ways. Let us never believe that the way in which the people in power tell us to look at the world is the only way we can look, because if we do that, then that's a kind of appalling self-censorship.

What you've written has been called insulting to Islam and a provocation to all Muslims. Did you take delight in provocation?

It depends what you mean by provocation. Any writer wishes to provoke the imagination. You want to make people think about what you're writing. One of the reasons for writing, I believe, is to slightly increase the sum of what it's possible to think, to say 'Let's look at it a different way.' If it works, then people are provoked, and maybe they don't like it.

Almost all the people who are being so insulted and provoked and disgusted have not really read the book. But I get letters every day from Muslims who do like the book. They write to me to say we're not all like those people who burn books. They say they're ashamed of what the imams are doing, about the way in which they're bringing shame on the Muslim community in this country by behaving in this extremely uncivilised way. So the idea that what I'm saying is somehow outside Islam is one that I resist. I come from a Muslim tradition, and in my family in the Indian subcontinent, there was an absolute willingness to discuss anything, there were not these anathemas, these rules, about what you must not talk about. I know about Islam as well, and these people's Islam is not the only Islam.

You've been known primarily as a world writer – perhaps sometimes as an Indian or Pakistani writer, sometimes as a British writer – but with this book it seems that you've become a Muslim writer.

Anybody who reads any of my books knows how powerful the influence of Islam has been. The fact that I would not call myself a religious person doesn't mean that I can reject the importance of Islam in my life. If you come from India or Pakistan, how can you reject religion? Religion is the air everyone breathes. If you're trying to write about that world, you can't make a simple rejection of religion. You have to deal with it because it's the centre of the culture.

The heart of what they're angry about is not the specific insults, it's to do with the whole notion of doubt.

Doubt, it seems to me, is the central condition of a human being in the twentieth century. One of the things that has happened to us in the twentieth century as a human race is to learn how certainty crumbles in your hand. We cannot any longer have a fixed certain view of anything – the table that we're sitting next to, the ground beneath our feet, the laws of science, are full of doubt now. Everything we know is pervaded by doubt and not by certainty. And that is the basis of the great artistic movement known as Modernism. Now the fact that the orthodox figures in the Muslim world have declared a jihad against Modernism is not my fault. It doesn't invalidate an entire way of looking at the world which is, to my mind, the most important new contribution of the twentieth century to the way in which the human race discusses itself. If they're trying to say that this whole process has gone out of the window – that you can't do that, all you have is the old certainties – then, yes, I do argue.[47] □

On 14 February 1989, St Valentine's Day in Britain, the Iranian religious leader Ayatollah Khomeini declared a fatwa against Rushdie. This decree called for Rushdie's death, and a bounty was put on his head. Soon after, Rushdie went into hiding under the protection of the British Special Branch. The American novelist Ralph Ellison responded to these events by suggesting: 'A death sentence is a rather harsh review.'[48]

After February 1989, the literary merits of *The Satanic Verses* were overshadowed by the text's perceived insult to the Islamic faith. As John Leonard observes, it became impossible to discuss *The Satanic Verses* as a literary work without referring to the fatwa.

■ Headlines kept getting in the way of this review. In Pakistan, reactionary nuts are using Salman Rushdie – and the dead bodies of some true believers – to destabilize Benazir Bhutto's government. In Iran, the Ayatollah Ruhollah Khomeini . . . has put out another $5.2 million contract on the novelist. In South Africa, Saudi Arabia and at Waldenbooks of Stamford, Connecticut, *The Satanic Verses* is banned. For a couple of minutes, let's try to see the book through the bonfires of its burning.

As much as Islam, Salman Rushdie blasphemes Thatcherism. He's unkind, too, to V. S. Naipaul. 'Pitting levity against gravity,' altogether impious, *The Satanic Verses* is one of those go-for-broke 'metafictions' – a grand narrative and a Monty Python send-up of history, religion and popular culture; Hindu cyclic and Moslem dualistic; postcolonial identity crisis and modernist pastiche; Bombay bombast and stiff-upper-liposuction; babu baby talk and ad agency neologism; cinema gossip, elephant masks, pop jingles, lousy puns, kinky sex and *Schadenfreude* [the malicious enjoyment of another's misfortune] a sort of *Sammy and Rosie Get Laid* [Hanif Kureishi, 1987] in Doris Lessing's *The Four-Gated City* [1969] – from which the sly-boots Author-God tip-and-twinkletoes away with a cannibal grin. 'Who am I?' he asks us. 'Let's put it this way: who has the best tunes?'

As we shall see, he's disingenuous. And already, like the Mojtabais and Mukherjees, I've made the novel sound as daunting as the kipper that the poor displaced protagonist Chamcha has to face, so many miles from home, at his first appalling public-schoolboy breakfast: 'England was a peculiar-tasting smoked fish full of spikes and bones, and nobody would ever tell him how to eat it.' How, indeed? [. . .]

Rushdie may say now whatever he wants to about 'the fictional dream[s] of a fictional character, an Indian movie star, and one who is losing his mind at that.' He can say that his book 'isn't actually *about* Islam'; it's about, instead, 'migration, metamorphosis, divided selves, love, death.' But that's not what he was saying last fall. To Madhu Jain in the *India Today* of September 15: 'Actually, one of my major themes is religion and fanaticism. I have talked about [Islam, which] I know the most about.' To Shrabani Basu in the September 18 edition of *Sunday*: 'It is a serious attempt to write about religion and revelation from the point of view of a secular person . . . Besides, Mohammed is a very interesting figure. He's the only prophet who exists even remotely inside history.'

I'm not saying that for this impudence Rushdie deserves Khomeini's eleventh-century sort of criticism by assassination. I *am* saying he has played fast and loose. ('Writers and whores,' observes his own Mahound: 'I see no difference here.') Having said that, let me add I'm sorry that so much attention's been paid to less than a third of the novel and so little to the rest of it, which has brilliant things to say about the hatred of women in history; the triumph of the machinery of images – in movies, television and advertising – over ancient myth,

classical literature and political science; the displacement and deracination of the modern intelligence in a world of permanent migration
and mindless hybridizing; the loss of self and death of love in a time
without decency or roots; wog-bashing in the racist theocracy of the
Mad Thatcher.[49] □

Leonard, like so many reviewers, compares *The Satanic Verses* unfavourably to Rushdie's earlier novels. He does, however, add that the novel 'is
infinitely more interesting than those hundreds of neat little novels we
have to read between Rushdies.'[50] The last review in this chapter also
finds it impossible to ignore the politics surrounding the novel. This
review, Michael Wood's 'The Prophet Motive', published in *The New
Republic* on 6 March 1989, attempts to defend Rushdie at a time when his
enforced hiding made it impossible for the author to defend himself.

■ The book has been publicly burned in Bradford, withdrawn from
bookstores, made the subject of a mass protest march. It is about to be
taken up in parliamentary debate. (It also has been banned in India,
Pakistan, Saudi Arabia, and South Africa.) Why? Because it is said to
blaspheme against Islam, and to insult the already much insulted
Muslim Community in Britain. But it can't blaspheme, because only
believers can blaspheme, as Rushdie himself says in the novel, and
this is a novel about doubt. (We may well wonder, as Rushdie did in
an eloquent article in the *Observer*, why a supposedly civilized and
modern country is considering extending its blasphemy laws instead
of abolishing them.) The book doesn't insult, either; but we are deep
in the hospital ward here, skins are understandably thin. [. . .]
    Only edgy or beleaguered or tyrannical people should take irrever-
ence as insult. We should ask not what Rushdie has done to the
Muslims in Britain. We should wonder, rather, what Britain has done
to them, to make them so eager to turn their (admittedly mischievous)
friend into their scapegoat. If they had read Rushdie's novel, they
would have learned that the solemn religious respect that they want
(and that he lacks) is the first step to the ghetto. Ghettos are made
partly of unquestioned orthodoxies, partly of prejudice masked as
tolerance. Tropical London is a lot more attractive than that.[51] □

It is clear from the reviews contained in this chapter that Rushdie's
works give rise to an enormous range of debates. He is, perhaps, the most
controversial author in the history of literature in English. As this chapter
has indicated, much of this controversy emerges from questions of cultural allegiance. The next chapter in this Guide explores these questions
at the level of literary criticism in terms of Rushdie's formal and textual
affiliations.

CHAPTER TWO

'Of What Fusions, Translations, Conjoinings Is It Made?': Intertexts and Questions of Tradition

IN THE previous chapter, Edward Said appeared to question Rushdie's motivation in writing *The Satanic Verses*. Said made the point that many Muslims believed Rushdie had betrayed his own people to side with the 'legions of Orientalists'. Said does not, however, hold this view himself. Instead, he offers a more complex understanding of Rushdie. While not denying the hurt that Rushdie's novels have caused, Said argues that it should be possible to acknowledge Rushdie's brilliance as well as his apostasy. One, indeed, cannot exist without the other; for Rushdie's novels operate in that space between sureties, outside fixed allegiances. It is, therefore, in the nature of his writing that it will offend. Yet at the same time, that offence reveals the true subject matter of Rushdie's work – namely the emergence of migrancy and hybridity as the defining characteristics of the twentieth century. Said points to this when he suggests that, 'the point is there is no pure, unsullied, unmixed essence to which some of us can return, whether that essence is pure Islam, pure Christianity, pure Judaism or Easternism, Americanism, Westernism.'[1]

Issues of origins, essence, migrancy, and hybridity, will be explored in greater depth in the following chapters of this Guide. These issues, however, also clearly impact upon the subject of this chapter, that of the intertextuality of *Midnight's Children* and *The Satanic Verses* – the manner in which Rushdie's texts stand in discursive relation to yet other texts. For if there can be no pure cultural essence, no accessible point of origin to which to return, then this is equally true of, indeed reflected within, Rushdie's writing itself. As Said argues, 'Rushdie's work is not just about the mixture, it is that mixture itself.'[2] This is, of course, true of any text inasmuch as intertextuality is inevitable if we accept the notion that 'the space into which a text inscribes itself is always a space that is already inscribed.'[3] In Julia Kristeva's conception of intertextuality, the figure of the author is in effect removed from any understanding of their text. The author is no longer seen to be either autonomous or intentional. Intertextuality is seen to be an inevitable and general quality of all texts.[4] For many critics, however, Rushdie's works not only accept the inevitability of intertextuality, but are also seen to celebrate it deliberately and self-consciously on both a thematic and structural level.

Rushdie describes himself as a migrant – as a man existing between and across cultures. It is perhaps inevitable that critics of his works should seek to identify similar qualities in his novels. Rushdie's status as a man between cultures is translated into Rushdie the writer between literary traditions. Rushdie himself does little to clarify these discussions. He willingly acknowledges a host of literary and cultural influences from both the East and the West, but refuses to privilege one above the other. Rushdie leaves that exercise to literary critics.

The first article included in this chapter, Philip Engblom's 'A Multitude of Voices: Carnivalization and Dialogicality in the Novels of Salman Rushdie', locates Rushdie's works within the framework of literary postcolonial resistance.[5] Engblom writes of Rushdie, 'He, more than anyone, has come to epitomize (to paraphrase his own words slightly) "the Empire writing back with a vengeance"'.[6] Rushdie is seen to be 'writing back' through formal invention and experimentation. He is seen to challenge literary conventions and redefine 'prevalent, complaisant ideas about the art of the novel.'[7] For Engblom, Rushdie's novels represent a response not only to colonialism but also to the artistic practices complicit in that oppression. Rushdie himself claims a 'determination to create a literary language and literary forms in which the experience of formerly colonized, still-disadvantaged peoples might find full expression.'[8] Yet in this article, Engblom presents a reading of Rushdie's works in the light of Western literary concepts; he points to Rushdie's literary exuberance and play to suggest a form of postmodernism best understood in relation to Mikhail Bakhtin's notion of the carnivalesque. Engblom declares:

■ We find, then, both carnival and dialogue, carnivalization and dia-logicality, in Rushdie's work. And with these terms we can quite profitably recast the entire discussion in the frame of analysis created by Mikhail Bakhtin. These are, of course, two of the governing ideas of his criticism, as he defines them specifically in *Problems of Dostoevsky's Poetics* [1929]. They have been applied in recent years to contexts quite distant from Dostoevsky's fiction; and perhaps through them we can see Rushdie, too, in a new light.[9] □

In Chapter One of this Guide, a number of reviewers were seen to attack both *Midnight's Children* and *The Satanic Verses* for being structurally 'loose'. Reading Rushdie's novels in the light of concepts such as the carnivalesque and Menippean satire may represent a response to such attacks.[10] The expansiveness and exuberance of Rushdie's subject matter, the conflicting perspectives contained by his writing, and his apparent refusal to provide closure to his novels, though it draws criticism from some critics, is celebrated in a Bakhtinian conception of the carnival. For Bakhtin, such qualities are transgressive; they subvert systems of authority founded upon a narrow, 'monologic', view of the world.

Bakhtin's conception of the carnival emerged out of his reading of François Rabelais' work, *Gargantua and Pantagruel* (1532–64). Rabelais was a Franciscan monk of the sixteenth century, yet his writings betray none of the piety one might expect from such a figure. *Gargantua and Pantagruel* is a great sprawling collection of novels full of irreverence, full of bodily and social excess. Both Bakhtin and Rabelais were writing out of periods of revolution. The Renaissance for Rabelais, and the political upheavals of the Russian revolution for Bakhtin, signal one world's death and another world's birth. Implicit in Engblom's article is the suggestion that the collapse of colonial empire represents a similar potential for re-birth.

The potential for re-birth is central to Bakhtin's conception of the carnival space. The carnival is a place of laughter. The ambivalence of this laughter serves to provide 'a gay parody of official reason, of the seriousness of official truth.'[11] In such a space, laws are suspended and power may be subverted; the king is un-crowned; the clown is made king. Binaries between high and low, sanctioned and unsanctioned, are disturbed. This is a space of grotesque bodies. Emphasis is placed upon orifices and protuberances. In the carnival, bodies are multiple. They escape representation by remaining unfinished. The carnival is fertile because it is unofficial, unfixed and therefore represents a realm of becoming.

Like Bakhtin, Engblom links the carnivalesque to oxymoronic combinations, the bringing together of opposites, through the metamorphosis, madness, and dreams of Menippean satire. In this article, Engblom slides easily from one concept to the other in his discussion of Rushdie's works. Both concepts not only embrace an understanding of self-hood as unstable, but also celebrate polyphony and heteroglossia – the existence of many voices, different sorts of voices in continuous dialogue. In such a space, no single authorative voice may hope to prevail. As Carlos Fuentes observes, 'Rushdie's work perfectly fits the Bakhtinian contention that ours is an age of competitive languages. The novel is the privileged arena where languages in conflict can meet . . . establishing a dialogic encounter, a meeting with the other.'[12]

■ In this context of pervasive carnival freedom, Rushdie develops the multivoicedness that is the mark of the polyphonic novel, the main evidence of which is the voice of none other than the narrator, Saleem Sinai. The question arises of how a novel with a first-person narrative throughout, such as *Midnight's Children*, can be dialogic or multivoiced. One answer is that the dialogicality is (to follow Bakhtin's own terminology) internal or hidden, *within* the voice of the narrator. Saleem's narration is not linear: it is anything but a straightforward telling of the narrative – in the manner, for instance, of the narrator of Conrad's *Lord Jim* [1900]. Saleem's narration is constantly questioning itself and this self-questioning is a habitual, harried anticipation of some other, usually unspecified person's outraged objection to his narration. Right from page one we find how Saleem's anticipation of this 'other' determines the way in which he speaks:

> I was born in the city of Bombay . . . once upon a time. No, that won't do, there's no getting away from the date: I was born in Doctor Narlikar's Nursing Home on August 15th, 1947. And the time? The time matters, too. Well then: at night. No, it's important to be more . . . On the stroke of midnight as a matter of fact. [3/11][13]

Saleem quite clearly is *talking* to someone. A dialogue is taking place, even if one side is silent – indeed, not even present in body – and is simply anticipated by the speaking voice. On occasion this 'other' may assume the body and voice of Padma, the illiterate pickle-factory worker, who is Saleem's only *acknowledged* audience. But even during Padma's absence, when she storms out in disgust midway through the novel, this unspecified 'other' is still present for Saleem to address and anticipate. It provides the constant basis for the hidden, internal dialogicality that is symptomatic of Saleem's narrative.

The dialogicality in *Midnight's Children* is by no means limited strictly to Padma, however, or to this amorphous 'other.' There are at least 115 specific voices in the novel that speak through the voice of the 'other' and that constantly challenge Saleem's veracity and authority as sole narrator. Saleem splinters, in other words, into each one of the characters of his narrative. Each is invested with a vigorous, often feisty voice of his or her own. Saleem does not have the last word. Indeed, it is part of the pathos of his character that everyone else seems to speak and act for him. This is certainly true of his double and nemesis, Shiva. Here we have two ideas, embodied, expressed, and lived by the fundamental, irreducible duality that is Saleem/Shiva, in a struggle unto death itself. Although we hear principally Saleem on the surface, Shiva is the constant counterpoint we hear beneath the dominant melody of the narrative. This is the polyphony of *Midnight's Children*. [. . .]

The carnival continues in *The Satanic Verses*. Here, too, there are over a hundred named characters, and the stage has grown to intercontinental proportions. The action is spread out between Bombay and London, but it also includes the dream-worlds of Gibreel Farishta – an Arabian Jahilia, an Iranian 'Jerusalem,' and an Indian Peristan. Even so, there is not quite the same frenetic movement between land-scapes as there is in *Midnight's Children*. By far the largest part of the book takes place in London, and that too within the special London of immigrants in the East End. But if the picaresque movement has diminished, the directly identifiable Menippean elements are, by con-trast, even greater in *The Satanic Verses* than in *Midnight's Children*. In *The Satanic Verses* every one of the Menippean elements that Bakhtin so carefully enumerates is so prominently on display that it would not be far wrong to call the novel a modern Menippean satire.

That the novel at the very least plays quite consciously off the tradition of the Menippean satire is suggested clearly by one promi-nent and specific allusion (which Rushdie puts in the mouth of Muhammad Sufyan, immigrant from the former East Pakistan, and East End proprietor of the Shaandaar Café) to one of the defining Latin Menippean satires, the *Metamorphoses* [second century AD, also known as *The Golden Ass*] of Apuleius. In what is in effect an act of solidarity with a 'colonial of an earlier Empire'[14] – the second-century Moroccan, Apuleius – [Sufyan] quotes directly from the *Metamorphoses*, as he seeks an explanation for Chamcha's transformation into a goat-footed Satan. This evocation of Apuleius and of the *Metamorphoses* not only legiti-mizes the device of human metamorphosis into animal form; it also gives licence to all the other Menippean elements of fantasy, dreams, insane vision, slum naturalism, social and racial misalliances, and eccentric behaviour and speech, which constitute the very fabric of the novel. *The Satanic Verses*, for all its postmodernist debunkings, its icon-oclasm, establishes for itself a legitimizing literary lineage, that of the Menippean satire.

The Menippean satire is, first and foremost, the test of an idea and of the hero who espouses that idea. All the vulgarity and profanation is a deliberate test, which asks, 'What kind of idea is this?' Or, to rephrase it as *The Satanic Verses* itself poses the test at several critical points in the novel: *'What kind of idea are you?'* This is the question asked of Mahound, of Ayesha, and of the mad dreamer himself, Gibreel Farishta. All of them answer by rejecting compromise. But there is a second part of the test, which asks, 'How do you behave when you win?' And here all of them answer, in deeds if not words, 'With mercy.' The only visionary character in the novel's dream-sequences who does not submit to this test is the Iman. His idea is fulfilled and legitimized only by blood, by the extirpation of the other-than-the-idea.

In the almost overwhelming carnival and Menippean freedom of

The Satanic Verses, what polyphony do we find? The narrative technique differs substantially in some ways from that in *Midnight's Children*. There is a first-person narrator, but we encounter him, as a character, little more than a dozen times throughout the novel and then usually for scarcely more than a sentence or two. The rest of the novel we read for long stretches from what we cannot help but regard as a fairly typical third-person omniscient point of view. We do not have the radical double-voicedness of the narrator himself to cue us to the polyphony. Even so, strong traces of hidden dialogue (anticipatory discourse) emerge out of the represented speech and thoughts of the main characters. Questions and self-admonitions are constantly erupting into the train of their thought, frequently italicized to emphasize the otherness of the questioning voice.

But the main polyphony emerges from the dialogic positions assumed by the novel's principal pair of parodic doubles – Gibreel and Chamcha. Their fates are irrevocably tied by their fall together from the paradise of the exploding airplane, the *Bostan*, at the start of the novel. But although they both fall, in this episode, out of the 'real' into the carnival realm, they remain opposites. Indeed, their oppositions become increasingly exaggerated as the novel develops. They not only express, but come actually to embody, fundamentally different worlds of value – a difference that is underscored by the one temporarily metamorphizing into an angel and the other into a satan. Yet they are forced together by their common immigrant status and thus juxtaposed as each other's dialogic other. The confrontation, indeed the collision, of their ill-matched worlds provides the armature of the novel. Within its polarized field, the sacred (in the novel's terms, the angelic) and the profane (in the novel's terms, the Satanic), Mahound and Baal, harem and brothel assume their own dialogic oppositions. As Rushdie himself puts it: 'The two struggling worlds, pure and impure, chaste and coarse, are juxtaposed by making them echoes of one another?' ('In Good Faith,' 54).[15] They not only echo each other but are forced, against their own wishes, to recognize each other and to *talk*, within the 'great dialogue' of the novel.

In a review of *The Satanic Verses*, D.J. Enright complains that the novel is 'copious in thesis and antithesis, but [. . .] synthesis hovers beyond it.'[16] And in his summation (after conceding the considerable pleasures of the book) he concludes: 'No doubt rather more in the way of order and (what art can and ought to give us, although and because life doesn't) of clarity would have been appreciated too' (Enright, 26). But, as we have seen, it is precisely synthesis – reduction to one grand clarifying 'Truth' – that the polyphonic novel most strenuously resists. In the carnivalesque world of *Midnight's Children* and *The Satanic Verses*, it is riotous plurality (not order), variety and difference (not clarity) that are valued and celebrated. Speaking on behalf of his fellow Indo-British writers, Rushdie makes the claim:

> One of the changes [in our writing] has to do with attitudes towards the use of English. We can't simply use the language in the way the British did: [. . .] it needs remaking for our own purposes. [. . .] we can find in that linguistic struggle a reflection of other struggles taking place in the real world, struggles between the cultures within ourselves and the influences at work upon our societies. To conquer English may be to complete the process of making ourselves free. ['Imaginary Homelands,' 17][17]

It is in the fluidity, the unfinalizable openness of carnivalization and dialogicality that Rushdie himself finds the means to break out of the imperial containments of official, metropolitan, monologic versions of the Western novel.[18] □

Engblom clearly acknowledges Rushdie's political commitment, and suggests it may find literary expression in carnivalised space. At no point in this article, however, does Engblom question the usefulness of applying the carnivalesque to Rushdie's brand of postcolonialism. For although Bakhtin's work gained enormous popularity in literary and cultural studies in the 1980s and early 1990s, it would be fair to say that some of that popularity has waned. Critics are now more inclined to question the efficacy of an approach that on the surface appears to celebrate temporary chaos and confusion at the expense of a more stable and politically engaged perspective. Terry Eagleton, for example, can find little to say of the carnival that is positive. Eagleton argues that, 'Carnival, after all, is a licensed affair in every sense, a permissible rupture of hegemony, a contained popular blow-off as disturbing and relatively ineffectual as a revolutionary work of art.'[19]

The next article included in this Guide also examines the relationship between Rushdie's writing and Western literature. Patricia Merivale's 'Saleem Fathered by Oskar: Intertextual Strategies in *Midnight's Children* and *The Tin Drum*', is not so much interested in locating *Midnight's Children* within a formal landscape, as it is in establishing the novel's connections to specific texts.[20] In this article, Merivale follows the example of numerous reviewers and critics by discussing how writers such as Gabriel García Márquez and Günter Grass have influenced Rushdie's work.[21] Merivale is then able to link *Midnight's Children* to *One Hundred Years of Solitude* (1970) and *The Tin Drum*, texts that she describes as 'Western' fictions.

There are, indeed, many similarities between *Midnight's Children* and *The Tin Drum*. The most apparent similarity is between the novel's central characters, Saleem and Oskar. Both are intimately linked to the history of their homelands. Saleem is born just as India reclaims its independence. Oskar's birth and stunted development corresponds to that of Nazi Germany. Both characters recount their tales upon reaching the biblically significant age of 30. Both Saleem and Oskar are outsiders, picaresque characters, able to comment on their worlds yet impotent. Both are grotesquely deformed. Yet, for Merivale, Rushdie is not simply mimicking Grass. Though she acknowledges his influence on *Midnight's Children*, Merivale argues that this influence is then translated 'into the "Indian" terms of Rushdie's own narrative.'[22]

■ At the very beginning of his story, Rushdie pays conspicuous though oblique tribute to Grass in his account of the German connections of Saleem's supposed grandfather, Aadam Aziz. He spent five years in Germany; his nose yields three drops of blood (*Children* 10)[23] in seeming echo of the three Parsifalian drops on snow (*Drum* 459);[24] his German anarchist friends, Oskar – who, incidentally, 'died . . . like a comedian' (*Children* 29) – and Ilse, unsettle his Muslim and Indian presuppositions, yet at the same time distance him with their 'Orientalist' notion 'that India – like radium – had been "discovered" by the Europeans . . . that he [Aziz] was somehow the invention of their ancestors' (*Children* 11). Thus Rushdie, although he valorizes many of Grass's literary strategies throughout, makes clear that he will 'transpose' or 'translate' them on his own terms.[25] □

Though Merivale points to Rushdie's valorisation, or emulation, of Grass, she does not detect the same relationship between Rushdie and Márquez. Rushdie himself adopts a similar position. He admits to a deep interest in both writers, yet appears to favour Grass's works. In his introduction to Grass's own essay on *The Tin Drum*, Rushdie provides a glowing tribute to Grass's novel.[26] In this introduction, Rushdie talks of those works that most influenced his early writing and suggests that *The Tin Drum* was the kind of novel that encouraged young writers such as himself to 'become the sort of writers they have it in themselves to be.'[27] For Rushdie, Grass is a migrant like himself; cut off from his past; separated from the city of his birth.[28] On the other hand, Rushdie points to important differences between himself and Márquez. He celebrates Márquez's writing, yet identifies in works such as *One Hundred Years of Solitude* a somewhat stable, perhaps even nostalgic, 'village view of the world.'[29] Rushdie's texts, by contrast, tend to focus upon urban environments as sites of flux and hybridity.

■ Both Rushdie and Grass (unlike García Márquez) tell a first-person, seemingly episodic story in a sequence of chapters, grouped in each case into three books: of eight, fifteen, and seven chapters respectively

in *Midnight's Children*, of sixteen, eighteen, and twelve chapters respectively in *The Tin Drum*. In Rushdie, the chapters, which correspond to
pickle-jars (of which, as Saleem would say, more later), explicitly add
up to Saleem's age as he ends the book: thirty. In Grass, the last of his
forty-six chapters is called 'Thirty,' for the same reason. Each chapter
in both books has a title which captures pithily and emblematically a
key object or situation, and many of Rushdie's titles are sufficiently
similar to Grass's to remind us of some thematic resemblances (I give
the Rushdie title first in each pair). Titles like 'The Perforated Sheet'
and 'The Wide Skirt,' 'Accident in a Washing Chest' and 'In the
Clothes Cupboard,' and 'Under the Carpet' and 'Under the Raft,' suggest, among other similarities of plot, the womb-like retreats suited to
the voyeurism and escapism of these largely passive heroes; 'All-India
Radio' and 'Special Communiqués' suggest the metaphor of telecom-
munications as the means by which 'news' makes itself known,
available for turning into 'history.' 'Mercurochrome' and 'Disinfectant'
suggest the key role of hospitals in each hero's life, and Oskar subtitles
his penultimate chapter 'Adoration of a Preserving Jar.'

Saleem and Oskar are writing, telling, or reading out their stories
within a frame narrative, to a clearly delineated listener, a 'narratee,'
who is a stand-in for the implied reader and a perpetual reminder of
the present tense of narrating time. Bruno, Oskar's warder in the
insane asylum, and Padma, Saleem's fellow-pickler in the pickle-
factory, eventually his fiancée, but chiefly his 'necessary ear' (149), are
both permitted to interrupt and even to contribute short sections of
their own; both provide – as Padma does through her 'paradoxical
earthiness of spirit' (150) – some Panzaic 'realism,'[30] some reader-
responsiveness from within the text, to keep the narrator's tale on
track and his Quixotic feet on the ground.[31]

Critics have praised Grass for his 'sensitivity to the magic qualities
of things' and for his 'realistic precision [in the] pursuit of fantasy as
part of reality';[32] they are already rightly praising Rushdie for the same
qualities. But further keys to mimesis in Grass and Rushdie may be
found in their (largely epic) figures of speech.

The two authors share an encyclopedic taste, like García Márquez,
for 'swallowing the world' through inclusiveness and exactness of
description, especially in the form of lists – the tables of contents are
the first 'lists' in each book to establish a sense of 'the supremacy of
the inanimate.' Sometimes such lists provide cryptic anticipations of
the story to come, as in the prophetic verses uttered just before
Saleem's birth: 'Washing will hide him – voices will guide him/ . . .
Spittoon will brain him – doctors will drain him' (87). Often they
serve as a recapitulation of the plot so far, as in Oskar's Hamletic rumi-
nation in the graveyard:

> My grandmother's four skirts . . . the maze of scars on Herbert
> Truczinski's back, the blood-absorbing mail baskets at the Polish
> Post Office, America – but what is America compared to Streetcar
> Number 9 that went to Brösen? (444)

His final peroration to the shadow of the Black Witch has a similar
function:

> The Witch, black as pitch, . . . had always been there, [in] all words
> . . . and all stones . . . and all the shattered glass . . . and all the
> groceries, all the flour and sugar in blue pound and half-pound
> bags . . . cemeteries I stood in, flags I knelt on, coconut fiber I lay
> on . . . (571)

Such Rabelaisian catalogues are largely made up of talismanic objects,
like Saleem's spittoon or Oskar's drum, constantly recurring leitmotifs, in both their descriptive roles and their symbolic references,
synecdochically mimicking all-inclusiveness by a canny selection of
apparently random items. The telepathic catalogue of Saleem's vision
from the Bombay clocktower (*Children* 173) becomes an olfactory catalogue of his experience of Karachi:

> Formlessly . . . the fragrances poured into me: the pustular body
> odours of young men in loose pajamas holding hands in Sadar
> evenings . . . the aroma of contraband cigarettes and 'black-money'
> . . . Mosques poured over me the itr of devotion . . . (317)

Then his 'overpowering desire for form assert[s] itself': synesthetically,
Saleem classifies the scents by colour, then shapes them into a 'general
theory of smell' and then into a 'science of nasal ethics' (318), a key set
of Rushdie's rhetorical strategies for making the moral and emotional
concrete. Saleem's marvellous nose can identify 'the nauseating odor
of defeat' (317) and 'the old aroma of failure' (202), or detect that
'unfairness smelt like onions' (370). 'Smells assail [Oskar]' throughout as well (568); again Rushdie *multiplies* a Grassian trope.

All three authors are linked through such figures of speech as the
hyperboles of amnesia, or of Rushdie's charming variation on a theme
by García Márquez: 'for forty days, we were besieged by the dust'
(*Children* 271), characteristically testifying to an aesthetic of abun-
dance, the feature which most clearly distinguishes their work from
the sparer imaginings of Kafka and Borges, their immediate predecessors in the interweaving of the tangible and the marvellous. One of
Rushdie's minor characters encapsulates this aesthetic destiny: 'a
painter whose paintings had grown larger and larger as he tried to get

the whole of life into his art . . . wanted to be a miniaturist and . . . got elephantiasis instead!' (*Children* 48).

Perhaps the most concentratedly 'magical' of such metaphors are those of abstractions reified: the infectious weeping in Oskar's Onion Cellar, the objective correlative of the collective pseudo-remorse (following the collective amnesia) of the Germans, is like the 'pigmentation disorder' (*Children* 179) which occurs among those prosperous Indians who turn white upon inheriting colonial prerogatives from the departing British, each ailment serving as a compact moral allegory for a collective historical phase.

Oskar's 'carnival make-believe' (*Drum* 452), the telepathic connections among the Midnight's Children, the games that the Delhi magicians play with illusion, all suggest in context that 'Reality can have metaphorical content; that does not make it less real' (*Children* 200), but rather, in terms of Magic Realism,[33] more real:

> [T]he magicians were people whose hold on reality was absolute; they gripped it so powerfully that they could bend it every which way in the service of their arts, but they never forgot what it was. (*Children* 399)

Saleem seems to contrast an Indian Magic Realism, like that exemplified by these magicians, with a Pakistani fantasy, devaluing the latter:

> [In my Indian childhood] I was beset by an infinity of alternative realities, while in [my Pakistani adolescence] I was adrift, disorientated, amid an equally infinite number of falsenesses, unrealities, and lies. (326)

Such an attitude has political consequences:

> Karachiites had only the slipperiest of grasps on reality, and were therefore willing to turn to their leaders for advice on what was real and what was not. [They were] beset by illusionary sand-dunes and the ghosts of ancient kings . . . (308)

What seems to be Saleem's description of his own style likewise suggests a commitment to Magic Realism:

> Matter of fact descriptions of the outré and bizarre, and their reverse, namely heightened, stylized versions of the everyday – these techniques . . . are also attitudes of mind . . . (218)

'Heightened, stylized' descriptions can be found, for example, in insertions of refrain-structured prose poems (very similar in form to some of Oskar's incantatory flights) into Saleem's first-person narration, already crammed with matter-of-fact descriptions of the outré and bizarre.

The Magicians, who are – like Saleem but in their different medium – bending reality without ever forgetting what it is, are Magic Realists and thus evidently artists. But so, in a more humble way, is Saleem's foster-mother, Mary Pereira: 'nobody makes achar-chutney like our Mary . . . because she puts her feelings inside [it].' She does so with the feelings of others also: very early in his life 'she stirred [Saleem's] guilt into green chutney' too (458). She resembles in this respect Oskar's supposed father, Matzerath, whose epitaph is that 'he, an impassioned cook, had a knack for metamorphosing feelings into soup' (*Drum* 36). These several parent figures supply our artist-heroes with a method for metaphor based on the emotional significance of material things, on food as art, the homeliest yet most pervasive of the innumerable metaphors in these books for the operations of the creative imagination.[34]

The primary self-reflexive image for the creative imagination in *Midnight's Children* seems to be Saleem's telepathic powers, but it is quickly replaced by the more widely diffused (although non-eponymous) olfactory image, which, in turn, modulates into the gastronomic images of his jars of chutney, which constitute, lined up, the chapters of the book itself. Similarly, Oskar, who can create an art work simply by coughing and sneezing (349), is chiefly known for his drumming; it is mirrored in Herbert Truczinski's historical back-scars (a tip of the hat to Kafka's 'In the Penal Colony' [1919]?), which are, in turn, reproduced in Bruno's string constructions, a *mise en abyme*,[35] like the 'ever so fragile house of cards' (*Drum* 232), literally exchangeable with Oskar's own storytelling: 'every time I tell him some fairy tale, he shows his gratitude by bringing out his latest knot construction' (9).

Speaking more abstractly than usual, Oskar says, 'inevitably the thread of events wound itself into loops and knots which became known as the fabric of History' (373); evidently Bruno can, with his string art, like that later artist, Eddie Amsel, in Grass's *Hundejahre*, [1963, *Dog Years* 1965] who turned History into scarecrows, reify the metaphoric 'fabric of history' into the concrete loops and knots of 'a figure, which in accordance with Mr. Matzerath's [Oskar's] story . . . I [Bruno] shall call "Refugee from the East"' (408). And there follows a recapitulation of Oskar's adventures in the familiar catalogue-form – all turned into string: that is, History. It climaxes in Bruno's attempt to delineate, in the form of 'a single [string] figure which, moreover, should present a *striking resemblance to himself* [Oskar]' (emphasis added), that Goethe–Rasputin dialectic – 'how many miles of string I have tied into knots, trying to create a valid synthesis of the two extremes' (412), Bruno complains – which has shaped Oskar's artistic life. He has thus made a *mise en abyme*, in string, of Oskar's 'new book,' *The Tin Drum*, itself the synthesis of Oskar's two sacred texts. And Rushdie has multiplied, like so much else in the patterns adapted from Grass, his allegories of inter-textual origins.

The two chief avatars of the Artist in these books are those of the Artist-as-Entertainer (their chief role within the *action* of each book) and of the Artist-as-Historian (their chief role in the *narration* of each book). The two roles overlap in an image like Oskar's painting of 'the blockade of Berlin on the table-top with champagne' (454). Both heroes are aware of themselves in motley, as court jesters, as fools in the carnival tradition (see, for example *Drum* 452). Their most direct influence upon history is in such scenes as the incitements of the language riots in Rushdie and the Pied Piping of the Onion Cellar in Grass, where their enacting of their 'historical role' (*Children* 86) is chiefly manifested in their role as entertainers; Art is powerful. Such power implies responsibility (in both senses), which further implies the possibility of guilt.

'Entertainers would orchestrate my life' (101), says Saleem. Bebra, the master-entertainer of the troupe of dwarfs with whom Oskar is briefly affiliated, likewise orchestrates Oskar's. Both heroes make their living largely as entertainers, though again art and history overlap in Oskar's employment as a carver of epitaphs upon gravestones. As narrators they are also entertainers; they are very conscious of the need to hold their audience, which consists, in the first instance, of their reader-surrogates, Bruno and Padma. Saleem, as Nancy Batty has emphasized, is particularly struck (as is García Márquez) by the analogy of his role as storyteller to that of Scheherazade and of his story to the frame narrative of the *Arabian Nights*.

The 'literal' connections between the heroes and history are deliberately strained; it is a necessary fiction for both narrators to see themselves as 'protagonists' yet, paradoxically, also as 'victims.' But however remote or indirect Saleem's 'first attempt at rearranging history' (260) or however strained the 'metaphoric' grounds for supposing that (for instance) the 1965 Indo–Pakistani 'war happened because I dreamed Kashmir into the fantasies of our rulers' (339), and, conversely, that 'the hidden purpose of the . . . war was . . . the elimination of my benighted family from the face of the earth' (338), that they both see themselves acting upon history, while synchronously being its central victims, is a self-delusion appropriate to Magic Realism, empowering the subjective distortions and the grotesque shifts of perspective that touch the Historical with the Marvellous.

'My [glass-shattering] number was conceived along historical lines'

(*Drum*, 318); their obligations as historians override in the end their obligations as entertainers. The gastronomic metaphors for art become metaphors for history, as Saleem finally puts *his* whole 'number' together. 'Pickle-fumes . . . stimulate the juices of memory' (166), and it is an almost Proustian taste of chutney that brings Saleem back to his Bombay heritage, very much as Oskar, in the asylum, must re-collect his life, through the process of re-drumming its events, in order to compose his story. The making of art or story is thus a perfect image of the operations of Magic Realism: 'It happened that way because that's how it happened' (461) is Saleem's final – historian's – justification for whatever most strains credulity in his account. But what is true is also 'what the author can manage to persuade his audience to believe' (*Children* 270–71), and thus, if you are skilled at incorporating 'memories, dreams, ideas' into your chutney, and possess 'above all a nose capable of discerning the hidden languages of what-must-be-pickled,' you may, like Saleem, create magic through the mimetic, in a 'chutnification of history; the grand [pseudo-Proustian] hope of the pickling of time!' (459–60).

In this essay, I have only touched on the variety of Rushdie's inter-textual strategies and the astonishing density of allusions to and echoes of *The Tin Drum* in *Midnight's Children*. And I have just hinted at Rushdie's bricolage of other texts, both Western and Indian. To what purpose or effect is his voraciously appropriative pastiche (I adapt Jean Franco's terms here) of Günter Grass, amounting to, in Bader's pithy, non-judgemental formulation, 'an Indian Tin Drum'? Given that, as Franco puts it, there 'is no innocent relationship between discourses' (105) what are we to make of Rushdie's totalizing intertextuality?[36] A satire or critique of Grass is not in evidence. Is Rushdie inverting the processes of 'colonial' domination, or is he dis-playing the 'overt cosmopolitanism' of which Brennan, more judgementally, speaks? His mimicry seems, rather, to be a celebration, with Grass's help, of 'people who had been translated, who had . . . entered the condition of metaphor,' of 'writing . . . at the frontier between . . . cultures' (Grass 1987, 63, 59).[37] Perhaps Grass, by now well-travelled in the East, will soon repay Rushdie's intertextual com-pliment with a German *Midnight's Children*.[38] □

If Merivale only touches upon the variety of Rushdie's intertextual allu-sions, then this lack is more than compensated for by M. Keith Booker in his article '*Finnegans Wake* and *The Satanic Verses*: Two Modern Myths of the Fall'.[39] In this article, Booker suggests an enormous array of textual affiliations that may be detected in Rushdie's work – although, like so many of Rushdie's critics, he confines himself almost entirely to Western influences. Booker argues that, 'No writer in the past decade has made more effective use of the Western literary tradition than that erstwhile scion of the east, Salman Rushdie.'[40] His article dedicates just a few lines of text, one footnote and a single supporting quote from Maria Couto, to acknowledge Rushdie's appeal to Eastern literary and cultural traditions.

Like Merivale, Booker identifies similarities between Rushdie, Grass, and Márquez. He does not, however, stop there but goes on to suggest a bewildering array of authors who, he argues, have influenced Rushdie's writing. This list includes figures such as Lucretius, Apuleius, Ovid, Machiavelli, Shakespeare, Defoe, Wordsworth, Blake, and Dickens. More contemporary authors include Kafka, Borges, Beckett, Saul Bellow, Nabokov, Calvino, Isaac Bashevis Singer, and Ray Bradbury. Booker also points to Rushdie's allusions to contemporary Western popular cultural icons such as Batman, Superman, and the singer Bob Dylan.

Booker observes: 'Many approaches are possible to the complex text of *The Satanic Verses*, and no doubt literary scholars (preferably ideal readers suffering from an ideal insomnia) will be exploring its intricacies for years to come.'[41] This article restricts itself to an examination of *The Satanic Verses* in relation to the work of James Joyce. Booker establishes links between *The Satanic Verses* and works such as *Dubliners* (1914), *A Portrait of the Artist as a Young Man* (1916), and *Ulysses* (1922). He is, however, particularly keen to stress the connections between Rushdie's novel and Joyce's *Finnegans Wake* (1939) – boldly asserting that a familiarity with *Finnegans Wake* 'is fundamental to the ability to understand the postmodern world. Such a familiarity also goes a long way towards providing an understanding of *The Satanic Verses*.'[42] Booker explains:

■ *Finnegans Wake* and *The Satanic Verses* have much in common. Both books rely heavily on the metaphor of the dream to aid in an escape from the restrictions of realistic representation, and they embody a complex writing practice that operates simultaneously in several textual modes – parody, allegory, poetry – and on several ontological levels – dreams, hallucinations, myth, film. The texts of each are highly reflexive and concerned with their own composition and that of texts in general. Each presents a world where characters undergo wild metamorphoses and where uncertain ontological conditions powerfully challenge the traditional notion of the unified, stable, autonomous subject. Both employ an impressive range of multinational cultural references and allusions . . . and all cultures seem dissolved in a rich intertextual soup of signification.[43] □

Like *Finnegans Wake*, *The Satanic Verses* defies easy categorisation. The sheer range of its references and allusions confounds any attempt to impose the sort of stable reading perspective normally required for classification. Booker suggests, however, that like *Finnegans Wake*, *The Satanic*

Verses may fruitfully be read in terms of its allusions to mythical and biblical falls from grace.

Finnegans Wake and *The Satanic Verses* open with depictions of falls. Similar falls are repeated throughout their narratives. These narratives are, indeed, structured around such falls. As Booker observes, 'The *Wake* begins with a polysyllabic, multilingual crash that is not only the sound of thunder and the voice of God but also the clamor of a universal fall'.[44] Characters fall and are injured or killed. Wall Street crashes. Reference is made to Humpty Dumpty falling from his wall. In similar fashion, *The Satanic Verses* opens with a description of Gibreel Farishta and Saladin Chamcha falling from the stricken airliner *Bostan*. Gibreel and Saladin, however, do not die, they are not even injured, and so perhaps Rushdie suggests the possibility that redemption and rebirth may follow a fall. Booker examines just this possibility, and its implications for an understanding of both *Finnegans Wake* and *The Satanic Verses*.

■ **The affirmation of renewal in both Joyce and Rushdie suggests that the cultural fall resulting from our loss of faith in the past is a fortunate and liberating one that opens up a variety of exciting possibilities for the future. And the notion of a fortunate fall has strong theological reverberations as well. Joyce makes this connection explicit through his evocation of the fall of Adam in the *Wake* and through the links he constructs between Stephen Dedalus and that other archetypal faller, Satan.[45] In *Portrait* Stephen openly cites Satan as one of his heroes, adopting Satan's *non serviam* [I will not serve] as a personal motto (117).[46] Stephen's choice is entirely appropriate. The proud, rebellious Satan is the very embodiment of both exile and the motif of the fall. Significantly, the narrator of *The Satanic Verses* turns out to be none other than Satan himself but may also be God or the archangel Gabriel; it is difficult if not impossible to distinguish among such figures in Rushdie's book.[47] This narrator clearly indicates a satanic component in his identity when he compares his own fall to that of Farishta and Chamcha from the airplane: 'You think *they* fell a long way? In the matter of tumbles, I yield pride of place to no personage, whether mortal or im-' (133).[48] This invocation of the fall of Satan inevitably recalls the primordial fall of man. Although there is, we are told, a basic difference:**

> **The fall of angels, Gibreel reflected, was not the same kettle as the Tumble of Woman and Man. In the case of human persons, the issue had been morality. Of the fruit of the tree of knowledge of good and evil they shouldst not eat, and ate . . . Whereas the angels' crash was a simple matter of power: a straightforward piece of celestial police work, punishment for rebellion. (332)**

The political emphasis given here to the fall of Satan is typical of Rushdie's writing. Gibreel follows this line of thought to meditate on the implications of the fact that the fall of mankind resulted from eating the fruit of the Tree of Knowledge of Good and Evil:

> Then how unconfident of Itself this Deity was, Who didn't want Its finest creations to know right from wrong; and Who reigned by terror, insisting upon the unqualified submission of even Its closest associates, packing off all dissidents to Its blazing Siberias, the gulag-infernos of Hell. (332)

Rushdie's linkage of the authoritarian practices of his significantly genderless Deity and those of modern-day Soviet Russia again shows his constant emphasis on the political implications of his fiction.

Such passages help to explain the uproar over Rushdie's book among certain segments of the religious world and indicate why a recent *New York Times Magazine* article on Rushdie was subtitled 'Fiction's Embattled Infidel.'[49] Compared to the sometimes outrageous methods of Joyce (think of Buck Milligan's 'Ballad of Joking Jesus' early in *Ulysses*), Rushdie's attacks on religious authority seem relatively tame, almost clichéd in some cases, at least to Western eyes. But more eyes than Western ones are on Rushdie and his work, as recent events have proved.

It comes as no surprise that the biblical fall figures prominently in both the *Wake* and *Verses*, especially given the heavy incidence of religious commentary (particularly parody) in both books. Conventional Christian or Muslim religious attitudes are among the myths of the past that Joyce and Rushdie would have us clear away to make room for the future.[50] □

Booker then shifts the terms of his discussion from a biblical fall from faith or grace towards a more postcolonial understanding of *Finnegans Wake* and *The Satanic Verses* in terms of a fall into exile. Both Joyce and Rushdie are, for Booker, voluntary exiles. Both authors exhibit ambivalence towards notions of 'roots' and 'home'. Booker's conception of a postcolonial fall also refers to the fall of colonial authority, and the fall of the English language that served as the tool of that authority. Both Joyce and Rushdie interrogate the role played by the English language in colonial oppression, while at the same time employing and transforming that language to their own ends.

■ This politicization of the myth of the fall is strengthened in both authors because they often recast the motif of death and rebirth into exile and return. Stephen is perhaps the prototypical exile figure of modern literature; I have already noted the parallel between the exile of Stephen from Ireland and that of Saladin Chamcha from India.[51] Moreover, the narrator in *The Satanic Verses* clearly invokes this connection between death and rebirth and exile and return in his description of the 'Imam,' an exile in London who ironically bears some striking resemblances to Rushdie's great popularizer, the Ayatollah Khomeini, in the days prior to the Iranian revolution:

> Who is he? An exile. Which must not be confused with, allowed to run into, all the other words people throw around: émigré, expatriate, refugee, immigrant, silence, cunning. Exile is a dream of glorious return. Exile is a vision of revolution: Elba, not St Helena. It is an endless paradox: looking forward by always looking back. (205)

Not only does this passage invoke the implied cyclicity of the death-rebirth motif, but Rushdie, by choosing to combine the terms 'silence,' 'cunning,' and 'exile,' provides an explicit verbal link to Joyce's Stephen, who proclaims:

> I will not serve that in which I no longer believe whether it call itself my home, my fatherland or my church: and I will try to express myself in some mode of life or art as freely as I can and as wholly as I can, using for my defence the only arms I allow myself to use – silence, exile, and cunning. (*Portrait* 246–47)[52]

This well-known passage takes on new life in the context of Rushdie's work because it stands so clearly as a central statement of the nature of both Stephen's and Rushdie's projects as artists. Rushdie, like Stephen and Joyce, is a voluntary exile from both the nation and the religion of his forefathers; and he, too, seeks to fill with his art the void created by that exile. Significantly, Rushdie cites this same passage in his response to the violent reaction of Muslim fundamentalists to *Verses*:

> The Muslim world is full of censors these days, and many of its greatest writers have been forced into silence, exile or submission. (The Joycean option of cunning seems unavailable at present.) ('Burning' 26)[53]

In the case of Rushdie, the myth of the fall is further politicized by the central importance in his work of the fall of the British raj and of the British Empire in general. *Midnight's Children*, whose narrator is born at the stroke of midnight on the day of Indian independence, is explicitly constructed from events surrounding this fall, but the sense of writing from within the framework of a former colonial culture informs all of

Rushdie's work in important ways, particularly at the level of language itself. Rushdie is a great lover of the English language, noting in an article in the *Times* (London) that 'I don't think there's another language large or flexible enough to include so many different realities.'[54] In this same article he also shows a profound appreciation for the historicity and political context of language, arguing that the vestiges of empire are still to be found in the 'cadences' of the English language itself. On the other hand, he sees that the political charge that inheres in language is potentially energizing. He argues that much 'vitality and excitement' can be derived from attempts to 'decolonize' the language, citing the great Irish writers Joyce, Beckett, and Flann O'Brien as predecessors in the effort and contemporary writers such as Chinua Achebe and Ngugi wa Thiong'o as ones who are resisting the history of imperialism retained within the language by 'busily forging English into new shapes':

> But of course a good deal more than formal, stylistic alteration is going on in this new fiction. And perhaps above all, what is going on is politics . . . There are very few major writers in the new English literatures who do not place politics at the very centre of their art. (8)[55] □

Though Booker's point is for the most part well made, it should be noted that Rushdie's appreciation of Ngugi is not without its reservations. Ngugi calls for the rejection of the language of the colonial power and for a return to suppressed indigenous languages, arguing: 'our languages were suppressed so that we, the captives, would not have our own mirrors in which to observe ourselves and our enemies.'[56] In a similar vein, Aruna Srivastava argues that Indian writers such as Rushdie who employ the language of colonial authority are in danger of displacing their own rich traditions, 'that they are, to put it bluntly, not only working in, but also valorizing, the language of their (former) colonizers to the detriment of others.'[57] Yet other critics, and indeed Rushdie himself, argue for a more complicated interpretation of his use of English. Rushdie describes himself as somewhat bemused by Ngugi's insistence upon addressing the audience of a literary conference in Swahili, when no one in the audience was familiar with the language.[58] Ngugi himself, moreover, is aware that insistence upon suppressed languages may restrict both range of expression, and audience reception.[59] Rushdie's use of English is not so much about disloyalty or complicity. Nor is it about perpetuating opposition. It is about the blurring of boundaries. Booker's article, however, seems more inclined to side with Ngugi.

■ Rushdie's emphasis on the particular positioning of the former colonial within the English language recalls the famous passage in *Portrait* in which Stephen, intensely aware of the political orientation of language, compares his own speech to that of the English dean of studies:

> The language in which we are speaking is his before it is mine. How different are the words *home, Christ, ale, master,* on his lips and on mine! I cannot speak or write these words without unrest of spirit. His language, so familiar and so foreign, will always be for me an acquired speech. (189, Joyce's emphases)[60]

One could see the radical linguistic experimentation of *Finnegans Wake* as Joyce's attempts to engage in a dialogue with the echoes of colonization and British imperial history embedded in the English language. Jacques Derrida reads the language of the *Wake* as a sort of allegory of resistance to linguistic imperialism in very much the mode that Rushdie describes as 'decolonization.' Derrida notes the Babelian multilingualism of the *Wake* and suggests that the interaction in the text of English as the dominant language with the other secondary languages is a mirror of the sort of imperialism that England imposed on Ireland:

> English tries to erase the other language or languages, to colonize them, to domesticate them, to present them for reading from only one angle. But one must also read the resistance to this commonwealth, not only pronounce oneself but also write oneself against it. Against Him. And this is indeed what happens. Between islands of language, across each island. Ireland and England would be only emblems of this. What matters is the contamination of the master by the language he claims to subjugate, on which he has declared war. (156)[61]

The language of *The Satanic Verses* is far less radical in its conception than that of the *Wake*, but nonetheless Rushdie seems to be engaged in a similar multilingual project, practising linguistic decolonization as well as preaching it. In particular Rushdie employs the linguistic energies of his native India to revitalize the English in which he writes, investing it with new accents, new rhythms, and new political orientations. Maria Couto, discussing *Midnight's Children*, notes the way Rushdie's English is spiced with an Indian flavor:

> Rushdie uses phonemes [distinct units of sound that distinguish one word from another] and word patterns to suggest the vigour and liveliness of folk culture, the pace and variety of Indian life, the mythology of Bombay films, the brash exuberance of affluence, the

violence simmering and on the boil . . . His prose, liberally sprin-
kled with Urdu, Hindi, and Sanskrit names, the deliberately
uncontrolled flow of sentence with repetition and sonorous content, suggests the chant of Indian traditional texts. (63)[62]

Gerald Marzorati describes the language of *Verses* in a similar way,
emphasizing the strong connections between Rushdie's language and
his contemporary social and political context:

Rushdie's prose – the lustrous, alloyed English he's fused from
street slang, Great Books, rock songs, and jingles, immigrant patois,
everything – has a way of keeping us in the crowded, gritty here and
now, even in the book's most phantasmagoric pages. (27)[63]

In short, as Mikhail Bakhtin would put it, Rushdie's texts are replete
with heteroglossia. Otto Cone's description in *Verses* of the modern
world stands not only as a nearly perfect textbook definition of heteroglossia, but as a useful description of both *Finnegans Wake* and *The
Satanic Verses* as well:

The world is incompatible, just never forget it: gaga. Ghosts, Nazis,
saints, all alive at the same time; in one spot, blissful happiness, while
down the road, the inferno. You can't ask for a wilder place. (295) [. . .]

Joyce and Rushdie also see the Babelian state of modern language as a
godsend. However, they ask us to accept this gift without the assur-
ance that God's providence will help us to use it wisely and to face the
future bravely without the illusory comforts offered by the patriarchal,
authoritarian mystifications of the past. Both artists employ the myth
of the fall and its associated archetypal pattern of death and rebirth as
central tropes for the representation of this effort to bury the past in
order to clear the way for the future. And both assume with courage
and grace the role assigned to the poet by the satirist Baal in *The Satanic
Verses*: 'To name the unnamable, to point at frauds, to take sides, start
arguments, shape the world and stop it from going to sleep' (97).[64] ☐

Though Engblom, Merivale, and Booker acknowledge both Rushdie's
problematic status as a migrant writer and his thematic engagement with
cultural hybridity, they prefer to read Rushdie's works in relation to Western
literary forms and traditions. Yet the hybridity they discuss, and 'heteroglossia' to which they point, should also allow for a broader recognition
of Eastern influences in Rushdie's writing. Rudolf Bader explains why
Western critics of Rushdie's works may perhaps pass over Rushdie's use
of a non-Western tradition. Bader argues that many 'implications of this

tradition are inaccessible for the majority of European scholars in the field of international English literature,[65] and thus the text [of Rushdie's novels] cannot become "experienceable" or "readable" for them.'[66]

A number of critical works, however, do attempt to compensate for this 'inaccessibility'. Bader's article is one such example. Perhaps a more notable example is C. Kanaganayakam's 'Myth and Fabulosity in *Midnight's Children*'.[67] In this article, Kanaganayakam charts a broad range of Eastern cultural, religious, and mythic traditions to be found in *Midnight's Children*, declaring of Rushdie: 'He has shown the writer how the modern Indian novel might be written; and he has shown the reader how the modern Indian novel can be read.'[68]

■ The use of myth is so pervasive and so overt a technique in the latter part of the novel that it would be profitable to dwell on it at some length. The narrator's predilection for recording his narrative in mythical terms surfaces in his metafictional observations. For example, after Padma deserts him, he observes:

> when Valmiki, the author of *Ramayana*, dictated his masterpiece to the elephant-headed Ganesh, did the god walk out on him halfway? He certainly did not (Note that, despite my Muslim background, I'm enough of a Bombayite to be well up in Hindu stories, and actually I'm very fond of the image of trunk-nosed flap-eared Ganesh solemnly taking dictation!). (149)

Here Saleem both confesses his love of myth and his intention to use myth in a half-ironic, playful manner in keeping with the overall pattern of narration.

The idea that myth is being played off against history becomes clear in the names of the three important Midnight's Children – Saleem Sinai, Shiva and Parvati. The name Saleem Sinai lends itself to a variety of interpretations, one of them being the association with Mount Sinai and Moses. Shiva, according to the narrator, was named after 'the god of destruction and procreation.' Parvati is the wife of Lord Shiva. Extended further, Saleem's sister is called the Brass Monkey which brings in the idea of Hanuman. Hanuman's feat of setting fire to Ceylon finds a comic parallel in the Brass Monkey's compulsive habit of setting fire to shoes. If one were to extend the parallel further, one would find that for a long time Saleem's sister is loyal to Saleem as Hanuman was to Rama. Then there is an inversion because the brother and sister tread different paths. The Brass Monkey sings for the benefit of the Pakistani army while Saleem returns to India. At the end of the novel there is a final betrayal when the Brass Monkey abandons Saleem altogether.

The inversion of myth reinforces the narrator's claim that the present era is Kali-Yuga (the epoch of evil). The motif of betrayal which inverts myth also draws attention to the constant occurrence of betrayal in the novel. Amina, Pia, Leela, Parvati and Indira Gandhi are all guilty of betrayal. And all these failures are seen in relation to the epic *Ramayana* which, above all, exalts the virtues of loyalty.

In harmony with the multiple myths which characterize the heritage of India, the narrator weaves together a number of myths. Saleem, whose association with Moses has been mentioned earlier, refers to his nose being 'elephantine as the trunk of Ganesh' (154). It is significant that earlier he refers to Padma's role as being similar to that of Ganesh. Later, Parvati's child too takes on the appearance of Ganesh. This bewildering confusion of myth makes sense when one considers the narrator's task of creating a meaningful pattern out of the multiplicity of India.

The framework of myth deliberately includes not merely the Children but also Padma, the listener. Speaking of her Saleem observes: 'Padma, the Lotus Calyx, which grew out of Vishnu's navel, and from which Brahma himself was born; Padma the source, the mother of Time!' (192). Padma thus becomes, on the level of myth, the source of life and the goddess of wealth. Ironically, Padma is poor in the novel, and her main grudge is that Saleem is impotent and that she cannot bear his child. The inversion of myth operates in her case too, as elsewhere.

An interesting example of mythologising history occurs in the person of Shiva, the 'alter-ego' of Saleem Sinai. The reference to alter ego is significant in that it recalls the two brothers in the *Ramayana*, Ravana and Vibishaka, who stood on opposite sides. However, Saleem's intention of linking Shiva not only with God but also with epic heroes is evident when he says that

> to Shiva, the hour had given the gifts of war (of Rama, who could draw the undrawable bow, of Arjuna and Bhima; the ancient prowess of Kurus and Pandavas united, unstoppably in him!). (196)

And so Shiva is symbolically the god of procreation, destruction and preservation, and the hero whose strength vanquishes the forces of evil.

Shiva's fecundity and destructive potential are never in question. He has no count of his illegitimate children. While his function as destroyer links him to Lord Shiva, it is equally clear that Shiva, unlike the Hindu god, destroys good and not evil. He is determined to destroy Saleem. And this is consistent with the political and social events where traditional roles are abandoned and there is a pervasive sense of disintegration.

It is interesting that the whole episode in the Sundarabans in Bangladesh, where Saleem (now called the buddha) gets lost for a period of time, can only be understood in relation to myth. The reference to the Buddha is a little unclear unless it is taken to mean that Saleem is going through a period of enlightenment. This reading is beautifully undercut in the episode in which Saleem is very nearly murdered by a farmer for attempting to seduce his wife. The jungle also refers to the Muslim Paradise as we encounter the houris. Strangely enough the houris materialise in the temple of the goddess Kali, who represents the wrathful aspect of divinity. One might also suggest that Saleem's sojourn in the jungle is not unlike the period of exile imposed on the Pandavas in the *Mahabharata*. Shiva's presence in Bangladesh and his failure to spot Saleem are not very different from the attempts made to spot the Pandavas before the allotted time and consign them to a further period of exile. Subsequently, Saleem returns to India and is called upon to confront Shiva. Saleem, instead of vindicating the cause of justice by destroying Shiva, runs in abject terror and is all but killed by the latter. It is not accidental that this happens during the period of Emergency imposed by Indira Gandhi when pessimism was at its highest and the possibility of renewal seemed most remote. Here too, as in other places, the inversion of myth emphasizes the dichotomy between the harmony of the past and the chaos of the present.

The framework of myth rights itself at the end. Parvati is very much in love with Saleem, but consummation is not possible as Saleem is impotent. She is eventually taken away by Shiva, seduced and abandoned. But she bears the child of Shiva, and when the child is born, Saleem says that

> he was the great-grandson of his great-grandfather, but elephantiasis attacked him in the ears instead of the nose – because he was the son of Shiva-and-Parvati; he was the elephant-headed Ganesh. (405)

The birth of Ganesh during the Emergency brings in a ray of hope. There is the suggestion that good is born out of evil and that the present collapse might lead to a future unity. And this glimmer of hope is reinforced by the fact that Saleem survives; and his jars of pickle (which represent both the chapters of the novel and the presentation of history) survive; also, the novel survives.[69] □

The final article included in this chapter, Feroza Jussawalla's 'Rushdie's

Dastan-E-Dilruba: *The Satanic Verses* as Rushdie's Love Letter to Islam', looks to Rushdie's use of Eastern traditions to defend Rushdie against his more ferocious critics.[70] In this article, moreover, Jussawalla argues that critics who discuss Rushdie's status as a hybrid postcolonial writer simply in terms of Indian independence from British rule merely betray their eurocentricism. Their position, suggests Jussawalla, fails to comprehend the true extent of an Indian history already characterised by hybridity well before the arrival of British colonial rule. Jussawalla presents a more complex understanding of Rushdie's work, one in which 'the very hybridity Rushdie manifests results from his being not only a "post-British" colonial but also a "post-Mughal" colonial.'[71] Jussawalla presents the very interesting argument that Rushdie's reference to Eastern myths, traditions and religions should not merely be seen in relation to the former British rule of India, but in terms of a deeper historical understanding of Indian culture.

In using the term 'post-Mughal', Jussawalla is referring to the hybrid culture that emerged out of the Muslim colonisation of Hindu India, a colonisation that reached its height in the Mughal empire of the sixteenth and seventeenth centuries. The resulting confluence of Persian, Arabic and Hindi gave birth to Urdu, 'a new language for the poetry, literature, arts, and in general the "high culture" of today's Indian Muslims.'[72] Rushdie himself is keen to declare his connections to this culture: 'My grandfather, my father's father, was a good Urdu poet. My father is not a writer but he's a very literary and literate man, a student of both Arabic and Persian Literature and Western Literature.'[73] Thus, argues Jussawalla, it is necessary to examine Rushdie in the light of this culture and the artistic and religious traditions that feed into it. Such a perspective might also, as the title of this article suggests, allow for a less damning appreciation of *The Satanic Verses*.

■ Therefore, facts of Mughal–Islamic religion, history, culture, and literature as they were syncretized in India are important for more than a simple exegesis of *The Satanic Verses*. They are important in understanding Salman Rushdie's current dilemma and in pointing to new directions for theoretical interpretations of cross-cultural 'hybrid' writers from the Indian Subcontinent.

Rushdie is the victim not only of the condition of postmodernity, where meaning is wrenched from the author's hands to rest in the hands of readers like the Ayatollah Khomeini, but of the indeterminacy of meaning outside certain cultural contexts. For instance, in looking at *The Satanic Verses* as manifesting an Islamic narrative form, we also have to consider that this form is from an Indo-Islamic tradition that is not as fundamentalist as some Islamic traditions – like those of the Persian or Arab Shiites – that did not get mixed and merged with the

Indian soil.[74] India's Islam is that of *khawali* (bawdy oral narrative) and of *baed-bazi* (debate) through the recitation of poetry, an Islam merged with Hinduism, as of the poet Kabir, an Islam whose presumptions might seem more blasphemous to the undiluted strain. Of Rushdie's use of Urdu *ghazal* (lyrical love poetry) in *The Satanic Verses*, Sara Suleri writes, 'it links Rushdie to a highly wrought tradition in which a recurrent trope is the rejection of Islam for some new object of epistemological and erotic devotion' [609].[75] In fact, in the Indo-Mughal tradition, love for one's religion, whether Hindu or Muslim, is expressed as love for a beloved, both in lyric poetry and longer oral narratives, which is not only why the *dastan-e-dilruba* (a love song for a beloved) is an appropriate metaphor for *The Satanic Verses* but, as I will show in the latter half of the essay, the form of the *dastan*, a long prose narrative delivered as a complaint to the beloved, is the form or the genre of *The Satanic Verses*. Continuing with this metaphor of the beloved, I would say that it is not the 'rejection of Islam'– the beloved – for 'ironized submission to the alterities' [Suleri 609] that Rushdie represents as much as love for the Islam – the religion – of the subcontinental soil, where it flourished under the Mughals and came into question at the end of Mughal dominance, where it was and is practised in an atmosphere of mixing and merging. [. . .]

Traditionally, the *dastan*, as it was narrated in Persia and later brought to India by the late Mughal emperors (particularly Jehangir, who had his own storyteller), was an oral narrative form. As it turned into an Urdu literary form, its orality was emphasized even more, because Urdu was the language of the illiterate people whereas Persian was the language of the literati of high culture. It wasn't until the late nineteenth century that the Indian entrepreneur Nawal Kishore thought of publishing the orally transmitted *dastans*. So they retain(ed) the characteristics of oral transmission. However, William Hanaway makes a distinction that is particularly applicable to *Midnight's Children* and *The Satanic Verses*:

> *The stories begin at the beginning and proceed in a fairly straight line to the end. There are, with one minor exception in* Samak-i-Ayyar, *no flashbacks. The stories are never begun in* medias res [to enter the middle of a story without preamble] *or work backwards and forward as they* [do] *in Modern Literature. The open-endedness and flexibility of the form result in a lack of internal cohesion. The integrated progression of the modern plot is absent. In its place we find a loose stringing together of episodes which in their lack of organic connection seem at times almost random.* [142][76]

While Gibreel Farishta and Saladin Chamcha's fall can be construed as an *in medias res* beginning, the story of both those characters does begin there, and their story unfolds almost in an episodic, picaresque fashion. While Rushdie does give us glimpses of their childhood, the story of their immigration as also the story of the Prophet's immigration progresses from beginning to end. In fact, the beginning of *The Satanic Verses* is very similar to that of *Midnight's Children*. It is almost as though there is an *ayah* (maidservant) telling a little boy the story of Gibreel and Saladin. 'Baba, if you want to get *born again*' [3, my emphasis],[77] she seems to say, listen to this story. 'It was so and it was not so.' The 'born again' metaphor is interesting. Is Rushdie applying to Islam a metaphor from contemporary America? From his long discussion in '"In God We Trust"' [387–92][78] of 'born again' Christianity in America, it would seem so.

From there we go to the story of the Prophet Mohammed. This is not a flashback, but a story within a story, a frame tale. The narrative voice is like that of the *ayah* Padma in *Midnight's Children*, who says, 'Once upon a time it was so and not so as the *old stories* say' [35].[79] There is therefore no attention to 'structural matters,' as Hanaway calls such strategies as *pacing*, the laying out of climaxes or the setting up of flashbacks. Rushdie, like the *dastan* narrators of yore, brings these together in loosely knit episodic form, a rambling story always going forward. Hanaway also writes, 'Much of the length of the Dastan comes from exhaustive catalogues of people and places as also from elaborate plays on words and multiple repetition' [142].

What Frances Pritchett says of the classical Urdu *dastan*, the *Dastan-e Amir Hamza*, is true of Rushdie's work: 'The language is rhythmic, repetitive, almost hypnotic, and gives the narrator's vision a dreamlike power and authority' [6].[80] Pritchett adds, 'The classical Urdu dastan became so inconceivably long and so elaborately fantastic that it exhausted its own possibilities' [6].

With Rushdie's novels, the fantastic is often attributed to postmodernism. But it is in looking at the form of the *dastan* that one finally understands the origins of Rushdie's fantastic and what he calls 'fantabulous.' *Dastans* are peopled by 'paris,' usually fairies or winged creatures. The hundreds of yellow butterflies that clothe the visionary Ayesha in *The Satanic Verses*, which have been attributed to García Márquez's yellow butterflies, are characteristic of this supernatural element. Ayesha herself may be considered a 'Pari' – Mohammed had always called his favorite wife an 'angel.' There are magically animated puppets – Saladin Chamcha turns into one, as does his penis, and like a true *dastan* hero he lives in a world full of 'marvellous events – mysterious inexplicable and magical' [Pritchett 9]. Ironically, much of this is controlled by black magic, which in the eyes of a good Muslim is always evil. Saladin thinks the Welsh policemen who captured him practised some black magic, and English black magic causes the migrant *mohajir* to sprout horns and turn into an evil character. Here Rushdie develops a post-European colonization metaphor: he seems expressly to disapprove of the postcolonial who turns European. He is asserting that transmogrification into the foreign culture is dangerous, which in itself can be taken as a call to retain one's religious and cultural identity.

Moreover, it is those who are rooted in their own culture who provide deliverance for Saladin Chamcha. Therefore the *clever spies* and secret agents, the *ayyar*, so vital to the *dastan* hero are, in *The Satanic Verses*, the Indians and Muslims of Bradford and Brick Lane like Mishal and Hind [Sufyan], who eventually transform the *dastan* hero Saladin from a cross-cultural monstrosity in suit and tie and bowler hat with long penis into a human being. Read in this way the fantastic, one of the characteristics of the *dastan*, *is* meant to be liberatory for the Muslims of Bradford and Brick Lane. This does not mean that Rushdie is satirizing these Muslim immigrants as 'fantastic and unbelievable,' as the Western press had made it seem he had. He is simply deploying one of the techniques of his chosen genre. *Dastan* narrators make 'so much use of marvellous events that in a sense such events lose their marvellousness and become the "normal"' [Pritchett 11]. And, in showing how the fantastic has become normal, Rushdie meant not to be criticizing the uprooted Muslims but urging them both into secularizing reform of strictures and into greater 'faith,' as Hali and Sir Sayed Ahmed Khan meant to in the nineteenth century. In fact, it was Sir Sayed Ahmed's travel to England that turned him deeper toward Islam, yet he brought back a sense of British secularism and was able to merge the two.

Islam has not been a stranger to criticism or satire. While panegyric was part of *maqamas* (eloquence), so was *hija* (satire), a form that came to the Islamic poets from the pre-Mohammedan [Meccans]. When the Persian poet Firdausi Tusi was paid only in silver for the *Shahnameh*, the complaint he registered through satire was rewarded by the gold he should have received. A complaint or a satire was not always punished. Like a modern-day Hali, Rushdie genuinely meant his satire to be reformist, not a target satire but a satire that was actually delivered out of love for his religion, fraught as it is with contemporary cross-cultural problems not only in Bradford and Brick Lane but in international diplomacy and policy.[81] □

Unlike Engblom, Merivale, Booker, and a host of other critics, Jussawalla clearly questions the suitability of Western forms and traditions as tools for understanding Rushdie's works. Jussawalla concludes this article by stressing the importance of reading works such as *The Satanic Verses* within their specific localised national contexts, and the hybrid space of post-

Mughal Indian culture represents just such a context. Such a position is squarely at odds with the work of critics such as Timothy Brennan who argue that 'the nation-centred origins of literary studies distorts [sic] the coverage of the vast realm of experience arising from imperial contacts.'[82] Jussawalla concedes that her position is vulnerable to such criticism, yet insists upon the need for 'nation-centered and context-based criticism which can in turn provide important insights into imperial contacts, particularly those contacts often ignored because of a lack of historical or contextual knowledge.'[83] This 'knowledge', and Rushdie's relationship to it, is examined in the next chapter of this Guide.

CHAPTER THREE

'It Was and It Was Not So . . . It Happened and It Never Did': History, Historicism and Nation

IN THE previous chapter, Feroza Jussawalla sought to locate *The Satanic Verses* in relation to Indian cultural traditions. In doing so, Jussawalla also placed Rushdie's novel in relation to Indian history in so much that it is out of this history that such traditions have emerged. The articles included in this chapter also examine the relationship between Rushdie's work and Indian history. They are not, however, concerned so much with establishing Rushdie's literary affiliations. These articles set out, instead, to explore Rushdie's depiction of that history, and examine his treatment of history itself as a concept mobilised to place and express nationhood and subjecthood.

It should be of little surprise that historical debate and notions of nationhood and subjecthood should feature so prominently in the criticism surrounding Rushdie's writing. Rushdie is, after all, described by many of his critics as a postcolonial writer and concepts such as history, nation and the self hold special significance for postcolonial debate. Emerging as they do out of European modernity, they are not only coterminous with the rise of colonialism, but were employed to justify the very project of colonisation itself. History was something 'possessed' by the European imperial powers, yet somehow lacking elsewhere. The possession of history assured colonialism of its supremacy, even as history was employed to construct that supremacy and present it as part of the natural order. The European development of a concept of nation, each equipped with its own history, allowed distinct European colonial powers to view themselves, and represent themselves, as coherent and stable entities suited to rule over others. Situated and validated by history and nation, the European 'self' was empowered to justify its assumed authority by regarding the colonial subject as a historyless, nationless 'other'. These concepts, moreover, continue to exercise their authority over what might loosely be termed the postcolonial period.[8]

Different critics, however, adopt different approaches to Rushdie's depiction of the Indian colonial and postcolonial experience. Uma Parameswaran, for example, in numerous reviews and articles, restricts her reading of *Midnight's Children* to an examination of the novel's historical veracity.[1] Such an approach, by failing to identify the historically constructed nature of nationhood and subjectivity, lacks much of the theoretical sophistication of articles that appear later in this chapter. Parameswaran is, however, a prolific and influential critic of Rushdie's works and her article 'Autobiography as History: Saleem Sinai and India in Rushdie's *Midnight's Children*' provides an early example of, and a useful opening to, a discussion of Rushdie's treatment of Indian history.[2] Parameswaran's article explores the relationship between individual, or personal, histories and the history of India as a nation. For Parameswaran, *Midnight's Children* is not simply the autobiography of Saleem 'but also the history of India'.[3] This conflation of the individual with the national is achieved, according to Parameswaran, through Rushdie's deliberate and 'ingenious literary device' of depicting the lives of Saleem and his family interacting with, reflecting, or expressing, the life of 'modern' India.[4] Such a view of the novel appears to coincide with that of Anita Desai who, in her review of *Midnight's Children*, suggests that Rushdie's writing reveals that 'while individual history does not make sense unless seen against its national background, neither does national history make sense unless seen in the form of individual lives and histories.'[5] This collapsing of the distinction between the private and the political spheres might also, at least potentially, link Parameswaran's reading of *Midnight's Children* to Fredric Jameson's suggestion that third-world texts perform the function of 'national allegories'.[6] Despite the somewhat pejorative connotations of the term 'third-world', Jameson's argument that *the story of the private individual destiny is always an allegory of the embattled situation of the public third-world culture and society'* does initially seem to lend itself to Parameswaran's approach to Rushdie's novel.[7]

■ The first event in the novel related to history is the Jallianwala Bagh massacre. In 1919, the government (this was during the British raj, we must remember) passed the Rowlatt Acts, which gave it unlimited powers, including 'doing away with ordinary legal procedure and authorizing imprisonment without trial'.[8] Mahatma Gandhi called for nationwide protest meetings. On April 13, 1919, about 500,000 people assembled at Jallianwala Bagh, an enclosed park in Amritsar. General R.E. Dyer, Martial Law Commander of Amritsar, ordered his troops to fire. They 'fired 1600 rounds of ammunition into the unarmed crowd that had no means of exit. Even according to official estimates 379 persons were killed, and 1200 wounded'.[9] In *Midnight's Children*,

> Brigadier Dyer's fifty men put down their machine guns and go away. They have fired a total of one thousand six hundred and fifty rounds into the unarmed crowd. Of these, one thousand five hundred and sixteen have found their mark, killing or wounding some person.

Saleem's grandfather, Dr. Aadam Aziz, treats as many as he can.

This incident tells us two important things about Rushdie's handling of history: he is fairly accurate about the historical facts he uses; and he makes historical events of personal significance to Saleem by involving a member of his family in the event. One other point is that there may or may not be any apparent connection between the event and Saleem's life, but if one looks deeper one might find some significance; this incident, for instance, is related to Saleem's life at a later point.

The next historical event – or movement – is the rise and fall of Sheikh Abdullah, Sher-e-Kashmir (the Lion of Kashmir). While the Muslim League was firmly established and intent upon the creation of Pakistan, Sheikh Abdullah, a Kashmir Muslim, founded the Muslim National Conference, which leaned towards Gandhi's undivided India and against the Muslim League. Sheikh Abdullah lived long after Independence, but Rushdie's Mian Abdullah, founder of Free Islam Convocation, is killed by six assassins, 'six crescent knives held by men dressed all in black,' but before he dies there is a supernatural aura given to him. The Hummingbird, as he is called in the novel, hums his body into steel so that the 'long curved blades had trouble killing him'; he [hummed] in decibels beyond human hearing till all the glass in the windows shattered, till all the dogs in the city 'came like wild things, leaping through the windows' and tore the assassins with their teeth so that 'nobody could say who they were.' The personal link in the story is Abdullah's secretary, Nadir Khan, who escapes and seeks refuge at Aadam Aziz's house, and later marries Aadam's daughter Amina, who is forced to divorce him after two years when Aadam finds out that they have not yet consummated their marriage. (Amina then marries Ahmed Sinai, and Saleem is their son.)

August 14, 1947. Pakistan came into being a moment past the midnight of August 13. And Vanita, Wee Willie Winkie's wife, who had been seduced by Methwold, starts her labour pains at exactly the same moment. Twenty-four hours later, on the stroke of midnight as India entered freedom, she gives birth to a ten-pound baby boy. At the same moment, in the same nursing home, Amina Sinai gives birth to a baby – also male, also ten pounds. Mary Pereira, bamboozled by her lover's

Marxist ideas, switches babies, contributing her bit to the levelling up of society's haves and have-nots. Thus Vanita (Mother India) and William Methwold (England) have brought into existence Saleem (Pakistan); this parallel does not hold all the way unless one is to see the Sinais as representative of Jawaharlal Nehru, the Kashmiri who unwittingly condemned India (Shiva) to a life of destitution and faulty ideology. Saleem grows up in the luxury of the Sinai household while the real Sinai baby, Shiva, grows up in the slums.

The assassination of Mahatma Gandhi is mentioned in passing, but nothing of historical significance is dwelt upon until the linguistic reorganization of states late in 1956. Dr. Narlikar, the doctor who delivered Saleem, has ambitions of reclaiming land from the sea by making stilts with a line of concrete tetrapods and then building upon it; this is a joint project by Ahmed and the doctor, and they place the first of the tetrapods on an embankment overlooking the sea. One day, while Narlikar is looking at his concrete brainchild, irate language marchers push him out of their way; he is pushed into the sea, still clinging to the concrete tetrapod, which soon drowns him. His drowning is Saleem's first experience of death. It is linked to the linguistic division of the country, perhaps one of the worst political decisions made. Narlikar's death is also linked more personally to the beginning of the financial and moral degeneration of Saleem's father. Of the national implications, Saleem says,

India had been divided anew, into fourteen states and six centrally-administered territories. But the boundaries of these states were not formed by rivers, or mountains, or any natural features of the terrain; they were, instead, walls of words. Language divided us.

Rushdie goes on to summarize the antagonism between Gujarati and Marathi-speaking people in the state of Bombay. One day, in a bicycle accident, Saleem is thrown in the midst of angry Marathi demonstrators who taunt him to speak Gujarati. He repeats the only rhyme he knows – learnt from a Goanese schoolmate, Keith Colaco – which makes fun of the rhythms of Gujarati language patterns: 'How are you? I am well. I'll take a stick and thrash you to hell.' Thus Rushdie has Saleem as the originator of a popular slogan of the time. 'In this way I became directly responsible for triggering off the violence which ended with the partition of the state of Bombay,' says Saleem. Though at the literary level the narrative is funny, its ironic intent is clear: major political events quite often have their sources in trivia.

In the spring of 1957, elections were held in India, and the Communist party won a large number of seats. Language oriented parties – such as the Marathi and Gujarati groups – divided the electorate, reducing still further the number of seats that the All India Congress had hoped to win.

There are two links more direct than the death of Suresh Narlikar between the story of Saleem and the story of India at this juncture. Shiva and Saleem's mother are partly responsible for the outcome of the election. Shiva and his gang, called 'Cowboys,' intimidate the voters, and later enter the polling booths, break open the ballot boxes and 'fix' the results so that the Congress wins. Saleem identifies the Congress only indirectly: 'only one party had really large sums to spend.' The Communist cause is served by Saleem's mother, Amina Sinai. Amina has been meeting her ex-husband Nadir, whom she has never ceased to love. He has now become a Communist; she campaigns for him and his party, donating time and money to the destitute who in return vote Communist.

Rushdie's links are a literary device and he uses it ingeniously. The elections of 1957 took place in the spring of the year but Saleem has his mother campaigning in the summer of 1957. The discrepancy is not an oversight, because Saleem realizes it, 'And then it occurs to me that I have made another error – that the election of 1957 took place before, and not after, my tenth birthday.' Thus Rushdie adds complexity to his narrative technique.

The next public event that occurs is the manslaughter of Homi Catrack, Lila Sabarmati's lover, by Commander Sabarmati of the Indian Navy. This incident was in the headlines of Indian magazines and newspapers at that time. The real names of Saleem's characters are well known to his contemporaries – as are the battles between the Navy and the Law as to whether Commander Nanavati should be in a civil jail or in naval custody. As with the language slogan, Saleem is personally responsible for triggering off the manslaughter, but whereas the former event was purely accidental, this one is premeditated, though Saleem obviously did not realize how serious his interference would become. Saleem, in order to teach his mother the lesson that she should stop her strange liaison with Nadir (they do not at any time have sexual intercourse), decides to expose another pair of lovers – Homi Catrack and Lila Sabarmati. Thus, a very personal problem precipitates a social and political scandal. [. . .]

The war between India and China, with public reaction and newspaper headlines, is documented by Saleem, as is also the infiltration of Pakistan into Kashmir and the subsequent Indo-Pakistani war of 1965. Saleem uses a series of ambiguous statements and questions to show how each side claimed all kinds of feats and conducted all kinds of treacheries. He uses factual accounts from newspapers and interweaves news of air raids with news of his own family, culminating in the night of September 22, 1965, when, in different places, all the members of his family die, except for Jamila Singer, his sister who is now a singing star, and Uncle Mustapha's family who are in Delhi.

Next, Saleem moves from 1965 to 1970, when he becomes a citizen of Pakistan. He is sent with sixty others to lead sixty thousand Pakistani soldiers in mufti to East Pakistan, which was about to secede and become Bangladesh. Saleem is their tracker, and like Bonzo the dog before him, he smells the terrain and leads the unit safely. Saleem's telepathic powers have been replaced by olfactory powers after an ear operation. Saleem records in passing that Indira Gandhi's New Congress Party had just won a landslide victory, with 350 out of a possible 515 seats in Lok Sabha.

On March 25, 1971, Saleem the tracker sniffs out Sheikh Mujib-ur-Rahman, who is then arrested and flown to West Pakistan. Saleem also describes, in summary, the loot, rape and massacre of those days as the West Pakistani soldiers went on a rampage. Saleem, pretending to be chasing someone, runs away from the war area into the swamp area, the Sunderban. With him there are three others – all boy-soldiers; when they return to Dacca several weeks later, there are only two others, the third having been killed by a sniper's bullet.

Throughout the time that Saleem is in the invading army, he calls himself the buddha and narrates in the third person. He is in a state of amnesia after his incestuous declaration to Jamila, but just how genuine the amnesia is remains an ambiguity. The name 'buddha' has two levels depending on its pronunciation, as he explains; his young colleagues call him 'budda,' with a hard *d*, meaning 'old man,' but he is also obviously the buddha, the enlightened one. At this time, Saleem does not *act*. Shiva, on the other hand, acts quite unequivocally. Saleem's inaction, at the metaphoric level, connects to history, while it is also consistent with his personal problem. Saleem's inaction is related to Shiva's action; Shiva, of the Indian army, is described by a Bangladesh carpetbagger as:

> They have one mighty soldier fellow, he can kill six persons at one time, breaks necks *khrikk-khrikk* between his knees.

The episode has to be read thus: Shiva is actually the son of Ahmed and Amina Sinai, and Amina has always been a Pakistani at heart and she is at this time an immigrant in Pakistan. The Bangladesh episode in history was a civil war, the eastern arm of Pakistan rising against the west-based government and the western arm trying to put it down; it was a civil war – of Muslims killing fellow Muslims. Thus Shiva, born of Muslim parents and fighting for East Pakistan, is a Muslim killing his fellow Muslims. Saleem, who is actually of Hindu and English parentage, does not actively participate after betraying

Sheikh Mujib. This betrayal might be linked, somewhat implausibly, to Saleem's English side, to Britain's divide-and-rule policy that believed in causing trouble and ill will between two groups and then standing aside while they fought it out. Saleem's Indian side does not seem relevant to the episode in any historical context, since India went to great lengths to help Bangladesh refugees, even at the risk of depleting the national coffers. As Saleem records, India welcomed refugees and spent '$200,000,000 a month on [refugee] camps.'

Saleem, who has forgotten his name, is then found by Parvati-the-witch, another midnight child, in Dacca, where she has come as part of an entertainment crew for the Indian soldiers. She calls him by name and thus recalls his identity to him. She arranges his escape, in a wicker basket, and they fly back to Delhi, arriving on February 23, 1973. On May 15, 1974, Major Shiva returns from the east and three days later meets Parvati. Major Shiva, a war hero, has had many liaisons, leaving a trail of bastard children among the rich and the poor; he now has a liaison with Parvati and abandons her once she gets pregnant. Shiva's increasing corruption can be paralleled to the deterioration of the country's economy and the corruption of its politicians under Indira Gandhi's government. The progress of Parvati's pregnancy is parallel to the growing strength of the Janata party under the leadership of Jaya Prakash Narayan and Morarji Desai. Parvati's labour pains start on June 12, 1975, the day the Allahabad High Court found Prime Minister Indira Gandhi guilty of two counts of campaign malpractice during the election of 1971.

The thirteen days of Indira Gandhi's political career following this verdict see Parvati (who is, of course, Mother India) going through protracted labour pains, and

> the evening of the thirteenth day they screamed Yes, yes she has begun to push, come on Parvati, push push push, and while Parvati pushed in the ghetto, J.P. Narayan and Morarji Desai were also goading Indira Gandhi . . . so in a sense they were forcing Mrs. Gandhi to push . . .

And at midnight of June 25, 1975, just as Parvati brings forth her child, Indira Gandhi brings forth hers – Emergency Rule. The baby, Aadam, does not cry at all for the first year of his life, though he is tubercular; this parallels the nation's silent acceptance of the new dictatorship.

Then, in 1976, Sanjay Gandhi, who had been behind the Prime Minister, stepped forward and rose to meteoric power. Two of his projects were carried out with swift and ruthless action: clearance of Delhi slums and pavements, and mass vasectomy camps to reduce population growth. Both are historical events, and Rushdie portrays both with racy and potent compression. He describes how vans and bull-dozers break down the slum tenements and how quickly the slums transplanted themselves elsewhere. Anyone who was in Delhi in the summer of 1976, as I was, would have witnessed the bulldozers clear-ing away the pavement shops of Karol Bagh [an area of Delhi], and similar sights elsewhere. Exactly as Rushdie says, the slums resurrected themselves as quickly as they were mown down. Rushdie ascribes magical powers to the magicians' ghetto, as it is called, but that is only one of his ways of recording history.

Sanjay Gandhi's second nationwide project was not so easily reversible – vasectomy. Camps and units were set up everywhere and men vasectomized under force – bribed with radios or money, pressured into it by employers, or physically forced into it. Saleem describes the horrors in several passages, a surrealistic passage about the Widow's hand, a stoic excerpt on 'what cannot be cured must be endured,' and in pathetic, funny or horrifying reference to his own ectomization.

The last historical event mentioned in the novel is the election of 1977, when Indira Gandhi's Congress was defeated by the Janata Party. But Saleem does not foresee any permanence in a party led by a wheelchaired Jaya Prakash Narayan, and Morarji Desai. He has only the bleakest of prophecies for his son; and for future generations:

> Yes, they will trample me underfoot reducing me to specks of voiceless dust, just as, all in good time, they will trample my son who is not my son, and his son who will not be his until a thou-sand and one midnights have bestowed their terrible gifts and a thousand and one children have died because it is the privilege and the curse of midnight's children to be both masters and victims of their time and to be unable to live or die in peace.

One should, perhaps, end this study with this, the last paragraph of the novel, for nothing is more powerful in modern storytelling than to end on a note of total hopelessness, an existential *nada*, but since this study attempts to correlate history and the narrative of a novel, one must end on a note of warning and observation – that Salman Rushdie's *Midnight's Children* is an excellent novel, that it gives us a variety of ideas and techniques, that it gives a fairly authentic history of contemporary India in the matter of facts, but that its interpretation of history is not always reliable.[10] ☐

Although Parameswaran's article certainly explores a relationship between personal and political histories, 'historical significance' remains above, if not always beyond, the individual. For Parameswaran, history is something large and rarely, if at all, 'ordinary'. The connections Parameswaran charts, between Saleem and the forces of history, are for the most part incidental or accidental and almost always fraught with danger. Unlike Desai and Jameson, moreover, Parameswaran remains somewhat sceptical of the validity of establishing such connections in fiction. Parameswaran's reviews and criticism of Rushdie's works are for the most part enthusiastic. Yet in one review, she directly attacks Rushdie's technique of conflating the private lives of fictional characters such as Saleem with historical 'reality', suggesting it creates a sense of 'spectacle but does not give a meaningful analysis of causes or results.'[11]

Perhaps Parameswaran holds this view because of the many factual errors and inconsistencies contained in *Midnight's Children*. Her argument that Rushdie's novel provides only a 'fairly authentic history of contemporary India', and that his 'interpretation of history is not always reliable', suggests that Parameswaran subscribes to the existence of an absolutely 'authentic' and fully interpretable history. When set against such a conception of history, *Midnight's Children* appears to lack the potential for full historical engagement. Yet for many critics, Rushdie's use of error and distortion allows for a sophisticated discussion of both 'historical' India and history itself.

Rushdie himself emphasises Saleem's role within the novel as that of an unreliable narrator. He readily concedes that Saleem very often gets things wrong. Such errors are not, for the most part, simple mistakes, but designed to point to the theoretical tension that exists between conceptions of history as a series of verifiable facts, and history as an act of narration. As an act of narration, history may be seen to resemble fiction. For Rushdie, indeed, history is a kind of fiction. Of course, this approach to history is not unique to Rushdie, but also clearly present within historical debate itself. Hayden White, for example, in his enormously influential essay 'The Fictions of Factual Representation', argues for a similar blurring of the distinction between history and fiction.[12] Though the development of history as an academic discipline led to its 'truth value' being placed over and against that of fiction, White argues that 'the aim of the writer of a novel must be the same as that of a writer of history. Both wish to provide a verbal image of "reality."'[13] White then goes on to suggest that 'history is no less a form of fiction than the novel is a form of historical representation.'[14]

Saleem's narration is an act of reminiscence; his version of history emerges from memory. Indeed, memory is a recurrent theme in Rushdie's writing. In his essay 'Imaginary Homelands', Rushdie explains that *Midnight's Children* was first conceived as an attempt to 'unlock the gates of lost time so that the past reappeared as it actually had been, unaffected by the distortions of memory'.[15] Rushdie was soon forced to concede to himself, however, that the novel was 'a novel of memory and about memory, so that my India was just that: "my" India, a version and no more than one version of all the hundreds and millions of possible versions.'[16]

In his essay '"Errata": Or, Unreliable Narration in *Midnight's Children*', Rushdie directly responds to those who find fault in his depiction of Indian's past, and explains the importance of narration and memory to his conception of history. Though Rushdie claims that *Midnight's Children* is not 'historical', this essay clearly reveals his view that history, like any discourse, is vulnerable to appropriation; it is something that should be distrusted. Yet it is also something that can, perhaps even should, be played with.

■ According to Hindu tradition, the elephant-headed god Ganesha is very fond of literature; so fond that he agrees to sit at the feet of the bard Vyasa and take down the entire text of the *Mahabharata*, from start to finish, in an unparalleled act of stenographic love.

In *Midnight's Children*, Saleem Sinai makes a reference, at one point, to this old tradition. But his version is a little different. According to Saleem, Ganesha sat at the feet of the poet Valmiki and took down the *Ramayana*. Saleem is wrong.

It is not his only mistake. During his account of the evolution of the city of Bombay, he tells us that the city's patron-goddess Mumbadevi has fallen out of favour with contemporary Bombayites: 'The calendar of festivals reveals her decline . . . Where is Mumbadevi's day?' As a matter of fact, the calendar of festivals includes a perfectly good Mumbadevi Day, or at least it does in all versions of India except Saleem's.

And how could Lata Mangeshkar have been heard singing on All-India Radio as early as 1946? And does Saleem not know that it was not General Sam Manekshaw who accepted the surrender of the Pakistan Army at the end of the Bangladesh War – the Indian officer who was Tiger Niazi's old chum being, of course, Jagjit Singh Arora? And why does Saleem allege that the brand of cigarettes, State Express 555, is manufactured by W.D. & H.O. Wills?

I could continue. Concrete tetrapods have never been used in Bombay as part of any land reclamation scheme, but only to shore up and protect the sea wall along the Marine Drive promenade. Nor could the train that brings Picture Singh and Saleem from Delhi to Bombay possibly have passed through Kurla, which is on a different line.

Etcetera. It is by now obvious, I hope, that Saleem Sinai is an unreliable narrator, and that *Midnight's Children* is far from being an authoritative guide to the history of post-independence India. But this isn't quite how unreliable narration usually works in novels. Conventionally unreliable narrators are often a little stupid, less able to work out what's going on around them than the reader. In such narratives, one deciphers the true meaning of events by 'seeing through' the narrator's faulty vision. However, the narrator of *Midnight's Children* is neither particularly stupid, nor particularly unaware of what's happening.

Why, then, all the errata? One answer could be that the author has been sloppy in his research. 'If you're going to use Hindu traditions in your story, Mr Rushdie,' I was asked by an irate and shiny-headed gentleman in Bangalore – he had spotted the Valmiki/Vyasa confusion – 'don't you think you could take the trouble to look it up?' I have also received letters arguing about Bombay bus routes, and informing me that certain ranks used by the Pakistan Army in the text are not in fact used by the Pakistan Army in Pakistan. In these letters there is always an undertone of pleasure: the reader's delight at having 'caught the writer out'.

So let me confess that the novel does contain a few mistakes that are mine as well as Saleem's. One is to be found in the description of the Amritsar massacre, during which I have Saleem say that Dyer entered the Jallianwala Bagh compound followed by 'fifty white troops'. The truth is that there were fifty troops, but they weren't white. When I first found out my error I was upset and tried to have it corrected. Now I'm not so sure. The mistake feels more and more like Saleem's; its wrongness feels *right*.

Elsewhere, though, I went to some trouble to get things wrong. Originally error-free passages had the taint of inaccuracy introduced. Unintentional mistakes were, on being discovered, not expunged from the text but, rather, emphasized, given more prominence in the story. This odd behaviour requires an explanation.

When I began the novel (as I've written elsewhere) my purpose was somewhat Proustian. Time and migration had placed a double filter between me and my subject, and I hoped that if I could only imagine vividly enough it might be possible to see beyond those filters, to write as if the years had not passed, as if I had never left India for the West. But as I worked I found that what interested me was the process of filtration itself. So my subject changed, was no longer a search for lost time, had become the way in which we remake the past to suit our present purposes, using memory as our tool. Saleem's greatest desire is for what he calls meaning, and near the end of his broken life he sets out to *write himself*, in the hope that by doing so he may achieve the significance that the events of his adulthood have drained from him. He is no dispassionate, disinterested chronicler. He wants so to shape his material that the reader will be forced to concede his central role. He is cutting up history to suit himself, just as he did when he cut up newspapers to compose his earlier text, the anonymous note to Commander Sabarmati. The small errors in the text can be read as clues, as indications that Saleem is capable of distortions both great and small. He is an interested party in the events he narrates.

He is also *remembering*, of course, and one of the simplest truths about any set of memories is that many of them will be false. I myself have a clear memory of having been in India during the China War. I 'remember' how frightened we all were, I 'recall' people making nervy little jokes about needing to buy themselves a Chinese phrase book or two, because the Chinese Army was not expected to stop until it reached Delhi. I also know that I could not possibly have been in India at that time. I was interested to find that *even after I found out that my memory was playing tricks* my brain simply refused to unscramble itself. It clung to the false memory, preferring it to mere literal happenstance. I thought that was an important lesson to learn.

Thereafter, as I wrote the novel, and whenever a conflict arose between literal and remembered truth, I would favour the remembered version. This is why, even though Saleem admits that no tidal wave passed through the Sundarbans in the year of the Bangladesh War, he continues to be borne out of the jungle on the crest of that fictional wave. His truth is too important to him to allow it to be unseated by a mere weather report. It is memory's truth, he insists, and only a madman would prefer someone else's version to his own.

Saleem Sinai is not an oracle; he's only adopting a kind of oracular language. His story is not history, but it plays with historical shapes. Ironically, the book's success – its Booker Prize, etc – initially distorted the way in which it was read. Many readers wanted it to be the history, even the guidebook, which it was never meant to be; others resented it for its incompleteness, pointing out, among other things, that I had failed to mention the glories of Urdu poetry, or the plight of the Harijans, or untouchables, or what some people think of as the new imperialism of the Hindi language in South India. These variously disappointed readers were judging the book not as a novel, but as some sort of inadequate reference book or encyclopaedia.

The passage of time has smoothed out such wrinkles. I'd just like to clear up that mistake of Saleem's about the god Ganesha. It happens just after Saleem has been boasting about his own erudition. In spite of coming from a Muslim background, he tells us, he's well up on the Hindu stories. That he should instantly perpetrate a howler about the myth which is, after all, most central to himself (Ganesha's elephantine nose, and dubious parentage, prefigure his own) was, I thought, a way of deflating that narratorial pomposity; but it was also – along with Saleem's other blunder about the date of Mahatma Gandhi's assassination – a way of telling the reader to maintain a healthy distrust. History is always ambiguous. Facts are hard to establish, and capable of being given many meanings. Reality is built on our prejudices, misconceptions and ignorance as well as on our perceptiveness and knowledge. The reading of Saleem's unreliable narration might be, I believed, a useful analogy for the way in which we all, every day, attempt to 'read' the world.[17] □

Similarly, Ralph J. Crane suggests: 'Rushdie has managed to make the relationship between Saleem and India in itself a metaphor for the relationship between any human being and his or her world.'[18] Like Rushdie himself, Crane argues that this is a relationship founded upon both error and creativity. Saleem, as a subject of first India, then Pakistan, is part of a material world that exists independently of his ability or inclination to represent it accurately. Yet this is a world which is also at the same time a product of Saleem's memories and imagination. Perhaps the most stimulating aspect to Crane's excellent reading of *Midnight's Children* is the manner in which it, albeit implicitly, links Rushdie's novel to contemporary theories of nationhood. For his suggestion that Saleem's experience of the world reflects that of us all, and that our experience of the world cannot be separated from our invention of it, shares much in common with Benedict Anderson's conception of nationhood as 'an imagined political community'.[19] Anderson argues that nationhood is best understood as imaginary because 'the members of even the smallest nation will never know most of their fellow-members, meet them, or even hear of them, yet in the minds of each lives the image of their communities'.[20] As the characters of *Midnight's Children* demonstrate, however, different members of that community may imagine different versions of it.

Gayatri Chakravorty Spivak, in her article 'Can the Subaltern Speak?: Speculations on Widow Sacrifice', describes how a British version of the history of India had served to construct a 'continuous and "homogenous" "India" in terms of heads of state and British administrators . . . [consequently] . . . "India" can then be "represented", in the other sense, by its imperial masters'.[21] Rushdie accepts this argument, but is clearly of the opinion that attempts to homogenise India have ultimately failed. This is, moreover, as true of the postcolonial period as it was of the colonial period.

In 'The Riddle of Midnight: India, August 1987', Rushdie supports this opinion by providing a view of India as an 'imagined community'. And just as Saleem's relationship to history is problematic, so too is India's status as a nation 'imagined' in relation to history less than straightforward. In this essay, Rushdie points to a 'sense' of Indian history that spans thousands of years, yet observes that in all that time 'there never was such a thing as a united India.'[22] Not even the British were able to fully impose coherence on its many disparate parts. Even after the passing of midnight, 15 August 1947, when India formally achieved a state of national independence, India remained something more imagined than real. Rushdie writes: 'And then that midnight, the thing that had never existed was suddenly "free". But what on earth was it? On what common ground (if any) did it, does it, stand?'

For Rushdie, both colonial and postcolonial conceptions of India have emerged from a process of narratisation. And so at the heart of so much of his writing is an attempt to engage with the question of narrative 'truth'; of the nature of the relationship between the act of representation and that which is being represented. The character of Saleem clearly illustrates this aspect of Rushdie's work; Saleem's unreliable narration encourages us to distrust the very act of narration itself. So history, and nationhood, as products not only of memory but also of narrative, are presented as suspect and contested concepts.

For many critics, *Midnight's Children* is not a failed attempt at historical correspondence, but a work that seeks to undermine the authority of history by occupying what David Lipscomb describes as 'a strange middle ground', where fantasy may represent a kind of truth and where '"real" history is just another ideological fantasy.'[23] For Dieter Reimenschneider, the 'truth' of fantasy finds expression through Rushdie's appeal to Indian philosophical traditions. Such an appeal, for Reimenschneider, represents a rejection of a Eurocentric, imperial and empirical, conception of history. Reimenschneider suggests of Rushdie that, 'by rejecting the belief in man's ability to write and think objectively about history, he demonstrates that reality can only be grasped through myth – or literature.'[24]

For Aruna Srivastava, Rushdie does not so much reject historical objectivity outright, but places it alongside a number of different philosophical approaches to history. In *Midnight's Children*, Srivastava argues, Saleem experiences India's recent past through the 'trials and tribulations of his body'.[25] Such a reading of the novel seems to suggest that the character of Saleem represents a physical or 'felt history'.[26] Yet at the same time, Saleem is also placed in relation to competing philosophical systems of thought.

■ As he writes the novel, Saleem wrestles with a chronological view of history, passed on by the ruling British and now part of the Indian national consciousness, and (to him) a more ephemeral, (Mahatma) Gandhian, mythical view of history – properly and traditionally Indian, but suppressed by more 'progressive' ideas about history and its relation to time. The first historical model (and 'model' is a very apposite term) needs the linear narrative, the act of plotting, to describe its cause-and-effect basis. Far from being objective, this type of history-telling is an act of 'remembering forward' in Barthesian terms (White, 'Question' 13), of knowing the end result, and linking it retrospectively to its beginning.[27] Historical events then have no immanent structure, but only one imposed by an ideologically conditioned historian. The act of creating histories, then, is an ideological act, designed to support political and moral systems.[28] □

As Srivastava observes, an 'imperialist venture, like that of the British in India, depends on such a traditional view of history for its sustenance.'[29] And, for the early sections of the novel, Saleem appears to subscribe to such a view himself. Not only is Saleem attempting to trace the linear path of his paternity, but his relationship to his British father might also bind him to a 'chronological, British-born(e) manipulation of history'.[30] Yet Saleem is the son of two fathers, one British and the other Indian, and as a consequence of this ambiguity his story becomes increasingly disordered. Saleem finds it impossible to structure his narrative along the line of a single chronologically determined lineage. As the novel progresses, Saleem's story adopts a less confining and more 'Indian', all-encompassing, approach to history. Yet this approach is not without its risks.

■ Saleem thus begins to come to terms with the role of the first, traditional historical mode, as well as recognizing that beyond lies a much larger, almost mythical, view of history found in Indian philosophy and religion from which the Indian concept of *maya*, or the illusoriness of life, derives, and only foreign sensibilities (or those of the colonized, completely estranged from their original cultures) find it alien, nihilistic, and frightening. For a man like Gandhi, this second mode of historical thinking is essential. For him 'that which is permanent eludes the historian of events. Truth transcends history' (quoted in Gokhale 217).[31] What he termed 'inner history' could not be seen in terms of dates, events, and quantifiable time, but rather in terms of time 'quite different from those of conventional history for they have a larger rhythm and a larger interval; the word used is *Yuga*, an entire age or aeon' (Gokhale 224). Saleem also considers this concept when he argues for a sense of proportion in the telling of stories:

> Think of this: history, in my version, entered a new phase on August 15th, 1947 – but in another version, that inescapable date is no more than one fleeting instant in the Age of Darkness, Kali-Yuga [which] . . . began on Friday, February 18th, 3102 B.C.; and will last a mere 432,000 years! Already feeling somewhat dwarfed, I should add nevertheless that the Age of Darkness is only the fourth phase of the present Maha-Yuga cycle which is, in total, ten times as long; and when you consider that it takes a thousand Maha-Yugas to make just one Day of Brahma, you'll see what I mean about proportion. (194)[32]

In this passage, we can see Saleem's understanding of the transcendental view of history, alongside the mundane concern with accuracy in numbers and dates. In an excellent article on Gandhi's philosophy of history, Balkrishna Gokhale discusses Franklin Edgerton's analysis of two strands of Indian philosophy: the interpenetration of the 'ordinary' and the 'extraordinary' (224). This combination of two levels of thought is what is so disturbing to a Western mind resolutely entrenched in just one, the 'ordinary.' These double strands also account for the totally different concept of time which is also essential to a transcendental view of history. With some irritation, Saleem remarks that 'no people whose word for "yesterday" is the same as their word for "tomorrow" can be said to have a firm grip on the time' (106), and the narrator in *Shame* also pinpoints this as the central problem in his attempt to narrate the story of [Khayyam], remarking that 'it seems that the future cannot be restrained, and insists on seeping back into the past' (24).[33]

And yet, this view of history, while potentially liberating, is extremely threatening. The impulse to narrate and to create stories is an impulse to order, to make sense of an apparently chaotic world, to create a coherent sense of self. *Midnight's Children* is about Saleem's struggle to make himself and his country into a unified subject, to assert his lineage, his family and national ties, and alliances. According to David Carroll, questioning conventional history threatens the very basis of subjectivity:

> The uncertainty of the representation of the past (of history and memory) when the origin and end of history are no longer assumed to be present, when the sense or direction of history is in question, cannot simply be dismissed as constituting a subjectivist view of history . . . for it is the subject itself, as an individual or collectivity (type) that depends on teleological views of history for its support. The derivation of the individual subject . . . the subject as unified presence . . . is problematical when history is not accepted in its 'domesticated,' rational, metaphysical form as the optimistic resolution of contradictions. (112)[34]

Both Saleem Sinai's and Omar [Khayyam's] obsession with place and, in particular, family (the search for lineage, the outlining of ancestry, the adoption if necessary of 'foster' family) can also be seen, in Carroll's terms, as this desire for a unified and coherent subjectivity. The desire for origin is for Carroll a desire to immortalize and retain the past. The family and the family home are the foci of this desire:

> The context of this subject is the family, which defines a structure,

an enclosure where the subject takes on an identity and becomes what it is, equal to itself. Memory within this enclosure protects the identity of the subject and is a means of recalling the sense of the subject to itself . . . The family is one as the subject is one. The family seems to have overcome the problem of the reconstruction of the past by offering a substantial, 'natural' context in which the reconstruction can take place. (149)

Clearly, both [Khayyam] and Sinai share this desire to be able to place the family home, family name, and family context. And, just as clearly, their lack of knowledge about their fathers, their very origins, thwarts any such attempts to reconstruct – for themselves, India, or Pakistan – a unified, coherent, sense of self, nationality or ethnicity. Saleem says as much of the personality of Pakistan when he suggests that

at the deep foundations of their unease lay the fear of schizophrenia, of splitting, that was buried like an umbilical cord in every Pakistani heart. In those days, the country's East and West wings were separated by the unbridgeable land-mass of India; but past and present, too, are divided by an unbridgeable gulf. Religion was the glue of Pakistan, holding the halves together; just as consciousness, the awareness of oneself as a homogeneous entity in time, a blend of past and present, is the glue of personality, holding together our then and our now. (351)

It is this dilemma of history that the narrator/Rushdie laments of the Pakistanis in *Shame*. 'All migrants leave their pasts behind,' he writes; 'it is the fate of migrants to be stripped of history' (63). Given that their origins are obscure, and are for all practical purposes nonexistent, both Sinai and [Khayyam] have to confront squarely the problem of identity and history. After he has destroyed the objects associated with his childhood, [Khayyam] gazes in dismay at what he describes as his 'massacred history' (32). For Saleem Sinai, the impetus is external; when the bulldozer robs him of his silver spittoon, he comments: '[I was] deprived of the last object connecting me to my more tangible, historically-verifiable past' (432). A few pages later, Saleem tiredly admits that he is indeed 'no longer connected to history' (442).

Both [Khayyam] and Saleem fear being annihilated from and by history altogether. [Khayyam] is afraid of 'never emerging from the disintegrating history race' (32), and the amnesiac buddha-Sinai talks of 'seceding from history' (351). Both point up the place of and necessity for discontinuity in a historical way of thinking that does not oppress, confine, and rigidify. Both India/Saleem and Pakistan/[Khayyam] are indeed in danger of disappearing entirely from a conventional historical approach. In strikingly Foucauldian terms, Rushdie reveals [Khayyam], just before his massacre of his history, to be exploring 'beyond history into what seemed the positively archaeo-logical antiquity of "Nishapur" [also known as Neyshabur, a town in north-eastern Iran and the birth place of the Persian poet Omar Khayyam (1050–1122)]' (31). In his essay 'Nietzsche, Genealogy, History,' Foucault opposes conventional history to the search for genealogy, or the analysis of descent, which he also shows to be a very disquieting alternative, for 'it disturbs what was previously consid-ered immobile; it fragments what was thought unified; it shows the heterogeneity of what was imagined consistent with itself' (147). Foucault adds that 'descent attaches itself to the body' (147), a state-ment again striking in its applicability to *Midnight's Children*. Saleem suffers history through his body. He is concerned always with its decay, which grows more and more rapid as his novel progresses. The history of India, and his own, is dependent on his nose, depleting body parts, his transistor-like head. In *Midnight's Children* the body is, as Foucault describes it,

> the pretext of . . . insurmountable conflict . . . the inscribed surface of events (traced by language and dissolved by ideas), the locus of a disassociated Self (adopting the illusion of a substantial unity), and a volume in perpetual disintegration. Genealogy, as an analy-sis of descent, is thus situated within the articulation of the body and history. Its task is to expose a body totally imprinted by history and the process of history's destruction of the body. (148)[35]

Foucault thus derogates the impulse of traditional history to create a unified subject, its attempt to dominate the past. Using Nietzsche's terms, Foucault prefers an 'effective' history, suggesting that 'History becomes "effective" to the degree that it introduces discontinuity into our very being' (154). What is liberating, despite the threat of frag-mentation and discontinuity, is the fact that such a view of history does not allow humans to hide behind ideas of destiny, or fate. Here (in spite of some important philosophical differences), Foucault comes closest in his view of history to Gandhi's. Indeed, Gandhi is one of Foucault's 'successes of history' – someone who is able to subvert the rules of the dominant group to his own ends. Although Foucault's view of humanity is far more pessimistic than Gandhi's, their views on the history of the human race show remarkable similarities. Foucault writes that 'humanity installs each of its violences in a system of rules and this proceeds from domination to domination' (151). In such a system of rules, like traditional history, Gandhi felt that 'the spirit of man lay buried under such events as wars and revolutions, empires and domination of one race by another' (Gokhale 217). Yet, in Gandhi's 'effective' history, there is room for optimism and relief. He too believes that a sense of fate is crippling. Individuals must recognize that they have, and must exercise, their freedom to make choices. With this freedom comes the ability to confront the self (and recognize its fragmentary nature) and thus to come to terms with a type of history in which 'All conflicts will be finally resolved, and history will transcend its own time-bound nature' (Gokhale 223).

To Gandhi, then, as to Nietzsche (Foucault seems to valorize only genealogy as a pursuit), all modes of historical thinking are necessary, although some are more limiting than others. In *The Use and Abuse of History*, Nietzsche argues for a combination of three modes of historical consciousness – the unhistorical, which comprises the power of 'forgetting,' of limiting one's horizon (43); the historical, which is what we understand by conventional history – the mode from which Nietzsche feels we suffer an excess (this is the paralysing 'burden of history' which is the source of Saleem's impotence [42]); finally, the superhistorical – a sense that allows for a greater cultural vision, one which encompasses art and religion (43).[36] In this way, Nietzsche hopes to combat the 'disguised theology' that traditional history has become (49). In fact, the initial effects of his 'remedy' to the ills of the 'historical' mode are described by Nietzsche at the end of his short work in terms strikingly similar to Saleem's at the end of *Midnight's Children*. Nietzsche writes:

> The unhistorical and the superhistorical are the natural antidotes against the overpowering of life by history; they are the cures for the historical disease. We who are sick of the disease may suffer a little from the antidote. But this is no proof that the treatment we have chosen is wrong. (70)

And this is Saleem:

> One day, perhaps, the world may taste the pickles of history. They may be too strong for some palates, their smell may be overpowering, tears may rise to the eyes; I hope nevertheless that it will he possible to say to them that they possess the authentic taste of truth . . . that they are, despite everything, acts of love. (461)

The Gandhian view of history is even more encompassing, however, than Nietzsche's three modes of history, although the impulse is the same: to free people from stultifying concepts of progress and time. What is striking about Gandhi's view is its biaxial nature; it is indeed a very similar conceptual model to the structuralist one of synchronic and diachronic historical axes; but in fact subsumes both those indices into one: in Gandhi's scheme, Foucault's and Nietzsche's effective history and three modes of historical consciousness are within the realm of conventional history. Both the synchronic and diachronic, archaeology and chronology, are placed on the vertical axis, while a transcendent concept of history must also encompass, along the horizontal axis, what Gandhi calls myths and mythologies, or fictions. [. . .]

This model clearly reveals the complexity of historical thinking with which Saleem is attempting to come to terms. By the end of the novel, he comes to accept the uncertainty of the forever-empty pickle jar, and acquiesces to the fact of his (and his country's) disintegration in conventional (bio) historical terms. He has, in fact, managed to see, for all its terror, a larger picture and context, and recognizes a different sense of proportion. Still, his is not the passive acceptance that outsiders see the doctrine of *maya* leading to. Like any good son of the British Empire, he is terrified at the prospect of annihilation:

> Yes, they will trample me underfoot, the numbers marching one two three, four hundred million five hundred six, reducing me to specks of voiceless dust, just as, all in good time, they will trample my son who is not my son, and his son who will not be his, and his who will not be his, until the thousand and first generation, until a thousand and one midnights have bestowed their terrible gifts and a thousand and one children have died, because it is the privilege and the curse of midnight's children to be both masters and victims of their times, to forsake privacy and be sucked into the annihilating whirlpool of the multitudes, and to be unable to live or die in peace. (463)[37] □

Srivastava concludes her article by pointing to Rushdie's political intent. Novels such as *Midnight's Children* and *Shame* may well contain numerous conflicting historical narratives, they might also disturb the distinction between history and fiction, but they do not merely do so in play. As Srivastava argues, 'Rushdie's brand of metafiction is not vainly narcissistic, nor does it fall into the nihilism of linguistic determinism that much "postmodern" fiction does.'[38] Rushdie's novels may well move beyond the confines of 'traditional history', yet they do not move beyond the realms of the real and history altogether. Linda Hutcheon describes such novels as 'historiographic metafictions'; novels that 'are intensely self-reflexive but that also both re-introduce historical context into metafiction and problematize the entire question of historical knowledge.'[39] Hutcheon observes, of novels such as *Midnight's Children* and *Shame*, that they are not an attempt 'to void or avoid history'.[40] For Rushdie's concern is to problematize the authority of historical knowledge, not to dispense with history. To do so would not only be to ignore the reality of India's colonial and postcolonial experience, but also to make himself vulnerable to accusations of historical revisionism. One only has to read essays such as 'Outside the Whale' and 'Attenborough's Gandhi' to gain a sense of how strongly Rushdie feels about the dangers of revisionist accounts of India's history.[41] In these essays, Rushdie is quick to criticise 'the refurbishment of the Empire's tarnished image' evident in works such as M. M. Kaye's *The Far Pavilions* (1978) and E. M. Forster's *A Passage to India* (1924), and their subsequent adaptation for television and film.[42] Rushdie criticises Richard Attenborough's *Gandhi* as 'inadequate as biography, appalling as history, and often laughably crude as a film'.[43] Rushdie goes on to condemn the film's rewriting of Indian political history as not only nonsense, but 'dangerous nonsense.'[44]

The articles in this chapter have, so far, concentrated on *Midnight's Children*. This is simply a reflection of the criticism. Rushdie himself admits that *The Satanic Verses* lacks the historical framework of his earlier novel.[45] The final article included in this chapter, Rukmini Bhaya Nair's 'Text and Pre-Text: History as Gossip in Rushdie's Novels', is one of the rare examples of criticism that examines Rushdie's most controversial novel in the light of its historical engagement.[46] Nair discusses the linguistic qualities of *The Satanic Verses* and its use of gossip as a narrative form to express history. For Nair, 'gossip' is a term that usefully encompasses a variety of qualities excluded from the realm of official and authoritative discourse. Gossip is, instead, oral, fragmented and at times even trivial. It requires no 'facts' for validation. It must, however, appear plausible if it is successfully to fulfil its function of observing the frailties and 'lapses of real people, historical figures and the like.'[47] Consequently, for Nair, *The Satanic Verses* is a novel characterised by formal irreverence, yet remains very much concerned with historical engagement.

■ 'Language' claims the narrator of *SV* 'is courage: the ability to conceive a thought, speak it, and by doing so make it true.' The argument advanced in this essay is that *SV* is the last and most risky step that Rushdie takes in his enterprise of creating a language, a form of discourse, namely gossip, which uses history as both a pre-text and a pretext. The three novels *MC*, *S* and *SV* [*Midnight's Children*, *Shame*, and *The Satanic Verses*] can be read as a single text, re-fashioned in the apparently rag-tag garb of gossip, from the standard texts of Indian, Pakistani and Islamic history and sharing certain discourse features in common.

Within the linguistic space of these novels, Rushdie's native cassandras and tiresiases [both Cassandra and Tiresias are soothsayers from Greek myth], liberated by their fantastical powers to penetrate and dissolve personality, to traverse time and space with ease, may home in unannounced on the most private of public moments. Multifarious births, copulations and regenerative deaths come within their purview. Not surprisingly therefore, narration in Rushdie's novels is shaped as gossip, an undervalued form of everyday talk that is now creatively empowered to reclaim the metaphors of an elite history. In *SV*, Rushdie, tongue very much in cheek, presents the following case through one of his minor characters, an intellectual Bengali woman.

> Society was orchestrated by what she called *grand narratives*; history, economics, ethics. In India, the development of a corrupt and closed state apparatus had 'excluded the masses of people from the ethical project'. As a result, they sought ethical satisfactions in the oldest of the grand narratives, that is, religious faith [*SV*, 537].[48]

Subversion/sub-versions of the grand narratives of history and religion might be effectively achieved through gossip, since the *raison d'être* of this mode of discourse is the creation of doubt about established versions of facts. A primarily non-literary genre, which Rushdie has adapted to the form of the novel with amazing facility and even more amazing consequences. [. . .]

Of course, the grand narratives of history and religion may also be reformulated, not as the intimate discourse of gossip favoured by Rushdie, but in terms of each other. In *SV*, Rushdie portrays, by no means wholly unsympathetically, the Ayatollah Khomeini in exile, who 'feels emanating from his fingertips, the arachnid strings with which he will control the movement of history . . . No, not history: something stranger.' The Imam speaks through his muezzin, Bilal.

> We will make a revolution . . . that is a revolt not only against a tyrant but against history . . . We will unmake the veil of history and when it is unravelled, we will see Paradise standing there, in all its glory and light. 'Burn the books and trust the Book; shred the papers and hear the World . . . explicated by your interpreter and Imam' [*SV*, 210–11].

On this view of textual interpretation, the narrator of *SV* seems to say, most of history is not so much retold, rewritten, as eradicated, expunged. In its place is a pure, timeless universe. The author/narrators of *SV*, *S* and *MC* clearly choose another route to historical truth, that of scandalous gossip, of *hearsay*. It is an accidental bounty of the English language, as Rushdie would no doubt appreciate, that hearsay sounds so close to *heresy*. [. . .]

Gossip is a spectator sport. Notwithstanding their absolute involvement in history, the narrators of gossip needs must remain apart, preserve their perspective on matters of history; they must retain their individuality. Rushdie achieves this by making the several protagonists of *MC*, *S* and *SV* slightly fantastic. Saleem Sinai of *MC* is all nose, his alter-ego Shiva all knees, his sister Jamila all voice, his son Aadam all ears. Omar Khayyam Shakil of *S* is 'dizzy, peripheral, inverted, stargazing, fat', his wife Sufiya [Zinobia] retarded, unnaturally lovely, prone to fits, his mother-in-law Bilquis Hyder obsessively fearful of the wind, his brother-in-law Talwar a stiff-necked clairvoyant, his 'mothers' a 'trinity' – Chunni, Munni-in-the-middle and 'little' Bunny all rolled in one. In *SV*, Ayesha is dressed in a garb of butterflies, Saladin Chamcha metamorphosises into a horned beast, Gibreel Farishta wears an unlikely halo, Rekha Merchant rides a magic carpet, Allie Cone meets restless ghosts on Everest.

Fantasy in Rushdie's novels is thus purposeful, it distinguishes the protagonists from millions of others whose stories they represent; fantasy is harnessed in service of the truth, of reality. Being grotesque as well as fantastically gifted allows one to stand apart yet 'swallow the world'. Like Márquez, Borges and other contemporary writers in the 'magic realist' tradition, Rushdie himself insists that the fantasy elements in his novels 'are only enabling devices to talk about actuality'. It may be argued that gossip is an enabling mode of discourse for the same purpose, the discussion of historical complexity:

> Islam is, after all, one of the greatest ideas that ever came into the world . . . and the chance to study the birth of a great historical idea is interesting . . . (but) the historical record is (fragmented). So I thought, well, let's not try and pretend to be writing a history. Let's take the themes I am interested in and fantasise them and fabulate them and all that, so that we don't have to get into the issue: did this really happen like this or did [it] not? [*Bandung File*].[49]

Fantasy can be seen as seriously reporting political reality only when readers and author share a version of how things really happened, a certain view of the facts. Rushdie has noted that Dickens was his master in this method, for Dickens 'uses a kind of background or setting for his works which is completely naturalistic, down to the tiniest details. And on top of this completely naturalistic background, he imposes totally surreal images – like the Circumlocution Office rooted in a recognisable real world, the fantasy works.'

Numerical exactitude is an innovative feature relating fact to fantasy that Rushdie adds to the Dickensian arsenal. This is a device that gives shape and texture to the flow of gossip in the novels. In his 1983 interview, Rushdie demonstrated this fascination with figures when he said, 'it seemed to me that the period between 1947 and 1977 – the period from Independence to Emergency – had a kind of shape to it, it represented a sort of closed period in the history of the country. That shape became part of the architecture of the work.'[50] Within *MC*, *S* and *SV*, numbers keep popping up. There are 1001 children of midnight (recalling [Scheherazade's] 1001 Arabian tales) of whom 420 fail to survive (this number being associated 'since time immemorial with fraud deception and trickery'); Sufiya [Zinobia]'s sense of shame betrayed leads her to decapitate 218 turkeys, and the fecund Naveed Hyder, in contrast to the Virgin Ironpants, produces 27 children, first twins, then triplets, quartets, quintuplets, sextets and finally septuplets; Gibreel Farishta, aboard the hijacked and doomed 'Flight AI-420, the Boeing 747 *Bostan*', recites endlessly:

> Tenth highest peak in the world is . . . Xixabangma Feng, eight oh one three metres. Annapurna ninth, eighty seventy-eight . . . One, Chomulungma, eight eight four eight. Two, K2, eighty-six eleven. Kanchenjunga, eighty-five ninety-eight, Makalu, Dhaulagiri, Manaslu. Nanga Parbat, metres eight thousand one hundred and twenty-six [*SV*, 82].

The authentication of gossip is also achieved in other ways, For example, in *SV*, details of Islamic medieval texts and history are alluded to constantly. Rushdie has claimed that 'almost everything in those sections – the dream sections (dealing with Mohammed's life) – starts from a historical or quasi-historical basis'. In *MC* and *S*, historical place-names, dates and personages are accurately recalled:

> On September 6th, Indian troops crossed the Wagah border [*MC*, 339].[51]

> One last fact: after the death of my grandfather, Prime Minister Jawaharlal Nehru fell ill and never recovered his health. This fatal sickness finally killed him on May 27th, 1964 [*MC*, 278].

> Voices of women singing 'Our Golden Bengal', . . . in the centre of the city, on the podium of his defeat, General Tiger Niazi awaited General Manekshaw. (Biographical details: Sam was a Parsee. He came from Bombay. Bombayites were in for happy times that day . . .) [*S*, 377].[52]

Serious acceptance is ensured by casually mentioning important political figures of the day and their foibles. We are told that Morarji Desai drinks his own urine, that Mountbatten had a 'chicken-breast-eater of a wife', that Jinnah scoffed at horoscope-mongers on the eve of independence 'secure in the knowledge that his Pakistan will be born in just eleven hours, a full day before independent India', that Sanjay Gandhi's wife was an ex-model. Many of these details may be publicly corroborated. Not only do they assist the main function of the narration as gossip, they also promote a less reverential attitude towards such public people.

In *SV*, however, Rushdie has extended the discourse of gossip to include not only politics but the Prophet, not only governments but God. As is inevitable in the discourse of gossip, he has thus had to humanise sacred figures in order to offer explications of their behaviour. Gossip functions as explanation rather than revelation. As is obvious from reactions to *SV*, the consequences of this authorial decision to explain the workings of the divine have been devastating because it invites a classic clash of sacred versus secular ideals. During the course of the novel, Rushdie's narrator himself uses the description 'humanised' to describe a process which radically alters certain characters in the novel, e.g., Allie, Gibreel, Saladin, whose supernatural counterparts Al-Lat, Gibreel, Shaitan cannot otherwise be properly comprehended. Such humanisation primarily seems to mean, for the narrator of SV, the experiencing of human *emotions*, learning to love and hate.

> . . . and at the centre of the carnage, sleeping like a baby, no mythological creature at all, no iconic Thing of horns and hellsbreath, but Mr Saladin Chamcha himself, apparently restored to his old shape, mother-naked but of entirely human aspect and proportions, *humanised* – is there any option but to conclude? – by the fearsome concentration of his hate [*SV*, 294].

By casting both Saladin and [Gibreel], his major protagonists in *SV*, as public characters, a radio-artiste and a film actor, Rushdie, who has in fact admitted his conceptual debt to film gossip magazines in India, is able, moreover, to construct the ideal arena for gossip, where the private side of the public is laid bare.[53] □

History and nationhood remain important themes in Rushdie's novels. Yet, the next chapter of this guide will demonstrate that, following the publication of *The Satanic Verses,* and as a reflection of developments in postcolonial debate, critics increasingly broadened their discussion of Rushdie's writing to include issues of migrancy and hybridity.

CHAPTER FOUR

'Mutability of the Essence of the Self': Writing the Migrant Experience

I N HIS essay, 'The Location of Brazil', Rushdie writes of a migrant sensibility, 'whose development I believe to be one of the central themes of this century of displaced persons'.[1] Rushdie's perspective on the social and political relevance of this issue is forged from personal experience. Rushdie was born in Bombay, but was sent to study in England when he was fourteen. Since that time, he has spent most of his life studying and working in England. In numerous essays and interviews, Rushdie describes himself as a migrant writer and much of the 'difficulty' of his work emerges from his migrant status. Rushdie asks:

■ What does it mean to be an 'Indian' outside India? How can culture be preserved without becoming ossified? How should we discuss the need for change within ourselves and our community without seeming to play into the hands of our racial enemies? What are the consequences, both spiritual and practical, of refusing to make concessions to Western ideas and practices? What are the consequences of embracing those ideas and practices and turning away from ones that came with us?[2] □

Rushdie's use of the expression 'racial enemies' seems to lend a somewhat antagonistic tone to his questioning. Yet, for Rushdie, the experience of migrancy is too complex to be simply located within a purely confrontational dynamic. In his discussion of migrant writers, Rushdie observes: 'Sometimes we feel that we straddle two cultures; at other times, that we fall between two stools. But however ambiguous and shifting this ground may be, it is not an infertile territory for a writer to occupy.'[3]

Timothy Brennan, in his influential study of Rushdie, *Salman Rushdie and the Third World: Myths of the Nation*, adopts a similar view.[4] Brennan links Rushdie to authors such as Mario Vargas Llosa, Derek Walcott,

Isabel Allende and Bharati Mukherjee, whom he describes as 'Third-World cosmopolitans'. These authors, argues Brennan, occupy a space that is both inside and outside of the cultures they depict. They have been chosen by the literary establishment of the West to act as 'the interpreters and authentic public voices of the Third World – writers who in a sense, allow a flirtation with change that ensured continuity, a familiar strangeness, a trauma by inches.'[5] These authors might appear compromised, in so much that they seem to occupy a privileged and authoritative space from which they may produce typically cosmopolitan 'sceptical readings of national liberation struggles'.[6] However, their assimilation of Western cosmopolitanism is neither complete nor unequivocal; they retain their ability to criticise the very powers that privilege them. Brennan argues: 'Being invited to speak as "Third-World" intellectuals, they took the opportunity to chastise too, and with the aid of their global awareness stated in clear accents that the world is one (not three) and that it is unequal.'[7]

These intricate relations of affiliation and potential compromise are explored in *Midnight's Children* through the figure of the 'chamcha'. Meaning 'spoons', chamchas point to intimacy and, indeed, complicity between the authority of colonialism and its colonial subjects. These are, moreover, relations that continue into the postcolonial context through 'the rise of the domestic collaborators, the corrupt neo-colonial élite.'[8] The figure of the chamcha, therefore, raises issues of colonial subjectivity, and postcolonial responsibility and, as Brennan appears to suggest, Rushdie does not necessarily exclude himself from such debates. Through his writing, Rushdie is seen to explore his own migrant status.

■ As a critic not only of India, Pakistan and England but of the 'fictions' of national discourse, Rushdie has been aware of the privileges separating Third-World authors from the realities they describe. So, he wonders, with what native authority can the colonial exile speak? Rushdie has been obsessed by this dubious position, which he expresses in the experiences of his many Westernised characters – for example, Aadam Aziz in *Midnight's Children*, who had been 'branded as an alien' for studying medicine in Germany, and was 'therefore a person not completely to be trusted' by the village poor. In the more recent novel, *Shame*, the sense of being foreign is even stronger, and its rebukes are directed for the first time against the author personally, who imagines the Pakistani commoners saying: 'Outsider! Trespasser! You have no right to this subject. We know you, with your foreign language wrapped around you like a flag: speaking about us in your forked tongue, what can you tell but lies?'[9]

So, it is with a sense of self-reproach that Rushdie declares himself an enemy of the *'chamchas'* in a *Times* article of 1983. Literally 'spoons', the *chamchas* are for Rushdie those collaborators under independence who have propped up the post-colonial status quo; even after the departure of the Raj, Rushdie observes, the Empire continues to grow fat by being 'spoon-fed'.[10]

In a novel like *Shame*, dependent on the mode of fantasy, there was the danger, especially among Western audiences, of simply continuing the warped vision of the European explorer by viewing the land as a spectacle, a fund of imagery. Although he writes about his native land, he carefully abstracts its features and makes them exotic, as if to reflect the uncomfortable similarities between himself and an adventurer stationed in London selling Oriental wares to a public whose tastes he knows from several decades of travel.

This tentative, but explicit, comparison between the early reconnaissance work of imperialism's first scouts and Rushdie's own novels of information, reveals his awareness of the contradictory sides of his impact in Britain. Not only is he potentially an 'impostor' to his Pakistani readers, but a potential traitor as well. Translating the coercive acts of European conquerors into the forms of his writing did not necessarily mean correcting them. García Márquez's playful recognition of an imperial legacy in style becomes in Rushdie an identification of motive as well: 'I too, like all migrants, am a fantasist. I build imaginary countries and try to impose them on the ones that exist.'[11]

There is no necessary connection between the cosmopolitan author and the post-colonial élite, yet on an imaginative level Rushdie repeatedly associates the two – for example, in *Shame*'s Omar Khayyam Shakil. As his name implies, Omar is a character only articulated *through* the English, just as the *Rubaiyat* [a collection of verses by the Persian poet, mathematician, philosopher and astronomer, Omar Khayyam (1050–1122)] is known to us only through the free revisions of the Victorian poet, Edward Fitzgerald. We see the pattern of Omar's significance to the novel before we see his precise role. Tainted by the English in name, Omar comes from a family whose entire heritage has English blemishes. An illegitimate child with three mothers, he has a father who is most likely 'an Angrez sahib'. Omar's grandfather has a reputation for learning that is based on a library secretly purchased from an English colonel.

Omar's stylish clothes, his cigars, his European education are obvious marks of his foreign identity, but they are not the decisive ones in his pervasive English makeup. The Shakil household betrays a history of collaboration, in which many of the English imperial habits are symbolised. His family's livelihood depends on pawning furniture that had been acquired by their 'rapaciously acquisitive forebears'. Like an imperious Westerner empowered by technology, Omar looks down on the town of Q from an upper floor of his ancestral home

('Nishapur') using a telescope through which he sees 'the world . . . as a bright disc, a moon for his delight' (*Shame*, p. 30).

The ability of the colonial power structure to impose its forms *in absentia* is reflected in a cultural system designed to enforce consent. Thus, Omar learns to manipulate his friends with the techniques learned from a European do-it-yourself hypnosis manual. And, more like the English than in any other way, knows no shame – there is no counterpart in English, says Rushdie, for the word *'sharam'* (shame). For this reason, Omar, like the English, cannot comprehend certain 'dialects of emotion' like 'embarrassment, discomfiture, decency, modesty, shyness, sense of having an ordained place in the world'. He belongs to that stratum of colonial society that has to be trained to lack a conscience, to deflect the uneasiness resulting from questions of his disgraceful origins, his tarnished birthright. But, in spite of these alliances, he is not the social equal of the Angrez sahibs. The only access that he and the other residents of 'Nishapur' have to the outside world is a dumbwaiter, a mark of their subservience.

Omar's erudition, his privileges, his cultural proximity to the English are all prefigured in Rushdie's earlier fictional counterpart, Saleem Sinai. However, *Midnight's Children* being a more explicitly historical work than *Shame*, Rushdie adds a theory of collaboration to the portrait of the Anglicised native – one that is central to his understanding of the failure of nationalism in India and Pakistan. At the heart of the theory is the *'chamcha'*, first raised in the portrait of Saleem's uncle Mustapha Aziz, whose wife,

> the half-Irani would-be socialite Sonia . . . had been driven certifiably insane by a life in which she had been required to begin 'being a chamcha' (literally a spoon, but idiomatically a flatterer) to forty-seven separate and successive wives of number-ones whom she had previously alienated by her manner of colossal condescension when they had been wives of number-threes. (*MC*, p. 467)

In *Midnight's Children*, we find the image of the *chamcha* in those 'leaders whose fortunes [were] built originally on the miseries of fleeing Hindu families', the same group described by Rushdie's contemporary, Tariq Ali, as the Punjabi bureaucrats and Muslim aristocrats who declared the viability of Pakistan with little other motive than to enrich themselves, speaking Urdu and writing in Persian to a peasantry that spoke Bengali, Punjabi, Sindhi and Pushtu, all the time claiming that they constituted a community. In *Midnight's Children*, Saleem's English parentage and his membership in the Aziz household (obviously patterned on Rushdie's own) slowly merges with the actions of the landholders, religious charlatans and military henchmen who control the state. Estrangement becomes collaboration.

The *chamcha* does not merely utilise the appeal to the nation but epitomises the appeal's oppressive legacy. Fashioned as a weapon against occupation, it merely completes the occupation by recasting the Empire in native form. Thus, in one scene from *Midnight's Children*, the war over the Rann of Kutch, highlighted by desperate communiqués summoning popular support against efforts 'to subvert the state' (p.404), is shown to be a cynical swindle. The real motives behind the war 'didn't get into the papers: the pressures of internal political troubles in Pakistan – Ayub's government was tottering, and a war works wonders at such times' (p.404).

The logic of Rushdie's harsh self-treatment is at first hard to grasp. Personal privileges do not after all amount to betrayal. But his affiliations with the vilest of *chamchas* makes [sic] some sense when one considers his and their roles in communicative fictions. In the conflicting official radio accounts of the war, 'Nothing was real; nothing certain' (p.406). Sincere, patriotic sacrifice is forged in 'the fantasies of our rulers' (p.405).

If the *chamcha* continues the logic of imperial domination, he does so using indigenous forms: the Christian civilising mission becomes 'Jehad . . . Holy War . . . the mujahid philosophy of Syed Ahmad Barilwi', who invites the Pakistani troops marching into Kashmir 'to make sacrifices "as never before"', promising that, if they are martyred, they will be 'bound for the perfumed garden! Where the men would be given four beauteous houris, untouched by man or djinn; and the women, four equally virile males!' (pp.405–6). And the culminating wars – the war for Bangladesh and the Indian 'Emergency' – were wars *within* the nation. Far from being exempt from cruelty, these home-made wars show the 'patriots' to be more furious than their predecessors. Rushdie reserves the most shocking descriptions and the bitterest emotions for his treatment of the fraternal conflicts:

> Bloodhounds track the fleeing enemies of national unity . . . And newspaper offices, burning with the dirty yellowblack smoke of cheap gutter newsprint, and the offices of trade unions, smashed to the ground, the roadside ditches filling up with people who were not merely asleep – bare chests were seen, and the hollow pimples of bullet-holes . . . [O]ur boys, our soldiers-for-Allah, our worth-ten-babus jawans held Pakistan together by turning flame-throwers machine-guns hand-grenades on the city slums. (*MC*, p.426)

In exploring his own culpability for the events of the novel, Saleem determines responsibility not only by his acquiescence ('nor was I to blame for Sino-Indian border skirmishes in the Aksai Chin region of Ladakh . . . [but] I did nothing to alleviate it'), or by his sharing of the desires and human failings of the visible culprits, but specifically as a writer – a creator of communicative fictions. Guilt is centred in, and emanates from, the author himself, extending to all his creations. This conforms to the book's central trope in which Saleem contains India's multitudes within him (p. 457). Authorial ambiguity translates into bipolar morality in which every group has a good and a bad expression.

In a celebrated passage of the novel, Saleem's parents, fleeing the horrors of Partition, move to Bombay where they buy an estate from the Englishman, William Methwold, a descendant of an East Indian Company officer who in 1633 (when their Portuguese rivals still had a foothold in India) had had a vision of 'a British Bombay . . . defending India's West against all comers'. Methwold stipulates that Ahmed and Amina may have the house cheaply but must leave everything just as it is – furniture, dishes, paintings . . . everything – in the same way that, under similar conditions, Lord Mountbatten signs over the British claim to India.

The genealogy of guilt thus begins with Empire, which, like the natives, is split into two parties: benevolent 'civilisers' like the Englishman, Methwold (with their pinkish skin, bibulous habits, mercenary intentions and carefully parted toupés) and cold-hearted keepers-of-order, like the infamous perpetrator of the Jallianwallah Bagh massacre, General Dyer (with their waxed moustaches, ingenuous pronouncements of white supremacy and willingness to kill for the sake of propriety).[12] In their wake come the Westernised and nativist Indians, neither of whom represent a wholly positive or negative political force.

As a follower of European humanism and Western democracy, the hero of the book's opening chapters, Aadam Aziz, represents in one sense genuine progress, a break from small-town prejudice and oppressive social practices, having studied medicine in Heidelberg and having been unable to retain his Muslim faith upon returning to India; he frees his wife from the chadoor and struggles to limit the influence of religious sectarianism.[13] On the other hand, his European idealism – repeated in the novel in other guises, especially by Aadam's college friend the German anarchist Oskar Lubin and his rival in love, Quasim the Red – fuels what Rushdie calls the 'disease of optimism', religious fanaticism's reverse image and the complement to nationalism in its Eastern form.[14] □

This next extract from Brennan, 'Pitting Levity against Gravity', also taken from *Salman Rushdie and the Third World: Myths of the Nation*, examines Rushdie's treatment of migrancy in *The Satanic Verses*. Brennan had read the novel in its manuscript form prior to its publication, and this essay was written before the fatwa was declared against Rushdie. Though he acknowledges its controversial content and the anger of the Muslim community, Brennan argues that *The Satanic Verses* should not be 'seen through the distorting images of the protests or what the media made of them since they overestimate the Islamic themes of a novel that is, after all, primarily about a very secular England.'[15] His essay presents a different view of the migrant's condition of 'insider/outsider'. Brennan broadens his discussion to include an examination of the migrant writer's relationship with his adopted 'home'.

■ Among Rushdie's novels, only *The Satanic Verses* does not end in oblivion. The countries of the earlier work had been countries 'of the mind'; they could be thought of in terms of apocalypse because they were the ones left behind. But forced to take a stand abroad in the England of *The Satanic Verses*, the immigrant is left with nothing but survival.

At first sight, then, the novel looks more oppositional – more a product of that art of communal resistance suppressed in the earlier work – simply because its survival is won at the expense of English institutions: the British bobby, the BBC newscaster, and the government of a Prime Minister congenially referred to as 'Mrs Torture' and 'Maggie the Bitch'. If the black communities are given the same savage scrutiny – if Asian middle-class hostel owners bilk their West Indian tenants, complain of being stuck in a country 'full of Jews and strangers who lump [them] in with the negroes', or who can think of the English only in the bigoted terms of the mad barber of Fleet Street, with a stiff upper lip on the outside but a secret obsession for kinky sex and death – a mood of specifically anti-institutional anger remains, and one that is not altogether cancelled by the ironies of the earlier work. Following Fanon's criteria, we are not surprised to see this slightly new perspective produce subtle shifts in the narrative. [Brennan is referring to Frantz Fanon's description of cosmopolitan writers who, as they condemn the notion of national culture, reveal their estrangement from their own cultural past. Such writers, according to Fanon, would be a '"race of angels" colorless, stateless, rootless . . . taking up a "universal standpoint" at the cost of psycho-affective injuries'.[16]] Although 'translating' just as heavily from a borrowed Islamic tradition, the novel no longer simply targets that tradition for rebuke; as a part of what makes the new immigrant different from the English, it is something that can be learned from, even emulated, at the cultural level. Because here Rushdie is dealing with a life not only remembered and longed-for but experienced first-hand. England is where Rushdie lives (not India or Pakistan), and so the immediacy of the account takes us away from those snapshots of emotion, and those distanced descriptions of lives actually lived, that fill the pages of the earlier novels. Those works were essentially thinking pieces whose only really vivid human interactions took place where the personal narrator spoke directly to the reader; the plotting of the characters was essentially an orchestration of parodic vignettes that collectively made up an argument. By contrast, the metafictional strategies of *The Satanic Verses* are not nearly so pronounced; the characters are for the first time people living in the world, acting out their lives in a story of their own. The story is not *about* events, but in them . . .[17] □

These events are largely political in nature. In essays such as 'Outside the Whale', Rushdie had already argued for a political role for fiction.[18] He had also attacked the nostalgia for empire evident in British film and television productions such as *A Passage to India* (1984) and *Jewel in the Crown* (1984). *The Satanic Verses* should be read against such a background of British conservatism. For as Brennan observes, this was also a period out of which emerged 'increasingly hostile and restrictive anti-immigration laws, the growth of the National Front, and the "feel-good" ideology of empire in the speeches of Margaret Thatcher, depressingly demonstrated in the war with Argentina over the Falklands (Malvinas) islands'.[19]

■ In another essay written a year earlier for *New Society*, Rushdie had taken on the question of racism itself: 'Britain is undergoing the critical phase of its post-colonial period. This crisis is not simply economic or political. It is a crisis of the whole culture, of the society's entire sense of itself.'[20] It was the postwar immigrations that had given the imperial pose new life:

> The British authorities, being no longer capable of exporting governments, have chosen instead to import a new empire, a new community of subject peoples of whom they can think, and with whom they can deal, in very much the same way as their predecessors thought of and dealt with 'the fluttered folk and wild', the 'new-caught sullen peoples, half-devil and half-child'.[21]

Noting 'the huge, undiminished appetite of white Britons for . . . the Great Pink Age', he went on to consider the unusually varied 'vocabulary of abuse' in the English language itself (wog, frog, kraut, paky), the way the word 'immigrant' in England's public debate invariably means 'black immigrant', and Margaret Thatcher's use of 'we' in a speech recalling the days when England ruled one quarter of the world – a 'we' that naturally excluded England's two million formerly colonised peoples.

The novel, however, does not develop these polemical observations. It sets out instead to capture the immigrants' dream-like disorientation, their multiform, plural 'union-by-hybridization' (*SV*, p.319).[22] *The Satanic Verses* is the most ambitious novel yet published to deal with the immigrant experience in Britain, but it is not by any means the first. Both its originality and its departures are visible only in terms of the enormously varied work that came before it, especially in the post-war period. These include the novels of the West Indian diaspora of the 1940s and 1950s – Samuel Selvon's *The Lonely Londoners* [1956], Edward Braithwaite's *To Sir with Love* [1957], George Lamming's *The Emigrants* [1954] and many others.[23] G. V. Desani's *All About H. Hatterr . . .* had been published as early as 1948. Even in the first postwar generation, novels such as these were operating within a larger milieu of union activism, community organising and the founding of the first black publishing houses, all of which were to lead in the 1970s and 1980s to an ever more vocal and visible movement exemplified today by the novels of Caryl Phillips, the poetry of Grace Nichols and Linton Kwesi Johnson, the plays of Mustapha Matura and the films of Menelik Shabazz.[24] 'Blacks' had, after all, been a presence in Britain for centuries as African musicians in the court of Henry VII, as Indian servants or *ayahs* accompanying returning colonial nabobs, or as sea-going *lascars* settling in the port towns of Cardiff, Bristol and Liverpool. The sudden increase in the numbers of blacks coming to a labour-starved England following the Second World War – from the West Indies, the Punjab, Pakistan, Africa and elsewhere – made a self-consciously 'British' community of the 1970s and 1980s possible. As *Race and Class* editor A. Sivanandan put it, they became 'a people for a class' with a 'legacy of holism [that] made our politics black'.[25]

Although, intellectually and politically, Rushdie does not share these views of Sivanandan, he remains sympathetic to many of them, and has in fact lent his support through jacket blurbs and introductions to some of the books that document the emergent black communities.[26] He is, however, simply not a part of that movement which, in a military metaphor, has called itself the artistic 'frontline'. The circles in which he travels are much closer to those of playwright and screenwriter Hanif Kureishi, whose *My Beautiful Laundrette* [1985] and *Sammy and Rosie Get Laid* [1987] have enjoyed the same international acclaim as Rushdie's novels, and which typically concern themselves with middle-class Asians who own small businesses and have influential relatives from the home country visiting an England that has come to look, as Kureishi once put it, 'very much like a Third World country'. The contrast between this kind of focus and that, say, of Bombay-born British author Farrukh Dhondy, is startling. A member of the British Black Panthers in his teens, a former teacher in the

East End, and currently director of programming for Channel 4, the alternative television station, Dhondy is only one of several current writers (and perhaps the best) to look at the very different world of Southall streetlife and the working-class Asian youths of the housing estates. In other words, as we have been saying, the differences are not the result of simple place or privilege – the fact, for example, that the Asian communities themselves tend to be more middle-class than the West Indian – it is a difference expressed in a larger political aesthetic.

'Pitting levity against gravity' is a phrase that helps explain this difference. Taken from the novel's opening pages (in a procedure that is typical of Rushdie's methods), the phrase embeds within a passing comment important clues to his narrative strategy. Staring in the face of misery, and with serious doubts about the future of the human race, Rushdie insists on the comic. The first thing to strike any reader of Rushdie is that, while engaged and pedagogical, his novels are simply funny. At the same time, the phrase echoes the idea that the 'weight-lessness' of the migrant sensibility is universal both in the sociological sense of the effects postwar immigrations and mass media have had on our collective thinking, and in another sense. He is, in other words, attacking the creation of a racial or ethnic 'other' by suggesting that we are all, in a way, migrants because we have all migrated to earth from our home 'out there'.[27] □

The racial or ethnic 'otherness' of the immigrant is perhaps most clearly undermined in *The Satanic Verses* through its exploration of cultural hybridity. Brennan's observation that *The Satanic Verses* attempts to 'capture the immigrants' dream-like disorientation, their multiform, plural "union-by-hybridization"', is key to an understanding of the novel.[28] Rushdie himself takes such a view when he places himself in opposition to advocates of cultural purity or essentialism, and describes *The Satanic Verses* as a celebration of hybridity. For Rushdie the novel embraces the inevitable consequences of mass migration in terms of 'impurity, inter-mingling, the transformation that comes of new and unexpected combinations of human beings, cultures, ideas, songs. It rejoices in mongrelization and fears the absolutism of the Pure . . . It is a love-song to our mongrel selves.'[29]

Within postcolonial debate, Homi K. Bhabha is the critic most closely associated with the theorisation of cultural hybridity. Rushdie himself directly refers to Bhabha's work in his fiction, while Bhabha, in turn, identifies Rushdie as one of a group of writers who, through their fictional working out of the migrant experience, have directly influenced his for-mulation of the concept.[30] It is, indeed, possible to follow the develop-ment of Bhabha's theories in his critical responses to Rushdie's work. In his 1990 essay 'DissemiNation: Time, Narrative, and the Margins of the

Modern Nation',[31] for example, Bhabha discusses Rushdie's treatment of hybridity in terms of cultural 'mimicry'. Similar to Brennan's figure of the 'chamcha',[32] the mimic is a hybrid figure inasmuch that he or she reflects or appears to adopt the qualities and values of colonial authority.

In his 1985 essay 'Signs Taken for Wonders: Questions of Ambivalence and Authority Under a Tree Outside Delhi, May 1817', Bhabha had already illustrated this complex set of relations by describing the native reaction to one of the great symbols of colonial expansion – the Bible.[33] In this work, Bhabha refers to a missionary register of 1818 that describes the excitement experienced by natives upon encountering the printed word of God. According to Bhabha, the natives enthusiastically engage with the ideas contained in the text and adopt many of the conventionalised expressions of belief devised by the Christian Church. The natives, moreover, literally re-write the Bible so that they might possess more copies for themselves. For Bhabha, however, mimicry by the colonial native represents a process that incorporates both resemblance and disturbance of colonial authority. It both reaffirms authority and menaces such authority. As Benita Parry observes, 'what the native re-writes is not a copy of the colonialist original, but a qualitatively different thing-in-itself, where misreadings and incongruities expose the uncertainties and ambivalences of the colonial text and deny its authorizing presence'.[34] Though the enthusiastic reception of the Bible might at first seem a triumph for the colonial authority it is employed to validate, that triumph is soon cast into doubt. For the native adapts it, expresses it differently; accepts some parts and denies others. The very symbol of colonial authority is undermined. Consequently, Bhabha argues: 'The colonial presence is always ambivalent, split between its appearance as original and authorative and its articulation as repetition and difference.'[35]

In 'DissemiNation', Bhabha adapts his conception of the colonial mimic and applies it to the postcolonial, hybrid migrants of *The Satanic Verses*. The following extract from that essay observes the importance of repetition for the maintenance of national 'integrity' – an 'integrity' essential to both colonial authority, and postcolonial nostalgia for that authority. The migrant, however, is seen to repeat 'differently' and so opens up a space of uncertainty out of which appears the empowered figure of the 'avenging migrant'.

■ **Salman Rushdie's *The Satanic Verses* attempts to redefine the boundaries of the western nation, so that the 'foreignness of languages' becomes the inescapable cultural condition for the enunciation of the mother-tongue. In the 'Rosa Diamond' section of *The Satanic Verses* Rushdie seems to suggest that it is only through the process of dissemi*Nation* – of meaning, time, peoples, cultural boundaries and historical traditions – that the radical alterity of the national culture** will create new forms of living and writing: 'The trouble with the English is that their history happened overseas, so they don't know what it means'.[36]

S.S. Sisodia the soak – known also as Whisky Sisodia – stutters these words as part of his litany of 'what's wrong with the English'. The spirit of his words fleshes out the argument of this essay. I have suggested that the atavistic national past and its language of archaic belonging marginalizes the present of the 'modernity' of the national culture, rather like suggesting that history happens 'outside' the centre and core. More specifically I have argued that appeals to the national past must also be seen as the anterior space of signification that 'singularizes' the nation's cultural totality. It introduces a form of alterity of address that Rushdie embodies in the double narrative figures of Gibreel Farishta/Saladin Chamcha, or Gibreel Farishta/Sir Henry Diamond, which suggests that the national narrative is the site of an ambivalent identification; a margin of the uncertainty of cultural meaning that may become the space for an agonistic minority position. In the midst of life's fullness, and through the representation of this fullness, the novel gives evidence of the profound perplexity of the living. Gifted with phantom sight, Rosa Diamond, for whom repetition had become a comfort in her antiquity, represents the English *Heim* or homeland. The pageant of a 900-year-old history passes through her frail trans-lucent body and inscribes itself, in a strange splitting of her language, 'the well-worn phrases, *unfinished business, grandstand view*, made her feel solid, unchanging, sempiternal, instead of the creature of cracks and absences she knew herself to be'.[37] Constructed from the well-worn pedagogies and pedigrees of national unity – her vision of the Battle of Hastings is the anchor of her being – and, at the same time, patched and fractured in the incommensurable perplexity of the nation's living, Rosa Diamond's green and pleasant garden is the spot where Gibreel Farishta lands when he falls out from the belly of the Boeing over sodden, southern England.

Gibreel masquerades in the clothes of Rosa's dead husband, Sir Henry Diamond, ex-colonial landowner, and through this post-colonial mimicry, exacerbates the discursive split between the image of a continuist national history and the 'cracks and absences' that she knew herself to be. What emerges, at one level, is a popular tale of secret, adulterous Argentinian amours, passion in the pampas with Martin de la Cruz. What is more significant and in tension with the exoticism, is the emergence of a hybrid national narrative that turns the nostalgic past into the disruptive 'anterior' and displaces the his-torical present – opens it up to other histories and incommensurable narrative subjects. The cut or split in enunciation – underlining all acts of utterance – emerges with its iterative temporality to reinscribe the figure of Rosa Diamond in a new and terrifying avatar. Gibreel, the migrant hybrid in masquerade, as Sir Henry Diamond, mimics the collaborative colonial ideologies of patriotism and patriarchy, depriving those narratives of their imperial authority. Gibreel's returning gaze crosses out the synchronous history of England, the essentialist memories of William the Conqueror and the Battle of Hastings. In the middle of an account of her punctual domestic routine with Sir Henry – sherry always at six – Rosa Diamond is overtaken by another time and memory of narration and through the 'grandstand view' of imperial history you can hear its cracks and absences speak with another voice:

> Then she began without bothering with once upon atime and whether it was all true or false he could see the fierce energy that was going into the telling . . . this memory jumbled rag-bag of material was in fact the very heart of her, her self-portrait . . . So that it was not possible to distinguish memories from wishes, guilty reconstructions from confessional truths, because even on her deathbed Rosa Diamond did not know how to look her history in the eye.[38]

And what of Gibreel Farishta? Well he is the mote in the eye of history, its blind spot that will not let the nationalist gaze settle centrally. His mimicry of colonial masculinity and mimesis allows the absences of national history to speak in the ambivalent, ragbag narrative. But it is precisely this 'narrative sorcery' that established Gibreel's own re-entry into contemporary England. As the belated post-colonial he marginalizes and singularizes the totality of national culture. He is the history that happened elsewhere, overseas; his postcolonial, migrant presence does not evoke a harmonious patchwork of cultures, but articulates the narrative of cultural difference which can never let the national history look at itself narcissistically in the eye. For the liminality [occupying a position at, or on both sides of, a boundary] of the western nation is the shadow of its own finitude: the colonial space played out in the imaginative geography of the metropolitan space; the repetition or return of the margin of the postcolonial migrant to alienate the holism of history. The postcolonial space is now 'supplementary' to the metropolitan centre; it stands in a subaltern, adjunct relation that doesn't aggrandise the *presence* of the west but redraws its frontiers in the menacing, agonistic boundary of cultural difference that never quite adds up, always less than one nation and double.

From this splitting of time and narrative emerges a strange, empowering knowledge for the migrant that is at once schizoid and subversive. In his guise as the Archangel Gibreel he sees the bleak history of the metropolis: 'the angry present of masks and parodies, stifled and twisted by the insupportable, unrejected burden of its past, staring into the bleakness of its impoverished future'.[39] From Rosa Diamond's decentred narrative 'without bothering with once upon atime' Gibreel becomes – however insanely – the principle of avenging repetition: 'These powerless English! – Did they not think that their history would return to haunt them? –´ "The native is an oppressed person whose permanent dream is to become the persecutor" (Fanon) . . . He would make this land anew. He was the Archangel, Gibreel – *And I'm back*'.[40]

If the lesson of Rosa's narrative is that the national memory is always the site of the hybridity of histories and the displacement of narratives, then through Gibreel, the avenging migrant, we learn the ambivalence of cultural difference: it is the articulation through incommensurability that structures all narratives of identification, and all acts of cultural translation.

> He was joined to the adversary, their arms locked around one another's bodies, mouth to mouth, head to tail . . . No more of these England induced ambiguities: those Biblical-satanic confusions . . . Quran 18:50 there it was as plain as the day . . . How much more practical, down to earth comprehensible . . . Iblis/Shaitan standing for darkness; Gibreel for the light . . . O most devilish and slippery of cities . . . Well then the trouble with the English was their, Their – In a word Gibreel solemnly pronounces, that most naturalised sign of cultural difference . . . The trouble with the English was their . . . in a word . . . their weather.[41] [. . .]

To end with the English weather is to invoke, at once, the most changeable and immanent signs of national difference. It encourages memories of the 'deep' nation crafted in chalk and limestone; the quilted downs; the moors menaced by the wind; the quiet cathedral towns; that corner of a foreign field that is forever England. The English weather also revives memories of its daemonic double: the heat and dust of India; the dark emptiness of Africa; the tropical chaos that was deemed despotic and ungovernable and therefore worthy of the civilizing mission. These imaginative geographies that spanned countries and empires are changing; those imagined communities that played on the unisonant boundaries of the nation are singing with different voices. If I began with the scattering of the people across countries, I want to end with their gathering in the city. The return of the diasporic; the postcolonial.

Handsworth Songs; Fanon's manichean colonial Algiers; Rushdie's tropicalized London, grotesquely renamed *Ellowen Deeowen* in the migrant's mimicry: it is to the city that the migrants, the minorities, the diasporic come to change the history of the nation. If I have suggested that the people emerge in the finitude of the nation, marking the liminality of cultural identity, producing the double-edged discourse of social territories and temporalities, then in the West, and increasingly elsewhere, it is the city which provides the space in which emergent identifications and new social movements of the people are played out. It is there that, in our time, the perplexity of the living is most acutely experienced.[42] □

In his 1994 essay 'How Newness Enters the World: Postmodern Space, Postcolonial Times and the Trials of Cultural Translation', Bhabha returns to *The Satanic Verses* to illustrate his conception of cultural hybridity.[43] Bhabha's discussion of Rushdie's novel remains focused upon the migrant's experience of metropolitan centres, but perhaps more explicitly presents his understanding of the hybrid migrant as a figure who by revealing difference might also represent 'newness'. However, such is the complexity of the following extract from this essay, that some form of introduction to Bhabha's ideas may be required.

Bhabha's conception of migrant hybridity in terms of difference is most clearly outlined in his 1988 essay 'The Commitment to Theory'.[44] In this essay, Bhabha observes the doubleness of colonial discourse as a process whereby both coloniser and colonised are ambivalently re-inscribed. For Bhabha, hybridity is a complex dynamic, involving what Benita Parry describes as 'a configuration of discursive transactions.'[45] By suggesting an active interaction between coloniser and colonised, Bhabha's conception of hybridity clearly resembles that proposed by Rushdie himself. For, in *The Satanic Verses,* the character of Saladin only achieves the salvation offered by the end of the novel by accepting an identity forged out of different cultures. Saladin is not British, yet nor can he return to India as if his life in Britain had left no mark. Saladin exists, like Rushdie, between 'two stools' and occupies what Bhabha terms the 'Third Space'.[46] Bhabha employs this term as part of his argument that hybridity exists not only at the level of the individual, but also at a cultural level. So Saladin is not simply formed between two fixed or essential cultures, but his fluctuating sense of self is formed out of cultures which are themselves in flux. Bhabha supports his position by first arguing for a distinction between 'cultural difference' and 'cultural diversity'. He suggests that diversity evokes the notion of cultures formed in isolation, essential by nature, that may subsequently be arranged in relation to each other, yet in no significant sense may one be seen to impact upon the other. Bhabha suggests that such a simplistic plotting of cultural boundaries gives rise to the sort of anodyne 'liberal notions of multiculturalism' to which Rushdie is so opposed.[47] Bhabha argues for the more hopeful notion of 'cultural difference'. He writes:

■ Through the concept of cultural difference I want to draw attention to the common ground and lost territory of contemporary critical debates. For they all recognize that the problem of the cultural emerges only at the significatory boundaries of cultures, where meanings and values are (mis)read or signs misappropriated.[48] □

Bhabha argues that all cultures are inherently unstable simply because the act of enunciating those cultures involves the same slippage experienced by all utterances. Bhabha is, in effect, proposing poststructural perspectives on language as a means to gain insight into the mechanisms of cultural expression and identity. He is suggesting that culture is not something that can be fully communicated or possessed, but is something open to interpretation and performance. This is because, as is the case for all utterances, the first space of 'I' and the second space of 'you' is bridged via the third space of language and context. The inevitable result, as the following extract suggests, is ambivalence, and any attempts to homogenise culture, or suggest cultural purity, are doomed.

■ What does the narrative construction of minority discourses entail for the everyday existence of the Western metropolis? Let us stay with televisual subjects of channel-switching and psychic splitting – that [Fredric] Jameson deems late capitalist – and enter the postmodern city as migrants and minorities. Our siren song comes from the Jewish ad-woman Mimi Mamoulian, talking over the phone from New York to Saladin Chamcha, erstwhile London based voice-over artiste, now a Satanic goatman, sequestered in an Indian-Pakistani ghetto in London's Brickhall Street. The scenario comes, of course, from *The Satanic Verses*, and the voice is Mimi's:

> I am conversant with postmodernist critiques of the West, e.g. that we have here a society capable only of pastiche: a flattened world. When I become the voice of a bubble bath, I am entering flatland knowingly, understanding what I am doing and why . . . Don't teach me about exploitation . . . Try being jewish, female and ugly sometime. You'll beg to be black. Excuse my french: brown.[49]

At the [Shaandaar] Café today all the talk is about Chamcha the Anglophile, famed for his voice-over on the Slimbix ad: *'How's a calorie to earn a salary? Thanks to Slimbix, I'm out of work.'* Chamcha, the great projector of voices, the prestidigitator of personae, has turned into a Goat and has crawled back to the ghetto, to his despised migrant compatriots. In his mythic being he has become the 'borderline' figure of a massive historical displacement – postcolonial migration – that is not only a 'transitional' reality, but also a 'translational' phenomenon. The question is, in Jameson's terms, whether 'narrative invention . . . by way of its very implausibility becomes the fibre of a linear possible [cultural] praxis' (p. 369).[50]

For Chamcha stands, quite literally, in-between two border conditions. On the one hand lies his landlady Hind who espouses the cause of gastronomic pluralism, devouring the spiced dishes of Kashmir and the yogurt sauces of Lucknow, turning herself into the wide land mass of the subcontinent itself 'because food passes across any boundary you care to mention'.[51] On Chamcha's other side sits his landlord Sufyan, the secular 'colonial' metropolitan who understands the fate of the migrant in the classical contrast between Lucretius and Ovid. Translated, by Sufyan, for the existential guidance of postcolonial migrants, the problem consists in whether the crossing of cultural frontiers permits freedom from the essence of the self (Lucretius), or whether, like wax, migration only changes the surface of the soul, preserving identity under its protean forms (Ovid).

This liminality of migrant experience is no less a transitional phenomenon than a translational one; there is no resolution to it because the two conditions are ambivalently enjoined in the 'survival' of migrant life. Living in the interstices of Lucretius and Ovid, caught in-between a 'nativist', even nationalist, atavism and a postcolonial metropolitan assimilation, the subject of cultural difference becomes a problem that Walter Benjamin has described as the irresolution, or liminality, of 'translation', *the element of resistance* in the process of transformation, 'that element in a translation which does not lend itself to translation'.[52] This space of the translation of cultural difference *at the interstices* is infused with that Benjaminian temporality of the present which makes graphic a moment of transition, not merely the continuum of history; it is a strange stillness that defines the present in which the very *writing* of historical transformation becomes uncannily visible. The migrant culture of the 'in-between', the minority position, dramatizes the activity of culture's untranslatability; and in so doing, it moves the question of culture's appropriation beyond the assimilationist's dream, or the racist's nightmare, of a 'full transmissal of subject-matter';[53] and towards an encounter with the ambivalent process of splitting and hybridity that marks the identification with culture's difference. The God of migrants, in *The Satanic Verses*, speaks unequivocally on this point, while of course, equivocal between purity and danger:

Whether We be multiform, plural, representing the union-by-hybridisation of such opposites as "Oopar and Neechay", or whether We be pure, stark, extreme, will not be resolved here.[54]

The indeterminacy of diasporic identity, '[that] *will not be resolved here'* is the secular, social cause for what has been widely represented as the 'blasphemy' of the book. Hybridity is heresy. The fundamentalist charge has not focused on the misinterpretation of the Koran, as much as on the offence of the 'misnaming' of Islam: Mohamed referred to as Mahound; the prostitutes named after the wives of the Prophet. It is the *formal* complaint of the fundamentalists that the transposition of these sacred names into profane spaces – brothels or magical realist novels – is not simply sacrilegious, but destructive of the very cement of community. To violate the system of naming is to make contingent and indeterminate what Alisdair Macintrye, in his essay on 'Tradition and Translation', has described as 'naming for: the institutions of naming the expression and embodiment of the shared standpoint of the community, its traditions of belief and enquiry'.[55] The conflict of cultures and community around *The Satanic Verses* has been mainly represented in spatial terms and binary geopolitical polarities – Islamic fundamentalists [vs.] Western literary modernists, the quarrel of the ancient (ascriptive) migrants and modern (ironic) metropolitans. This obscures the anxiety of the irresolvable, borderline culture of hybridity that articulates its problems of identification and its diasporic aesthetic in an uncanny, disjunctive temporality that is, at once, the *time* of cultural displacement, and the *space* of the 'untranslatable'.

To blaspheme is not simply to sully the ineffability of the sacred name. ' . . . [B]lasphemy is by no means confined to the Islamic chapters', Sara Suleri writes in her fine reading of *The Satanic Verses*. '[A] postcolonial desire for deracination, emblematized by the protagonist Saladin Chamcha, is equally represented as cultural heresy. Acts of historical or cultural severance become those blasphemous moments that proliferate in the narrative . . . '[56] Blasphemy goes beyond the severance of tradition and replaces its claim to a purity of origins with a poetics of relocation and reinscription. Rushdie repeatedly uses the word 'blasphemy' in the migrant sections of the book to indicate a theatrical form of the staging of cross-genre, cross-cultural identities. Blasphemy is not merely a misrepresentation of the sacred by the secular; it is a moment when the subject-matter or the content of a cultural tradition is being overwhelmed, or alienated, in the act of translation. Into the asserted authenticity or continuity of tradition, 'secular' blasphemy releases a temporality that reveals the contingencies, even the incommensurabilities, involved in the process of social transformation.

My theoretical description of blasphemy as a transgressive act of cultural translation, is borne out by [Yunas] Samad's reading of blasphemy in the context of the real event of the fatwah.[57] It is the *medium* Rushdie uses to reinterpret the Koran that constitutes the crime. In the Muslim world, Samad argues, poetry is the traditional medium of censure. By casting his revisionary narrative in the form of the novel – largely unknown to traditional Islamic literature – Rushdie violates the poetic licence granted to critics of the Islamic establishment. In Samad's words, 'Salman Rushdie's real crime, in the eyes of the clerics, was that he touched on early Islamic history in a critical, imaginative and irreverent fashion but with deep historical insight.' It could be argued, I think, that far from simply misinterpreting the Koran, Rushdie's sin lies in opening up a space of discursive contestation that places the authority of the Koran within a perspective of historical and cultural relativism. It is not that the 'content' of the Koran is directly disputed; rather, by revealing other enunciatory positions and possibilities within the framework of Koranic reading, Rushdie performs the subversion of its authenticity through the act of cultural translation – he relocates the Koran's 'intentionality' by repeating and reinscribing it in the locale of the novel of postwar cultural migrations and diasporas.

The transposition of the life of Mohamed into the melodramatic theatricality of a popular Bombay movie, *The Message*, results in a hybridized form – the 'theological'[58] – targeted to Western immigrant audiences. Blasphemy, here, is the slippage in-between the intended moral fable and its displacement into the dark, symptomatic figurations of the 'dreamwork' of cinematic fantasy. In the racist psychodrama staged around Chamcha, the Satanic goatman, 'blasphemy' stands for the phobic projections that fuel great social fears, cross frontiers, evade the normal controls, and roam loose about the city turning difference into demonism. The social fantasm of racism, driven by rumour, becomes politically credible and strategically negotiable: 'priests became involved, adding another unstable element – the linkage between the term *black* and the sin *blasphemy* – to the mix.'[59] As the unstable element – the interstice – enables the linkage black/blasphemy, so it reveals, once more, that the 'present' of translation may not be a smooth transition, a consensual continuity, but the configuration of the disjunctive rewriting of the transcultural, migrant experience.

If hybridity is heresy, then to blaspheme is to dream. To dream not of the past or present, nor the continuous present; it is not the nostalgic dream of tradition, nor the Utopian dream of modern progress; it is the dream of translation as 'survival' as Derrida translates the 'time' of Benjamin's concept of the after-life of translation, as *sur-vivre*, the act of living on borderlines. Rushdie translates this into the migrant's dream of survival: an *initiatory* interstices [*sic*]; an empowering condition of hybridity, an emergence that turns 'return' into reinscription or redescription; an iteration that is not belated, but ironic and insurgent. For the migrant's survival depends, as Rushdie put it, on discovering 'how newness enters the world'. The focus is on making the linkages through the unstable elements of literature and life – the dangerous tryst with the 'untranslatable' – rather than arriving at ready-made names

The 'newness' of migrant or minority discourse has to be discovered *in medias res*: a newness that is not part of the 'progressivist' division between past and present, or the archaic and the modern; nor is it a 'newness' that can be contained in the mimesis of 'original and copy'. In both these cases, the image of the new is iconic rather than enunciatory; in both instances, temporal difference is represented as epistemological or mimetic distance from an original source. The newness of cultural translation is akin to what Walter Benjamin describes as the 'foreignness of languages' – that problem of representation native to representation itself. If Paul de Man focused on the 'metonymy' of translation, I want to foreground the 'foreignness' of cultural translation.

With the concept of 'foreignness' Benjamin comes closest to describing the performativity of translation as the staging of cultural difference. The argument begins with the suggestion that though *Brot* and *pain* [in the German and French languages] intend the same object, *bread*, their discursive and cultural *modes of signification* are in conflict with each other, striving to exclude each other. The complementarity of language as communication must be understood as emerging from the constant state of contestation and flux by the differential systems of social and cultural signification. This process of complementarity as the agonistic supplement is the seed of the 'untranslatable' – the foreign element in the midst of the performance of cultural translation. And it is this seed that turns into the famous, overworked analogy in the Benjamin essay: unlike the original where fruit and skin form a certain unity, in the act of translation the content or subject matter is made disjunct, overwhelmed and alienated by the form of signification, like a royal robe with ample folds.

Unlike Derrida and de Man, I am less interested in the metonymic fragmentation of the 'original'. I am more engaged with the 'foreign' element that reveals the interstitial; insists in the textile superfluity of folds and wrinkles; and becomes the 'unstable element of linkage', the indeterminate temporality of the in-between, that has to be engaged in creating the conditions through which 'newness comes into the world'. The foreign element 'destroys the original's structures of reference and sense communication as well'[60] not simply by negating it but by negotiating the disjunction in which successive cultural temporalities are 'preserved in the work of history and *at the same time* cancelled . . . The nourishing fruit of the historically understood contains time as a precious but tasteless seed.'[61] And through this dialectic of cultural negation-as-negotiation, this splitting of skin and fruit through the *agency* of foreignness, the purpose is, as Rudolf Pannwitz says, not 'to turn Hindi, Greek, English into German [but] instead to turn German into Hindi, Greek, English'.[62]

Translation is the performative nature of cultural communication. It is language *in actu* (enunciation, positionality) rather than language *in situ* (*énoncé*, or propositionality).[63] And the sign of translation continually tells, or 'tolls' the different times and spaces between cultural authority and its performative practices.[64] The 'time' of translation consists in that *movement* of meaning, the principle and practice of a communication that, in the words of de Man, 'puts the original in motion to decanonise it, giving it the movement of fragmentation, a wandering of errance, a kind of permanent exile'.[65]

Chamcha is the discriminatory sign of a performative, projective British culture of race and racism – 'illegal immigrant, outlaw king, foul criminal or race hero'.[66] From somewhere between Ovid and Lucretius, or between gastronomic and demographic pluralisms, he confounds nativist and supremacist ascriptions of national(ist) identities. This migrant movement of social identifications leads to the most devastating parody of Maggie Torture's Britain.

The revenge of the migrant hybrid comes in the Club Hot Wax sequence,[67] named, no doubt, after Sufyan's translation of Ovid's waxy metaphor for the immutability of the migrant soul. If Gibreel Farishta, later in the book, transforms London into a tropical country with 'increased moral definition, institution of a national siesta, development of vivid and expansive patterns of behaviour',[68] then it is the deejay, prancing Pinkwalla, who stages the revenge of black history in the expressivist cultural practices of toasting, rapping and scratching. In a scene that blends Madame Tussaud's with Led Zeppelin, the sepulchral wax figures of an excised black history emerge to dance amidst the migrants of the present in a postcolonial counter-masque of a retrieved and reinscribed history. Waxy Maggie Torture is condemned to a meltdown, accompanied by the Baldwinian chants of 'the fire this time'. And suddenly through this ritual of translation, Saladin Chamcha, the Satanic goatman, is historicized again in the movement of a migrant history, a metropolitan world 'becoming minority'.[69] □

Bhabha's argument, that the 'difference' of hybridity is a source of uncertainty in terms of both resistance and transformation, has been taken up by a number of critics of *The Satanic Verses*. Vijay Mishra's article 'Postcolonial Differend: Diasporic Narratives of Salman Rushdie',[70] for example, draws on many of Bhabha's ideas in its reading of Rushdie's fiction. The following extract from Mishra is, however, particularly interesting for the ways it adapts and develops those ideas. Mishra suggests that different sorts of discourses have emerged out of the postcolonial diaspora, and that it is in terms of the tensions and interplay between these discourses that *The Satanic Verses* is best understood. Most notably, Mishra makes the distinction between a discourse of the 'millenarian' (one frozen by resistance to change and nostalgic for the past and for 'home'), and that of the diasporic (characterised by mutation and 'newness').

■ [L]et me underline once again that *The Satanic Verses* is *the* text about migration, about the varieties of religious, sexual, and social filiations of the diaspora.[71] The work is the millenarian routed through the space of travel (the aeroplane replaces the ship) and then problematically rooted in the new space of the diaspora. In this respect the text's primary narrative is a tale of migrancy and the ambiguities of being an Indian (or Pakistani) in Britain. In the process, the work explores the disavowal of so many fundamental assumptions and values because of a massive epistemic violence to the intellect. The narrative, in fact, begins with people who have already lost their faith in religion and who now have a truly diasporic relationship with India. As Rushdie has explained, these people are the new travellers across the planet; having lost their faith, they have to rethink what death means to the living and how desire can find expression when people cannot love (Interview with Blake Morrison 120–21).[72] One of the key phrases that recurs deals with being born again (to be born again, you have to die, says Gibreel to Saladin), and the diasporic world is very much the world in which one undergoes a rebirthing. In the case of Gibreel and Saladin, the context in which this occurs combines the fantastic free-fall from an exploding plane (AI 420 from the height of Mt. Everest, a full 29,002 feet[73]) with the realistic narrative of terrorism and hijacking. The combination of these two generic modes is striking, since it forecloses the possibility of naturalistic readings because the work reveals a kind of simultaneous *karma* and reincarnation: two people die and are immediately reborn as they were at the moment of their deaths. The rebirthing of Gibreel and Saladin, then, parallels, say, the rebirth of Amba as Shikhandin in the *Mahabharata*, the founding Indian text that is simultaneously diachronic and synchronic: it happened then, it happens now. One becomes someone else but keeps the earlier history/biography intact.[74] □

Yet it is the character of Saladin, not that of Gibreel, who is ultimately reborn by embracing transformation and change. Mishra observes: '[N]ostalgia for the past (a house, one's ancestral religion, and so on) is not something one can live by but something to which, in an act of both homage and acceptance of his father Changez Chamchawala, Saladin returns.'[75]

■ It is through Saladin/Salman (Rushdie) that the new themes of diasporic interaction are explored. Saladin sees in the relics of Empire in the heart of London, 'attractively faded grandeur.' Gibreel, on his part, only sees a 'wreck, a Crusoe-city, marooned on the island of its past.' When asked about his favourite films, Saladin offers a cosmopolitan list: *'Potemkin, Kane, Otto e Mezzo, The Seven Samurai, Alphaville, El Angel Exterminador'* (439),[76] whereas Gibreel (the larger-than-life Bombay film actor modelled on Amitabh Bachchan and N.T. Rama Rao, the latter a hero-god in countless mythological films turned politician) offers a list of successful commercial Hindi films: *'Mother India, Mr India, Shree Charsawbees:* no Ray, no Mrinal Sen, no Aravindan, or Ghatak' (440). The lists, the choices made, the implied discriminations, the negotiations with the migrant's new land, all indicate the complex ways in which two diaspora discourses (the millenarian and the diasporic) work. Gibreel, for his part, does not undergo mutation but remains locked in the worlds of memory and fantasy. Saladin thus becomes the figure that is both here and elsewhere, and his return to the Motherland to be at his father's deathbed is perhaps the more cogent statement about the diasporic condition. Gibreel, on the other hand, acts out his actor's fantasies and becomes the conduit through whom (in his imagination) the Prophet receives the *Quran*. Blasphemy, therefore, falls not to the hybrid mutant but to the nostalgia-ridden Gibreel. Further, the mutant condition of Saladin (names in the diaspora are similarly mutated, a Hobson–Jobson discourse gets replayed)[77] is both linguistic as well as physical: the he-goat with an erratic pair of horns and the owner of a name that moves between the Indian Chamchawala to the trans-Indian Spoono (English for *chamcha*, 'spoon,' though in Hindi/Urdu a *chamcha* is a sycophant gleefully doing his/her master's work). In all this, two ideas – the idea of newness and that of love – keep cropping up. For Dr Uhuru Simba, 'newness will enter this society by collective, not individual actions' (415). As for love, the combinations it takes – Gibreel/Rekha Merchant/Allie Cone; Saladin/ Pamela Lovelace/Zeeny Vakil/Mimi Mamoulian – get complicated by other alignments: Jumpy Joshi/Pamela; Saladin/Allie Cone; Billy Battuta/Mimi; Hanif Johnson/Mishal Sufyan. All these relationships are part of the new diasporic combinations, a kind of necessary re-programming of the mind in the wake of the diasporic newness. At the point of interaction where the old and the new come together – as is the case with the diaspora's encounter with the vibrant politics of the metropolitan centre – new social meanings get constructed, especially in the domain of psycho-sexual politics. Thus the capacious Hind and not the bookish Muhammad effectively runs the Shaandaar café: her great cooking is what improves the material condition of the family rather than Muhammad's Virgilian rhetoric, which has no use value in Britain. Gender relations therefore get repositioned in the diaspora, and women begin to occupy a different, though not necessarily more equitable, kind of space. The manner in which a diasporic restaurant culture in Britain is actually based on wives as cooks is quite staggering. In another world, in the world of Jahilia, however, it is Hind, the powerful wife of the patriarch Abu Simbel, who has to battle with another new idea: 'What kind of an idea are you?' (335), is the question asked of the Prophet. Yet the idea of the 'new' (the idea of the 'post' in any modernity) also has a tendency to get fossilized, which is where another narrative of the diaspora, the millenarian, becomes the attractive, and easy, alternative. As a heterogeneous, 'unread' text, *The Satanic Verses* has been appropriated, positively and negatively, towards both diasporic (hybrid) and essentialist ends . . . [78] □

Mishra then goes on to examine how these tensions are exacerbated by the violence of British racism, and further complicated by the existence of multiple narratives of diaspora from other parts of the world. From the complexity of these relations emerges a critique of 'Britishness' itself as something similarly suspended between nostalgia for an imaginary homogeneity and an awareness of its long history of cultural and ethnic heterogeneity.

■ The late 1960s saw the emergence of a new racism in Britain for which Enoch Powell was the best-known, but not the only, spokesperson. In what seemed like a remarkable reversal of old Eurocentric and imperialist readings of the black colonized as racially inferior, the new racists began to recast races on the model of linguistic difference. This 'difference,' however, had to be anchored somewhere, and the easiest means of doing this was by stipulating that nations were not imagined communities constructed historically but racial enclaves marked by high levels of homogeneity. Thus a race had a nation to which it belonged. The British had their nation and belonged to an island off the coast of Europe, and so on. In the name of racial respect and racial equality, this version in fact gave repatriation theorists such as Enoch Powell a high level of respectability in that, it was argued, what Powell stood for was not racism but a nationalism that the immigrants themselves upheld. What the argument simplified was the history of imperialism itself and the massive displacement of races that had taken place in the name of Empire. Nowhere was this more marked than in the Indian, African, and Chinese diasporas of the Empire. More importantly, however, the new racism was used to defend Britishness itself, to argue that multiculturalism was a travesty of the British way of life, which was now becoming extremely vulnerable. The only good immigrant was one that was totally assimilable, just as the only good gay or lesbian was someone who led a closet life. Writes Anna Marie Smith:

> Only the thin veneer of deracializing euphemisms has shifted over this period, with blatantly racist discourse on immigration being recoded in discourse on criminality, inner-cities' decay and unrest, anti-Western terrorism, and multiculturalism. Indeed, the fundamentally cultural definition of race in the new racism allows for this mobile relocation of the racial-national borders to any number of sociopolitical sites.[79]

In *The Satanic Verses*, it is by way of the Sufyan family (Muhammad, the Bangladeshi schoolmaster with a weakness for European classics, his wife, Hind, and their daughters Mishal and Anahita) that we enter into changing demographic patterns and race relations in Britain, as well as see how homeland family norms negotiate the new gender politics of diasporas. The Sufyan family lives in Brickhall Street, the old Jewish enclave of tailors and small-time shopkeepers. Now it is the street of Bangladeshi migrants or Packies/Pakis ('brown Jews' [300]) who are least equipped for metropolitan life. Thus, in Brickhall, synagogues and kosher food have given way to mosques and halal restaurants. Yet nothing is as simple as it seems in this world of the diaspora. The space of the Shaandaar Café B&B becomes the space of new labour relations between husband and wife but also of new forms of sexuality. Mishal becomes pregnant by the second-generation diaspora Hanif Johnson, while Jumpy Joshi has sex with Pamela, even as her husband Saladin sleeps under the same roof. The diaspora here finally crumbles and falls apart because the pressures come not only from the newly acquired socio-sexual field of the participants in the diasporic drama but also because that drama has to contend with racist hooliganism as the diaspora becomes progressively an object of derision to be represented through the discourse of monsterism. It is through this brand of fascism that death finally comes to the diaspora and to those associated with it. Both the café and the community centre are burned down. Hind, Muhammad, as well as Pamela, die, and suddenly there is no room for nostalgia, no room for the discourse of mysticism (469) that had sustained the discourses of the homeland. Instead, the imperative is to transform one's memory into modes of political action because the world is far too Real (469). It is at this point in the narrative that diasporic identities become complicated by the presence in Britain of people who have already gone through the diasporic experience in other parts of the world. Having co-existed with Afro-West Indians, the Indian diaspora of the West Indies, for instance, is already a hybrid form. Thus Sewsunker Ram (Pinkwalla), the DJ, and John Maslama, the club proprietor, have political and cultural orientations that bring them close to the kinds of diasporic politics endorsed by a Dr. Uhuru Simba. The alignments at work here – Bengali, Afro-Caribbean, East Indian Caribbean, East African Indian, Sikh, Indian, Pakistani, Bangladeshi, and so on – gesture towards new forms of diasporic awareness and coalitional politics. From the Africanist ideal of Dr. Uhuru Simba to the multifaceted, decentred, simulative worlds of the Sufyan girls, Jumpy Joshi and Hanif Johnson, one now begins to see not one legitimation narrative of the diaspora but many.

'The trouble with the Engenglish is that their hiss hiss history happened overseas, so they dodo don't know what it means,' stutters S.S. Sisodia (343). When those who were instrumental in creating that history (as subject peoples on whose behest the Empire believed it was acting) are within the metropolitan centres of the Empire itself, the idea of Britishness is threatened. Both the challenge and the threat are summarized elegantly by Iain Chambers, who writes:

> It is the dispersal attendant on migrancy that disrupts and inter-rogates the overarching themes of modernity: the nation and its literature, language and sense of identity; the metropolis; the sense of centre; the sense of psychic and cultural homogeneity. In the recognition of the other, of radical alterity, lies the acknowledge-ment that we are no longer at the centre of the world.[80]

Chambers's 'we' here is British, but the definition that he gives of the British is very much an intermediate one. It is a definition in which the subjects of the centre – the British as an ethnic entity – also begin to find that subjectivity is 'interactively' constructed, on the move, so to speak. The cultural imperative that underlies Chambers's move is that the diaspora now invades the centre and makes prior, essentialist definitions of nation-states based on notions of racial purity (Enoch Powell), a historical relic of imperialism itself. It is the privileged site of that imperialist history and its constructions of Britishness that get replayed in the doctrines of purity in postcolonial Britain. Yet, as I say this I think what is implicit in the Chambers thesis – the need for a radical pedagogy about ethnic identities – is precisely what needs underlining. How does one make decisive interventions in the curriculum so that Britishness itself is opened up for debate? It is the agenda of the agents who would transform the apparatuses of control through which the idea of the self is constructed that requires further examination.

A 'post-diaspora community' in Britain, to use Rushdie's own phrase

(*Imaginary Homelands* 40), now becomes a site from which a critique of Britishness itself (and the imperial relationship between the British and Indians that has a 300-year long history) is now being mounted. The migrant living here and elsewhere would find it difficult to fit into, say, Margaret Thatcher's imperious definition of a Briton during the Falklands War. As Chambers again has stressed, any attempt to decipher this appeal to 'Britishness' necessarily draws us to a complex, contradictory, and even treacherous terrain, in which the most varied elements, 'entwine, coexist and contaminate one another'.[81] For the Indian diaspora, this trope of 'Britishness' has multiple identities and can be expressed in a variety of ways. To be British in a post-diaspora Britain is to be conscious of multiple heritages and peoples' conflicting participation in the long history of Britain. For many, an easy, unproblematic re-insertion into a utopic or linear narrative of the British nation is impossible. In *The Satanic Verses*, we get a strong affirmation of the undesirability of this version of linear history.

We are therefore faced with 'the possibility of two perspectives and two versions of Britishness' (Chambers, *Border Dialogues* 27). One is Anglocentric, frequently conservative, backward-looking, and increasingly located in a frozen and largely stereotyped idea of the national, that is, English, culture. The other is excentric, open-ended, and multi-ethnic. The first is based on a homogeneous 'unity' in which history, tradition, and individual biographies and roles, including ethnic and sexual ones, are fundamentally fixed and embalmed in the national epic, in the mere fact of being 'English.' The other perspective suggests an overlapping network of histories and traditions, a heterogeneous complexity in which positions and identities, including those relating to the idea of the 'citizen,' cannot be taken for granted and are not 'interminably fixed but tend towards flux' (Chambers, *Border Dialogues* 27).[82] □

Rushdie's preference for the 'flux' of hybridity, however, does not always receive a positive reception. One only has to look to some of the criticism directed at Bhabha to understand why this might be the case. Benita Parry, for example argues that Bhabha's complex conceptualisation of a 'Third Space', and his foregrounding of ambivalence, serves to elide the more confrontational set of relations of the colonial and postcolonial period. Parry writes of those who have experienced, or might still be engaged in, the struggle against colonial imperialism and suggests they 'could well read the theorizing of discourse analysts with considerable disbelief at the construction this puts on the situation they are fighting against and the contest in which they are engaged.'[83] For Parry, emphasis upon hybridity at the expense of struggle and confrontation represents little more than an academic favouring of theory over practice; Bhabha's image of the re-writing of the colonial Book might well represent some sort of destabilisation of colonial authority, but not 'an alternative text.'[84]

Rushdie, however, demonstrates awareness of this sort of criticism in his novel *The Moor's Last Sigh*. One of the central characters of the text is the artist Aurora Zogoiby and Rushdie's sarcastic description of a study of Aurora's work entitled 'Imperso-Nation and Dis/Semi/Nation: Dialogics of Eclecticism and Interrogation of Authenticity in A.Z.' is made directly at the expense of Bhabha's discussion of *The Satanic Verses* in his essay 'DissemiNation'.[85] Rushdie seeks to expose the potential danger of academic formulations of hybridity allowed to run riot. He playfully parodies a poststructuralist tendency to create language puns out of its subject matter, and, more seriously, draws attention to the manner in which academic discourses, through ever more convoluted use of theory, might rarefy that subject matter out of existence altogether. In his interview with Maya Jaggi, Rushdie provides an even stronger warning when he suggests that there is a 'flip side to pluralism; the down side can be confusion, formlessness, chaos, a lack of vision or singleness of purpose. There are some very strong, monolithic, brutal views around, and sometimes those who have a clearer view get further.'[86]

Yet even though Rushdie is clearly concerned at the manner in which the concept has sometimes been appropriated and applied, he also warns against any knee-jerk rejection of hybridity.[87] Hybridity remains both a thematic and formal feature of his work. Catherine Cundy makes just this point when she suggests that Rushdie's work represents a mutation of the Western novel into 'something else entirely; the hybrid post-colonial text.'[88] For Cundy, and indeed for most of the critics included in this chapter, hybridity, despite its theoretical complexity, offers the hope of something new emerging out of old conflicts and oppositions. Cundy's support for Rushdie, however, is far from complete. As is evident in the following chapter of this Guide, Cundy responds less generously to Rushdie's engagement with gender issues – particularly his representations of women.

CHAPTER FIVE

'How Are We to Understand My Too-Many Women?': The Issue of Gender in Rushdie's Fiction

IN THE previous chapter, Vijay Mishra suggested the possibility that new sorts of gender relations may emerge out of the hybrid 'newness' of the postcolonial diaspora, but warned that these relations are not 'necessarily more equitable'.[1] Such relations, according to Mishra, are explored in *The Satanic Verses*. If this is so, it might explain Homi K. Bhabha's observation that despite all the controversy associated with *The Satanic Verses*, feminist groups have, for the most part, refused to condemn the novel. Bhabha argues, indeed, that the 'most productive debates, and political initiatives, in the post-fatwah period, have come from women's groups like Women Against Fundamentalism and Southall Black Sisters[2] in Britain.'[3] These groups, argues Bhabha, have not 'fetishized' Rushdie's naming of the prostitutes after Mohammed's wives, but prefer instead to draw attention 'to the politicized violence in the brothel and the bedroom, raising demands for the establishment of refuges for minority women coerced into marriage.'[4] For both Mishra and Bhabha, the gender issues raised by Rushdie form an integral part of his examination of the colonial and postcolonial experience.

Considering the mass of criticism that surrounds Rushdie's writings, it is somewhat surprising that so few critics choose to examine Rushdie's treatment of gender. Most of the criticism that does adopt such an approach tends to focus upon Rushdie's third novel *Shame*.[5] Yet such an approach is also important for a fuller understanding of both *Midnight's Children* and *The Satanic Verses*. Timothy Brennan, for example, though he suggests, as Catherine Cundy observes later in this chapter, that Rushdie's depictions of women can be regarded as offensive, also identifies the structural importance of the character of Padma in *Midnight's Children*.[6] For Brennan, Padma's primary function within the text emerges out of her relationship with Saleem as the narrator of the novel. Padma, throughout the course of *Midnight's Children*, passes comments, often disparaging in their nature, upon Saleem's narrative. Brennan argues: 'In this supra-narrative role, Padma also literally intervenes in the composition of the book Saleem is writing, by presenting in her comments an alternative popular aesthetics.'[7] Padma acts as a literary critic 'whose authority rests on her being a member of the lower classes.'[8] Consequently, according to Brennan, the authority of Padma's plebeian or popularist sentiments, coupled to her obvious willingness to criticise Saleem, serves partially to compensate for the novel's 'shameful cosmopolitanism'.[9]

In her article 'The Art of Suspense: Rushdie's 1001 (Mid-) Nights', Nancy E. Batty suggests a similarly privileged position for Padma. Like Brennan, Batty observes that Padma serves as a foil to Saleem's narrative.

■ In a sense, the reader is seduced into a judgement of the worth of Saleem's narrative on the basis of Padma's response, and this is further reinforced by Saleem's explicit dependence on Padma as a conduit for his narrative. But Padma, as Saleem points out, is not always easy to please, and it becomes obvious as the novel progresses that Padma not only serves as an index to Saleem's successes and failures as an autobiographer but also plays an important role in the creation of his story.[10] □

Through his narrative, Saleem attempts to validate his life. He needs Padma to affirm his existence. Yet more importantly, for Batty, Padma's role as narratee also reveals the 'political exigency of the narrative act.'[11] In this article, Batty compares Padma's relationship with Saleem to the emotionally fraught relationship between King Shahryar and Scheherazade of *A Thousand and One Nights*. Such a comparison is designed to reveal that, like Scheherazade, Saleem is 'engaged in a desperate political act'.[12] For, like Scheherazade, Saleem is oppressed by an overwhelming sense of impending doom. Only through the act of story-telling may Saleem hope to avert that doom. To do so, however, he must retain Padma's attention.

■ [H]is narrative takes shape from the demands of Padma as an explicit audience. Just as Scheherazade's tales are ostensibly intended to appease young Dunyazade's rehearsed demand to hear them, their real meaning is to deflect King Shahryar from his murderous goal. If, as Macherey implies, the aim of narration is to defer its own resolution, then its method must be that of concealment: 'Here is the double movement: the mystery must be concealed before it is revealed . . . the entire elaboration of the narrative consists in the disruption and organization of this delay'.[13] Like the perforated sheet through which

Aadam Aziz views the various parts of Naseem's body, narrative must always reveal something while concealing everything else. Saleem's narrative self-consciously employs deferment of disclosure – 'But I mustn't reveal all my secrets at once'[14] – and nowhere is this more evident than in Book One of the novel, which begins with a notice of Saleem's portentous birth, but is composed almost entirely of a retrospective of the thirty-odd years that preceded it. The structure of Book One is a prototype for the pattern of disclosure and concealment which governs the entire novel. Deferral of disclosure follows a rigid pattern of promise and fulfilment: the implicit contract between narrator and narratee is made explicit and self-conscious. Saleem laments Padma's impatience and her desire for 'linear narrative' (38) and posits 'a more discerning audience, someone who would understand the need for rhythm, pacing, the subtle introduction of minor chords which will later rise, swell, seize the melody' (102): in short, someone who will comprehend the need for concealment in narrative.

The tension between Padma's 'what-happened-nextism' (39) and Saleem's need to conceal propels, and to a large extent shapes, the entire narrative. In a discussion of the relationship between what is 'real' and what is 'true,' Saleem confesses his narrative philosophy: '*True*, for me, was . . . something hidden inside the stories Mary Pereira told me . . . *True* was a thing concealed just over the horizon towards which the fisherman's finger pointed in the picture on my wall' (79). If *true*, for Saleem, is what is concealed, then *real* is essentially secondary and contingent: 'in autobiography, as in all literature, what actually happened is less important than what the author can manage to persuade his audience to believe' (270–71). But it is also what that audience can persuade the author to reveal: Saleem's story, or much of it, is also Padma's, as the following passage strongly suggests:

> . . . And certainly Padma is leaking into me. As history pours out of my fissured body, my lotus is quietly dripping in, with her down-to-earthery, and her paradoxical superstition, her contradictory love of the fabulous – *so it's appropriate that I'm about to tell the story of the death of Mian Abdullah*. (38; emphasis added)

Padma's role as Saleem's 'necessary ear' (149) should not obscure her status as co-creator of his narrative. Parameswaran underestimates this function, I think, when she compares Padma to 'the chorus in a Greek drama – always on the stage, but never initiating action'.[15] If we regard Saleem's narration as the supreme act of the novel, in the sense that Genette refers to the act of narrating as 'an act like any other',[16] then Padma's role in *Midnight's Children* is indeed paramount. Saleem confirms this when he asks:

> How to dispense with Padma? How to give up her ignorance and
> superstition, necessary counterweights to my miracle-laden omni-
> science? I should speak plainly, without the cloak of a question
> mark: our Padma has gone, and I miss her. (150)

The integral relationship between Saleem and Padma is complex and
complementary, and Padma cannot be reduced to a 'convenient reader
surrogate' as Wilson suggests.[17] I would argue that the uneasy and reci-
procal relationship between 'reality' and 'truth' in narrative resides in
the mutual pact between narrator and audience: the narrator promises,
in his own good time, to reveal all that has previously been concealed;
the audience submits to this demand as long as the narrator retains
credibility and interest, or as long as revelation justifies its concealment. Ross Chambers describes the narrator–narratee relationship in
slightly different, though relevant, terms:

> . . . at the bottom the narrator's motivation is like that of the narra-
> tee and rests on the assumption of exchanging a gain for a loss.
> Where the narratee offers attention in exchange for information, the
> narrator sacrifices the information for some sort of attention.
> Consequently, there is a sense in which the maintenance of narra-
> tive authority implies an act of seduction.[18]

When the exchange of information is accomplished – when the narrative act is consummated, so to speak – the very basis for narrative is
destroyed. The narrator's employment of retardatory structure defers
this consummation. But the narrator–narratee contract is a tenuous
one – what Meir Sternberg calls a 'double-edged sword.'[19] The success
of retardatory structure 'hinges on the artist's own skill in counter-
acting the reader's natural inclination to dash forward,'[20] or, in Padma's
case, to dash out. Having waited impatiently for Saleem to arrive at the
place where he began his narrative – the night of his auspicious birth –
Padma is shocked to discover the seeming irrelevance of Saleem's
lengthy exploration of his short-circuited genealogy. Padma's brief
departure from Saleem's life (but not his narrative) is ostensibly
triggered by a disagreement regarding Saleem's use of the word
'love' to describe her feelings toward him; it is, however, no less a
response to a disagreement regarding the relative value of narrative
digression.

Saleem's manipulation (or seduction) of his audience, informed
by his conflicting desires to be secretive and at the same time to retain
Padma's interest in his narrative, is transparent, exploitative and
coquettish, as when he comments on his inability to control exposition:

> Interruptions, nothing but interruptions! The different parts of my somewhat complicated life refuse, with a wholly unreasonable obstinacy, to stay neatly in their respective compartments. (187)

Such coyness is deceptive: Saleem's narrative, for all that it stutters, stumbles and digresses – *because* it stutters, stumbles and digresses – strikes a carefully poised balance between concealment and disclosure. Saleem's pronouncement – 'I know now that [Padma] is . . . hooked. . . . [M]y story has her by the throat' (38) – is premature but is nonetheless borne out. Padma does return to Saleem's side and she *does* fulfil her role as narratee, but this should not surprise us. Saleem tailors his narrative for Padma: like a lover engaged in making a sexual conquest, Saleem adjusts his strategies of seduction according to the response which those strategies elicit. Padma's incredulous response to the story of the midnight children, for example, engages Saleem in a defence of his narrative, but it also teaches him a valuable lesson: 'It's a dangerous business to try and impose one's view of things on others' (212). He brackets the events of the subsequent chapter with the familiar and soothing overtures of the fairy tale: 'Once upon a time . . . ' (213, 320).

Padma's desire to know 'what happened next,' in conflict with Saleem's need to conceal, is routinely satisfied by what Parameswaran calls 'periodic previews of events to come'.[21] Genette, who has offered a formidable vocabulary of narratological terms, would describe this technique as 'repeating prolapses',[22] but neither Parameswaran nor Genette captures the peculiar self-conscious nuance of this device as it is used in *Midnight's Children*. Saleem himself provides us with a more accurate term when he compares this technique to the employment of 'trailers' in episodic cinema; in effect, these explicit foreshadowings are the foundation of Saleem's pact with Padma – Saleem explains: 'the promise of exotic futures has always seemed, to my mind, the perfect antidote to the disappointments of the present' (346). Saleem's employment of trailers, as we shall see, is pervasive, and it is complemented by yet another cinematic narrative device which Saleem does not consciously identify. A close examination of *Midnight's Children* reveals that the chapter-by-chapter progression of the novel resembles the structure of an episodic film, or serial, in which synopses of previous events provide a rhythmical counterpoint to the teasers for events to come. The comparison of Saleem's technique to that employed by episodic cinema is a relevant one: just as the cliffhanger serial is ruthless in manipulating the expectations of its audience, often resorting to misleading clues in its trailers, Saleem employs sensationalism in order to hold the interest of his audience. Narrative synopses provide Saleem with a means of compensating for this sensationalism by imposing order and significance on past events, but these synopses also slow the narrative pace, thereby functioning to retard exposition and abet concealment.

A paradigm of the complementary function of trailer and synopsis in *Midnight's Children* is found at the end of the chapter entitled 'Wee Willie Winkie' and the beginning of the subsequent chapter. Promising that he will finally reveal the details of his birth to Padma, Saleem describes elaborate preparations for the event. 'Wee Willie Winkie' ends with 'the sound of seconds passing, of an approaching, inevitable midnight' (106). The title of the following chapter, 'Tick-Tock,' links the narrative idea of a countdown with its opening line: 'Padma can hear it: there's nothing like a countdown for building suspense' (106). But Saleem, relishing his control over his audience, launches into a lengthy synopsis of the previous narrative – a synopsis that ends ironically with Padma's naïve praise: '"At last . . . you've learned how to tell things really fast . . ."' (109). Saleem does not, however, confine his trailers to the ends of chapters (or the end of the writing session, as each chapter would seem to correspond to a night in the fictional present): the narrative is replete with trailers which appear in various forms, and with varying degrees of significance.

Saleem's trailers can be divided roughly into two categories: those which (seemingly) inevitably arise from the reflective nature of his project (these are clearly what Genette terms repeating prolapses) and those which are self-consciously employed to create suspense. Repetitive prolapses occur when an event in the narrated present triggers a 'remembrance' of a future event, as when Saleem says:

> (. . . And already I can see the repetitions beginning; because didn't my grandmother also find enormous . . . and the stroke, too, was not the only . . . and the Brass Monkey had her birds . . . the curse begins already, and we haven't even got to the noses yet!). (12)

Such prolapses, of course, contribute to the creation of suspense in Saleem's narrative, but Saleem also self-consciously employs this technique in a sensationalistic manner. Having narrated the death of his family in Pakistan, Saleem senses that Padma's interest is waning, and he quickly inveigles her back into his narrative world:

> 'I'm not finished yet! There is to be electrocution and a rainforest; a pyramid of heads on a field impregnated by leaky marrowbones; narrow escapes are coming, and a minaret that screamed! Padma, there is still plenty worth telling.' (346) [. . .]

Clearly, to Padma at least, Saleem's stories are at times only tentatively connected to his 'real' existence. However, there is a point at which the content of Saleem's narrative impinges on Padma's 'reality': a point at which she can no longer deny the veracity, if not all of the details, of the story Saleem is telling. This point, I will argue, is the anti-climax of the novel, akin to, but an inversion of, the cessation of Scheherazade's tales and her plea to King Shahryar to spare her life and those of her three sons. It is the moment at which Saleem's promise to Padma is fulfilled: the point at which suspense yields not to consummation but to a confession of impotence.[23] □

For Batty, 'this moment of disclosure marks the critical focus of the text.'[24] For Saleem's confession ultimately reveals the source of the sense of impending doom that has haunted him throughout the novel. Batty observes: 'If Saleem's destruction is at the heart of the novel's meaning, then what is most closely associated with this doom is the Widow.'[25] Saleem's confession also points to the existence of an implied listener beyond Padma, but one Saleem lacks the courage to confront directly.

■ When Saleem confesses his Widow-induced castration to Padma, he provides her with the reason for his impotence and proves to her the existence of the fictional Saleem:

> But Padma knows what I can no longer do; Padma, who once, in her anger, cried out: 'But what use are *you*, my God, as a *lover*?' That part, at least, can be verified: in the hovel of Picture Singh, I cursed myself with the lie of impotence . . . (440)

With a parodic echo of the *Arabian Nights*, Saleem offers his castration to Padma as proof of the value of his life. Like King Shahryar, Padma is compelled to take pity on and wed her narrative suitor. Not only is Saleem's marriage to Padma, built on its foundation of impotence rather than fertility, a parody of Scheherazade's marriage to Shahryar, Padma herself is a parody of the knife-wielding despot. Padma's superstitious nature links her structurally with the Widow, who Saleem says is 'obsessed with the stars' (427), but there are other textual clues that suggest their association. Saleem warns Padma that if she marries him, 'it will turn you into a widow' (444), and, in an even more telling passage, Saleem describes awakening from his vivid dream of the Widow:

> For two days (I'm told) Padma has been sitting up all night placing cold wet flannels on my forehead, *holding me through my shivers and dreams of Widow's hands*; for two days she has been blaming herself for her potion of unknown herbs. (208; emphasis added)

Padma, hoping to undo the Widow's curse and restore Saleem's virility, almost succeeds in silencing his protest: she is both ally and adversary, possessing the will to redress but the power to destroy. Saleem's sexual impotence is the price he must pay for political awareness, but by addressing his story to the wrong widow (Padma is politically ignorant and ineffective), Saleem scarcely escapes what he fears the most: absurdity. Saleem's sexual impotence is a metaphor for his political impotence. Padma is not the Widow: Saleem has missed the spittoon.[26] □

In Batty's view, Padma not only influences the formulation of Saleem's narrative, but her role as narratee ultimately reveals Saleem's political impotence. A number of critics have, however, attacked Rushdie for his depictions of women. Gayatri Chakravorty Spivak, for example, argues: 'One of the most interesting features about much of Rushdie's work is his anxiety to write woman into the narrative of history. Here again we have to record a failure'.[27] Spivak does not question Rushdie's intent to subvert established structures of power, be they political, social or religious. Yet, according to Spivak, when it comes to issues of gender, Rushdie's work does little more than repeat the dynamics of women's oppression. She observes that in *Shame* 'women seem powerful only as monsters', and that the two central male protagonists of *The Satanic Verses*, Gibreel Farishta and Saladin Chamcha, 'are tortured by obsession with women, go through them, even destroy them, within a gender code that is never opened up, never questioned'.[28]

The following extract, from Charu Verma's 'Padma's Tragedy: A Feminist Deconstruction of Rushdie's *Midnight's Children*', applies a similar, though perhaps more aggressive, reading to Rushdie's second novel. The title of this article is particularly interesting in that it suggests a literary reading of *Midnight's Children* through the compound lens of postcolonial and feminist thought. In doing so, it draws attention to the similarities that exist between these two theoretical/critical perspectives. In their interrogation of the politics of domination and exploitation, both not only identify similar dynamics of 'othering', but also seek to reinstate the 'other' in the face of such oppression. According to Verma, however, Rushdie's depiction of Padma serves only to re-inscribe the double marginalisation that results from her status as an Indian woman. By confirming Padma's marginality, Rushdie is validating the centrality of the masculine experience.

■ Padma is a victim of this male hegemonic view. Occasionally, she appears to be the reader's surrogate in the book, but the first thing to remember about her is – should be – that she is a woman. Her characterization is managed through two prominent strategies: strategies of absences and those of presences. In Padma's case, most presences are openly derogatory, while the inferrable positives in her being are simply absenced.

Padma is most presented in the narrative through her animal physicality. Saleem introduces her as 'Padma – our plump Padma . . . sulking magnificently. (She can't read . . . Padma: strong, jolly, a consolation for my last days. But definitely a bitch-in-the-manger.)'[29] This exposition does not create a positive image of her, and it is followed by a still more damaging insinuation: 'She attempts to cajole me from my desk: "Eat, na, food is spoiling." I remain stubbornly hunched over paper. "But what is so precious," Padma demands, her right hand slicing the air updownup in exasperation, "to need all this writing-shiting?" . . . Padma snorts. Wrist smacks against forehead. "Okay, starve starve, who cares two pice?" Another louder, conclusive snort. . . . Thick of waist, somewhat hairy of forearm, she flounces.' (24) It is noteworthy that for one good detail (a consolation for my last days), several derogatory and diminishing details are piled up one after another. She is compared to a bitch, she cajoles, snorts; moves her hand updownup and so on. This suggests a temperamental reluctance on the part of Saleem to allow her anything more than a comic status. She is not only illiterate and ignorant but is ugly as well. She is described as fat, 'thick of waist' – and 'somewhat hairy of forearm.' [. . .]

Padma's functions reinforce her as a mere stereotype. She cooks food for Saleem, makes his bed, sulks when she is ignored and performs all Martha's tasks. Her functions are all taken too much for granted, devalued, marginalized, they are considered to be so petty as to deserve no notice or appreciation. Her honest, simple responses deserve to be refined by 'the' man who claims that he knows better. Writing is Saleem's territory, and she is alien here. His writing activity and his manly 'penly' preoccupation with, say, history, time and politics, are arbitrarily privileged. [. . .] She is good only as audience, a receiver, for Saleem is the giver. Saleem often mocks her for being silly, and tries to assert his dominance by saying: 'I attempt to educate her.' (38) Saleem, like Rushdie behind him claims that he knows India, her people, politics, sociology. How is it that he should be content with describing Padma as an illiterate without also pointing to the socioeconomic conditions which keep women uneducated here? This is clearly a case of sexual separatism. Roles, traits, qualities, profession, etc. are divided along the sexual lines. Cooking food, washing clothes, raising children are all woman's jobs; the world out there is regarded as man's area. [. . .]

Although Padma is Saleem's constant companion and audience, interlocutor and critic, the moments of crucial decisions or intensity in the narrational perspective simply leave her out. The two most crucial 'narrational' moments – his decision to begin the narrative in chapter 1 and his reluctance to come out with the emergency truths in chapter 29 – do not include Padma. The strategy used at these intense moments is that a woman will be a nuisance, for no woman can understand man's deep agony. Therefore, Padma too cannot sympathize with Saleem. Hence her erasure at these points. One recalls how Grass's *The Tin Drum*, a major influence on *Midnight's Children*, begins by introducing Bruno, Oskar's keeper in the narrational perspective, and how much dignity Oskar awards to him by asking him to do a whole chapter of the narrative. Padma, by contrast, is consistently diminished. It is safe to assume that Saleem's narrative, like Saleem, believes that it can easily do without her: 'Padma must take a back seat.' (385).

Padma's portrait is composed more of gaps and absences than of presences. Her absences relate to such crucial matters as her background, her past, her family, her social contexts. She seems to be characterized only as a footnote to Saleem the narrator [. . .] She is negated when Saleem discusses politics or history. Her story is discardable like dung. Saleem ignores her, but we cannot and we should not. Saleem, in fact, goes three generations back to start his story and claims that in order to know him, we will have to swallow a multitude of lives; but he does not feel any need to perspectivize Padma in time or space at all. 'Grieve for Saleem . . . ' (345) But what about Padma's tragedy? Where is Padma's past, where are her parents, her earlier locations, her adventures? Where is her story? They are all lost in the man's story which alone is considered worth telling.

How do we reconcile the above analysis with the textual fact that Padma is described as the lotus-goddess? Perhaps there is no paradox at all. All male dominant ideologies need to compensate man's actual degradation and exploitation of woman by doling out to her some imaginary, mystified space in which she is worshipped as a goddess. This mystified space is the opinion of her sex. This unreal space is a device to legitimatize her actual exploitation day in, day out. Padma's description as the lotus-goddess is no compliment to her, though she may think it is, because she is a willing dupe of the sexist politics of India. She is Saleem's despised other, usable, exploitable, disposable. She is, in other words, a mere commodity. She is not only a slave but also a perfect fool. It is disturbing to see Saleem making so much of his victimization and tragedy but simply marginalizing the tragedy that is Padma's. Since women constitute a half of India, Padma's tragedy finds its echo in this other India's tragedy. Padma's tragedy is no less terrifying than Saleem's but the narrative being phallocentric, her tragedy is wholly, though arbitrarily, appropriated by that of Midnight's son.[30] □

For Verma, the term 'woman' exists in binary opposition to that of 'man'. The inequality inherent in all binaries is reflected in relations of power between the two genders: 'Patriarchy established itself as a social constant and the male set himself as the human "norm" . . . woman is the "other"'.[31] In the following article, included in full, Catherine Cundy develops this idea, but suggests that Rushdie's fictions demonstrate that these terms are fluid and may contain many, and often contradictory, characteristics. Despite this fluidity, and Rushdie's protestations, the shadow of patriarchal authority remains, for Cundy, a feature of all Rushdie's fictions.

■ In the process of defending himself and his text *The Satanic Verses* against the barrage of criticism that has assailed both, Salman Rushdie inadvertently exposed a weakness in his personal politics which, though certainly not as dramatic in its repercussions as his alleged affront to Islam, forms the subject of this discussion. In stark contrast to the clustered 'blasphemies' of his latest major work of fiction, which offered themselves up so readily to the xeroxes and scissors of his enemies, Rushdie's problematic depictions of women appear as a thread running through his work, seemingly trivial in isolation but disturbing with their cumulative weight. The defence in question is his essay 'In Good Faith' which seeks in part to explain the idea behind the text's controversial depiction of a brothel where the whores adopt the names of the prophet Mohammed's twelve wives. He writes:

> I sought images that crystallized the opposition between the sacred and profane worlds. The harem and the brothel provide such an opposition . . . Harem and brothel are antithetical worlds . . . what happens in the brothel . . . is that the men of 'Jahilia' are enabled to act out an ancient dream of power and possession . . . That men should be so aroused by the great ladies' whorish counterfeits says something about them, not the great ladies, and about the extent to which sexual relations have to do with possession.[32]

This passage encapsulates some of the confusions and ambivalences that attach to so many of Rushdie's textual representations of women. He fails to see that harem and brothel, far from being antithetical, are in fact related aspects of the same desire for possession and control of women – one culturally sanctioned and one, ostensibly, not.

For the Islamic cultures of which he writes in both *Shame* and the *Verses*, and of which he himself is a product, the harem and the brothel figure the innocent/whore binarism in which women are caught and constructed. The significance of the image to Rushdie himself is that, despite his declared projects to reinstate women and their lives into history, this binarism and the confusion of responses that it implies, resides at the heart of his own attitudes to the women he creates, both Moslem and non-Moslem. The brothel as 'a place of refuge'[33] is a concept that appears in Rushdie's first novel *Grimus* as well as the *Verses*. The problematic nature of such a refuge is that it offers man shelter from the outside world (which threatens the safety both of the travellers in *Grimus* and the poet Baal in the *Verses*) at the same time as it reminds him of his own weakness. Writing which has difficulty elevating itself above the level of soft-core pornography in *Grimus*, attempts to address ideas of submission and domination in the *Verses*, but falters on the rocks of its own inability to disentangle the fantasies of the whores from those of Baal and the author himself sufficiently to make its arguments clear. The brothel in the *Verses* is named 'The Curtain' after the *Hijab* that protects Moslem women from the male gaze. Rushdie's dangerous pun, however, provides an inadvertent echo of his presentation of the incestuous relationship of the hero of *Grimus*, Flapping Eagle, with his sister Bird-Dog – the first in what was to become a series of disturbing images of women in his work:

> The hole between her legs yawned: its hairs were like ropes . . . She was a house, a cavern lying red and palpitating before him, the curtain of hair parting. He heard her booming voice, – Why resist, she was saying. Give up, little brother. Come in. Give up. Come in.[34]

Here the 'curtain' of hair is both an enticement and man's last defence against the abyss of female sexuality that threatens to swallow him.

The image of the refuge that is simultaneously the abyss for man recurs in *Midnight's Children* in the form of the basket used by Parvati-the-witch to make men disappear until she wills them to return, and which she uses to secure Saleem Sinai's safe return to India from Bangladesh. It is another 'basket of invisibility'[35] in the narrative, just like the washing-chest in which Saleem conceals himself, but one where, far from being the observer empowered by his own invisibility, he is instead preserved in a curious state of limbo:

> Present, but insubstantial, actual, but without being or weight . . . I hung in a sphere of absence at whose fringes, like faint reflections, could be seen the spectres of wickerwork.[36]

This scenario differs from Saleem's concealment in the washing-chest in that it is controlled by a woman. Like the brothels of K in *Grimus* and Jahilia in *The Satanic Verses*, women and their sexuality offer both security and the threat of loss of identity. Woman is prepared to aid man's escape and secure his safety, but through the exercise of her power and ultimate control. As with the characters of Liv Jones and

Bird-Dog in *Grimus* (both texts demonstrate the treachery of wives and sisters), Parvati's power is illustrative of the nurturer/destroyer dichotomy that Rushdie so often depicts in women:

> In the grip of Parvati's sorcery, I felt my hold on the world slip away – and how easy, how peaceful not to never to return! . . . in short I was in mortal danger.[37]

Woman can therefore confer and destroy the sense of a man's identity. As with the four female demons encountered by Saleem and his fellow soldiers at Kali's temple in the Sundarbans, women promise the fulfilment of men's dreams which then serve as the agent of their destruction.

Rushdie's exploration of the writer's peripheral position in society through the various 'invisible' observers in his texts, such as Saleem and Baal, becomes linked to the fascination/obsession with the domestic and sexual power of women more strongly in *Shame* than anywhere else. The text's declared project to voice the silenced stories of Pakistan's oppressed women is often admired by critics without consideration of the way it is undercut by the representation of the women themselves. Anuradha Dingwaney Needham, for example, celebrates 'the complex ways in which women and their histories are recovered and inserted into the "alternate" history of Pakistan.'[38]

But in the figure of *Shame*'s putative hero, Omar Khayyam Shakil, and the resentment he bears at his peripheral position in relation to his three 'mothers', we have yet another instance of the blend of confusion, frustration and even outright hostility towards the relative autonomy of women which surfaces in Rushdie's fiction. Rape often bursts through as the ultimate signification of this resentment – Flapping Eagle's rape of the goddess Axona in *Grimus*, for example, and in *Shame*, Omar's assault on the hypnotised Farah Zoroaster. Sexuality is explored and exploited by rendering the woman in the equation effectively powerless. Omar's resentment of his mothers' closeness, figured in sexual terms, has an extra edge of unpleasantness to it when viewed alongside other instances of such resentments in Rushdie's texts:

> . . . he hated them for their closeness, for the way they sat with arms entwined on their swinging, creaking seat, for their tendency to lapse giggling into the private languages of their girlhood . . . [39]

One is reminded of the 'mood' of this confrontation in *The Satanic Verses* when Saladin takes an instant dislike to the '. . . self-contained . . . essence' of Allie Cone.[40]

The suggestion is offered to us that 'all [Omar's] subsequent deal-ings with women were acts of revenge against the memory of his mothers.'[41] This impulse is highlighted in a reference to the shared adulteries of Omar and Iskander Harappa. Here, Omar's ability to hypno-tise women for sexual purposes – an extreme representation of male manipulation of women – is undercut by the ambivalence of the authorial voice at these actions. The objects of Omar's attentions are merely 'white women of a certain type' who possess 'admittedly scanty inhibitions';[42] the perversity of their semi-rape undermined by the authorial voice's value-judgements on women.

Rushdie's treatment of the 'arrested sexuality'[43] of the three women depicts them as sexually naïve, but this is counterbalanced by the prurience with which the authorial voice ponders on the nature of the sisters' solidarity. The bond, it is suggested, may have been sealed in menstrual blood – a seal representative in itself of secrecy, otherness and a vague menace. This image may stem in itself from the strictures of the *Quran*, which is clear in its prohibitions on women experiencing the temporary pollution of menstruation:

> They ask you about menstruation. Say: 'It is an indisposition. Keep aloof from women during their menstrual periods and do not touch them until they are clean again.'[44]

We are told that the sisters inhabit their father, Old Shakil's, 'labyrinthine' mansion and, as in the *Verses*, this concept of the labyrinth seems somehow feminised. Just as the whores of 'The Curtain' wait at the centre of their labyrinthine brothel and protect Baal in the *Verses*, so the Shakil sisters, once their collective pregnancy becomes known, withdraw into the secret corners of their own labyrinth, sealing themselves off from the penetrating gaze and prying curiosity of the outside world. The stiletto blades that lurk lethally inside the dumb-waiter – the only means of access into their protected stronghold – come to represent what we are persuaded is the twisted sexuality of the sisters; something destructive rather than creative. Should man ever succeed in penetrating the defences a woman con-structs around her, there might still be a surprise in store for him, waiting to destroy him.

The woman-centred claustrophobia of the Shakil house, 'Nishapur', is presented as a womb to which Omar seeks to cling. Omar's acciden-tal glimpse of the outside world through a crumbling wall strikes immediate fear into him and sends him running back indoors – back to the womb – rather than risk venturing forth. That Rushdie slips into such a clichéd use of a womb to represent Omar's home illustrates both the structural imperatives imposed on the text by its desire for circularity and to resonate symbolic meanings, and also, once more, the idea that a female refuge from the dangers of the outside world would represent a threat as well as a haven. The 'womb' of 'Nishapur' serves more as a revelation (albeit involuntary) of Rushdie's psychology than as an interesting elaboration of the narrative.

How far then is Rushdie guilty of self-deception in his apparent belief in himself as a champion of women? It is certainly true that there is a male/female split in the storyline of *Shame* as there is in his other texts, and that this does serve in many respects to point up and humanise the stories of his heroes. But this formal manoeuvre and superficial even-handedness finds itself time and again in conflict with other forces, presumably stemming from the same culture-and gender-based prejudices and conditioning which Rushdie purports to explode. In Chapter Seven of *Shame*, the authorial voice intervenes to declare its understanding of the Moslem fathers who feel compelled to murder their 'shameless' westernized daughters. (It is of course surprising that this empathy with the Moslem mind did not prevent his more serious breach of Islamic *izzat* [Urdu word for honour, reputation or prestige – derived from the Arabic word *izza,* meaning glory] with the presentation of Mahound in *The Satanic Verses*.) Rushdie imagines just such a daughter whom he calls Anahita [Muhammad]:

> She danced behind my eyes, her nature changing each time I glimpsed her: now innocent, now whore, then a third and a fourth thing. But finally she eluded me.[45]

It is an image he returns to in *The Satanic Verses*. The 'Anahita' of Anahita [Muhammad] and the 'Sufiya' of Sufiya Zinobia are taken up again to create the two worldly British Asian sisters, Anahita and Mishal [Sufyan] who live at the [Shaandaar] Café [in *The Satanic Verses*]. The way in which Anahita is imagined in *Shame*, 'now innocent, now whore', cuts deep to a culturally conditioned belief that will not allow him to conceive of women except in extreme terms. It also exposes his sense of frustration at being unable to control this image – unable ultimately to bid a woman to be one thing or another. The innocent/whore binarism extends beyond the actual women who appear in the text to embrace abstractions and inanimate objects. Karachi itself is shown to age from 'slender girlish town' to 'obese harridan' – a 'painted lady' of 'overblown charms'.[46] Bilquis Hyder's father, Mahmoud, comments on the emotions and images that attach to the word 'Woman':

> Is there no end to the burdens this word is capable of bearing? Was there ever such a broad-backed and also such a dirty word?[47]

Therein lies the root of . . . both the innocent/whore and shame/shamelessness binarisms in the text – that the concept of Woman like women themselves can embody both sides of each of these coins. In societal terms, it is the understanding that, for example, great sexual repression and extremes of uninhibited and unconstrained sexual activity can not only occur within the same society but are interdependent, equal and opposite forces, with repression fanning the flame of abandon. Even Sufiya Zinobia herself – the embodiment of the desire for revenge against the nation's collective shame – also serves as the ultimate manifestation of the destructive capabilities of female sexuality. Destroying those who seek sexual union with her, she becomes as much like the black widow spider as she does Nemesis – indeed, an amalgam of the black burqa of shame and oppression and the 'shameless' autocracy of the 'black widow' Indira Gandhi as we see her in *Midnight's Children*.

Aijaz Ahmad in his recent study *In Theory* sees Sufiya becoming 'the oldest of the misogynist myths: the virgin who is really a vampire, the irresistible temptress who seduces men in order to kill them . . . '[48] Inderpal Grewal shares Ahmad's distrust of Rushdie's aims in his depiction of Sufiya:

> Though Sufiya's genocidal mimicry is meant to be a critique of patriarchal culture, it fails because its horror can only operate by playing on a patriarchal fear of women and by showing the potential for destruction that is contained within women.[49]

Even the text's too-perfect Moslem daughter, Arjumand Harappa, becomes one of a number of Rushdie's characters whose obsessive love refuses to recognise the taboos of kinship. Her near-identification with her father Iskander as lover – rejecting the needs of her body to punish it into becoming the repository of his memory – mirrors Saleem Sinai's incestuous love for Jamila Singer in *Midnight's Children*, Flapping Eagle's sexual relationship with Bird-Dog in *Grimus* and the cloying closeness of Gibreel Farishta and his mother in *The Satanic Verses*. As Ahmad again says:

> . . . throughout, every woman, without exception, is represented through a system of imageries which is sexually overdetermined; the frustration of erotic need, which drives some to frenzy and others to nullity, appears in every case to be the central fact of a woman's existence.[50]

Returning to Rushdie's defence of *The Satanic Verses* in 'In Good Faith', he writes that it is 'a proper function of literature'[51] to point up such social injustices as the oppression or devaluing of women; a feature, as Rushdie sees it, of Islamic societies and of the teachings of the *Quran* itself. The incident of the 'satanic verses' around which the text is structured, and which in itself draws attention to this question of woman's 'value', is accepted by some historians and contested by others. The scholar and translator of the *Quran*, N.J. Dawood, describes the accepted prehistory of Islam thus:

> Long before Muhammad's call, Arabian paganism was showing signs of decay. At the Ka'bah the Meccans worshipped not only Allah, the supreme semitic God, but also a number of female deities whom they regarded as the daughters of Allah. Among these were Al-Lat, Al-Uzza, and Manat, who represented the Sun, Venus, and Fortune respectively.[52]

In *The Satanic Verses* Uzza, we are told, represents beauty and love; Manat, Fate; while Lat is the omnipotent mother-goddess, Allah's female counterpart.[53] The point of contention among historians of the *Quran* is whether verses were inserted into the holy book in the early days of Islam, in order to placate the polytheistic peoples of Mecca and bring about greater tolerance of the new religion. The historian al-Tabari (839–923) stated that Mohammed received the verses praising the intercession of the goddesses but that these were removed from the *Quran* when the angel Gabriel informed the prophet that they were verses inspired by the devil.[54] The recitation and subsequent rescinding of the verses are separated by just ten pages in *The Satanic Verses*. 'Mahound', the dream-prophet of the text, is offered tolerance in return for acceptance of the goddesses. He provides it:

> Have you thought upon Lat and Uzza, and Manat, the third, the other? . . . They are exalted birds, and their intercession is desired indeed.[55]

That the goddesses were a significant obstacle to Islam's development is clear from the fact that they still appear in the *Quran* itself. Within the text of Dawood's translation of the holy book, there is reference to the pagan triumvirate, in surah 53:20–26 entitled 'The Star':

> Have you thought on Al-Lat and Al-Uzza and on Manat, the third other? Are you to have the sons and He the daughters? This is indeed an unfair distinction! They are but names which you and your fathers have invented: God has vested no authority in them.[56]

The Verses does not set itself up as a project to espouse the cause of women in the same way as *Shame*, but it quite deliberately hinges the course of events in the text on the actions and interventions of its many female characters.

That said, however, the crucial role which Rushdie assigns to his hero Saladin's Indian lover, Zeeny Vakil, is even here undercut by his presentation of her, and by the continuing and now ingrained tendency to demonize the female. Timothy Brennan in *Salman Rushdie and the Third World* senses that Rushdie's characterisations of women in the *Verses* are 'strangely demeaning',[57] but seems unable to pin down the cause of his reservations. The *Verses* shows Rushdie caught once again between the threat and the promise offered by women. The body of Tavleen, the Sikh extremist who causes the explosion that destroys the hijacked aircraft at the opening of the text, is in many ways the ultimate figuring of woman as destruction in Rushdie's fiction:

> . . . they could all see the arsenal of her body, the grenades like extra breasts nestling in her cleavage, the gelignite taped around her thighs . . . [58]

Beauty and destructiveness, fear and desire, coincide in an image that is, to put it mildly, 'sexually overdetermined.'

Gibreel Farishta, Saladin's fellow traveller on the exploding plane, is presented as both the 'beneficiary' and the 'victim' of female emotional and sexual generosity[59] – a victim in the sense that he is allowed by his lovers to continue philandering and breaking hearts without being made aware of the consequences of his actions. But is this just a piece of sophistry on Rushdie's part? To locate Gibreel between these twin dilemmas apparently offered by unencumbered sexual gratification is to exonerate him from ultimate responsibility for his actions. Conscience, like gratification, becomes the gift and the responsibility of woman.

In his account of *The Satanic Verses* 'affair', Malise Ruthven is keen to suggest correspondences between the characters of Pamela Lovelace and Rushdie's first wife, Clarissa, and Allie Cone and the Australian travel writer Robyn Davidson with whom Rushdie was involved before his second marriage to Marianne Wiggins.[60] Such an overlaying of text onto life is rarely particularly useful, but in this instance it may shed some light on the depiction of Zeeny Vakil and her crucial role as the 'saviour' of Saladin's Indian self.

Zeeny is a doctor, a part-time art critic who mirrors Rushdie's own views on artistic eclecticism, and a committed and unselfish political activist to boot. The fact that Ruthven hazards no suggestion of a correspondence between Zeeny and a 'live' woman in Rushdie's own past or present contributes to the general air that Zeeny imparts of being a fantasy figure, strangely two-dimensional and not very far removed from the 'lurid painting of a bare-breasted myth-woman' that hangs in the [Shaandaar] Café.[61] The conflict apparent in Rushdie's representation of women is given a different dimension in Zeeny. One does not have to doubt the sincerity of Rushdie's belief in the force of love as the 'prime mover' in effacing the rebirth of identity to feel that Zeeny's role is too comfortably appropriate. It diverts attention from the fact that the crucially important love affair for Saladin is the one between himself and his father, Changez. The scenes around the latter's death bed convey a poignancy that is only hinted at in Zeeny's offer of support to Saladin at the end of the text. As the narrator declares, 'to fall in love with one's father after the long angry decades was a serene and beautiful feeling; a renewing, life-giving thing . . .'[62]

What this essay suggests is that a contradiction exists between Rushdie's non-fictional espousals of the cause of women and his fictional representations of them, and what, to go back to his own statement with which this piece opened, it says about him rather than the 'great ladies' concerned. It is a recurring feature of his work that women are invoked to prove a point about social injustices and inequities, and then effectively demeaned (or, in the case of Zeeny, marginalised) by the writing itself.[63] □

Cundy's point, that the allegedly blasphemous content of *The Satanic Verses* and the ensuing politics of the 'Rushdie Affair' have overshadowed Rushdie's representations of women, is well made. Yet as Cundy's essay suggests, and the final chapter of this Guide demonstrates, the politics of Rushdie's fiction and his depictions of women cannot be viewed as strictly separate issues.

CHAPTER SIX

'And if Rivers of Blood Flow from the Cuts His Verses Inflict': The Politics of Fiction

TO DESCRIBE *The Satanic Verses* as a disputed novel would be a masterpiece of understatement. Never before has the publication of a novel resulted in such fierce academic and religious argument, in such intense political manoeuvring, in such vehement threats and in such acts of terrible violence. 'The Rushdie Affair', as it is now called, seems a somewhat inadequate, almost polite, way to describe the extreme range of reactions to Rushdie's work. Even now, *The Satanic Verses* retains its reputation as a 'byword for trouble, trouble within and between cultures, religions, different sections of society.'[1]

This sort of 'trouble,' however, was not exactly new to Rushdie. It should be noted that one effect of the 'Rushdie Affair' has been to obscure the contentious, and at times seemingly belligerent, quality of Rushdie's earlier fiction. As Katherine Frank observes in her article 'Mr. Rushdie and Mrs. Gandhi', controversy also surrounded the publication of *Midnight's Children*. In this study, Frank explores the consequences of Rushdie's depiction of Indira Gandhi as a witch-like figure who, during India's Emergency Period, was responsible for false imprisonment, violent acts of slum clearance and programs of compulsory castration. Frank's article is particularly interesting in that it raises a question that would just a few years later be asked in more ominous tones of Rushdie's fiction – that of authorial accountability.

■ As far as we know, Salman Rushdie and Indira Gandhi[2] never laid eyes on each other – in the flesh at any rate – though if Margaret Thatcher had had her way, they would have lunched together at the 1982 Festival of India in London. Rushdie, however, declined Mrs. Thatcher's invitation to a luncheon in honor of the visiting Indian

Prime Minister, and thus he failed to meet the woman he pilloried in *Midnight's Children* as 'the Widow.' Because of Rushdie's absence, it was left to Mrs. Thatcher to praise the novel as 'a fine contribution to the Anglo–Indian cultural bond' while Gandhi sat, unflinching and impassive, at Thatcher's side. Gandhi had good reason to be furious at both her hostess and Rushdie, for unlike Thatcher and Thatcher's staff, Indira Gandhi had actually read *Midnight's Children* and the book had caused her sufficient pain to make her consider taking legal action against Rushdie and his publisher Jonathan Cape.

For the biographer of Indira Gandhi this episode – when Rushdie failed to come to lunch – points up the truth that sometimes the most provocative and telling incidents in a subject's life are those which are narrowly averted, deliberately spurned, or accidentally bypassed. Significance may lie hidden in what didn't as well as what did happen. But although he failed to meet Indira Gandhi in 1982, Rushdie 'engaged' with her in other ways, especially by writing a great deal about her: in *Midnight's Children*, which appeared in 1981 while Indira Gandhi was still in office, and also in a number of essays that Rushdie collected in *Imaginary Homelands*, published in 1991, seven years after Gandhi's assassination. [. . .]

[F]ar from cementing the 'Anglo–Indian cultural bond' close to Mrs. Thatcher's heart, Mr. Rushdie and Mrs. Gandhi became public enemies when *Midnight's Children* was published in 1981. Three years later the long-simmering animosity between them boiled over in a High Court in London when Indira Gandhi sued Rushdie for libel. In and out of court, Gandhi and Rushdie had, and continue to have, their camp followers, but what transpired between them in this case is significant for a number of nonpartisan reasons. Writers of fiction are seldom accused of libel, though Rushdie refers to Indira Gandhi by name in *Midnight's Children* as well as portraying her as the witch-like Widow with centre-parted, schizoid-colored hair who imprisons, castrates, and destroys the Children of Midnight. That the accusation of libel reached a lawcourt at all is worth pondering. This seems to imply that a novelist is legally responsible and accountable to real people and real events even when what he has written is patently a work of fiction.[3] [. . .] □

Though Frank recognises the fictional status of *Midnight's Children*, she also points to the novel's depiction of actual historical figures and events. For Frank, this is a 'problem' inasmuch that:

■ *Midnight's Children* and Rushdie's other writing on Indira Gandhi raise important questions about the relationship between biography and fiction. At issue are the novelist's accountability and the question of 'Whose life is it, anyway?' Does the individual – in this case, Indira Gandhi – have a privileged insight into the 'truth' of their own life? Is it possible that a biographer or a novelist might possess a greater understanding of it? Is there such a thing, as Rushdie argues, as 'imaginative truth,' which may have even greater validity than factual accuracy? These questions are perhaps fundamentally unanswerable, but the case of Mr. Rushdie and Mrs. Gandhi yields some interesting, if tentative responses.[4] [. . .] □

Despite the novel's political content, Frank suggests that Indira Gandhi's response to *Midnight's Children* was motivated more from a sense of personal injury. It was not so much Rushdie's description of Indira Gandhi's role in India's Emergency years that caused such offence, but his description of her as a heartless 'widow'. According to Frank, the experience of widowhood in Indian culture, since the abolition of 'suttee' (sometimes called 'sati' and referring to the former Hindu practice of a widow immolating herself on her husband's funeral pyre), is often characterised by marginalisation or exclusion. Frank observes that 'at best a widow is considered "inauspicious" . . . Often a widow is driven from her home and then, if she is fortunate, she may find her way to a widow's hostel. (Another alternative, if she is not too old, is prostitution.)'[5] Rushdie's depiction of Indira Gandhi, for Frank, falls into 'a time-honored literary activity . . . [of] . . . widow-baiting.'[6]

■ Hence, twenty-four years later, the peculiar and limited nature of Indira Gandhi's libel suit against Rushdie. She made no attempt to ban *Midnight's Children* in India, nor did she seek legal redress for Rushdie's portrayal of her in Saleem's nightmare as a talon-nailed, green and black devouring Widow with part-colored hair who rolls little children into balls and hurls them into the darkness. Rather than suppressing this direct frontal assault on herself, what Indira Gandhi sought damages for at the Old Bailey in 1984 was a brief passage – just one sentence, in fact – that is no longer to be found in the paperback edition of the novel. At the end of a thumbnail sketch of Gandhi's life, Rushdie's narrator says that Sanjay Gandhi, who is often referred to as 'Labia Lips' in the novel, accused his mother, the Widow, of causing his father's death by cruelly and selfishly neglecting him (406, Cape edition).[7] Among all the things that the Widow perpetrates in *Midnight's Children*, including genocide, several wars, and the castration and destruction of the Children of Midnight, neglecting her husband is scarcely her most serious crime. But it was the one that Indira Gandhi sued Rushdie for, and it doesn't take much psychological insight to see why.[8] [. . .] □

Frank then goes on to describe Rushdie's attempt to defend his novel as an act of literary imagination.

■ 'I tried to make it as imaginatively true as I could, but imaginative truth is simultaneously honourable and suspect' (10).[9] 'Imaginative truth' is Rushdie's rhetorical equivalent of the basket that Parvati uses to spirit Saleem out of Bangladesh: an idea that grants invisibility and freedom to the author and negates accountability. 'Human beings do not perceive things whole; we are not gods but wounded creatures, cracked lenses, capable only of fractured perceptions,' he explains. Then, more specifically: 'I wasn't trying to write about . . . the Emergency in the same way as I wrote about events half a century earlier. I felt it would be dishonest to pretend . . . that it was possible to see the whole picture. I showed certain blobs and slabs of the scene' (12–13).

Quite understandably, Indira Gandhi did not appreciate the blobs and slabs bearing her family name in *Midnight's Children*. But Rushdie again invoked aesthetic criteria. 'Literature,' he argued, 'is self-validating. That is to say a book is not justified by its author's worthiness to write it, but by the quality of what has been written' (14). Supremely confident of the literary merits of his novel, Rushdie felt it should be immune to any other sort of criticism. Rushdie of course lives in a society where free speech is a basic and legally protected right. The case of Gandhi versus Rushdie that was tried at the Old Bailey in July 1984, just three months before Indira Gandhi was killed, was concerned only with whether Rushdie had crossed the line that separates freedom of expression from libel. In court, the literary quality of *Midnight's Children*, and Rushdie's safe berth in North London far away from the people, events, and country he portrays in the novel, were not issues. He should have had nothing to fear, but Rushdie unfortunately had made a quite serious miscalculation by using real names in *Midnight's Children* – names which the general reader would assume were not arbitrary but rather signified real people in a real India.[10]

What the court had to decide in *Gandhi vs. Rushdie* was whether Rushdie had expressed a false assumption in *Midnight's Children* that Sanjay Gandhi had accused his mother of causing his father's fatal coronary by neglecting him. No one had witnessed such an accusation, and by the time of the trial no evidence could be obtained from Sanjay and Feroze Gandhi since they were both dead. It was Indira Gandhi's word against Salman Rushdie's. The court's verdict was for Gandhi. Rushdie and his publisher, Jonathan Cape, had to apologize publicly to Gandhi, promise to remove the libellous passage in future editions of the novel, and pay all court costs. Rushdie, then, was legally brought to his knees, but it is unlikely that Gandhi felt any great sense of triumph. Her victory cleared her of blame: it did not bring back the dead. *Midnight's Children* continued to sell like hotcakes, and few of those who read it were aware of the libel case, which despite the fame of the contestants, was scarcely reported in the press.

Though the offending sentence was eventually excised from *Midnight's Children* and a brief and rather perfunctory apology printed in the *Guardian*, the trial really only raised – rather than settled – the underlying issues of *Gandhi vs. Rushdie*. A precedent was set whereby in a court of law, fictional statements were as potentially libellous as factual ones. But basic questions concerning the relationship between fictional and 'real' worlds, the reconstruction or recreation of the past, the relative validity of what Rushdie calls 'imaginative' and historical truth, were still unresolved. Rushdie's penchant for hybridity, plurality, multiplicity – for mongrel books as well as mongrel selves – suggests that such questions should remain unanswered and that he is not troubled by his contradictory statements regarding his intention or purpose in writing *Midnight's Children*.[11] What does matter, he insists, is the aesthetic quality of the novel.

Read as literary construct, there is no question that *Midnight's Children* delivers. But a biographer will read the book with different eyes, seizing on the historical, political, and biographical information it incorporates, and for her (or him) *Midnight's Children* is, as the Indian woman journalist put it, 'not satisfactory.'[12] Perhaps inevitably so. Hybridity may be a liberating notion for the novelist, grafting an oral tradition and the conventions of Hindi film onto a postmodern narrative. But this artful blurring of the boundary between fact and fiction is far more problematic for the biographer. Turning from Rushdie and *Midnight's Children* to biographies that experiment with 'patches of straight fiction' – Peter Ackroyd's *Dickens* [1990] for example, and more recently Joe McGinnis's life of Ted Kennedy and Julia Blackburn's *Daisy Bates* [1994] – the same problem arises. Instead of being true hybrids, blending the best of various genres, these books take distracting liberties with invented characters or employ an unconvincing omniscience, and again are not satisfactory because they provoke conflicting expectations. The fact is we read fiction and biography differently. Reading novels we suspend disbelief; reading biography we suspend it not at all. Or as the by now familiar axiom states, 'biography is fiction under oath.'[13]

Rushdie, of course, has political as well as aesthetic commitments. In *Midnight's Children* he needs someone to blame for the mess India is in and Indira Gandhi is the obvious culprit.[14] But even more, he needs 'patches of straight history' as a kind of scaffolding for the tragicomedy of Saleem Sinai's fully realized fictional autobiography.[15] Rushdie's hatred of Indira Gandhi, his refusal to forgive her for the Emergency, his contempt for what the Gandhi name represents, all make sense fictionally because Saleem, the protagonist, requires an antagonist. Towards the end of the novel, on the same page as the libellous sentence, Saleem says, 'Mother Indira really had it in for me' (421). Saleem and the Widow are rivals and enemies because both of them are 'handcuffed to history,' both of them want to be indissolubly linked to the fate of their country. Saleem, then, is particularly incensed (as was Rushdie) by Gandhi's campaign slogan: 'India is Indira and Indira is India.' In Saleem's words, he and the Widow are 'competitors for centrality . . . gripped by a lust for meaning' (420). In court Gandhi won this particular contest, but Rushdie – still alive, still writing, still unable to forgive Indira Gandhi – continues to have the last word.[16] □

If the publication of *Midnight's Children* established Rushdie as the 'Bad Boy of literary London',[17] *The Satanic Verses* was to compound that reputation to an unprecedented degree. *The Satanic Verses* was launched in Britain on 26 September 1988. The novel had been short-listed for the Booker Prize, and, as one rather ironic newspaper article suggested, 'Viking, the publishers, were hoping for extensive press coverage.'[18] The coverage the novel received, however, can hardly have been what they had hoped for. Yet in the weeks leading up to its official publication, *The Satanic Verses* had already begun to receive the sort of attention that would soon almost completely overshadow the novel's literary merits.

In mid-September, two of India's news magazines, *India Today* and *Sunday*, had published interviews with Rushdie that clearly indicated the novel's inflammatory potential.[19] These interviews caught the attention of the Muslim MP Syed Shahabuddin. As a member of the opposition Janata party, Shahabuddin applied pressure on the Indian government to ban the book. Shahabuddin's intervention came at a critical time in Indian politics. With a general election less than a year away, Rajiv Gandhi's ruling Congress-I party was facing mounting unpopularity.[20] In such circumstances, the strategic electoral importance of India's 100 million Muslims was a factor that he could not ignore. So, on 5 October 1988, the Indian government contacted the publishers of *The Satanic Verses* to announce its decision to ban the novel.

On 10 October, Indian Radio broadcast 'An Open Letter to PM Rajiv Gandhi' in which Rushdie aggressively responded to this decision. In this letter, which subsequently appeared in various newspapers,[21] Rushdie attacks the Indian government, and in particular its prime minister, for political opportunism. He also raises an issue that, especially in the West, was to dominate debate about the novel – that of free speech. Rushdie asked:

■ What sort of India do you wish to govern? Is it to be an open, or a repressive society? Your action in the matter of *The Satanic Verses* will be for many people around the world, an important indicator. If you confirm the ban, I'm afraid I, and many others, will have to assume the worst. If, on the other hand, you should admit your Government's error and move swiftly to correct it, that will be an honourable deed and I shall be the first to applaud.[22] □

Despite Rushdie's protest against the banning of *The Satanic Verses*, its potentially offensive qualities must be acknowledged. The very title of the novel itself is a source of offence to many Muslims. As Marlena G. Corcoran observes: 'the willingness of devout Muslims to condemn a book of which they have only read the title is easier to understand if one realizes that the novel itself is named after a banned text'.[23] Corcoran is referring to an incident described by a ninth-century historian who tells us that certain verses were removed from the Qur'an because of their satanic origins. According to Islamic belief, Mohammed received the verses of the Qur'an from the angel Gabriel. The satanic verses, however, are said to have originated from the devil seeking to undermine Muslim monotheism by suggesting accommodation for three ancient Arab goddesses so they might serve as intermediaries between man and God. In *The Satanic Verses*, Rushdie seems to suggest that such an accommodation also serves a financial function, one that ensures that the revenues of the established pagan temples would not be lost.

Rushdie appears to question the foundations of Islam by placing prophetic inspiration alongside uncertainty. By casting into doubt the divine source of the holy text, the very authority of the Qur'an itself is challenged. For in *The Satanic Verses*, the role of Gabriel, God's messenger to Mohammed, is taken by the dreaming character of Gibreel, a twentieth-century human actor. Gibreel declares: '*Mahound comes to me for revelation, asking me to choose between monotheist and henotheist alternatives, and I'm just some idiot actor having a bhaenchud nightmare, what the fuck do I know, yaar, what to tell you, help, Help.*'[24] Gibreel's is not the only voice of *The Satanic Verses*. There is also the voice of Satan himself, intruding and thereby exposing himself as the narrator of the novel. Consequently, the reader is left unsure as to who is actually speaking the words of revelation. Is it Gibreel in a dream, or is it Satan directing the actor?

To assuage his doubts concerning the validity of the satanic verses, the Prophet returns for fresh guidance. Rushdie depicts him wrestling a new recitation from the angel, one that now denies any place for the goddesses. So it is not simply reference to the censorship of the satanic verses that offends. Nor is it only the doubt as to who is revealing the verses to the Prophet, Satan or the actor Gibreel. It is also Rushdie's apparent suggestion that the Prophet receives his revelation only after wrestling for it; that after a contest of wills Mohammed manipulates the voice of revelation. Rushdie writes of the prophet: 'he started weeping for joy and then he did his old trick, forcing my mouth open and making the voice, the Voice, pour out of me again, made it pour all over him, like sick.'[25] This suggestion strikes at the very core of Muslim belief that the source of every word in the Qur'an is God himself, not Mohammed.

Another source of offence is the choice of the name Mahound for the character of the Prophet. Though for some this might simply be regarded as an archaic version of Mohammed, Amin Malak argues that 'the choice of this name is anything but innocent . . . "Mahound" signifies, especially for Western medievalists, four meanings, all offensive: "false prophet"; "a false god"; "a hideous creature"; and "a name for the devil."'[26] Rushdie's depiction of the character Mahound as an, at times, manipulative and opportunist businessman served only to compound the sense of outrage.

Rushdie's irreverence is also directed at the wives of the Prophet. He names the prostitutes of Jahilia's most popular brothel after the Prophet's wives. Such an act is seen to be a direct attack upon those women known to Muslims as the 'Mothers of the believers.' That the brothel should also be called 'The Curtain' or *Hijab*, meaning veil in Arabic, signals for Malak the suggestion that Muslim men regard their wives as little more than prostitutes.[27] Malak argues: 'believers would legitimately consider such a wantonly contrived episode as the most vicious of Rushdie's offences. To them Rushdie's blend of blasphemy with quasi-pornography tastelessly verges on the obscene.'[28]

Soon after *The Satanic Verses* was banned in India, similar action was taken in Pakistan, Saudi Arabia, Egypt, Somalia, Bangladesh, Sudan, Malaysia, Indonesia, Qatar and South Africa. Even before the banning of *The Satanic Verses* in India, a number of prominent British Muslims had begun to organise their own protest against the novel. Encouraged by Aslam Ejaz, of the Islamic Foundation in Madras, Faiyazuddin Ahmad, a public relations director of the Islamic foundation in Leicester, had circulated photocopies of the novel's offending passages to leading Islamic organisations in Britain. By 15 October, Dr Syed Pasha, secretary of the Union of Muslim Organisations, an umbrella organisation for Islamic groups in Britain, had summoned the Union's nineteen council members for a crisis meeting to discuss what action might be taken against Rushdie's novel. As a result of that meeting, it was decided to mount a campaign to get *The Satanic Verses* banned in Britain. After unsuccessfully attempting to contact Rushdie's publisher, Pasha contacted the Prime Minister, Margaret Thatcher, and asked her to prosecute Rushdie and his publishers under the Public Order Act (1986) and the Race Relations Act (1976). Pasha wrote: 'Never have we encountered such a ferocious and savage attack on our Holy Prophet . . . the Muslim community is shocked and seething with indignation.'[29] Thatcher's response was to refuse to ban the book, declaring: 'It is an essential part of our democracy that people who act within the law should be able to express their opinions freely.'[30] She did, however, refer the book to the Attorney-General, Sir Patrick Mayhew, who judged that the book constituted no criminal offence. The frustration and outrage evident in the following short extract mirrors the feelings of many British Muslims.

■ If some writer uses my name and the names of some of my friends and also selects some situations and incidents of my life and distorts them and vilifies them, do I not have the right to charge that person for slander and defamation? Should not the Muslim community have the right to condemn this man for blasphemy because he is using a thin veil of fiction in order to vilify the Prophet and all that they hold dear to them? As the author is not interested in presenting his own realisation of any truth, as he is preaching an anti-Islamic theory in the guise of a novel, his liberty as a writer ends and he should be treated as anyone producing blasphemous writing is treated.[31] □

In British law, however, Rushdie cannot be charged with blasphemy. Much of the subsequent debate surrounding Rushdie and his novel was to focus on this legal point. For while British law affords protection against blasphemy to the Christian faith, it is denied to other religions. In 1976, for example, successful action was taken against the magazine *Gay News* after it published a poem that depicted Christ in a homosexual context. Muslims protesting against *The Satanic Verses* were denied similar recourse to the law for the novel's alleged attack upon the prophet Mohammed. Calls were made, but without success, to extend the blasphemy laws so that they encompassed different religions.

On 28 October, the UK Action Committee on Islamic Affairs issued a formal statement to British Muslims.[32] This document called for Muslims throughout Britain to demand that *The Satanic Verses* be withdrawn from sale and all copies of the novel destroyed, and that Rushdie himself should not only apologise to the world Muslim community, but that he should also pay damages to an agreed Islamic charity in Britain for the offence he had caused.

The growing protests against his novel soon began to affect Rushdie himself.

On 2 November 1988, a visit to a South African book fair, where he was to have presented a keynote speech on apartheid and censorship, had to be cancelled when its organisers withdrew the invitation. British protests against Rushdie gathered further momentum when, on 21 November, a ruling by Cairo's Al-Azhar, a combined mosque and university considered to be the seat of Islamic theology, called on British Islamic organisations to step up their campaign against *The Satanic Verses*. In early December, the novel was for the first time publicly burned when more than 7,000 demonstrators gathered in Bolton to stage a protest march against its publication. Though the British press largely ignored this demonstration, it took more notice when, on 14 January 1989, members of a smaller protest in Bradford burnt a copy of *The Satanic Verses* outside the police headquarters. This act sparked enormous debate within the British press, and, in terms of media coverage and public awareness, marked the beginning of the 'Rushdie Affair'.

Rushdie was quick to respond to the public burning of his novel. In 'Choice Between Light and Dark', published in *The Observer* on 22 January, Rushdie argued that his novel was not anti-religious, but then concluded: '"Battle lines are being drawn up in India today," one of my characters remarks. "Secular versus religious, the light versus the dark. Better you choose which side you are on."' Rushdie then went on to suggest: 'Now that the battle has spread to Britain, I can only hope it will not be lost by default. It is time to choose.'[33] Over the following weeks, however, the number of demonstrations and book burnings increased. On 28 January, over 8,000 demonstrators gathered in Hyde Park in protest against Rushdie and his novel.

In other parts of the world, the protests against Rushdie were of a more violent nature. Just days before the official publication of *The Satanic Verses*, Rushdie had declared 'it would be absurd to think that a book can cause riots. That's a strange view of the world.'[34] On 12 February, however, five people were killed and many more injured, when police opened fire on anti-Rushdie protesters as they attempted to storm the US Information Centre in the Pakistan capital of Islamabad. The very next day, in Kashmir, one person was killed and over a hundred injured in a similar demonstration. Days later, the Iranian religious leader Ayatollah Khomeini declared a fatwa against Rushdie that also threatened all those involved in the publication of his novel. The following announcement was made on Radio Tehran just before the afternoon news:

■ In the name of God Almighty. There is only one God, to whom we shall all return. I would like to inform all the intrepid Muslims in the world that the author of the book entitled *The Satanic Verses*, which has been compiled, printed and published in opposition to Islam, the Prophet and the Koran, as well as those publishers who were aware of its contents, have been sentenced to death.

I call on all zealous Muslims to execute them quickly, wherever they find them, so that no one will dare insult the Islamic sanctions. Whoever is killed on this path will be considered as a martyr, God willing.

In addition, anyone who has access to the author of the book, but does not possess the power to execute him, should refer him to the people so that he may be punished for his actions. May God's blessing be on you all.[35] □

A few days later Rushdie made a short apology.

■ As author of *The Satanic Verses* I recognise that Moslems in many parts of the world are genuinely distressed by the publication of my novel. I profoundly regret the distress that publication has occasioned to the sincere followers of Islam. Living as we do in a world of many faiths this experience has served to remind us that we must all be conscious of the sensibilities of others.[36] □

This apology was first rejected, then accepted, and then rejected again by various factions of the Iranian establishment. Ayatollah Khomeini's response, however, was unequivocal: 'Even if Salman Rushdie repents and becomes the most pious man of [all] time, it is incumbent on every Muslim to employ everything he has got, his life and his wealth, to send him to hell.'[37]

Khomeini's anger may also have been fuelled by a sense of personal insult. In *The Satanic Verses,* Rushdie depicts an Imam in exile in London. This figure is seen by some critics to represent the Ayatollah Khomeini himself, who had also spent time in exile before achieving power. Feroza Jussawalla points to Rushdie's description of the Imam of the novel as 'the great Haramzada in person.' Jussawalla explains how this description might appear harmless to a Western academic inasmuch that the word 'haram' may be taken to mean 'canonically forbidden' or even worse may simply be confused with *haram*, the hallowed area around the monuments of Mecca. Only the Indian audience knows the full import of the abuse. In 'richshawwallah' parlance, it simply means 'bastard'.[38] If we are to see this character as the Ayatollah Khomeini, Rushdie's novel acquires a prescient quality when the Imam thunders the words 'Apostate, blasphemer, fraud',[39] the very accusation that the Ayatollah was to level against Rushdie himself.

The effect of the fatwa was to inflame further the violence directed against *The Satanic Verses*. The next day, crowds threatened the British Embassy in Tehran. On 24 February, a further ten people died and many were injured during rioting in Bombay. Bookshops in Padua and London were attacked and the offices of Riverdale Press in New York were fire-bombed. On 29 March, Imam Abdullah Al-Ahdal, the leader of Belgium's Islamic community, and his assistant Salem el-Behir, were assassinated for making an apparently lenient statement on Belgian television about the Rushdie issue.

In 1988, Britain and Iran had agreed to normalise diplomatic relations for the first time since the overthrow of the Shah in 1979. Following the threat to the British Embassy, however, relations between the two countries took a downward turn. After unsuccessful meetings between the British chargé d'affaires, Nicholas Brown, and Iranian foreign ministry officials, Britain turned to Europe for support. The European Community issued a statement condemning the fatwa and declared its intention to recall ambassadors from Tehran and suspend diplomatic relations with Iran. The next day, Sweden, Canada, Australia, Norway and Brazil adopted similar positions.

In the USA, President Bush issued a statement of support for EEC foreign ministers. On 27 February, the US Senate unanimously passed Resolution 72 in which it condemned the Ayatollah Khomeini's fatwa as 'state-sponsored terrorism' and declared its commitment to support the publishers and booksellers of *The Satanic Verses*. While the Senate recognised 'the sensitivity of religious beliefs and practices', it called upon the President of the United States to take 'swift and proportionate action . . . in the event that violent acts should occur.'[40]

The position of the Christian churches underwent something of a shift as the 'Rushdie Affair' developed. On 15 February, the embassy of the Islamic Republic of Iran made an appeal to Pope John Paul II to demonstrate religious solidarity by blocking the publication of *The Satanic Verses* in Italy. A senior Vatican official responded by suggesting that such an appeal from Iran was 'rather out of place . . . It's their problem, not ours. We have enough of our own, especially with all the books and films which cast doubts on Jesus Christ himself. We have never asked for Moslem help in curbing their sale.'[41] This reluctance was, however, soon replaced by firm support. On 21 February, the Archbishop of Canterbury, Dr Robert Runcie, called for a strengthening of the law against blasphemy so that it might protect religions other than Christianity. While in France, Cardinal Decourtnay, Archbishop of Lyons, declared: '*The Satanic Verses* is an offence against religion.'[42] By March, it was reported that 'a Vatican official had condemned Salman Rushdie for blasphemy and spoken in curiously ambivalent tones of the threat to his life'.[43] A similar position was taken in Jerusalem by Jewish religious leaders. Rabbi Avraham Ravitz, the leader of the strictly Orthodox Degel Hataorah Party, for example, said that Rushdie should be condemned for his depiction of Mohammed, adding 'imagine what the response would have been if someone had written that about Moses.'[44]

Important members of the literary establishment also attacked Rushdie. In a letter to *The Times*, Roald Dahl described *The Satanic Verses* as an indifferent book and Rushdie himself as 'a dangerous opportunist.'[45] Auberon Waugh asked 'just how much we should exert ourselves, as deeply stained white imperialists, to protect him from his own people',[46] and Germaine Greer attributed Rushdie's predicament to a form of megalomania and said 'I refuse to sign petitions for that book of his, which was about his own troubles'.[47] Many more, however, rallied to Rushdie's side. On 15 February, the playwright Harold Pinter, supported by a group of writers, literary agents and publishers delivered a letter of protest to Margaret Thatcher. Pinter demanded that the government 'should confront Iran with the consequences of its statement and remind the Islamic community that it cannot incite people to murder.'[48] In America, Article 19, PEN (a worldwide association of writers) and the Author's Guild organised a public reading of *The Satanic Verses* and voiced their protest against the fatwa outside the Iranian Mission to the United States. They also staged a number of demonstrations outside selected bookshops that had chosen to remove copies of the novel from their shelves. On 1 March, a world writers' statement of support for Rushdie, containing the names of thousands of literary figures, was released to the press. One week later, Susan Sontag, on behalf of the 2,200 members of PEN American Centre, testified before the Subcommittee on International Terrorism, Senate Foreign Relations Committee. In this testimony, Sontag urged the Senate, and the President of the United States, to take firm action against Iran. Sontag argued that 'the matter of Salman Rushdie has made him the world's best-known endangered writer, but he is far from the only one. In all too many parts of the world, to take up one's pen is to risk violence'.[49]

During this period, relatively few academics chose to attack Rushdie for *The Satanic Verses*. One notable exception was Feroza Jussawalla. (Yet, as the extract contained in Chapter Two of this Guide illustrates, Jussawalla would later support Rushdie.) In a number of different articles, Jussawalla very usefully outlines both the novel's formal qualities, and its potentially offensive aspects. For Jussawalla, however, *The Satanic Verses* 'is less an exploration of artistic techniques than a cover for political or racial attitudes that the author holds.'[50] Jussawalla concludes by describing *The Satanic Verses* as a pre-meditated attempt to curry favour with the Western, particularly American, literary establishment.

Most academics, however, supported Rushdie. Edward Said, for example, called for a more tolerant response to *The Satanic Verses*, arguing: 'To dispute with him, to engage with his work does not, cannot, be the same thing either as banning it or threatening him with violence and physical punishment.'[51] Rushdie himself offered a defence of his novel in his now famous essay, 'In Good Faith'. In the following extract from this essay, Rushdie appears at first to adopt a somewhat conciliatory tone. Yet as the essay progresses, he becomes noticeably firmer in his resolve as he outlines the manner in which *The Satanic Verses*, and the controversy that surrounded its publication, was appropriated and manipulated for political purposes.

■ I set out to explore, through the process of fiction, the nature of revelation and the power of faith. The mystical, revelatory experience is quite clearly a genuine one. This statement poses a problem to the non-believer: if we accept that the mystic, the prophet, is sincerely undergoing some sort of transcendent experience, but we cannot believe in a supernatural world, then *what is going on?* To answer this question, among others, I began work on the story of 'Mahound'. I was aware that the 'satanic verse' incident is much disputed by Muslim theologians; that the life of Muhammad has become the object of a kind of veneration that some would consider un-Islamic, since Muhammad himself always insisted that he was merely a messenger, an ordinary man; and that, therefore, great sensitivities were involved. I genuinely believed that my overt use of fabulation would make it clear to any reader that I was not attempting to falsify history, but to allow a fiction to take off from history. The use of dreams, fantasy, etc. was intended to say: the point is not whether this is 'really' supposed to be Muhammad, or whether the satanic verses incident 'really' happened; the point is to examine what such an incident might reveal about what revelation is, about the extent to which the mystic's conscious personality informs and interacts with the mystical event; the point is to try and understand the human event of revelation. The use of fiction was a way of creating the sort of distance from actuality that I felt would prevent offence from being taken. I was wrong.

Jahilia, to use once again the ancient Arab story-tellers' formula I used often in *The Satanic Verses,* both 'is and is not' Mecca. Many of the details of its social life are drawn from historical research; but it is also a dream of an Indian city (its concentric street-plan deliberately recalls New Delhi), and, as Gibreel spends time in England, it becomes a dream of London, too. Likewise, the religion of 'Submission' both is and is not Islam. Fiction uses facts as a starting-place and then spirals away to explore its real concerns, which are only tangentially historical. Not to see this, to treat fiction as if it were fact, is to make a serious mistake of categories. The case of *The Satanic Verses* may be one of the biggest category mistakes in literary history.

Here is more of what I knew: I knew that stories of Muhammad's doubts, uncertainties, errors, fondness for women abound in and around Muslim tradition. To me, they seemed to make him more vivid, more human, and therefore more interesting, even more worthy of admiration. The greatest human beings must struggle against themselves as well as the world. I never doubted Muhammad's greatness, nor, I believe, is the 'Mahound' of my novel belittled by being portrayed as human.

I knew that Islam is by no means homogeneous, or as absolutist as some of its champions make it out to be. Islam contains the doubts of Iqbal, Ghazali, Khayyám as well as the narrow certainties of Shabbir Akhtar of the Bradford Council of Mosques and Kalim Siddiqui, director of the pro-Iranian Muslim Institute. Islam contains ribaldry as well as solemnity, irreverence as well as absolutism. I knew much about

Islam that I admired, and still admire, immensely; I also knew that Islam, like all the world's great religions, had seen terrible things done in its name.

The original incident on which the dream of the villagers who drown in the Arabian Sea is based is also a part of what I 'knew'. The story awed me, because of what it told me about the huge power of faith. I wrote this part of the novel to see if I could understand, by getting inside their skins, people for whom devotion was as great as this.

He did it on purpose is one of the strangest accusations ever levelled at a writer. Of course I did it on purpose. The question is, and it is what I have tried to answer: what is the 'it' that I did?

What I did not do was conspire against Islam; or write – after years and years of anti-racist work and writing – a text of incitement to racial hatred; or anything of the sort. My golem, my false Other, may be capable of such deeds, but I am not.

Would I have written differently if I had known what would happen? Truthfully, I don't know. Would I change any of the text now? I would not. It's too late. As Friedrich Dürrenmatt wrote in *The Physicists*: 'What has once been thought cannot be unthought.'

The controversy over *The Satanic Verses* needs to be looked at as a political event, not purely a theological one. In India, where the trouble started, the Muslim fundamentalist MP Syed Shahabuddin used my novel as a stick with which to threaten the wobbling Rajiv Gandhi government. The demand for the book's banning was a power-play to demonstrate the strength of the Muslim vote, on which Congress has traditionally relied and which it could ill afford to lose. (In spite of the ban, Congress lost the Muslims and the election anyway. Put not your trust in Shahabuddins.)

In South Africa the row over the book served the purpose of the regime by driving a wedge between the Muslim and non-Muslim members of the UDF. In Pakistan, it was a way for the fundamentalists to try and regain the political initiative after their trouncing in the general election. In Iran, too, the incident could only be properly understood when seen in the context of the country's internal political struggles. And in Britain, where secular and religious leaders had been vying for power in the community for over a decade, and where, for a long time, largely secular organizations such as the Indian Workers Association (IWA) had been in the ascendant, the 'affair' swung the balance of power back towards the mosques. Small wonder, then, that the various councils of mosques are reluctant to bring the protest to an end, even though many Muslims up and down the country find it embarrassing, even shameful, to be associated with such illiberalism and violence.

The responsibility for violence lies with those who perpetrate it. In the past twelve months, bookshop workers have been manhandled, spat upon, verbally abused, bookshop premises have been threatened and, on several occasions, actually firebombed. Publishing staff have had to face a campaign of hate mail, menacing phone calls, death threats and bomb scares. Demonstrations have, on occasion, turned violent, too. During the big march in London last summer, peaceful counter-demonstrations on behalf of humanism and secularism were knocked to the ground by marchers, and a counter-demo by the courageous (and largely Muslim) Women Against Fundamentalism group was threatened and abused.

There is no conceivable reason why such behaviour should be privileged because it is done in the name of an affronted religion. If we are to talk about 'insults', 'abuse', 'offence', then the campaign against *The Satanic Verses* has been, very often, as insulting, abusive and offensive as it's possible to be.

As a result, racist attitudes have hardened. I did not invent British racism, nor did *The Satanic Verses*. The Commission for Racial Equality (CRE), which now accuses me of harming race relations, knows that for years it lent out my video-taped anti-racist Channel 4 broadcast to all sorts of black and white groups and seminars. Readers of *The Satanic Verses* will not be able to help noticing its extremely strong anti-racist line. I have never given the least comfort or encouragement to racists; but the leaders of the campaign against me certainly have, by reinforcing the worst racist stereotypes of Muslims as repressive, anti-liberal, censoring zealots. If Norman Tebbit has taken up the old Powellite refrains and if his laments about the multi-cultural society find favour in the land, then a part of the responsibility at least must be laid at the door of those who burn, and would ban, books.

I am not the first writer to be persecuted by Islamic fundamentalism in the modern period; among the greatest names so victimized are the Iranian writer Ahmad Kasravi, stabbed to death by fanatics, and the Egyptian Nobel laureate Naguib Mahfouz, often threatened but still, happily, with us. I am not the first artist to be accused of blasphemy and apostasy; these are, in fact, probably the most common weapons with which fundamentalism has sought to shackle creativity in the modern age. It is sad, then, that so little attention has been paid to this crucial literary context; and that Western critics like John Berger, who once spoke messianically of the need for new ways of seeing should now express their willingness to privilege one such way over another, to protect a religion boasting one billion believers from the solitary figure of a single writer brandishing an 'unreadable' book.

As for the British Muslim 'leaders', they cannot have it both ways. Sometimes they say I am entirely unimportant, and only the book matters; on other days they hold meetings at mosques across the nation and endorse the call for my killing. They say they hold to the laws of this country, but they also say that Islamic law has moral primacy for them. They say they do not wish to break British laws, but only a very few are willing openly to repudiate the threat against me. They should make their position clear; are they democratic citizens of a free society or are they not? Do they reject violence or do they not?

After a year, it is time for a little clarity.

To the Muslim community at large, in Britain and India and Pakistan and everywhere else, I would like to say: do not ask your writers to create *typical or representative* fictions. Such books are almost invariably dead books. The liveliness of literature lies in its exceptionality, in being the individual, idiosyncratic vision of one human being, in which, to our delight and great surprise, we may find our own image reflected. A book is a version of the world. If you do not like it, ignore it; or offer your own version in return.

And I would like to say this: life without God seems to believers to be an idiocy, pointless, beneath contempt. It does not seem so to non-believers. To accept that the world, here, is all there is; to go through it, towards and into death, without the consolations of religion seems, well, at least as courageous and rigorous to us as the espousal of faith seems to you. Secularism and its work deserve your respect, not your contempt.

A great wave of freedom has been washing over the world. Those who resist – in China, in Romania – find themselves bathed in blood. I should like to ask Muslims – that great mass of ordinary, decent, fair-minded Muslims to whom I have imagined myself to be speaking for most of this piece – to choose to ride the wave; to renounce blood; not to let Muslim leaders make Muslims seem less tolerant than they are. *The Satanic Verses* is a serious work, written from a non-believer's point of view. Let believers accept that, and let it be. [. . .]

Do I feel regret? Of course I do: regret that such offence has been taken against my work when it was not intended – when dispute was intended, and dissent, and even, at times, satire, and criticism of intolerance, and the like, but not the thing of which I'm most often accused, not 'filth', not 'insult', not 'abuse'. I regret that so many people who might have taken pleasure in finding their reality given pride of place in a novel will now not read it because of what they believe it to be, or will come to it with their minds already made up.

And I feel sad to be so grievously separated from my community, from India, from everyday life, from the world.

Please understand, however: I make no complaint. I am a writer. I do not accept my condition. I will strive to change it; but I inhabit it, I am trying to learn from it.

Our lives teach us who we are.[52] ☐

Rushdie's expectation that readers of *The Satanic Verses* would adopt a 'literary' approach to his novel, and thereby avoid attributing offence, has been examined by a number of critics. As early as 1984, Keith Wilson was making just this point in his reading of *Midnight's Children* when he suggested that Rushdie enters into a 'participatory' contract with his readers, 'a contract premised on the reader's knowledge of the conventions and deceptions of the narrative act'.[53] In the final article of this Guide, K.M. Newton interrogates this suggestion in the light of the 'Rushdie Affair'. In doing so, Newton is clearly attempting to return discussion of *The Satanic Verses* to the realm of literary debate.

■ Does literary theory have anything to contribute to the Salman Rushdie affair? Up to now the conflict between him and his opponents has been discussed mainly in terms of such issues as free speech and free expression, but on its own the freedom question is not likely to have much impact on Muslim opinion. Muslims can easily point to anomalies and contradictions in the arguments of defenders of the right to free speech and free expression. For example, the fact that there is a law against blasphemy in this country which applies only to Christianity, even if it is almost never enforced, would appear to discriminate unfavourably against the Islamic religion. One also sees free expression curtailed in other areas without protest, a point made forcibly by a Rushdie supporter, Kathy Acker:

> Most of the western writers who have discussed the issues around *The Satanic Verses* have proclaimed, as writers and artists, their right to 'freedom of speech'. (A freedom not publicly applauded when the matter in hand isn't anti-Muslim, if that's what *The Satanic Verses* is, but is rather anti-Zionist, and, as in the case of Jean Genet's final book, pornographic, etc.)[54]

It may, therefore, be more productive to shift the ground from freedom of expression to the question of reading. Rushdie himself has moved the debate into this area: whereas Muslim readers interpret certain passages in *The Satanic Verses* as blasphemous Rushdie has asserted that this is an inappropriate way of reading the novel since it is a work of art and should not be read in such a literal manner. In his essay 'In Good Faith' he says that the novel 'aspires to the condition of literature' and that 'people on all sides of the argument have lost sight of this fact'.[55] He rejects the view that the novel is deliberately offensive to Muslims as this is to ignore its literary aspect: 'It has been bewildering to learn that people *do not care about art*' (p.397). Is it possible to demonstrate convincingly that Muslim interpreters of the novel are guilty of misreading or are they justified in reading the novel as they do? Though literary theory may have little or no direct influence on fanatics who are determined to kill Rushdie, it surely has a responsibility to attempt to resolve or at least to clarify the issues that are at stake in this conflict since clearly they have wide and important ramifications.

It may be useful to compare the conflict between Rushdie and Muslim readers as to how *The Satanic Verses* should be read with a dispute about reading between M.H. Abrams and J. Hillis Miller in regard to Wordsworth's lyric 'A Slumber Did My Spirit Seal'. In an essay called 'Construing and Deconstructing', Abrams attacked Miller's deconstructive reading of the poem as an 'over-reading' and advocated a return to 'construing' the plain meaning of the poem.[56] Miller replied as follows to Abrams's critique of his reading:

> The major misunderstanding in Abrams' essay might be approached by way of his title, 'Construing and Deconstructing'. If these two terms are translated into their more traditional equivalents, Abrams' title would be 'Grammar and Rhetoric' . . . Abrams' error is the aboriginal one of assuming that the grammar of a language . . . is a first and fundamental level of easily identifiable meaning to which figurative language, the deviant realm of tropes, is added as a nonessential layer open to what Abrams, in a nice little play of double meaning of his own, calls 'over-reading'. First there is under-reading, or the construing of plain grammar, and then, if you happen to want it (though why should you?) there is over-reading, the interpretation of figures, what is sometimes called deconstruction.

Miller goes on to argue that 'All good reading is . . . the reading of tropes at the same time as it is the construing of syntactical and grammatical patterns' and that 'there is no such thing as that plain under-reading which Abrams hypothesizes'.[57]

Using this model, Muslim readers of *The Satanic Verses* may be seen as 'under-readers' of the text who take the words on the page literally whereas Rushdie could claim that his text requires 'over-readers'. Another way of putting this is to say that Muslim readers read the text 'grammatically' whereas the text requires that one looks beyond the grammatical or literal to the rhetorical or the figurative. On the face of it, then, if one accepts Miller's argument, one can accuse Muslim interpreters of Rushdie's text of misreading it because they restrict its meaning to the grammatical level and refuse to recognise its more powerful rhetorical or figurative dimension. Rushdie himself, in defending the novel against Muslim attacks on it, has emphasised its figurative nature. The passages that have particularly offended

Muslims do not aim 'to vilify or "disprove" Islam, but . . . portray a soul in crisis' (p. 397); a reference to 'Salman the Persian' is not intended to 'insult and abuse' the Prophet's companion Salman al-Faris but is rather 'an ironic reference to the novel's author' (p. 399). Rushdie claims that 'such highlighting is a proper function of literature' (p. 400). Similarly, the 'shocking' representations of the Prophet's wives as whores are not to be taken literally but rather as images which juxtapose antithetically 'the sacred and profane worlds' (p. 401).

However, one difficulty of this parallel is that such an eminent critic as M. H. Abrams, if one accepts Miller's characterisation of him as an 'under-reader', becomes implicitly an ally of Muslim readers of *The Satanic Verses*, and one could find numerous critics who would much prefer to 'under-read' Wordsworth in the manner of Abrams than to 'over-read' him in the manner of Miller. Miller's dismissal of under-reading and his claim that 'There is only and always, from the beginning, one form or another of over-reading, the reading of grammar and tropes together, more or less adequately'[58] may therefore do the Rushdie case more harm than good unless we explore the issue further.

Now of course one cannot say that reading 'grammatically' without taking account of the rhetorical or figurative is wrong in itself. In most forms of discourse 'under-reading' is quite adequate to serve our normal purposes. Indeed to attempt to read all texts rhetorically would be absurd. But though it may be pragmatically necessary to restrict certain discourses to the level of the grammatical, this does not mean that Miller is wrong to assert that the rhetorical dimension can never be excluded from any text. A motorist who interprets a 'Keep Left' road-sign figuratively as a political slogan may find himself or herself in practical difficulties but this does not mean that the language of the text is not open to such a reading. Rather, pragmatic considerations demand that road-signs be restricted to a grammatical or literal interpretation with any possible rhetorical dimension of the text being ignored. Miller would not, I feel sure, deny this. His claim that good reading demands that the rhetorical have priority over the grammatical implicitly applies only to certain forms of discourse, most obviously literature. Nor, surely, would Abrams deny that rhetoric is crucial in any reading of a literary text; his difference with Miller is about how far one should go in interpreting literature rhetorically. Both Miller and Abrams would almost certainly agree that a rigidly grammatical reading of a literary text that ignored its rhetorical aspect was inadequate. Rushdie therefore, if *The Satanic Verses* is recognised as a work of literature, would be likely to have the backing of both in the conflict.

On the face of it, literary theory would appear to be on the side of

Rushdie since it can provide support for the view that the language of literary texts cannot be read in a straightforward, 'grammatical' manner. Certainly the claim that *The Satanic Verses* is a work of art and therefore a literary text is central to Rushdie's strategy in his fight against his opponents, and he continually asserts in speeches and interviews that the text has to be read as such. What Rushdie can be interpreted as asserting is that his novel is not open to accusations of blasphemy since in art or literature the figurative necessarily dominates. One could illustrate how such a view may affect reading by considering a canonical literary text, *Richard III* [*c.* 1593] which could also be accused of bias and factual inaccuracy. The question as to whether the historical Richard was in fact the psychopathic monster and murderer Shakespeare depicts him as being could be seen as irrelevant in any consideration of the play as a work of art. Read as a literary text, it may be argued, the play does not operate on such a factual or literal plane and anyone who condemned it on these grounds would be responding wrongly to it. Even if convincing documentary evidence emerged which indicated that Richard had not been responsible for the murder of the princes in the Tower, this would not undermine the power or interest of the play as a work of literature. Similarly, Muslim readers of *The Satanic Verses* who condemn it for its representation of the Prophet are like those who would condemn *Richard III* because they regard it as presenting a historically false picture of Richard. Both sets of readers are guilty of a category mistake: they respond inappropriately to literary discourse. [. . .]

However, it is too early to conclude that literary theory will help Rushdie win the conflict with his Muslim opponents, for his strategy of claiming literary status for his text is not without its dangers. A Muslim opponent familiar with literary theory might question whether Rushdie has the right to claim that his text is a work of art or literature and in consequence exists beyond the scope of grammatical readings. Can Rushdie as author unilaterally consign his text to the category of art or literature? John M. Ellis in his book *The Theory of Literary Criticism* argues that the term 'literature' denotes a special group of texts which are open to a distinctive form of reading: 'Literary texts are not treated as part of the normal flow of speech, which has a purpose in its original context and is then discarded after that purpose is achieved, and they are not judged according to such limited purposes'.[59] In practical terms this means that the figurative dimension assumes predominance in texts categorised as literary, enabling such texts to break with grammatical or literal signification. But Ellis also claims that the most that the author of a text that aspires to be literature can do is to offer it to the community as a literary text. It is up to the community to decide whether or not the text in question deserves to have this privileged status. The author has no power to make the community accept a particular text as literature. Until such acceptance is accorded by the community at large, it could be persuasively argued, it is legitimate to deny that the figurative dimension of the text has an intrinsic priority over the grammatical dimension.

Furthermore, even if a consensus of non-Muslims emerges which claims that the novel deserves to be categorised as a work of literature, it is still doubtful whether Rushdie's Muslim opponents would accept that such a judgement was made in good faith and not mere special pleading. Non-Muslims, it could be reasonably claimed, who support Rushdie in asserting that the text has to be accorded literary status are not expressing a disinterested literary judgement but are ideologically motivated by their desire to protect Western values of free speech and free expression from attack. But more interestingly, Muslims might also argue with some justification that the main reason that non-Muslim readers may find no difficulty in going beyond the grammatical aspect of the text to the figurative is simply a consequence of the fact that they don't care whether or not its representation of the life of the Prophet is an insult to the Muslim religion. If they did care might they not be less ready to accord the text the privileged status of art or literature? When Rolf Hochhuth's play *The Soldiers* [1967], which depicts Churchill as being responsible for the murder of a Polish politician, was first produced in London and was attacked as libellous, Kenneth Tynan defended the play by arguing that it was no different from *Richard III*. Tynan asserted that since theatre-goers did not reject the latter because it presented Richard as a criminal psychopath even though the historical evidence suggests that he was not, why should they refuse to accept Hochhuth's representation of Churchill as murderer? Both plays belonged to the category of art, Tynan implied, and therefore the figurative had priority over the literal or grammatical. But clearly the difference was that whereas in the case of Richard audiences had ceased to care about the historical figure, with Churchill they still did care and this made it difficult for audiences to respond to the play as a figurative representation, as they could with regard to Richard. The grammatical or literal thus had the greater power with the result that the play had to be taken off. Muslim opponents of Rushdie could exploit such cases in order to claim that the only difference between them and non-Muslim readers of *The Satanic Verses* is that they cannot be indifferent to Rushdie's depiction of the Prophet; the literal force of the text is too strong for them to set it aside in favour of the figurative.

It seems to me, therefore, that though it is understandable that Rushdie should attempt to counter Muslim attacks on the novel by claiming that it has to be interpreted as a work of art or literature in which the figurative has priority, this strategy will not be successful and indeed it may be counter-productive since Muslim readers, as I have suggested, have reasonable grounds for rejecting such a claim. However, even more worrying for defenders of Rushdie is the fact that contemporary critical theory casts doubt on the view that even in literary texts the figurative or rhetorical should have priority over the grammatical or literal.

J. Hillis Miller, in his discussion of the relation between grammar and rhetoric in literature, has almost certainly been influenced by Paul de Man's essay on this subject, 'Semiology and Rhetoric'. De Man, like Miller, sees rhetoric as crucial to any understanding of literature and states that he 'would not hesitate to equate the rhetorical, figural potentiality of language with literature itself'.[60] Yet there is a difference in emphasis between their views. Whereas for Miller the grammar and rhetoric of a text must be read together, with rhetoric having priority in literary texts at least, de Man rather places the greatest emphasis on the fact that neither the grammatical nor the rhetorical has intrinsic priority in either literary or non-literary texts. Indeed, he states that even in literary texts, literal meaning cannot be effaced by figurative meaning, as he shows in an analysis of Yeats's line from 'Among School Children', 'How can we know the dancer from the dance?' In de Man's view the meaning generated by neither the grammatical nor the rhetorical can totally prevail since the line can be read either as an ordinary question inviting an answer or as a rhetorical question, and this creates an undecidability of meaning which for him is characteristic of texts that deserve to be called literary. De Man thus stresses the irreconcilability of grammar and rhetoric, not, like Miller, the necessity of reading them together.

It would seem to follow from the de Man essay that the literal dimension even of literary texts cannot be set aside in favour of the figurative. If he is right then clearly the Muslim literal reading of *The Satanic Verses* cannot merely be dismissed as the consequence of a category mistake. And further, if one denies that *The Satanic Verses* is a work of literature or believes that it is too early to assign it such a status why should the figurative be accorded the greater force than the literal? Why should one accept the author's view that the text has to be read figuratively? Thus de Man's treatment of the grammar–rhetoric relation offers little protection to Rushdie in his conflict with Muslim readers.

One can also argue from a different point of view that it is impossible with any text, literary or non-literary, to assign priority either to the figurative or the literal. To claim intrinsic superiority for one method of reading is to essentialise reading since no account is taken of the social and cultural factors that necessarily have a determining influence on the construction of the reader and the reading process. The reader is not an abstract entity but a social and cultural product, and the particular methods of reading that are practised at a particular period cannot be seen in isolation from social, cultural and political forces. This is true both for methods of reading that are predominantly grammatical or rhetorical and also for de Manian deconstructive methods which play off the grammatical and the rhetorical. It would be easy, for example, to construct a social explanation as to why deconstruction was such a force during the 1970s and similarly explain why its power has greatly diminished in the past decade. Since social or cultural factors will have a determining influence on whether the grammatical, the figurative, or the deconstructive will tend to have greater force as a reading method at any particular historical moment, one cannot therefore categorically state that one method of reading is intrinsically superior to another. To adopt such a view is to assume that reading can be abstracted from the cultural situation within which all reading must take place.

Clearly, for devout Muslims it is virtually impossible for a text such as *The Satanic Verses* to be read in such a way that figurative meanings stand in place of the literal meaning of the text; the text is so offensive to them that the figurative dimension has little if any force. But there have been circumstances in which the rhetorical has seemed to dominate the grammatical with a similar degree of power for readers at particular periods. For example, for people under occupation or living in totalitarian states it is well known that certain literary texts when taken figuratively have such relevance to their cultural situation that the literal force of the language of the text is virtually abolished in favour of meanings produced by metaphorical or allegorical forms of reading. Modern productions of classic drama have tended similarly to exploit the figural in an effort to make such texts as directly meaningful as possible to a twentieth-century audience. There seems to me to be no justification for judging modes of reading that emphasise either the grammatical or the figurative as invalid in an intrinsic sense, as critics such as Abrams and Miller seem inclined to do. One cannot separate reading from the interests which govern it and from the cultural situations which shape those interests.

But perhaps what makes Rushdie's defence of *The Satanic Verses* as a literary text that must be read figuratively particularly problematic at the present time is that recent literary theory has seen a decided shift from the view that the figurative should be predominant in the reading of literary texts. The Rushdie position relies implicitly on a critical ideology which the most influential contemporary critical theory has rejected. The major tendency of critical theory over the last ten years or so has favoured a theorised and politicised historical criticism which contends that literature is not a discourse in which the figurative has an independent force that has priority over the grammatical but that even the works of a writer as canonic as Shakespeare must be read contextually and politically in a very specific sense. John M. Ellis's view that literary texts 'are defined as those that outgrow the original context of their utterance' and 'are not dependent on that context for meaning'[61] is rejected. For example, Jean E. Howard and Marion F. O'Connor describe as follows how such a critical approach deals with Shakespeare:

> By a political analysis we mean one which examines how Shakespearean texts have functioned to produce, reproduce, or contest historically specific relations of power . . . [The text] lives in history, with history itself understood as a field of contestation . . . [T]o posit a category of self-evidently literary works, somehow above ideology, is to ignore the historicity of the very category of the literary . . . [62]

Rushdie, in contrast, views literature as anti-ideological:

> If religion is an answer, if political ideology is an answer, then literature is an inquiry; great literature, by asking extraordinary questions, opens doors in our minds . . . [L]iterature is, of all the arts, the one best suited to challenging absolutes of all kinds. (pp. 423–4)

It would be a distortion to say that this new historical criticism rejects the rhetorical meaning of texts in favour of their grammatical meaning. In many respects this form of criticism is highly rhetorical in that it introduces into criticism a complex intertextuality founded on the belief that texts do not exist in isolation. As Stephen Greenblatt has put it, the aim of new historical criticism is to investigate 'both the social presence to the world of the literary text and the social presence of the world in the literary text'.[63] But one can argue that the aim of situating literary texts in their historical contexts is fundamentally grammatical in that their contemporary meaning is recovered and interpretations which exploit the figurative language of texts in order to read them in a more universal human context are attacked. Thus a critic such as Jonathan Dollimore, in discussing *King Lear* [*c.* 1604–6], rejects interpretations of the play which read it metaphorically as being about human nature or the human condition and insists on reading the play in relation to ideological issues in the Jacobean period. He dismisses readings which emphasise general humanist themes in favour of a reading which emphasises power and property within specific material conditions.[64]

Earlier I used *Richard III* as an example in discussing the view that a text had to be divorced from questions of historical fact, or the grammatical, in order to function as a literary text, so that those who attacked or condemned it on the grounds of perpetrating lies about Richard would not be treating it as a literary text but merely as an ordinary speech act. New historical criticism would take a different view. If there existed contemporary attacks on the play – for being, for example, a blatant piece of Tudor propaganda which employed lies and character assassination for political purposes – these could not be dismissed, new historical critics would surely argue, as anti-literary for they would show that literature does not exist outside of ideology but rather that the text lives in history as a 'field of contestation', as Howard and O'Connor put it. Critics who would take such a view can hardly therefore deny the legitimacy of the Muslim response to *The Satanic Verses*. Indeed from such a critical perspective is the Muslim way of reading the text not preferable to attempts to defend the text as a work of literature whose metaphorical force enables it to communicate in a more universal human context since the Muslim response in effect refuses to accept that the novel is a text which is beyond ideology?

If one were discussing a classic literary text, such as a play by Shakespeare, there would be no difficulty in accepting that the text can be read in different ways, depending on the interests and critical outlook of the reader or interpreter of the text, even though there may be great debate as to which critical approach is most valid. Such literary texts can be read figuratively, that is as texts which have transcended their originating contexts, grammatically as texts which participate in the ideological struggles of their historical moment, hermeneutically as texts in which there is a 'fusion of horizons' between the originating context and the situation of the modern reader, or deconstructively as texts in which there is an undecidable play of meaning between the rhetorical and the grammatical. But when it comes to discussing contemporary works such as *The Satanic Verses*, a novel whose literary status is still undecided, the grammatical critical perspective is surely the most powerful. In a hundred years time, if the work has been accorded literary status, it will no doubt be possible to read it figuratively or outside of any specific ideological or political context but such a reading hardly seems possible at present. The Muslim literal reading of the text refuses to accept figurative meanings that allow it to communicate in a wider human context and is therefore a form of grammatical reading, and in the present critical climate how can it be said to be illegitimate?

In a recent essay [published in 1991] Alan Sinfield writes:

The traditional goal of literary study assumed an essential humanity, informing both text and critic . . . It is now easy to see that this reading position was in fact that of the discourse of literary criticism, and that teaching amounted to persuading people who were attached to other discourses to abandon them and adopt ours. If a lower-class person, woman, student, person of colour, lesbian or gay man did not 'respond' to 'the text', we thought it was because they were reading partially, wrongly . . . We believed they – we – became fuller human beings. Perhaps we did; but it was at the expense of abandoning subcultural allegiances. The profession requires you to read not as a homosexual or a Black, but in accordance with its established criteria.[65]

Sinfield goes on to urge that academics 'should seek ways to break out of the professional subculture and work intellectually in dissident subcultures'.[66] This view has a powerful appeal but one should face the fact that there is no logical reason why 'Muslim fundamentalist' should not be added to Sinfield's list of 'lower-class person, woman, student, person of colour, lesbian or gay man'. Probably a majority of contemporary literary theorists would accept Sinfield's position, but how can they then avoid, as a consequence, supporting the Muslim point of view in *The Satanic Verses* debate?

If, as I have suggested, one can defend the Muslim reaction to *The Satanic Verses* by using arguments derived from de Manian deconstruction or new historical criticism, why then have contemporary theorists not registered their support of the right of Muslims to respond to the text in the way they do or indicated their disagreement with Rushdie's claim that the text's literary aspirations render such a reading invalid? Obviously literary theorists must sympathise with Rushdie's situation and do not therefore wish to be seen as offering support to his enemies. But though it is understandable that literary theorists do not want to make Rushdie's situation any worse than it is, it seems to me to be a mistake for literary theory to keep silent on this subject. Not only would it be morally wrong to withhold support from the Muslim manner of reading *The Satanic Verses* if it is more defensible than the claim that it has a protected literary status but, even more important, non-Muslims' untheorised partiality for the Rushdie case may have made matters worse. Not only do non-Muslim supporters of Rushdie proclaim that Muslims are wrong in seeking to have a book banned, a view I share, but more significantly they also appear to suggest that Muslims have no right even to find the book offensive since they are reading the text in an improper fashion. Thus Malise Ruthven in his book *A Satanic Affair* has no sympathy with a Muslim who believes in regard to *The Satanic Verses* that 'certain words have a certain plain meaning' and who is offended 'that lies should be propagated' because 'Islam stands for the propagation of truth'. For Ruthven this Muslim 'had a naïve, unscientific view of what was essentially a literary question' and he goes on to assert that

> fundamentalism . . . is hard, factualistic and philistine, impervious to the multilayered nuances of meaning that reside in texts, in fictions, in music and iconographies, in the cells of art and culture where modernity – that universal modernity created by a vibrant, still dynamic 'West' – stores its spiritual wealth.[67]

Literary critics and theorists would, I believe, make a positive contribution to the Rushdie affair if they openly admitted that Muslim readers are justified in finding *The Satanic Verses* offensive. To argue that the novel is a work of literature and therefore incapable of giving offence is not a view that it is reasonable to expect Muslim readers of the work to accept and, as I have suggested above, it is a view that many contemporary literary theorists would also, rightly I believe, reject. Instead of being urged to tolerate *The Satanic Verses* or to accord it the privileged status of literature, Muslim readers should rather be encouraged by literary critics and theorists to enter into debate with the book, to answer back as vigorously as they wish. If literary critics and theorists had adopted this policy from the beginning then it is possible that Muslim anger with the novel may have taken a different form. But the lack of sympathy of non-Muslims for Muslim outrage with the book, together with explicit and implicit accusations that the Muslim response was primitive and philistine, only served to create a build-up of frustration among Muslims that has led to many British Muslims supporting the Ayatollah's 'fatwa'. It may be too late to do anything to defuse the situation. Nevertheless I think critics and theorists, however late in the day, should make an effort to redress this situation by acknowledging that the Muslim response to the text is, from the standpoint of contemporary literary theory, legitimate even if *The Satanic Verses* is a text which aspires to be literature, since literary texts cannot be dissociated from ideological struggles and conflicts of various sorts and thus necessarily provoke opposition. It follows from this that literary critics and theorists should offer their support to Muslims who enter into ideological or political debate with the novel and consequently go beyond mere attack and condemnation. To be fair to Rushdie, despite his efforts to have the novel read figuratively in the manner of literary texts as he conceives them, he accepts that his opponents have the right to enter into dispute with the novel 'with the utmost passion' (p. 393).

What the Rushdie affair clearly demonstrates is that both Muslims and those who have inherited Western values need to make an effort to resist strong forces within their different traditions and should be prepared to enter into a dialogic relation with difference. This would help promote compromise rather than intolerance and conflict. Muslims, especially those who now reside in Western countries, have to strive to come to a *modus vivendi* with European Enlightenment values, especially the latter's encouragement of scepticism and critique. But inheritors of Western values should also learn to view works of art in a less idealistic spirit. The Romantic tradition encouraged the tendency to set works of art on a pedestal, as in Keats's 'What the imagination seizes as Beauty must be truth', and this valorisation of the work of art has continued in the twentieth century in such critical movements as the New Criticism and Leavisism. Thus Rushdie's appeal to art tends to have considerable force for the Western consciousness. In the debate over *The Satanic Verses*, however, the pressure has been almost entirely on Muslims to modify their position, but there is much more likelihood of persuading Muslims to do this if there is a corresponding modification in Western attitudes. If both sides could recognise the necessity for such a spirit of compromise then a more positive outcome to an apparently intractable conflict may still be possible.[68] □

Newton's point is well argued. Although the 'spirit of compromise' he argues for is not yet fully realised, the anger and violence of the 'Rushdie Affair' has receded. In September 1998, the Iranian government released a statement lifting the death threat to Rushdie's life. The fatwa itself, however, cannot be withdrawn. According to Islamic law, the only person with the authority to lift a fatwa is the person who issued it, and Ayatollah Khomeini died shortly after proclaiming Rushdie's sentence. Though some degree of threat remains, Rushdie has now returned to public life. The politics surrounding Rushdie's writing should not be forgotten. Yet, as this Guide illustrates, relocating his works within the realm of literary debate not only allows the literary merits of novels such as *Midnight's Children* and *The Satanic Verses* to be acknowledged, but also provides the necessary illumination for a full and intelligent understanding of the politics of Rushdie's writing.

NOTES

INTRODUCTION

1 Liz Calder, quoted in Ian Hamilton, 'The First Life of Salman Rushdie', *The New Yorker*, 25 December 1995–1 January 1996, p. 101.

2 Ian Hamilton, p. 101.

3 John Haffenden, *Novelists in Interview*, London: Methuen, 1985, p. 246.

4 John Haffenden, p. 246.

5 John Haffenden, p. 246.

6 In June 1975, Indira Gandhi was convicted of corrupt practices during her 1971 election campaign. Faced with the loss of her parliamentary seat, she declared a state of emergency. In an attempt to demonstrate popular support, a general election was called in 1977. Not only did Indira Gandhi lose her parliamentary seat, but also her Congress Party failed to retain power. The leader of the newly elected Janata Party, Morarji R. Desai, ended the Emergency period.

7 For an example of this position, see Philip Howard, 'Big Book on India Wins Booker Again', *The Times*, 21 October 1981, p. 1. For a more sophisticated treatment of this perspective see Maria Couto, '*Midnight's Children* and Parents: The Search for Indo-British Identity', *Encounter*, vol. 58, no. 2, 1982, pp. 61–6.

8 Salman Rushdie, '"Commonwealth Literature" Does Not Exist', *Imaginary Homelands: Essays and Criticism 1981–1991*, London: Granta Books, 1991, p. 70.

9 Salman Rushdie, 'Essays: Günter Grass', *Imaginary Homelands*, p. 277.

10 Ian Hamilton, p. 105.

11 John Haffenden, p. 240.

12 Ian Hamilton, p. 112.

CHAPTER ONE

1 Discussed in Lindsay Mackie, 'Indian wins the Booker', *The Guardian*, 21 October 1981, p. 1.

2 Valentine Cunningham, 'Nosing out the Indian Reality', *Times Literary Supplement*, 15 May 1981, p. 535.

3 Anita Desai, 'An Oriental Fantasy', *The Book Review*, vol. 6, no. 1, 1981, pp. 32–6. For an earlier version of this review see Anita Desai, 'Where Cultures Clash by Night', *The Washington Post*, vol. 11, no. 11, 15 March 1981, pp. 1, 13.

4 A copy of Rushdie's review of Desai's novel *In Custody* (1984) can be found in Salman Rushdie, *Imaginary Homelands: Essays and Criticism 1981–1991*, London: Granta Books, 1991, pp. 71–2.

5 Anita Desai, 'An Oriental Fantasy', p. 32.

6 Anita Desai, 'An Oriental Fantasy', pp. 35–6.

7 Clark Blaise, 'A Novel Of India's Coming of Age', *The New York Times Book Review*, 19 April 1981, [pp. 1, 18–19] p. 1.

8 Michael T. Kaufman, 'Author from 3 Countries', *The New York Times Book Review*, 13 November 1983, p. 22.

9 Clark Blaise, p. 1.

10 Clark Blaise, p. 1.

11 Clark Blaise, p. 19.

12 Clark Blaise, p. 19.

13 Robert Taubman, 'Experiments with Truth', *London Review of Books*, vol. 3, no. 8, 1981, pp. 3, 5–6.

14 Robert Taubman, pp. 3, 5.

15 Robert Taubman, pp. 5–6.

16 Chandrabhanu Pattanayak, 'Interview with Salman Rushdie', *The Literary Criterion*, vol. 18, no. 3, 1983, p. 20.

17 Salman Rushdie, *Shame*, London: Pan Books, 1984, p. 70.

18 Salman Rushdie, 'The Riddle of Midnight: India, August 1987', *Imaginary Homelands*, p. 26.

19 S. Krishnan, '*Midnight's Children*: An un-Indian book about all things Indian', *Aside* (Madras), vol. 6, part 3, 1982, [pp. 51, 53] p. 53.

20 Aparna Mahanta, 'Allegories of the Indian Experience. The Novels of Salman Rushdie', *Economic and Political Weekly*, vol. 19, no. 6, 1984, pp. 244–7.

21 Aparna Mahanta, p. 244.

22 Gayatri Chakravorty Spivak, *In Other Worlds: Essays in Cultural Politics*, New York: Methuen, 1987, p. 256.

23 Edward Said, 'Intellectuals in the Post-Colonial World', *Salmagundi*, vol. 70–71, 1986, p. 53.

24 Aparna Mahanta, p. 244.

25 Aparna Mahanta, p. 244.

26 Aparna Mahanta, p. 244.

27 Aparna Mahanta, pp. 245, 247.

28 Though Rushdie was born in India, after the partition of India to form the independent states of India and Pakistan, most of his family moved to Pakistan.

29 Michael T. Kaufman, p. 23.

30 Michael T. Kaufman, p. 23.

31 Iain Sinclair, 'Imaginary Football Teams', *New Statesman & Society*, 30 September 1988, p. 40.

32 Angela Carter, quoted in Madhu Jain, 'Salman Rushdie: Satanic Storm', *India Today*, vol. 14, no. 5, 1989, p. 22.

33 Roger Woddis, 'The Satanic Verses Review', *New Statesman & Society*, 30 September 1988, p. 4.

34 Robert Irwin, 'Original Parables', *Times Literary Supplement*, 30 September–6 October 1988, p. 1067.

35 Patrick Parrinder, 'Let's get the hell out of here', *The London Review of Books*, 29 September 1988, p. 11.

36 Patrick Parrinder, p. 12.

37 Sean French, 'Falling Towards England', *The Observer*, 25 September 1988, p. 43.

38 Malise Ruthven, 'A question of identity', *The Tablet*, 3 December 1988, p. 1401.

39 Edward Said, 'Rushdie and the Whale', *The Observer*, 14 February 1989, p. 14.

40 Michael Dummett, quoted in Geoffrey Wheatcroft, 'Foreign Affairs: The Friends of Salman Rushdie', *The Atlantic Monthly*, vol. 273, no. 3, 1994, p. 30.

41 Madhu Jain, 'My Theme is Fanaticism', *India Today*, 15 September 1988, p. 98.

42 Madhu Jain, p. 99.

43 Salman Rushdie, *The Satanic Verses*, [1988], Delaware: The Consortium, 1992, p. 97.

44 Syed Ali Ashraf, 'Nihilistic, Negative, Satanic', *Impact International*, vol. 18, no. 20, 1988, pp. 16–17.

45 Jonathan Yardley, 'Wrestling With the Angel', The Washington Post, 29 January 1989, p. 3.

46 Salman Rushdie, 'Fact, faith and fiction', *Far Eastern Economic Review*, 2 March 1989, p. 11.

47 Interview: Salman Rushdie, 'Bonfire of the Certainties', *Bandung File*, Channel 4, 14 February 1989, 9 p.m.

48 Ralph Ellison, quoted by Susan Sontag in her testimony before the Subcommittee on International Terrorism, Senate Foreign Relations Committee, 8 March 1989. An extract from this testimony is contained in Lisa Appignanesi and Sara Maitland (eds), *The Rushdie File*, London: Fourth Estate, 1989, pp. 166–8.

49 John Leonard, 'Who Has the Best Tunes?' *The Nation*, vol. 248, no. 10, 1989, [pp. 346–9] pp. 346, 348.

50 John Leonard, p. 349.

51 Michael Wood, 'The Prophet Motive', *The New Republic*, 6 March 1989, pp. 29, 30.

CHAPTER TWO

1 Edward Said, 'Rushdie and the Whale', *The Observer*, 26 February 1989, p. 14.

2 Edward Said, p. 14.

3 Rudolf Bader, '*The Satanic Verses*: An Intercultural Experiment by Salman Rushdie', *The International Fiction Review*, vol. 19, no. 2, 1992, p. 66.

4 See Jonathan Culler, *The Pursuit of Signs: Semiotics, Literature, Deconstruction*, London: Routledge and Kegan Paul, 1981, p. 101.

5 Philip Engblom, 'A Multitude of Voices: Carnivalization and Dialogicality in the Novels of Salman Rushdie', in M. D. Fletcher (ed.), *Reading Rushdie: Perspectives on the Fiction of Salman Rushdie*, Amsterdam and Atlanta, GA: Rodopi, 1994, pp. 293–304.

6 Philip Engblom, p. 293. Engblom is referring to Rushdie's assertion that the English language is in need of 'decolonisation' – see Salman Rushdie, 'The Empire Writes Back', *The Times*, 3 July 1982, p. 8.

7 Philip Engblom, p. 293.

8 Salman Rushdie, 'In Good Faith', *Imaginary Homelands: Essays and Criticism 1981–1991*, London: Granta Books, 1991, p. 394.

9 Philip Engblom, p. 296.

10 Menippean satire is a term derived from the works of the third-century-BC philosopher and cynic, Menippus. Applied to both prose and poetry, Menippean satires employ elements of caricature, parody and burlesque to expose and deflate man's follies and self-important posturing. It is, however, usually less aggressive than those works we would usually call satires.

11 Mikhail Bakhtin, *Rabelais and his World*, Bloomington: Indiana University Press, 1984, p. 39.

12 Carlos Fuentes, *The Guardian*, 24 February 1989, pp. 29–30.

13 Engblom is referencing two editions of the text: Salman Rushdie, *Midnight's Children*, London: Jonathan Cape, 1981; New York: Avon, 1982. The Cape edition is referenced in *italics*.

14 [Engblom's note] Salman Rushdie, *The Satanic Verses*, New York: Viking, 1989, p. 243.

15 [Engblom's note] Salman Rushdie, 'In Good Faith: A Pen Against the Sword', *Newsweek*, 12 February 1990, pp. 52–4.

16 [Engblom's note] D.J. Enright, 'So and Not So', *New York Review of Books*, vol. 36, no. 3, 1989, p. 25.

17 Salman Rushdie, 'Imaginary Homelands', *London Review of Books*, vol. 4, no. 17, 1982, pp. 18–19.

18 Philip Engblom, p. 300–3.

19 Terry Eagleton, *Walter Benjamin: Towards a Revolutionary Criticism*, London: Verso, 1981, p. 148.

20 Patricia Merivale, 'Saleem Fathered by Oskar: Intertextual Strategies in *Midnight's Children* and *The Tin Drum*', *Ariel: A Review of International English Literature*, vol. 21, no. 3, 1990, pp. 5–21.

21 See, for example: Rudolf Bader, 'Indian Tin Drum', *International Fiction review*, vol. 11, no. 2, 1984, pp. 75–83; Timothy Brennan, *Salman Rushdie and the Third World: Myths of the Nation*, London: Macmillan, 1989; Kumkum Sangari, 'The Politics of the Possible', *Cultural Critique*, vol. 7, 1987, pp. 157–86.

22 Patricia Merivale, p. 5.

23 Salman Rushdie, *Midnight's Children*, London: Picador, 1983 [1981].

24 Günter Grass, *The Tin Drum*, trans. Ralph Manheim, New York: Fawcett, 1966 [1963].

25 Patricia Merivale, pp. 6–7.

26 Salman Rushdie, 'On Günter Grass', *Granta*, vol. 15, 1985, pp. 179–85.

27 Salman Rushdie, 'On Günter Grass', p. 180.

28 Like Oskar, Grass was born in the free city of Danzig. Danzig lost its status as a free city during the Second World War and was occupied by German forces. At the end of the war it was liberated by the Russian army and, as a consequence of the post-war re-mapping of Europe, was incorporated into Poland and re-named Gdansk. After his release as a prisoner of war, Grass moved to the newly formed West Germany.

29 Chandrabhanu Pattanayak, 'Interview with Salman Rushdie', *The Literary Criterion*, vol. 18, no. 3, 1983, p. 20.

30 Merivale is refering to the character Sancho Panza who served as squire to Don Quixote in Cervantes' *Don Quixote* (1604–14). Throughout this work, Panza is called upon to provide a rational perspective on his master's frequently delusional impulses.

31 [Merivale's note] Wilson (25) [Keith Wilson, '*Midnight's Children* and Reader Responsibility,' *Critical Quarterly*, vol. 26, no. 3, 1984, pp. 23–37] makes a case for Padma's strengths and limitations as a reader-surrogate; he employs the useful formula that Rushdie is to Saleem as the reader is to Padma. Batty privileges Padma even further in her narratological analysis of Rushdie's Scheherazadean strategies, which, in her view, make *Midnight's Children* an act of sedition against (Indira Gandhi's) Indian state, with Gandhi herself as the ultimate 'implied reader' of the book. [See Nancy Batty's 'The Art of Suspense: Rushdie's 1001 (Mid)Nights', *Ariel: A Review of International English Literature*, vol. 18, no. 3, 1987, pp. 49–65. An extract from this article is contained in Chapter Five of this Guide.] This distinctly appealing interpretation is indeed corroborated to a degree by Gandhi's considerable annoyance with both the book and its author. She was, however, notably less vengeful than the Islamic Republic has been in respect to Rushdie's recent, and more explicit, (alleged) blasphemy against the Muslim faith.

32 [Merivale's note] Thomas (80) [R. Hinton Thomas and Wilfred van der Will, *The German Novel and the Affluent Society*, Manchester: Manchester University Press, 1968, p. 80] is translating from Günter Blöcker's review of *Hundejahre* (1963); Miles (49) [Keith Miles, *Günter Grass*, London: Vision, 1975, p. 49] quotes Grass himself (Interview, 29 [Günter Grass, 'Interview', *Encounter*, vol. 35, no. 3, 1970, pp. 26–9.]), who is specifying the influence on his work of Melville's *Moby-Dick*.

33 This is a term first applied to pictorial art in the 1920's. More recently, it has been associated with Latin American writers, but is increasingly employed to describe a broad range of authors from around the world. Magic Realism is most usually applied to texts that exhibit a formal tension between realism and the fantastic. For a discussion of *Midnight's Children* as a magic-realist novel see: Jean-Pierre Durix, 'Magic Realism in *Midnight's Children*', *Commonwealth Essays and Studies*, vol. 8, no. 1, 1985, pp. 57–63.

34 [Merivale's note] See Batty on Rushdean metaphors for narrative: 'narrative is a perforated sheet, concealing the whole while revealing a part' (61); it can also be, among other things, an episodic cinema, a symphony, and a labyrinth.

35 A term coined by the French writer André Gide that refers to a single element of a work that may stand in for, or express, that work as a whole.

36 Jean Franco, 'Pastiche in Contemporary Latin-American Literature', *Studies in Twentieth-Century Literature*, vol. 14, no. 1, 1989, p.105.

37 Günter Grass and Salman Rushdie, 'Writing for a Future', in Bill Bourne, Udi Eichler and David Herman (eds), *Voices: Writers and Politics*, Nottingham: Spokesman, 1987.

38 Patricia Merivale, pp.12–19.

39 M. Keith Booker, '*Finnegans Wake* and *The Satanic Verses*: Two Modern Myths of the Fall', *Critique*, vol. 32, no. 3, 1991, pp.190–207.

40 M. Keith Booker, p.190.

41 M. Keith Booker, p.191.

42 M. Keith Booker, p.191.

43 M. Keith Booker, pp.191, 192.

44 M. Keith Booker, p.192.

45 [Booker's note] One of the leitmotifs that runs throughout the *Wake* is that of *the felix culpa* [referring to an apparent error resulting in positive consequences, e.g. in Christian theology the sin of Adam ultimately results in the blessedness of redemption], which appears dozens of times in various forms, including several (e.g., 'phoenix culprit') that play on HCE's indiscretion in Phoenix Park and on the mythical phoenix as a symbol of rebirth. Also note that the 'Ballad of Perce-Oreille' features the falls of both Satan and man and is followed by the exclamation 'O fortunous casualitas!' (175. 29).

46 James Joyce, *A Portrait of the Artist as a Young Man*, New York: Viking, 1975 [1916].

47 [Booker's note] The divine and the diabolic are often conflated in the *Wake* as well. For example, when Shaun accuses Shem of attempting to set himself up as a godlike figure, he does so by attributing to him the motto of Satan (and Stephen Dedalus), *non serviam*: 'Do you hold yourself then for some god in the manger, Shehohem, that you will neither serve nor let serve, pray nor let pray?' (188.18–9). This passage also evokes that favorite Joycean motif, the conflation of 'god' with 'dog.'

48 Salman Rushdie, *The Satanic Verses*, New York: Viking, 1989.

49 Gerald Marzorati, 'Salman Rushdie: Fiction's Embattled Infidel', *New York Time Magazine*, 29 January 1989, pp.24–7, 44–9, 100.

50 M. Keith Booker, pp.195–6.

51 [Booker's note] Similarly, Ulysses is probably the prototypical exile figure of ancient literature, providing a further indication of Joyce's concern with the exile motif.

52 [Booker's note] *The Satanic Verses* includes other allusions to Stephen as well. For example, when Mrs. Pamela Chamcha hears of the airplane explosion, she naturally assumes that her husband is dead, describing herself as 'the widow Chamcha whose spouse is beastly dead' (188). The allusion here is obviously to Buck Mulligan's irreverent reference to Stephen in *Ulysses* as 'Dedalus whose mother is beastly dead' (7). Pamela's reference is equally irreverent, given that she is in the arms of her lover at the time she makes this statement. Mulligan also refers to Stephen in *Ulysses* by the nickname of 'Kinch' (3). Late in *Verses* there appears a police inspector named 'Stephen Kinch' (455).

53 Salman Rushdie, 'The Book Burning', *New York Review of Books*, 2 March 1989, p.26.

54 Salman Rushdie, 'The Empire Writes Back With a Vengeance', *The Times*, 3 July 1982, p.8.

55 M. Keith Booker, pp.200–1.

56 Ngugi wa Thiong'o, *Moving the Center: The Struggle for Cultural Freedoms*, London: James Curry, 1983, p.32.

57 Aruna Srivastava, '"The Empire Writes Back": Language and History in "Shame" and "Midnight's Children"', *Ariel: A Review of International English Literature*, vol. 20, no. 4, 1989, p.73.

58 Salman Rushdie, 'Commonwealth Literature Does Not Exist', *Imaginary Homelands: Essays and Criticism 1981–1991*, p.62.

59 Ngugi wa Thiong'o, p.21.

60 [Booker's note] This emphasis on the political investedness of language extends to Stephen's encounters with religion as well. R.B. Kershner notes that Stephen's 'relationship with the church is a linguistic affair . . . His religious crisis thus appears a clear case of possession by liturgical language. See R.B. Kershner, Jr., *Joyce, Bakhtin, and popular literature: Chronicles of Disorder*, Chapel Hill: University of North Carolina Press, 1989, p.162.

61 Jacques Derrida, 'Two Words for Joyce', in Derek Attridge and Daniel Ferrer (eds), *Post-Structuralist Joyce*, Cambridge: Cambridge University Press, 1984.

62 Maria Couto, '*Midnight's Children* and Parents', *Encounter*, vol. 58, 1982, p.63.

63 Gerald Marzorati, 'Salman Rushdie: Fiction's Embattled Infidel', *New York Times Magazine*, 29 January 1989, p.27.

64 M. Keith Booker, pp.201–2, 204–5.

65 See Bhikhu Parekh, 'Between Holy Text

and Moral Void', *New Statesman and Society*, 24 March, 1989, pp.29–33.

66 Rudolf Bader, p.65.

67 C. Kanaganayakam, 'Myth and Fabulosity in *Midnight's Children*', *Dalhousie Review*, vol. 67, no. 1, 1987, pp.86–98.

68 C. Kanaganayakam, p.98.

69 C. Kanaganayakam, pp.90–2.

70 Feroza Jussawalla, 'Rushdie's Dastan-E-Dilruba: *The Satanic Verses* as Rushdie's Love Letter to Islam', *Diacritics*, vol. 26, no. 1, 1996, pp.50–73.

71 Feroza Jussawalla, p.51.

72 Feroza Jussawalla, p.51.

73 Michael T. Kaufman, 'Author from 3 Countries', *New York Times Book Review*, 13 November 1983, p.22.

74 [Jussawalla's note] Islam's growth in the Indian soil was very different from the roots it lay down in Africa, for instance. The Somali writer Nuruddin Farah, who has also lived in India, describes his context in *Interviews with Writers of the Post-colonial World*: 'The reason why Islam appears to be more relentless is twofold. One is that for everything Muslims do, they resort to the holy book from which they seek divine approval The second is that Islamic societies have not been secularized [in Africa] in the same way as Christian societies have been'. From Feroza Jussawalla and Reed Dasenbrock, *Interviews with Writers of the Postcolonial World*, Jackson: University Press of Mississippi, 1992, p.561.

75 Sara Suleri, 'Contraband Histories: Salman Rushdie and the Embodiment of Blasphemy', *Yale Review*, vol. 78, no. 4, 1989, pp.604–24.

76 William L. Hanaway, Jr., 'Persian Popular Romances', *Review of National Literatures 2*, 1971, [pp. 139–60] p.142. (Hanaway's italics.)

77 Salman Rushdie, *The Satanic Verses*.

78 Salman Rushdie, *Imaginary Homelands*.

79 Salman Rushdie, *Midnight's Children*, New York: Knopf, 1981.

80 Frances W. Pritchett, *Marvellous Encounters: Folk Romance in Urdu and Hindi*, Riverdale, MD: Riverdale, 1985.

81 Feroza Jussawalla, pp.53–4, 69–71.

82 Timothy Brennan, 'The National Longing for Form', in Homi K. Bhabha (ed.), *Nation and Narration*, London: Routledge, 1990, p.61.

83 Feroza Jussawalla, p.71.

CHAPTER THREE

1 For a collection of her reviews and articles, see Uma Parameswaran, *The Perforated Sheet: Essays on Salman Rushdie's Art*, New Delhi: Affiliated East-West Press, 1988.

2 See Uma Parameswaran, 'Autobiography as History: Saleem Sinai and India in Rushdie's *Midnight's Children*', *Toronto South Asian Review*, vol. 1, no. 2, 1982, pp.52–60.

3 Uma Parameswaran, 'Autobiography as History', p.52.

4 Uma Parameswaran, 'Autobiography as History', p.53.

5 Anita Desai, 'Where Cultures Clash by Night', *The Washington Post*, vol. 11, no. 11, 15 March 1981, p.13.

6 Fredric Jameson, 'Third-World Literature in the Era of Multinational Capitalism', *Social Text*, vol. 15, 1986, pp.65–88.

7 Fredric Jameson, p.69 (Jameson's italics).

8 [Parameswaran's note] R.C. Majumdar et al., *An Advanced History of India*, Delhi: Macmillan, 1958, p.984.

9 [Parameswaran's note] R.C. Majumdar et al., p.984.

10 Uma Parameswaran, 'Autobiography as History', pp.53–6, 57–60

11 Uma Parameswaran, 'Midnight's Children', *Journal of South Asian Literature*, vol. 17, no. 2, 1982, p.249.

12 Hayden White, 'The Fictions of Factual Representation', in Angus Fletcher (ed.), *The Literature of Fact*, New York: Columbia University Press, 1976, pp.21–44. To trace the evolution of his conception of history see also: Hayden White, 'The Historical Text as Literary Artifact', in Robert Canary and Henry Kozicki (eds), *The Writing of History: Literary Form and Historical Understanding*, Madison: University of Wisconsin Press, 1978, pp.41–62. Hayden White, 'The Value of Narrativity in the Representation of Reality', *Critical Inquiry*, vol. 7, no. 1, 1980, pp.5–27. Hayden White, 'The Narrativization of Real Events', *Critical Enquiry*, vol. 7, no. 4, 1981, pp.793–8.

13 Hayden White, 'The Fictions of Factual Representation', p.22.

14 Hayden White, p.23.

15 Salman Rushdie, 'Imaginary Homelands', *Imaginary Homelands: Essays and Criticism 1981–1991*, London: Granta Books, 1991, [pp. 9–21] p.10.

16 Salman Rushdie, 'Imaginary Homelands', p.10.

17 Salman Rushdie, '"Errata": Or, Unreliable Narration in *Midnight's Children*', *Imaginary Homelands: Essays and Criticism 1981–1991*, London; Granta Books, 1991, pp. 22–25.

18 Ralph J. Crane, *Inventing History: A History of India in English-Language Fiction*, London: Macmillan Academic and Professional Ltd, 1992, p. 171.

19 Benedict Anderson, *Imagined Communities: Reflections on the Origin and Spread of Nationalism*, London: Verso, 1983, p. 6.

20 Benedict Anderson, p. 6.

21 Gayatri Chakravorty Spivak, 'Can the Subaltern Speak?: Speculations on Widow Sacrifice', *Wedge*, 7/8, 1985, p. 127.

22 Salman Rushdie, 'The Riddle of Midnight: India, August 1987', *Imaginary Homelands*, p. 27.

23 David Lipscomb, 'Caught in a Strange Middle Ground: Contesting History in Salman Rushdie's *Midnight's Children*', *Diaspora: A Journal of Transnational Studies*, vol. 1, no. 2, 1991, p. 182.

24 Dieter Riemenschneider, 'History and the Individual in Salman Rushdie's *Midnight's Children* and Anita Desai's *Clear Light of Day*', *Kunapipi*, vol. 6, no. 2, 1984, p. 66.

25 Aruna Srivastava, '"The Empire Writes Back": Language and History in "Shame" and "Midnight's Children"', *Ariel: A Review of International English Literature*, vol. 20, no. 4, 1989, pp. 62–3.

26 For John Burt Foster Jr. 'felt history' is revealed through its 'immediate feel, its physical impact upon the body and the senses. In essence, then, felt history refers to the eloquent gestures and images with which a character or lyric persona registers the direct pressure of events'. See, John Burt Foster Jr., 'Magic Realism in The White Hotel: Compensatory Vision and the Transformation of Classic Realism', *Southern Humanities Review*, vol. 20, no. 3, 1986, p. 210.

27 Srivastava is referring to: Hayden White, 'The Question of Narrative in Contemporary Historical Theory', *History and Theory*, vol. 21, no. 1, 1984, pp. 1–33.

28 Aruna Srivastava, p. 63.

29 Aruna Srivastava, p. 63.

30 Aruna Srivastava, p. 63.

31 Balkrishna Govind Gokhale, 'Gandhi and History', *History and Theory*, vol. 11, 1972, pp. 214–25.

32 Salman Rushdie, *Midnight's Children*, London: Pan, 1982.

33 Salman Rushdie, *Shame*, London: Jonathan Cape, 1983.

34 David Carroll, *The Subject in Question: The Languages of Theory and the Strategies of Fiction*, Chicago: University of Chicago Press, 1982.

35 Michel Foucault, 'Nietzsche, Genealogy, History', *Language, Counter-Memory, Practice*, Ithaca, NY: Cornell University Press, 1977.

36 Friedrich Nietzsche, *The Use and Abuse of History*, New York: Liberal Arts, 1957.

37 Aruna Srivastava, pp. 66–71, 72.

38 Aruna Srivastava, p. 77.

39 Linda Hutcheon, '"The Pastime of Past Time": Fiction, History, Historiographic Metafiction', *Genre*, vol. 20, no. 3–4, 1987, pp. 285–6.

40 Linda Hutcheon, p. 298.

41 Salman Rushdie, 'Outside the Whale', *Imaginary Homelands*, pp. 87–101; 'Attenborough's Gandhi', *Imaginary Homelands*, pp. 102–6.

42 Salman Rushdie, 'Outside the Whale', p. 91.

43 Salman Rushdie, 'Attenborough's Gandhi', p. 102.

44 Salman Rushdie, 'Attenborough's Gandhi', p. 105. For an interesting comparison between Rushdie's writing and Attenborough's film, see Feroza Jussawalla, 'Fact Versus Fiction: Attenborough's *Gandhi* and Salman Rushdie's *Midnight's Children*', in Kirpal Singh and Robert Yeo (eds.), *ACLALS Bulletin*, 7th Series, no. 4, Commonwealth Fiction (2), Singapore: The Association for Commonwealth Literature and Language Studies, 1986, pp. 70–78.

45 Sean French, 'Falling Towards England', *The Observer*, 25 September 1988, p. 43.

46 Rukmini Bhaya Nair, 'Text and Pre-Text: History as Gossip in Rushdie's Novels', *Economic and Political Weekly*, vol. 24, no. 18, 1989, pp. 994–1000. For another example, see also Christine Brooke-Rose's reference to *The Satanic Verses* in her essay 'Palimpsest History' in Stefan Collini (ed.), *Interpretation and Overinterpretaion: Umberto Eco with Richard Rorty, Jonathan Culler, Christine Brook-Rose*, Cambridge: Cambridge University Press, 1992. pp. 125–38.

47 Rukmini Bhaya Nair, p. 995.

48 Salman Rushdie, *The Satanic Verses*, London: Viking, 1988.

49 Salman Rushdie, 'The Bandung File Interview', Channel 4, February 1989, 9 p.m.

50 Nair is referring to C. Pattanayak, 'Interview with Salman Rushdie', *The Literary Criterion*, vol. 28, no. 3, 1983, p. 21.

51 Salman Rushdie, *Midnight's Children*,

London: Pan Books, 1982.

52 Salman Rushdie, *Shame*, New Delhi: Rupa Paperback, 1982.

53 Rukmini Bhaya Nair, pp. 995, 996–7.

CHAPTER FOUR

1 Salman Rushdie, 'The Location of Brazil', *Imaginary Homelands: Essays and Criticism 1981–1991*, London: Granta Books, 1991, p.124.

2 Salman Rushdie, 'The Indian Writer in England', in Maggie Butcher (ed.), *Eye of the Beholder: Indian Writing in English*, London: Commonwealth Institute, 1983, p.81.

3 Salman Rushdie, 'Imaginary Homelands', *Imaginary Homelands*, p.15.

4 Timothy Brennan, *Salman Rushdie and the Third World: Myths of the Nation*, London: Macmillan, 1989. See also: Timothy Brennan, 'India, Nationalism, and Other Failures', *Atlantic Quarterly*, vol. 87, no. 1, 1988, pp.131–46; Timothy Brennan, 'The National Longing for Form', in Homi K. Bhabha (ed.), *Nation and Narration*, London and New York: Routledge, 1990, pp.44–70; Timothy Brennan, 'Rushdie, Islam and Postcolonial criticism', *Social Text*, vol. 10, no. 2–3, 1992, pp.271–6.

5 Timothy Brennan, *Salman Rushdie and the Third World*, pp.viii–ix.

6 Timothy Brennan, p.ix.

7 Timothy Brennan, p.ix–x.

8 Timothy Brennan, p.85.

9 [Brennan's note] Salman Rushdie, *Shame*, New York: Vintage/Adventura, 1984, p.23.

10 [Brennan's note] See Rushdie's detailed discussion on the *Chamcha* in 'The Empire Writes Back with a Vengeance', *The Times*, 3 July 1983, p.36.

11 [Brennan's note] Salman Rushdie, *Shame*, p.92.

12 [Brennan's note] This dichotomy in its Pakistani guise reappears in the person of Iskander Harappa and Raza Hyder in *Shame*.

13 [Brennan's note] '[T]hen the day arrived when Aziz threw out the religious tutor. Thumb and forefinger closed around the mauvi's ear. Naseem and her husband leading the straggledbearded wretch to the door in the garden wall . . . Do you know what that man was teaching your children? He was teaching them to hate, wife. He tells them to hate Hindus and Buddhists and Jains and Sikhs and who knows what other vegetarians', in Salman Rushdie, *Midnight's Children*, New York: Avon, 1980, p.43.

14 Timothy Brennan, pp.85–90.

15 Timothy Brennan, 'Pitting Levity against Gravity', *Salman Rushdie and the Third World: Myths of Nation*, p.147.

16 Frantz Fanon, *The Wretched of the Earth*, New York: Grove Press, 1968, p.218.

17 Timothy Brennan, pp.147–8.

18 Salman Rushdie, 'Outside the Whale', *Imaginary Homelands*, pp.87–101.

19 Timothy Brennan, p.148.

20 [Brennan's note] Salman Rushdie, 'The New Empire Within Britain', *New Society*, 9 December 1982, p.420.

21 [Brennan's note] Salman Rushdie, 'The Empire Writes Back with a Vengeance', *The Times*, 3 July 1982, p.8.

22 Salman Rushdie, *The Satanic Verses*, New York: Viking Penguin, 1988.

23 [Brennan's note] For an account of the West Indian writer's community in Britain in this period, see George Lamming, *The Pleasures of Exile*, London: Michael Joseph, 1960.

24 [Brennan's note] The range of writers suggested by this short list – all of whom have published their work within the last twenty years – is extensive, and corresponds to the rise of black-run publishing houses such as the Race Today Collective, Bogle-L'Ouverture, New Beacon, Creation for Liberation and others. For some idea of the breadth of arts activity among the contemporary black communities, see Kwesi Owusu, *The Struggle for Black Arts in Britain: What We Can Consider Better Than Freedom*, London: Comedia Publishers Group, 1986.

25 [Brennan's note] A. Sivanandan, 'The Struggle for Black Arts in Britain', *Race and Class*, vol. 28, 1986, p.77.

26 [Brennan's note] See, for example, his introduction to Derek Bishton and John Reardon, *Home Front*, London: Jonathan Cape, 1984, and his book-jacket endorsements of Peter Fryer, *Staying Power: The History of Black People in Britain*, London and Sydney: Pluto Press, 1984.

27 Timothy Brennan, pp.148–51.

28 Timothy Brennan, p.149.

29 Salman Rushdie, 'In Good Faith', *Imaginary Homelands*, p.394.

30 Homi K. Bhabha, *The Location of Culture*, London: Routledge, 1994, p.ix.

31 Homi K. Bhabha, '"DissemiNation": Time, Narrative, and the Margins of the Modern Nation', in Homi K. Bhabha (ed.),

Nation and Narration, London: Routledge, 1990, pp. 291–322.

32 In the preface to *Salman Rushdie and the Third World*, Brennan acknowledges the influence of Bhabha on his work. Similarly, Bhabha appreciates the importance of Brennan's essay 'The National Longing for Form', by including a version of it in *Nation and Narration*, pp. 44–70.

33 Homi K. Bhabha, 'Signs Taken for Wonders: Questions of Ambivalence and Authority Under a Tree Outside Delhi, May 1817', *The Location of Culture*, pp. 102–22.

34 Benita Parry, 'Problems in Current Theories of Colonial Discourse', *Oxford Literary Review*, vol. 9, nos. 1 and 2, 1987, pp. 41–2.

35 Homi K. Bhabha, 'Signs Taken for Wonders', p. 107.

36 [Bhabha's note] Salman Rushdie, *The Satanic Verses*, New York: Viking, 1988, p. 337.

37 [Bhabha's note] Salman Rushdie, *The Satanic Verses*, p. 130.

38 [Bhabha's note] Salman Rushdie, The Satanic Verses, p. 145.

39 Salman Rushdie, *The Satanic Verses*, p. 320.

40 Salman Rushdie, *The Satanic Verses*, p. 353.

41 [Bhabha's note] Salman Rushdie, p. 354. I have slightly altered the presentation of this passage to fit in with the sequence of my argument.

42 Homi K. Bhabha, 'DissemiNation', pp. 317–20.

43 Homi K. Bhabha, 'How Newness Enters the World: Postmodern Space, Postcolonial Times and the Trials of the Cultural Translation', *The Location of Culture*, pp. 212–35.

44 Homi K. Bhabha, 'The Commitment to Theory', *The Location of Culture*, pp. 19–39.

45 Benita Parry, p. 42.

46 Homi K. Bhabha, p. 36.

47 Homi K. Bhabha, p. 34.

48 Homi K. Bhabha, p. 34.

49 [Bhabha's note] Salman Rushdie, *The Satanic Verses*, London: Viking, 1988, p. 261.

50 Bhabha is referring to Fredric Jameson's essay 'Secondary Elaborations', in *Postmodernism: Or, The Cultural Logic of Late Capitalism*, Durham: Duke University Press, 1991, pp. 297–418.

51 [Bhabha's note] Salman Rushdie, *The Satanic Verses*, p. 246.

52 [Bhabha's note] Walter Benjamin, *Illuminations*, trans. H. Zohn, New York: Shocken Books, 1968, p. 75.

53 [Bhabha's note] Walter Benjamin, p. 75.

54 [Bhabha's note] Salman Rushdie, *The Satanic Verses*, p. 319.

55 [Bhabha's note] Alisdair Macintyre, *Whose Justice? Which Rationality?*, London: Duckworth, 1988, p. 378.

56 [Bhabha's note] Sara Suleri, *The Rhetoric of English India*, Chicago: Chicago University Press, 1992, p. 192.

57 [Bhabha's note] [Yunas Samad], 'Book Burning and Race Relations: Political Mobilisation of Bradford Muslims,' *New Community*, vol. 18, no. 4, 1991, pp. 507–19. My discussion in this paragraph is a paraphrase of Samad's argument and research.

58 [Bhabha's note] Salman Rushdie, *The Satanic Verses*, p. 272.

59 [Bhabha's note] Salman Rushdie, *The Satanic Verses*, p. 288.

60 [Bhabha's note] See R. Gasché's brilliant essay on Benjamin's theory of language, 'The Saturnine Vision and the Question of Difference: Reflections on Walter Benjamin's Theory of Language', *Studies in 20th Century Literature*, vol. 2, no. 1, 1986.

61 [Bhabha's note] Walter Benjamin, *Illuminations*, p. 263.

62 [Bhabha's note] Rudolph Pannwitz, in Benjamin, *Illuminations*, p. 80.

63 [Bhabha's note] Gasché, 'The Saturnine Vision', p. 92.

64 [Bhabha's note] It is this disjunctive form of cultural interaction that David Lloyd describes as 'refractive, non-equivalent, translation', in his reading of the emergence of the 'minor' Irish national canon. See D. Lloyd, *Nationalism and Minor Literature*, Berkeley and London: University of California Press, 1987, pp. 110–11.

65 [Bhabha's note] Paul de Man, *The Resistance to Theory*, Minneapolis: Minnesota University Press, 1986, p. 92.

66 [Bhabha's note] Salman Rushdie, *The Satanic Verses*, p. 288.

67 [Bhabha's note] Salman Rushdie, pp. 291–3.

68 [Bhabha's note] Salman Rushdie, p. 354.

69 Homi K. Bhabha, 'How Newness Enters the World', pp. 223–8.

70 Vijay Mishra, 'Postcolonial Differend: Diasporic Narratives of Salman Rushdie', *Ariel: A Review of International English Literature*, vol. 26, no. 3, 1995, pp. 7–45.

71 [Mishra's note] '[T]he book isn't actually about Islam, but about migration, metamorphosis, divided selves, love, death, London

and Bombay,' wrote Rushdie to the Indian Prime Minister Rajiv Gandhi. In Lisa Appignanesi and Sara Maitland (eds), *The Rushdie File*, London: Fourth Estate, 1989, p. 44.

72 Blake Morrison, 'Interview with Salman Rushdie', *Granta*, vol. 31, 1991, pp. 113–25.

73 [Mishra's note] Air India Flight 182 exploded in 1985, one of the more audacious acts of Sikh terrorism that actually originated, it seems, in the Canadian Indian diaspora. [The figure of] 29,002 feet was compulsory knowledge for geography students in the colonies.

74 Vijay Mishra, pp. 16–17.

75 Vijay Mishra, p. 17.

76 Salman Rushdie, *The Satanic Verses*, London: Viking, 1988.

77 See Salman Rushdie, 'Hobson-Jobson', in *Imaginary Homelands*, pp. 81–83.

78 Vijay Mishra, pp. 18–20.

79 [Mishra's note] Anna Marie Smith, 'The Imaginary Inclusion of the Assimilable "Good Homosexual": The British New Right's Representations of Sexuality and Race', *Diacritics*, vol. 24, no. 2–3, 1994, p. 62.

80 [Mishra's note] Iain Chambers, *Migrancy, Culture, Identity*, London: Routledge, 1994, pp. 23–4.

81 [Mishra's note] Iain Chambers, Border Dialogues: Journeys in Postmodernity, London: Routledge, 1990, p. 27.

82 Vijay Mishra, pp. 20–3.

83 Benita Parry, p. 43.

84 Benita Parry, p. 43.

85 Salman Rushdie, *The Moor's Last Sigh*, London: Jonathan Cape, 1995, p. 329.

86 Maya Jaggi, 'The Last Laugh', *New Statesman and Society*, vol. 8, no. 369, 1995, p. 21.

87 See, for example, Colin MacCabe et al., 'Interview: Salman Rushdie Talks to the London Consortium About *The Satanic Verses*', *Critical Quarterly*, vol. 38, no. 2, 1996, p. 65.

88 Catherine Cundy, *Salman Rushdie: Contemporary World Writers*, Manchester: Manchester University Press, 1996, p. 26

CHAPTER FIVE

1 Vijay Mishra, 'Postcolonial Differend: Diasporic Narratives of Salman Rushdie', *Ariel: A Review of International English Literature*, vol. 26, no. 3, 1995, p. 19. An extract from this article is contained in Chapter Four of this Guide.

2 See G. Sahgal, 'Fundamentalism and the multicultural fallacy', in *Against the Grain: A Celebration of Survival and Struggle*, Middlesex: Southall Black Sisters, 1990. The statement of support for Rushdie from Women Against Fundamentalism can be found in Lisa Appignanesi and Sara Maitland (eds), *The Rushdie File*, London: Fourth Estate, 1989, pp. 241–2.

3 Homi K. Bhabha, 'How Newness Enters the World: Postmodern Space, Postcolonial Times and the Trials of Cultural Translation', *The Location of Culture*, London: Routledge, 1994, p. 229.

4 Homi K. Bhabha, p. 229.

5 For two excellent examples of this criticism see: Aijaz Ahmad, 'Salman Rushdie's *Shame*: Postmodern Migrancy and the Representation of Women', in Aijaz Ahmad, *In Theory: Classes, Nations, Literatures*, London: Verso, 1992, pp. 123–58; Inderpal Grewal, 'Salman Rushdie: Marginality, Women, and *Shame*', *Genders*, vol. 16, no. 2, 1988, pp. 210–27.

6 Timothy Brennan, *Salman Rushdie and the Third World*, London: Macmillan, 1989, p. 126.

7 The few critics who have written on Rushdie have missed this, seeing in Padma merely the personification of the audience in a general sense: a kind of chorus. See Uma Parameswaran, 'Handcuffed to History: Salman Rushdie's Art', *Ariel: A Review of International English Literature*, vol. 14, no. 4, 1983, pp. 34–45.

8 Timothy Brennan, p. 101.

9 Timothy Brennan, p. 101. See Chapter Four of this Guide for Brennan's discussion of Rushdie's cosmopolitanism.

10 Nancy E. Batty, 'The Art of Suspense: Rushdie's 1001 (Mid-) Nights', *Ariel: A Review of International English Literature*, vol. 18, no. 3, 1987, p. 53.

11 Nancy E. Batty, p. 50.

12 Nancy E. Batty, p. 50.

13 [Batty's note] Pierre Macherey, *A Theory of Literary Production*, (1966), trans. Jane E. Lewin, Ithaca, NY: Cornell University Press, 1990, p. 29.

14 [Batty's note] Salman Rushdie, *Midnight's Children*, London: Pan, 1982, p. 14.

15 [Batty's note] Uma Parameswaran, p. 44.

16 [Batty's note] Gérard Genetie, *Narrative Discourse: An Essay in Method*, 1972. Trans. Jane E. Lewin, Ithaca, NY: Cornell University Press, 1980, p. 234.

17 [Batty's note] Keith Wilson, 'Midnight's Children and Reader Responsibility', Critical Quarterly, vol. 26, no. 3, 1984, p.34.

18 [Batty's note] Ross Chambers, Story and Situation: Narrative Seduction and the Power of Fiction, Minneapolis: University of Minnesota Press, 1984, p.50.

19 [Batty's note] Meir Sternberg, Expositional Modes and Temporal Ordering in Fiction, Baltimore: Johns Hopkins University Press, 1978, p.162.

20 [Batty's note] Meir Sternberg, pp.162–3.

21 [Batty's note] Uma Parameswaran, p.38.

22 [Batty's note] Gérard Genette, p.73.

23 Nancy E. Batty, pp.53–8, 60–1.

24 Nancy E. Batty, p.61.

25 Nancy E. Batty, p.62.

26 Nancy E. Batty, pp.63–4.

27 Gayatri Chakravorty Spivak, 'Reading The Satanic Verses', Public Culture, vol. 2, no. 1, 1989, p.82.

28 Gayatri Chakravorty Spivak, p.83.

29 [Verma's note] Salman Rushdie, Midnight's Children, London: Picador, 1982, p.24; subsequent references appear in parentheses in the text.

30 Charu Verma, 'Padma's Tragedy: A Feminist Deconstruction of Rushdie's Midnight's Children', in Sushila Singh (ed.), Feminism and Recent Fiction in English, New Delhi: Prestige Books, 1991, pp.156–7, 159–60.

31 Charu Verma, p.155.

32 [Cundy's note] Salman Rushdie, 'In Good Faith', Imaginary Homelands: Essays and Criticism 1981–1991, London: Granta, 1991, pp.401–2.

33 [Cundy's note] Salman Rushdie, Grimus, London: Paladin, 1989, p.33.

34 [Cundy's note] Salman Rushdie, Grimus, p.71.

35 [Cundy's note] Salman Rushdie, Midnight's Children, London: Pan, 1982, p.385.

36 [Cundy's note] Salman Rushdie, Midnight's Children, p.381.

37 [Cundy's note] Salman Rushdie, Midnight's Children, p.381.

38 [Cundy's note] Anuradha Dingwaney Needham, 'The Politics of Post-Colonial Identity in Salman Rushdie', Massachusetts Review, vol. 29, no. 4, 1988/9, p.624.

39 [Cundy's note] Salman Rushdie, Shame, London: Pan, 1983, p.35.

40 [Cundy's note] Salman Rushdie, The Satanic Verses, Harmondsworth: Viking Penguin, 1989, p.428.

41 [Cundy's note] Salman Rushdie, Shame, p.40.

42 [Cundy's note] Salman Rushdie, Shame, p.128.

43 [Cundy's note] Salman Rushdie, Shame, p.13.

44 [Cundy's note] The Koran, trans. N.J. Dawood, Harmondsworth: Penguin, 1990, p.34.

45 [Cundy's note] Salman Rushdie, Shame, p.116.

46 [Cundy's note] Salman Rushdie, Shame, p.118.

47 [Cundy's note] Salman Rushdie, Shame, p.62.

48 [Cundy's note] Aijaz Ahmad, p.148.

49 [Cundy's note] Inderpal Grewal, p.37.

50 [Cundy's note] Aijaz Ahmad, p.144.

51 [Cundy's note] Salman Rushdie, 'In Good Faith', p.400.

52 [Cundy's note] N.J. Dawood, p.ix.

53 [Cundy's note] Salman Rushdie, The Satanic Verses, pp.99–100.

54 [Cundy's note] Quoted in W.J. Weatherby, Salman Rushdie: Sentenced to Death, New York: Carroll & Graf, 1990, p.26.

55 [Cundy's note] Salman Rushdie, The Satanic Verses, p.114.

56 [Cundy's note] The Koran, p.525.

57 [Cundy's note] Timothy Brennan, Salman Rushdie and the Third World, London: Macmillan, 1989, p.126.

58 [Cundy's note] Salman Rushdie, The Satanic Verses, p.81.

59 [Cundy's note] Salman Rushdie, The Satanic Verses, p.26.

60 [Cundy's note] Malise Ruthven, A Satanic Affair: Salman Rushdie and the Wrath of Islam, London: Hogarth, 1991, pp.21, 23.

61 [Cundy's note] Salman Rushdie, The Satanic Verses, p.184.

62 [Cundy's note] Salman Rushdie, The Satanic Verses, p.523.

63 Catherine Cundy, 'Rushdie's Women', Wasafiri, vol. 18, 1993, pp.13–17.

CHAPTER SIX

1 Catherine Cundy, Salman Rushdie: Contemporary World Writers, Manchester: Manchester University Press, 1996, p.65.

2 [Frank's note] Indira Gandhi's father was of course Jawaharlal Nehru, not Mahatma Gandhi, who was a close family friend, but unrelated to the Nehrus or to Indira Gandhi's

husband, Feroze Gandhi.

3 Katherine Frank, pp. 245–6, 247–8.

4 Katherine Frank, p. 248.

5 Katherine Frank, 'Mr. Rushdie and Mrs. Gandhi', *Biography: An Interdisciplinary Quarterly*, vol. 19, no. 3, 1996, p. 249.

6 Katherine Frank, p. 249.

7 Salman Rushdie, *Midnight's Children*, London: Jonathan Cape, 1981.

8 Katherine Frank, pp. 250–1.

9 Salman Rushdie, *Imaginary Homelands*, New York: Penguin, 1991.

10 [Frank's note] When Indira Gandhi's cousin Nayantara Sahgal attacked Gandhi in her Emergency novel *Rich Like Us*, she did not refer to Gandhi by name, and even trotted out the standard safe caveat at the beginning of the book: 'The characters and situations in this book are entirely imaginary and bear no relationship to any real person or actual happening.'

11 Frank is referring to Rushdie's declaration that *Midnight's Children* was designed to put the events of the Emergency 'on the record', (quoted in W.J. Weatherby, *Salman Rushdie: Sentenced to Death*, New York: Carroll and Graf, 1990, p. 47) and his apparently contradictory statement that Saleem's story 'is not history' (see Salman Rushdie, '"Errata": Or, Unreliable Narration in *Midnight's Children*', *Imaginary Homelands: Essays and Criticism 1981–1991*, p. 25. This essay is included in full in Chapter Three of this Guide).

12 For a description of this encounter, see: Peter Craven et al., 'Interview with Salman Rushdie', *Scripsi*, vol. 3, nos. 2–3, 1985, p. 113.

13 [Frank's note] Various critics such as Ira Nadel, as well as biographers like Julia Blackburn, have argued strenuously for a new biography that takes imaginative liberties with 'facts' and 'truths,' but for the general reader at least – and it is the general reader rather than the academic who has created the current boom in biographical writing – there is still the basic and pre-postmodern expectation that biography will reflect what really happened insofar as this is knowable. The prevailing belief is that biography reconstructs rather [than] constructs the past.

14 [Frank's note] According to a recent biographical essay on Rushdie by Ian Hamilton, [Ian Hamilton, 'The First Life of Salman Rushdie', *The New Yorker*, December 25 1995 – January 1 1996, pp. 90–113] Indira Gandhi dominated an earlier version of the novel entitled 'Madame Rama,' the main character of which bore 'some resemblance to Indira Gandhi whose state-of-emergency repressions had left Rushdie disillusioned and indignant: Nehru's legacy betrayed by Nehru's daughter.' Rushdie offered 'Madame Rama' to his publisher Gollancz, but to his surprise, his editor Liz Calder turned it down, though she conceded that 'it had some great stuff,' which Rushdie later 'plundered . . . for "Midnight's Children."' (102).

15 Frank is quoting Timothy Brennan, *Salman Rushdie and the Third World*, London: Macmillan, 1989, p. 117.

16 Katherine Frank, pp. 254–6.

17 Katherine Frank, p. 247.

18 Quoted in Lisa Appignanesi and Sara Maitland (eds), *The Rushdie File*, London: Fourth Estate, 1989, p. 56.

19 Madhu Jain, 'My Theme is Fanaticism: An Interview', *India Today*, 15 September 1988, pp. 98–9; and Sharabani Basu, 'Of Satan, Archangels, and Prophets: An Interview', *Sunday* (India), 18–24 September 1988, pp. 18–24.

20 The Congress-I party was named by Indira Ganhi as a direct reference to herself – the 'I' standing in for Indira.

21 For example, see: 'It's between Us, Mr PM: Rushdie', *The Times of India*, 18 October 1988, section 1, pp. 1, 10; 'Personal View', *The Sunday Times*, 16 October 1988, p. G4; 'India Bans a Book for Its own Good', *The New York Times*, 19 October, 1988, p. A27.

22 Salman Rushdie, 'Personal View', p. G4.

23 Marlena G. Corcoran, 'Salman Rushdie's Satanic Narration', *The Iowa Review*, vol. 20, no. 1, 1990, p. 156.

24 Salman Rushdie, *The Satanic Verses*, Delaware: The Consortium Inc., 1992, p. 109. (Rushdie's italics.)

25 Salman Rushdie, *The Satanic Verses*, p. 123.

26 Amin Malak, 'Reading the Crisis: The Polemics of Salman Rushdie's "The Satanic Verses"', *Ariel: A Review of International English Literature*, vol. 20, no. 4, 1989, pp. 177–8.

27 Amin Malak, p. 179.

28 Amin Malak, p. 180.

29 Syed Pasha, quoted in Sally Soames, 'Satanic Curses: Condemned to Die', *The Sunday Times*, 19 February 1989, p. A16.

30 Margaret Thatcher, quoted in Sally Soames, p. A16.

31 Syed Ali Ashraf, 'Nihilistic, Negative,

Satanic', *Impact International*, 10 November 1988. An extract from this review is contained in Chapter One of this Guide.

32 A copy of this document is included in Lisa Appignanesi and Sara Maitland (eds), pp. 57–60.

33 Salman Rushdie, 'Choice Between Light and Dark', *The Observer*, 22 January 1989, p. 11.

34 Sharabani Basu, 'Of Satan, Archangels, and Prophets: An Interview', p. 18.

35 Ayatollah Ruhollah al-Musavi Al-Khomeini, quoted in Lisa Appignanesi and Sara Maitland (eds), p. 84.

36 Salman Rushdie, 'The Fatwa', *The Observer*, 19 February 1989, p. 1.

37 Ayatollah Ruhollah al-Musavi Al-Khomeini, *Irna Iranian News Agency*, 19 February 1989.

38 Feroza Jussawalla, 'Resurrecting the Prophet: The Case of Salman, the Otherwise', *Public Culture*, vol. 2, no. 1, 1987, p. 107.

39 Salman Rushdie, *The Satanic Verses*, p. 209.

40 A copy of Senate Resolution 72 is contained in Lisa Appignanesi and Sara Maitland (eds), pp. 165–6.

41 Quoted in Lisa Appignanesi and Sara Maitland (eds), p. 107.

42 Cardinal Decourtnay, quoted in *The Independent*, 23 February 1989, p. 10.

43 John Harriot, 'The Tactics Behind the Vatican's Condemnation of Rushdie', *The Independent*, 8 March 1989, p. 20.

44 Quoted in Lisa Appignanesi and Sara Maitland (eds), p. 136.

45 Roald Dahl, 'Letter', *The Times*, 28 February 1989, p. 15.

46 Auberon Waugh, quoted in Geoffrey Wheatcroft, 'The Friends of Salman Rushdie', *Atlantic Monthly*, vol. 273, no. 3, 1994, p. 24.

47 Germaine Greer, quoted in Geoffrey Wheatcroft, p. 27.

48 Harold Pinter, quoted in Peter Murtagh, 'Writers Rally to Rushdie as Publishers Rethink', *The Guardian*, 16 February, 1989, p. 2. It should be noted that the religious leadership of British Muslims expressed strong opposition to any attempt to murder Rushdie. Dr Mughram Ali Al-Ghamdi, Chairman of UK Action Committee on Islamic Affairs, stated 'we do intend to fully abide by the law. We are not above the law. We do not condone violence of any kind by anyone under any pretext.' Quoted in Lisa Appignanesi and Sara Maitland (eds), p. 113.

49 Susan Sontag, quoted in Lisa Appignanesi and Sara Maitland (eds), p. 168.

50 Feroza Jussawalla, 'Post-Joycean/Sub-Joycean: The Reverses of Mr. Rushdie's Tricks in *The Satanic Verses*', in Viney Kirpal (ed.), *The New Indian Novel in English: A Study of The 1980s*, New Delhi: Allied Publishers Limited, 1990, p. 228. See also: Feroza Jussawalla, 'Resurrecting the Prophet: The Case of Salman, the Otherwise', *Public Culture*, vol. 2, no. 1, 1989, pp. 106–17.

51 Edward Said, 'Rushdie and the Whale', *The Observer*, 26 February 1989, p. 14.

52 Salman Rushdie, 'In Good Faith', *Imaginary Homelands: Essays and Criticism 1981–1991*, London: Granta, pp. 408–13.

53 Keith Wilson, '*Midnight's Children* and Reader Responsibility', *Critical Quarterly*, vol. 26, no. 3, 1984, p. 26.

54 [Newton's note] See 'Words for Salman Rushdie', *New Statesman and Society*, 31 March 1989, p. 25.

55 [Newton's note] Salman Rushdie, 'In Good Faith', p. 393. Subsequent page numbers are incorporated into the text.

56 [Newton's note] See M. H. Abrams, *Doing Things with Texts: Essays in Criticism and Critical Theory*, New York: W.W. Norton, 1989, pp. 297–32.

57 [Newton's note] J. Hillis Miller, *Theory Now and Then*, Hemel Hempstead: Harvester-Wheatsheaf, 1991, p. 188.

58 [Newton's note] J. Hillis Miller, p. 188.

59 [Newton's note] John M. Ellis, *The Theory of Literary Criticism: A Logical Analysis*, Berkeley: University of California Press, 1974, p. 111.

60 [Newton's note] Paul de Man, *Allegories of Reading: Figural Language in Rousseau, Nietzsche, Rilke and Proust*, New Haven: Yale University Press, 1979, p. 10.

61 [Newton's note] John M. Ellis, pp. 111–12.

62 [Newton's note] Jean E. Howard and Marion O'Connor, *Shakespeare Reproduced: The Text in History and Ideology*, New York: Methuen, 1987, pp. 3–5.

63 [Newton's note] Stephen Greenblatt, *Renaissance Self-Fashioning: From More to Shakespeare*, Chicago: University of Chicago Press, 1980, p. 5.

64 [Newton's note] See Jonathan Dollimore, *Radical Tragedy: Religion, Ideology and Power in the Drama of Shakespeare and his Contemporaries*, Brighton: Harvester Press, 1984, p. 197.

65 [Newton's note] Alan Sinfield, 'Englit

and Subcultures', *CUE News: The Newsletter of the Council for University English*, vol. 4, no. 1, 1991, p. 8.

66 [Newton's note] Alan Sinfield, p. 9.

67 [Newton's note] Malise Ruthven, *A Satanic Affair: Salman Rushdie and the Rage of Islam*, London: Chatto and Windus, 1990, pp. 138, 139, 142.

68 K. M. Newton, 'Literary Theory and the Rushdie Affair', *English: The Journal of the English Association*, vol. 41, no. 171, pp. 235–47.

SELECT BIBLIOGRAPHY

Works Cited

Letters and Reviews

Syed Ali Ashraf, 'Nihilistic, Negative, Satanic', *Impact International*, vol. 18, no. 20, 1988, pp. 16–17.

Clark Blaise, 'A Novel Of India's Coming of Age', *The New York Times Book Review*, 19 April 1981, pp. 1, 18–19.

Valentine Cunningham, 'Nosing out the Indian Reality', *Times Literary Supplement*, 15 May 1981, p. 535.

Roald Dahl, 'Letter', *The Times*, 28 February 1989, p. 15.

Anita Desai, 'An Oriental Fantasy', *The Book Review*, vol. 6, no. 1, 1981, pp. 32–6.

—— 'Where Cultures Clash by Night', *The Washington Post*, vol. 11, no. 11, 15 March 1981, pp. 1, 13.

Carlos Fuentes, *The Guardian*, 24 February 1989, pp. 29–30.

Robert Irwin, 'Original Parables', Times Literary Supplement, 30 September–6 October 1988, p. 1067.

S. Krishnan, 'Midnight's Children: An un-Indian book about all things Indian', *Aside* (Madras), vol. 6, pt. 3, 1982, pp. 51, 53.

John Leonard, 'Who Has the Best Tunes?', *The Nation*, vol. 248, no. 10, 1989, pp. 346–9.

Aparna Mahanta, 'Allegories of the Indian Experience: The Novels of Salman Rushdie', *Economic and Political Weekly*, vol. 19, no. 6, 1984, pp. 244–7.

Patrick Parrinder, 'Let's get the hell out of here', *The London Review of Books*, 29 September 1988, pp. 11–13.

Malise Ruthven, 'A Question of Identity', *The Tablet*, 3 December 1988, p. 1401.

Iain Sinclair, 'Imaginary Football Teams', *New Statesman & Society*, 30 September 1988, pp. 40–1.

Robert Taubman, 'Experiments with Truth', *London Review of Books*, vol. 3, no. 8, 1981, pp. 3, 5–6.

Roger Woddis, 'The Satanic Verses Review', *New Statesman & Society*, 30 September 1988, p. 4.

Michael Wood, 'The Prophet Motive', *The New Republic*, 6 March 1989, pp. 28–30.

Jonathan Yardley, 'Wrestling With the Angel', *The Washington Post*, 29 January 1989, p. 3.

Books

Benedict Anderson, *Imagined Communities: Reflections on the Origin and Spread of Nationalism*, London: Verso, 1983.

Lisa Appignanesi and Sara Maitland, *The Rushdie File*, London: Fourth Estate, 1989.

Homi K. Bhabha, *Nation and Narration*, London: Routledge, 1990.

—— *The Location of Culture*, London: Routledge, 1994.

Timothy A. Brennan, *Salman Rushdie and the Third World: Myths of the Nation*, London: Macmillan, 1989.

Ralph J. Crane, *Inventing History: A History of India in English-Language Fiction*, London: Macmillan Academic and Professional Ltd, 1992.

Catherine Cundy, *Salman Rushdie: Contemporary World Writers*, Manchester: Manchester University Press, 1996.

Terry Eagleton, *Walter Benjamin: Towards a Revolutionary Criticism*, London: Verso, 1981.

Frantz Fanon, *The Wretched of the Earth*, New York: Grove Press, 1968.

M.D. Fletcher, *Reading Rushdie: Perspectives on the Fiction of Salman Rushdie*, Amsterdam & Atlanta, GA: Rodopi, 1994.

Gayatri Chakravorty Spivak, *In Other Worlds: Essays in Cultural Politics*, New York: Methuen, 1987.

Ngugi wa Thiong'o, *Moving the Center: The Struggle for Cultural Freedoms*, London: James Curry, 1983.

Articles and Essays

Rudolf Bader, '*The Satanic Verses*: An Intercultural Experiment by Salman Rushdie', *The International Fiction Review*, vol. 19, no. 2, 1992, pp. 65–75

Nancy E. Batty, 'The Art of Suspense: Rushdie's 1001 (Mid-) Nights', *Ariel: A Review of International English Literature*, vol. 18, no. 3, 1987, pp. 49–65.

M. Keith Booker, '*Finnegans Wake* and *The Satanic Verses*: Two Modern Myths of the Fall', *Critique*, vol. 32, no. 3, 1991, pp. 190–207.

Timothy A. Brennan, 'The National Longing for Form', in Homi K. Bhabha (ed.), *Nation and Narration*, London: Routledge, 1990.

Marlena G. Corcoran, 'Salman Rushdie's Satanic Narration', *The Iowa Review*, vol. 20, no. 1, 1990, pp. 155–67.

Catherine Cundy, 'Rushdie's Women', *Wasafiri*, vol. 18, 1993, pp. 13–17.

Philip Engblom, 'A Multitude of Voices: Carnivalization and Dialogicality in the Novels of Salman Rushdie', in M.D. Fletcher (ed.), *Reading Rushdie: Perspectives on the Fiction of Salman Rushdie*, Amsterdam & Atlanta, GA: Rodopi, 1994, pp. 293–304.

Katherine Frank, 'Mr. Rushdie and Mrs. Gandhi', *Biography: An Interdisciplinary Quarterly*, vol. 19, no. 3, 1996, pp. 245–58.

Ian Hamilton, 'The First Life of Salman Rushdie', *The New Yorker*, 25 December 1995 – 1 January 1996, pp. 90–113.

John Harriot, 'The Tactics Behind the Vatican's Condemnation of Rushdie', *The Independent*, 8 March 1989, p. 20.

Linda Hutcheon, '"The Pastime of Past Time": Fiction, History, Historiographic Metafiction', *Genre*, vol. 20, no. 3–4, 1987, pp. 285–305.

Madhu Jain, 'Salman Rushdie: Satanic Storm', *India Today*, vol. 14, no. 5, 1989, pp. 14–18, 20, 22–4.

Fredric Jameson, 'Third-World Literature in the Era of Multinational Capitalism', *Social Text*, vol. 15, 1986, pp. 65–88.

Feroza Jussawalla, 'Resurrecting the Prophet: The Case of Salman, the Otherwise', *Public Culture*, vol. 2, no. 1, 1987, pp. 106–17.

—— 'Post-Joycean/Sub-Joycean: The Reverses of Mr. Rushdie's Tricks in *The*

Satanic Verses', in Viney Kirpal (ed.), *The New Indian Novel in English: A Study of The 1980s*, New Delhi: Allied Publishers Limited, 1990, pp. 227–38.

—— 'Rushdie's Dastan-E-Dilruba: *The Satanic Verses* as Rushdie's Love Letter to Islam', *Diacritics*, vol. 26, no. 1, 1996, pp. 50–73.

C. Kanaganayakam, 'Myth and Fabulosity in *Midnight's Children*', *Dalhousie Review*, vol. 67, no. 1, 1987, pp. 86–98.

Ayatollah Ruhollah al-Musavi Al-Khomeini, *Irna Iranian News Agency*, 19 February 1989.

David Lipscomb, 'Caught in a Strange Middle Ground: Contesting History in Salman Rushdie's *Midnight's Children*', *Diaspora: A Journal of Transnational Studies*, vol. 1, no. 2, 1991, pp. 163–89.

Lindsay Mackie, 'Indian wins the Booker', *The Guardian*, 21 October 1981, p. 1.

Amin Malak, 'Reading the Crisis: The Polemics of Salman Rushdie's "The Satanic Verses "', Ariel: A Review of International English Literature', vol. 20, no. 4, 1989, pp. 176–86.

Patricia Merivale, 'Saleem Fathered by Oskar: Intertextual Strategies in "Midnight's Children" and "The Tin Drum"', *Ariel: A Review of International English Literature*, vol. 21, no. 3, 1990, pp. 5–21.

Vijay Mishra, 'Postcolonial Differend: Diasporic Narratives of Salman Rushdie', *Ariel: A Review of International English Literature*, vol. 26, no. 3, 1995, pp. 7–45.

Peter Murtagh, 'Writers Rally to Rushdie as Publishers Rethink', *The Guardian*, 16 February 1989, p. 2.

Rukmini Bhaya Nair, 'Text and Pre-Text: History as Gossip in Rushdie's Novels', *Economic and Political Weekly*, vol. 24, no. 18, 1989, pp. 994–1000.

K. M. Newton, 'Literary Theory and the Rushdie Affair', *English: The Journal of the English Association*, vol. 41, no. 171, pp. 235–47.

Uma Parameswaran, 'Autobiography as History: Saleem Sinai and India in Rushdie's *Midnight's Children*', *Toronto South Asian Review*, vol. 1, no. 2, 1982, pp. 52–60.

—— 'Midnight's Children', *Journal of South Asian Literature*, vol. 17, no. 2, 1982, pp. 249–50.

Benita Parry, 'Problems in Current Theories of Colonial Discourse', *Oxford Literary Review*, vol. 9, nos. 1 and 2, 1987, pp. 27–58.

Dieter Riemenschneider, 'History and the Individual in Salman Rushdie's *Midnight's Children* and Anita Desai's *Clear Light of Day*', *Kunapipi*, vol. 6, no. 2, 1984, pp. 53–66.

Edward Said, 'Intellectuals in the Post-Colonial World', *Salmagundi*, vol. 70–71, 1986, pp. 44–64.

—— 'Rushdie and the Whale', *The Observer*, 14 February 1989, p. 14.

Sally Soames, 'Satanic Curses: Condemned to Die', *The Sunday Times*, 19 February 1989, pp. A15–A17.

Gayatri Chakravorty Spivak, 'Can the Subaltern Speak?: Speculations on Widow Sacrifice', *Wedge*, 7/8, 1985, pp. 120–30.

—— 'Reading *The Satanic Verses*', *Public Culture*, vol. 2, no. 1, 1989, pp. 79–99.

Aruna Srivastava, '"The Empire Writes Back": Language and History in

"Shame" and "Midnight's Children"', *Ariel: A Review of International English Literature*, vol. 20, no. 4, 1989, pp. 62–78.

Charu Verma, 'Padma's Tragedy: A Feminist Deconstruction of Rushdie's *Midnight's Children*', in Sushila Singh (ed.), *Feminism and Recent Fiction in English*, New Delhi: Prestige Books, 1991, pp. 154–162.

Geoffrey Wheatcroft, 'Foreign Affairs: The Friends of Salman Rushdie', *The Atlantic Monthly*, vol. 273, no. 3, 1994, pp. 22–30, 38–43.

Hayden White, 'The Fictions of Factual Representation', in Angus Fletcher (ed.), *The Literature of Fact*, New York: Columbia University Press, 1976, pp. 21–44.

Keith Wilson, '*Midnight's Children* and Reader Responsibility', *Critical Quarterly*, vol. 26, no. 3, 1984, pp. 23–37.

Suggested Further Reading

Books

Joel Kuortti, *The Salman Rushdie Bibliography: A Bibliography of Salman Rushdie's Work and Rushdie Criticism*, Frankfurt am Main: Peter Lang, 1997.

Alisdair Macintyre, *Whose Justice? Which Rationality?*, London: Duckworth, 1988.

Uma Parameswaran, *The Perforated Sheet: Essays on Salman Rushdie's Art*, New Delhi: Affiliated East-West Press, 1988.

Malise Ruthven, *A Satanic Affair: Salman Rushdie and the Rage of Islam*, London: Chatto and Windus, 1990.

Sara Suleri, *The Rhetoric of English India*, Chicago: Chicago University Press, 1992.

W. J. Weatherby, *Salman Rushdie: Sentenced to Death*, New York: Carroll & Graf, 1990.

Articles and Essays

Aijaz Ahmad, 'Salman Rushdie's Shame: Postmodern Migrancy and the Representation of Women', in Aijaz Ahmad, *In Theory: Classes, Nations, Literatures*, London: Verso, 1992, pp. 123–58.

Rudolf Bader, 'Indian Tin Drum', International Fiction Review, vol. 11, no. 2, 1984, pp. 75–83.

Timothy A. Brennan, 'India, Nationalism, and Other Failures', *Atlantic Quarterly*, vol. 87, no. 1, 1988, pp. 131–46.

—— 'The National Longing for Form', in Homi K. Bhabha (ed.), *Nation and Narration*, London and New York: Routledge, 1990, pp. 44–70.

—— 'Rushdie, Islam and Postcolonial Criticism', *Social Text*, vol. 10, no. 2–3, 1992, pp. 271–6.

Maria Couto, '*Midnight's Children* and Parents', *Encounter*, vol. 58, 1982, pp. 61–6.

Jean-Pierre Durix, 'Magic Realism in *Midnight's Children*', *Commonwealth Essays and Studies*, vol. 8, no. 1, 1985, pp. 57–63.

Inderpal Grewal, 'Salman Rushdie: Marginality, Women, and Shame', *Genders*, vol. 16, no. 2, 1988, pp. 210–27.

Feroza Jussawalla, 'Fact Versus Fiction: Attenborough's *Gandhi* and Salman Rushdie's *Midnight's Children*', in Kirpal Singh and Robert Yeo (eds), *ACLALS Bulletin*, 7th Series, no. 4, Commonwealth Fiction (2), Singapore: The Association for Commonwealth Literature and Language Studies, 1986, pp. 70–8.

Anuradha Dingwaney Needham, 'The Politics of Post-Colonial Identity in Salman Rushdie', *Massachusetts Review*, vol. 29, no. 4, 1988/9, pp. 609–24.

Uma Parameswaran, 'Handcuffed to History: Salman Rushdie's Art', *Ariel: A Review of International English Literature*, vol. 14, no. 4, 1983, pp. 34–45.

Bhikhu Parekh, 'Between Holy Text and Moral Void', *New Statesman and Society*, 24 March 1989, pp. 29–33.

Christine Brooke-Rose, 'Palimpsest History' in Stefan Collini (ed.), *Interpretation and Overinterpretaion: Umberto Eco with Richard Rorty*, Jonathan Culler, Christine Brooke-Rose, Cambridge: Cambridge University Press, 1992, pp. 125–138.

Yunas Samad, 'Book Burning and Race Relations: Political Mobilisation of Bradford Muslims,' *New Community*, vol. 18, no. 4, 1991, pp. 507–19.

Kumkum Sangari, 'The Politics of the Possible', *Cultural Critique*, vol. 7, 1987, pp. 157–86.

Alan Sinfield, 'Englit and Subcultures', *CUE News: The Newsletter of the Council for University English*, vol. 4, no. 1, 1991, p. 8.

Sara Suleri, 'Contraband Histories: Salman Rushdie and the Embodiment of Blasphemy', *Yale Review*, vol. 78, no. 4, 1989, pp. 604–24.

Salman Rushdie

Books

Grimus, London: Victor Gollancz, 1975.

Midnight's Children, London: Jonathan Cape, 1981.

Shame, London: Jonathan Cape, 1983.

The Jaguar Smile, London: Pan Books Ltd., 1987.

The Satanic Verses, London: Viking, 1988.

Haroun and the Sea of Stories, London: Granta Books/Penguin, 1990.

Imaginary Homelands: Essays and Criticism 1981–1991, London: Granta Books, 1991.

The Wizard of Oz, London: B.F.I. (British Film Institute) Publications, 1992.

East, West, London: Jonathan Cape, 1995.

The Moor's Last Sigh, London: Jonathan Cape, 1995.

The Ground Beneath Her Feet, Jonathan Cape, 1999.

Essays and Reviews

'The Empire Writes Back with a Vengeance', *The Times*, 3 July 1982, p. 8.

'Imaginary Homelands', *London Review of Books*, 20 October 1982, pp. 18–19. (Reprinted in *Imaginary Homelands*, pp. 9–21.)

'The New Empire within Britain', *New Society*, 9 December 1982, pp. 34–7. (Reprinted in *Imaginary Homelands*, pp. 129–38.)

'The Indian Writer in England', in Maggie Butcher (ed.), *Eye of the Beholder:*

Indian Writing in English, London: Commonwealth Institute, 1983, pp. 75–83.

'Truth Retreats When The Saint Goes Marching In: Gandhi by Richard Attenborough', *The Times*, 2 May 1983, p.10. (Reprinted in Imaginary Homelands, pp. 102–106.)

'"Errata": Or, Unreliable Narration in *Midnight's Children*', Gothenburg Conference on Commonwealth Literature, September 1983. (Reprinted in *Imaginary Homelands*, pp. 22–5.)

'"Commonwealth Literature" Does Not Exist (1983)', in *Imaginary Homelands*, pp. 61–70.

'In Custody by Anita Desai (1984)', in *Imaginary Homelands*, pp. 71–3.

'Outside the Whale', *Granta*, vol. 11, 1984, pp. 61–6. (Reprinted in *Imaginary Homelands*, pp. 87–101.)

'Hobson-Jobson (1985)', in *Imaginary Homelands*, pp. 81–83.

'The Location of Brazil', American Film, vol. 10, Jan/Feb 1985. (Reprinted in *Imaginary Homelands*, pp. 118–25.)

'On Günter Grass', *Granta*, vol. 15, 1985, pp. 179–85. (Reprinted in *Imaginary Homelands*, pp. 276–81.)

'Writing for a Future', co-written by Günter Grass, in Bill Bourne, Udi Eichler and David Herman (eds), *Voices: Writers and Politics*, Nottingham: Spokesman, 1987.

'The Riddle of Midnight: India, August 1987', Channel 4, 27 March 1988, 8.45 p.m. (Reprinted in *Imaginary Homelands*, pp. 26–33.)

'Personal View', *The Sunday Times*, 16 October 1988, p. G4.

'Choice Between Light and Dark', *The Observer*, 22 January 1989, p. 11.

'The Fatwa', *The Observer*, 19 February 1989, p. 1.

'The Book Burning', *New York Review of Books*, 2 March 1989, p. 26.

'In Good Faith: A Pen Against the Sword', *Newsweek*, 12 February 1990, pp. 52–7. (Reprinted in *Imaginary Homelands*, pp. 393–414.)

Interviews

Sharabani Basu, 'Of Satan, Archangels, and Prophets: An Interview', Sunday (India), 18–24 September 1988, pp. 18–24.

Peter Craven, et al., 'Interview with Salman Rushdie', *Scripsi*, vol. 3, nos. 2–3, 1985, pp. 107–26.

Jean-Pierre Durix, 'Interview with Salman Rushdie', *Kunapipi*, vol. 4, no. 2, pp. 17–26.

'Fact, faith and fiction: An Interview with Salman Rushdie', *Far Eastern Economic Review*, 2 March 1989, pp. 11–12.

Sean French, 'Falling Towards England', *The Observer*, 25 September 1988, p. 43.

Victoria Glendinning, 'Interview with Salman Rushdie', *The Sunday Times*, 25 October 1981, p. 38.

John Haffenden, *Novelists in Interview*, London: Methuen, 1985, pp. 231–61.

Maya Jaggi, 'The Last Laugh', *New Statesman and Society*, vol. 8, no. 369, 1995, pp. 20–1.

'Interview with Salman Rushdie: Bonfire of the Certainties', *Bandung File*,

Channel 4, 14 February 1989, 9 p.m.

Madhu Jain, 'My Theme is Fanaticism: An Interview', *India Today*, 15 September 1988, pp. 98–9.

Michael T. Kaufman, 'Author from 3 Countries', *The New York Times Book Review*, 13 November 1983, pp. 3, 22.

Mark Lawson, 'Fishing for Salman', *The Independent*, 10 September 1988, pp. 58–62.

Colin MacCabe et al., 'Interview: Salman Rushdie Talks to the London Consortium About The Satanic Verses ', *Critical Quarterly*, vol. 38, no. 2, 1996, pp. 51–70.

Gerald Marzorati, 'Salman Rushdie: Fiction's Embattled Infidel', *New York Times Magazine*, 29 January 1989, pp. 24–7, 44–9, 100.

Blake Morrison, 'Interview with Salman Rushdie', *Granta*, vol. 31, 1991, pp. 113–25.

Chandrabhanu Pattanayak, 'Interview with Salman Rushdie', *The Literary Criterion*, vol. 18, no. 3, 1983, pp. 19–22.

ACKNOWLEDGEMENTS

The editor and publisher wish to thank the following for their permission to reprint copyright material: *The Book Review* (for material from 'An Oriental Fantasy'); *The New York Times Book Review* (for material from 'A Novel of India's Coming of Age'); *Economic and Political Weekly* (for material from 'Allegories of the Indian Experience' and 'Text and Pre-text'); *Impact International* (for material from 'Nihilistic, Negative, Satanic'); Channel 4 (for material from 'Bonfire of the Certainties', in *Bandung File*); *The Nation* (for material from 'Who Has the Best Tunes?'); Rodopi (for material from 'A Multitude of Voices', in *Reading Rushdie*); *Ariel: A Review of International English Literature* (for material from 'Saleem Fathered by Oskar', '"The Empire Writes Back"', 'Postcolonial Differend' and 'The Art of Suspense'); *Critique* (for material from '*Finnegans Wake* and *The Satanic Verses*'); *Dalhousie Review* (for material from 'Myth and Fabulosity in *Midnight's Children*'); *Diacritics* (for material from 'Rushdie's Dastan-E-Dilruba'); *Toronto South Asian Review* (for material from 'Autobiography as History'); *Granta* (for material from '"Errata"' and 'In Good Faith', in *Imaginary Homelands*); Macmillan (for material from *Salman Rushdie and the Third World*); Routledge (for material from '"DissemiNation"', in *Nation and Narration*, and 'How Newness Enters the World', in *The Location of Culture*); Prestige (for material from 'Padma's Tragedy', in *Feminism and Recent Fiction in English*); *Wasafiri* (for material from 'Rushdie's Women'); *Biography: An Interdisciplinary Quarterly* (for material from 'Mr. Rushdie and Mrs. Gandhi'); *English: The Journal of the English Association* (for material from 'Literary Theory and the Rushdie Affair').

There are instances where we have been unable to trace or contact copyright holders before our printing deadline. If notified, the publisher will be pleased to acknowledge the use of copyright material.

The editor is most grateful to Jillian Robson for her invaluable assistance and unflinching support during the preparation of this Guide.

David Smale is a lecturer in the Department of English Literature and Cultural History, Liverpool John Moores University.

INDEX